THE MUSEUM
OF HORRORS

The Horror Writers Association Presents

THE MUSEUM OF HORRORS

EDITED BY DENNIS ETCHISON

LEISURE BOOKS NEW YORK CITY

A LEISURE BOOK®

June 2003

Published by

Dorchester Publishing Co., Inc.
276 Fifth Avenue
New York, NY 10001

ISBN: 0-8439-5077-3

The name "Leisure Books" and the stylized "L" with design are trademarks of Dorchester Publishing Co., Inc.

Printed in the United States of America.

Visit us on the web at www.dorchesterpub.com.

to Richard Laymon
1947-2001

CONTENTS

Contents

THE MUSEUM
OF HORRORS

It is not on any map.

You must have walked past it many times and never noticed it was there. . . .

But tonight you do.

The air in these streets is hotter than your room, stifling, so that you cannot get your breath; there is no hint of a breeze, not even at the intersections where the buildings give way to open space. Suddenly the shadowed doorway catches your eye—a dingy, unmarked storefront—and you pause to take a closer look.

Of course you do.

You have been walking aimlessly, in search of relief, and a moment ago, at the last corner, you even wondered if someone might be following you. Were those footsteps that stopped in the darkness when you turned around, or only the echo of your passing on this lonely block?

Now you see a hand-painted sign above the door, its letters so covered with grime that you can barely read them:

THE MUSEUM OF HORRORS

A wax museum? An old sideshow attraction, perhaps, a collection of oddities for those who seek bizarre entertainment.

But here?

This is not a boardwalk or fairgrounds but the heart of the city. It makes no sense.

You try the knob.

The door swings wide. . . .

There is no one on the other side. The homeless have not yet found this place. That is surprising, because it is much cooler inside, and strangely quiet, as if squealing tires and sirens and clicking heels cannot penetrate these walls. There are cardboard boxes and layers of dust on the floor, as if the museum, if that is what it is, was abandoned many years ago. It has not been open to the public for a very long time.

Ahead, a flickering.

You follow it into a large room, deceptively long, stretching as far as the eye can see. That must be an illusion, a trick of false perspective—you have seen corridors like this before, in carnivals, when you were a child.

What is the source of the light? It is faint and yellow, almost golden, the color of candles guttering somewhere near the ceiling or behind pillars, just out of sight.

Now your eyes begin to adjust, and you see rows of glass cases against the walls.

Some of the cases are low and flat, others larger and set on end, as tall as upright coffins. Their panes reflect and magnify the glow, like the mirrors of a funhouse.

You make out shapes and something glitters, as if the cases are filled with bright and dark jewels.

Dennis Etchison

There are title cards below each one.

According to the cards, some contain the preserved remains of world-class criminals, others the personal effects of their victims.

The shapes can't be real. They are wax dummies, department store mannequins, dressed in costumes and propped up inside the glass, nothing more.

That must be it.

But why?

Take a closer look.

You know about Jack the Ripper, Lizzie Borden, Vlad the Impaler and Jeffrey Dahmer. They were monsters, no doubt. But these? They appear ordinary, commonplace, like the people you see every day. One might be the man next door, another the child downstairs, that one the woman across the street who never goes out. They are the invisible ones, the unremarked, the unnoticed, who never call attention to themselves and pass their lives quietly, away from the watchful eye of the law. They could be your friends and neighbors.

You lean even closer in the mothlight.

Within the first case something shines. Or is it only a beam of stray light from outside, a passing car beyond the high, narrow windows? At the base of the figure there is a photograph, and it appears to be . . .

Shimmering.

Is it?

As you press closer, almost touching your face to the glass, the image begins to glow.

You see a country road, trees, a farmhouse, a porch, and another door that opens as the darkness inside shimmers brighter. . . .

THE MUSEUM OF DR. MOSES

by Joyce Carol Oates

1. 1956

"Mommy!"

The things flew at me out of the sky. I thought they were darning needles stabbing my face. Some were in my hair, and some had gotten inside the pink ruffled sundress Mommy had sewed for me. I was trying to shield my eyes. I was four years old, I knew nothing of self-defense, yet instinctively I knew to shield my eyes. A stabbing, stinging, angry buzzing against my face, my cheeks, my tender exposed ears! I screamed, "Mommy! *Mommy!*" And there came Mommy to rescue me, only just happening to worry about where I might be, having wandered off behind my grandfather's hay barn; only just happening, as she would say afterward, to tilt her head to listen attentively for the cry of a little girl that might easily have been confused with the sharp cries of birds or cicadas or the half-feral tomcats that lived in the barn.

"Mom*my!*"

She heard. She didn't hesitate for a moment. She ran swift and unerring as a young girl, though she was thirty-two years old and had not fully recovered from a miscarriage the previous spring, and was not in any case a woman accustomed to running. She heard my desperate cries and was herself panicked and yet had enough presence of mind to tear a bath towel off my grandmother's clothesline with which to wrap me, roughly, efficiently, as if putting out flames. Mommy shielded me from the wasps with both the towel and her bare, vulnerable flesh. She was being stung herself, a dozen times, yet tried to comfort me as I screamed in pain and terror—"It's all right, Ella! Mommy's got you." She half-carried me, half-ran with me out of the orchard, away from the pear tree disfigured by black knot and by a gigantic wasps' papery gray nest attached like a goiter to the tree trunk overhead at a height of about nine feet; away from the crazed cloud of wasps that had erupted out of nowhere.

Long afterward my mother would say with her breathy, nervous laugh that she hadn't felt much pain herself, at the time. Not until later. For nothing had mattered except rescuing me.

"My mother saved my life, when I was four years old."

This was a statement I would make often, to new friends, or to people who, for one reason or another, I hoped to impress. *I was so loved once. I was a very lucky child.*

"My mother gave me life, and my mother saved my life. When I was four years old."

Is this true? I wonder: could a child die of multiple wasp stings? I think probably, yes. I think a child could die of the shock of the stings, the trauma of the assault as well as the wasps' venom. Perhaps an adult woman could die of such an assault, too.

2. THE SUMMONS

Twenty-two years later, driving north to see Mother, from whom I'd been estranged for the past decade and to whom I hadn't spoken for several years, I was thinking of these things. Driving north to the town of my birth, Strykersville, New York, and beyond Strykersville into the abandoned farmland and foothills of Eden County, I told myself, as if to comfort myself, the familiar story: four-year-old Ella exploring Grandpa's pear orchard, wandering far from the adults seated on the veranda of the old farmhouse, attacked suddenly by wasps that seemed to fly at her out of the sky; screaming, "Mommy!"—and Mommy running desperately to save her. It was a fairy tale with a happy ending.

(But where in this story was Daddy? He had not yet left us. He must have been there, somewhere. Or had he, too, wandered off from the adults on the veranda, in another direction? Maybe he'd even gotten into the car and driven away, into Strykersville, restless for a change of scene. An hour's diversion in a local tavern. There was no Daddy in my story, and had never been.)

Like all beloved family stories, this story had been enhanced over the years. It had been enlarged to include a description of Ella's pretty pink sundress with the ruffled bodice which she'd worn for the first time that day, and Ella's blond-gold hair prettily braided, by Mommy, into two shoulder-length plaits entwined with pink satin ribbons. It had been enlarged to include an acknowledgment of my mother's physical condition, which hadn't been robust. *Yet Ginny never hesitated. How that woman ran! And none of us had even heard Ella crying.*

Snapshots of those lost years show my older brother Walter and me smiling and seemingly happy, and Mommy more somber, though attempting her usual earnest smile; a youngish woman with an oddly wide, sensual mouth; her dark hair parted on the left side of her head in the overly prim style of the Fifties. In a typical picture Mommy would be crouching between Walter and me, her arms tightly around us to steady us, or to prevent us from squirming; face blurred, eyes averted shyly from the camera (which had probably been held by Daddy, who'd liked mechanical things, and had not liked his picture taken, at least with his young family).

Poor Ginny. She hadn't been well. . . . Because, it was vaguely said, of the miscarriage; because she'd never gotten over giving birth to the little girl, a thirty-hour labor; because of certain "female weaknesses." (Meaning what? In that era in which breast, cervical, and ovarian cancer as well as more ordinary menstrual problems were mysteriously alluded to as "women's shame," it was difficult to guess what this ominous term meant.) And because, just possibly, though this was never uttered in my hearing, she had a husband with a quick temper and quick fists who'd tired of loving her during her first pregnancy. *But Ginny is so devoted. So forgiving.*

Forgiving! That was the primary reason I'd become estranged from my mother. Not just Mother had endured my father's crude, often dangerous behavior when Walter and I were growing up, but, after her divorce, when I was in high school, she fell into the same pattern with Walter. He'd dropped out of school and never kept a job for more than a few weeks; he was a "charming" boy but a chronic drinker while still in his teens. Mother pleaded with me to be more understanding. "Ella, you're too hard on your brother. Ella, he's *your brother*." And I would secretly think, embittered as only a good dutiful daughter can be, confronted with her mother's weak, hapless love for one who didn't deserve it, *No. He isn't my brother, he's your son.*

After my grandparents died, Mother inherited their farm. It was only eleven acres, yet a fairly large property by Eden County standards. This she'd sold piecemeal, year by year; she worked at various jobs in Strykersville, to support her family (receptionist for our family dentist, saleslady at Strykersville's department store, substitute junior high school teacher—a nightmare job she'd dreaded), and I'd taken part-time jobs while still in high school; but Walter drained our meager savings, my damned brother was always the issue, and when Mother paid a $2500 fine for him after an accident he'd had driving while intoxicated, an accident in which the other driver was seriously injured, I stopped speaking to Mother. *You've chosen between us. Good!* I was disgusted with family life and with small-town life. I left Strykersville at the age of seventeen, attended the State Teachers' College at Oneida on a scholarship, worked at part-time jobs to support myself for four years, and was proud of my independence. I associated Strykersville with the past and I had no nostalgic yearning for the past, I'm not a sentimental person. For what is sentiment but weakness, and usually female weakness. *I am not one of you.*

I lived now outside Philadelphia. I had a good, if demanding, teaching job in a private school. I told myself that I didn't miss my mother, and I certainly didn't miss my brother, who'd disappeared into America sometime in the mid-Seventies. I had friends, and I had lovers—to a degree. (No one has ever gotten too close to me. Except for my mother, which is the reason I don't entirely trust anyone.) If the subject of family came up, I explained that I was "estranged" from mine. That had a dignified 19th-century sound. But one evening, with an older woman friend, I began talking of my mother who'd "saved" my life, and I became emotional. I began telling my friend of the knitting, embroidering, sewing my mother had done, so many beautiful things, over the years; she asked if I had any of these things and I said yes, I'd taken a few articles of clothing when I'd left home, a knitted cashmere coat-sweater, a long-sleeved silk blouse, a wool jersey vest with mother-of-pearl buttons. My friend examined these items, and marveled over them— "Your mother is a wonderful seamstress. And she's never sewn for money?" I shrugged indifferently. Possibly I had not wanted to feel emotion. "I don't really wear this kind of clothing," I said. "It isn't my style." My friend was peering at the inside of the silk blouse, holding it to the light. "See this fine stitching? This is the Fortuny stitch. And this exquisite lace hem. What an interesting woman your mother must be!" I looked, and saw, yes, the stitching was fine, and intricate, but what was the point of it? And the lace hem: Why had my mother gone to so much trouble, to hem a blouse in lace, on the underside of the material where no one would ever see?

Driving north to Strykersville, a distance of several hundred miles from my home, I thought of these things as a way of not thinking of the present.

Driving north to Strykersville in the oppressive heat of August, after so many years, I thought of my mother as she'd been, as a way of not thinking of the woman she might be now.

She was fifty-four years old. To me, at twenty-six, *old*.

She was "Mrs. Moses Hammacher" now, she'd remarried abruptly, the previous March.

Wife of Dr. Moses!

After almost twenty years of being a divorced woman in a small town where divorce was rare, yet a divorced woman whose husband was known to have been an abusive alcoholic, so that sympathy was entirely with my mother, and no one would have dreamt of criticizing her, my mother had suddenly, without warning, remarried: a locally known retired physician and Eden County coroner named Moses Hammacher, familiarly called "Dr. Moses."

Dr. Moses! He'd been an old man, gaunt and white-haired, or so it had seemed to me, when I was in junior high.

Mother, how could you.

I had tried to call her. Finally, I'd written a brief letter to her, sending it in care of relatives to be forwarded. I had to assume the letter had been received by my mother though—of course—Mother hadn't answered it. Since then I had not slept well. My sleep was thin like mist or spray, disturbed by strange echoing voices and muffled laughter. And my mother's voice sudden, pleading—*Ella? Come to me! Help me.*

In Strykersville, I drove across the familiar jarring railroad tracks and it was as if I'd never left. Though I had been imagining my hometown as unpopulated, for some reason, a ghost town, yet of course there was traffic on the streets, there were people on the sidewalks downtown, and probably I would recognize some of these people if I lingered. I did take note of the number of FOR RENT FOR LEASE FOR SALE signs; I saw abandoned, boarded-up houses. I drove past our old church, the First Presbyterian, to which Mother had taken Walter and me, before we were old enough to rebel; I drove past my old high school, which had been renovated and enlarged; I felt my heartbeat quicken in apprehension and dread. *Why am I here? She doesn't want me. If she wanted me . . .*

Mother had not invited me to her wedding, of course. She had not even informed me she'd remarried, I had learned from relatives.

The shock of it! The shame. Learning that your mother has remarried, from relatives. And that she was now the wife of "Dr. Moses."

I'd instructed myself before I began my trip that I would not do this, yet here I was driving around Strykersville, staring with rapt, lovesick eyes. Did I miss my past, truly? Did I miss *this?* I'd thought

myself very shrewd—and very lucky—to have escaped this eco-
nomically depressed region of upstate New York as I'd escaped the
confinements of my former life, and it seemed to me a risky matter,
a sign of my own recklessness, that I'd been drawn back into it, like
a moth blindly flying into a gigantic cobweb.

"Mother! God damn *you*."

For there I was driving slowly past our old brown-shingled
house on Iroquois Street, with the flower beds Mother had worked
so hard to keep in bloom, and the flowering Russian olive tree she'd
kept watered through summer droughts, my eyes misting over with
tears. The house now belonged to strangers of course. I wondered
what price Mother had gotten for the property, and where the
money had gone: for according to my cousin Brenda, who'd been
the one to give me information about Mother, she'd sold everything
very quickly, including most of her long-cherished furniture, and
even her car, after her "private" wedding to Dr. Moses Hammacher,
and had gone to live with her new husband in his stone house in
the Oriskany hills nine miles northeast of Strykersville. The doctor
had had an office in Strykersville, in fact he'd had two offices, as a
G.P. and as Eden County coroner; but he'd long since retired. My
cousin Brenda believed that Dr. Moses, or Dr. Hammacher, still saw
some of his elderly patients; and that he'd turned part of his house
into a kind of museum. "Museum?" I asked incredulously, and
Brenda explained it was probably just an old man's hobby—"To
give him something to do, you know, in his retirement." "But is this
an actual *museum*? Open to the public?" Brenda said, "After the
Fowler House was taken over by the County Historical Society, and
all those old antiques, weaving looms, dressmakers' dummies,
washboards and butter churns and whatever were put on display,
Dr. Moses demanded money from the Society to start a museum of
his own. A history of medical arts in Eden County which means, I

suppose, a history of *Dr. Moses!* So the Society gave him a small grant, to humor him, but he wanted more, and broke off relations with the Society, and I guess he has this museum out in Oriskany, such as it is. Medical school things like skeletons and 'cadavers' made of plaster, old instruments, office equipment, things floating in formaldehyde . . . A few people went to see it out of curiosity when it opened about five years ago, but I never went." Brenda paused. She was conscious of speaking in an amused voice, and had suddenly to realize that she was talking about my new stepfather. "Ella, I'm sorry. I'm sure . . . your mother is happy with Dr. Moses." But she sounded doubtful.

I said, miserably, "Why on earth would Mother marry *Dr. Moses?* He's old enough to be her father." *And my grandfather. But I don't want another grandfather.*

Brenda said sympathetically, "I can imagine you're upset, Ella. We all were, at first. I mean . . . your mother is so *sweet.* So *trusting.* And Dr. Moses is, well . . . a kind of strong-willed man, I guess. He must be in his mid-eighties, yet he doesn't seem terribly old when you see him. Certainly his mind is sharp as always. Razor-sharp. Maybe your mother needs someone strong-willed to take care of her." Was this a reproach? Quickly Brenda amended, "Ella, your mother told me, when I happened to run into her downtown a few days before the wedding, that she was 'embarking upon a new life'—she was 'very happy'—she and Dr. Moses were driving to Mexico, where she'd never been, on their honeymoon. She said she had been 'very lonely'—but that was over now. I'm sure that she married Dr. Moses voluntarily; I mean, I don't think he coerced her in any way. You know what your mother is like, Ella!"

Did I? Even when I'd lived with my mother, had I known her?

As if hoping to console me, now that she'd upset me, Brenda

went on to say that Dr. Moses was still an individual of some reputation in the county. He still drove his fancy British car, a twenty-year-old silver-green Bentley, which was like no other car in the county; he'd also acquired a Land Cruiser, a combination van and trailer of the kind popular with retired people. Still he cut a gentlemanly, dapper figure in Strykersville with his dignified derby hats in cool weather and festive straw hats in warm weather. He wore his trademark pinstriped suits, white starched cotton shirts with monogrammed gold cuff links, striped neckties. People respected him, though they tended to joke nervously about him as they'd always done. (I recalled how, years ago, my high school girl-friends made a show of shuddering and shivering as Dr. Moses passed by us on the sidewalk, tipping his hat and smiling his white-toothed smile, "Good day, girls!" His gaze, mildly defracted by bifocal lenses, lingered on us. We had to wonder who would wish to be county coroner and examine dead, sometimes badly disfigured and mangled bodies extracted from wrecks? And for virtually no salary.) This tall white-haired gentleman had been both "Dr. Hammacher," a well-to-do physician with a general practice, and "Dr. Moses," the cheery county official who was invited into public schools in the district to give talks and slide presentations with such titles as "You and Your Anatomy" and "The Miracle of Eyesight." As Dr. Moses he exuded an air of civic responsibility like those fanatically active businessmen who ran the Strykersville Chamber of Commerce, the Rotary Club, the Royal Order of Moose, and other service organizations. I'd thought him older than my grandfather back in the mid-Sixties when he came to our junior high assembly to speak on "The Miracle of Eyesight."

For this, an energetic talk that left the more sensitive among us queasy, Dr. Moses used a large plaster-of-paris eyeball as a prop; it swung hideously open in sections to reveal the veiny interior of the eye, uncomfortably suggesting a dissection. I felt light-headed, and resistant. Yet Dr. Moses must have made a strong impression on me since I remembered long afterward certain parts of the eye: the "pupil"—the "cornea"—the "lens"—the "iris"—the "retina"—the "sclera"—the "aqueous humor"—the "vitreous humor"—the "optic nerve"—the "blind spot." Dr. Moses concluded his presentation by appealing to us, "So you see, boys and girls, the miraculous anatomy of the human eye alone teaches us that 'evolution'—the blind chance of natural selection, survival of the fittest—is simply not feasible. No organ so complex as the human eye could have 'evolved' in a hit-or-miss fashion as the Darwinists say. Nor could it have evolved out of some primal pro-toplasm. It would have to have been, like our souls, *created*." Dr. Moses squinted at us through his shiny bifocals. "By a *creator*." How dramatically the man spoke! In our naiveté some of us may have confused white-haired Dr. Moses in his gray pinstripe suit with *creator*. "Are there any questions, boys and girls?" Our mouths wanted to smile, to grimace and giggle, but could not.

And now, as in a malevolent fairy tale, Dr. Moses had married my mother.

Dr. Moses was my stepfather.

Dazed, I heard Brenda's cautious voice. She was asking, "Ella? You aren't crying, are you?" and I said quickly, incensed, "Of course I'm not crying! I'm laughing."

3. IN ORISKANY

Strange to be driving here alone.

I stopped in Strykersville only briefly, and continued out into the country toward Oriskany. As I ascended into the hills I felt as if

I were driving, under a strange half-pleasurable compulsion, into the past: there were farmhouses, barns, granaries I vaguely recalled, though a number of these were for sale or abandoned; there was the old Starlite Drive-In on the Oriskany Pike, a morose, funeral ruin jutting up above overgrown fields. About three miles north of Strykersville I crossed the high, humpbacked rusted-iron bridge above the Eden Creek which I vaguely recalled as one of the nightmare bridges of my childhood: below, the creek was diminished and mud-colored, its gnarled banks exposed in the languid heat of August. Descending the steep bridge ramp I saw, nailed to an oak tree by the side of the road, a small, darkly weathered sign:

MUSEUM OF EDEN COUNTY MEDICAL ARTS 6 miles

The museum of Dr. Moses existed! The next signs appeared at two-mile intervals, all of them small and undistinguished; finally, when the Oriskany Pike veered to the east, a sign at the crossroads indicated that the museum was a half-mile away, on a graveled single-lane county road. At the crossroads were a boarded-up Sunoco gas station and a dilapidated bait shop. Nearby was an abandoned farm; the land surrounding it had long since reverted to tall grasses, nettles, scrub trees. Yet the landscape here in Oriskany was starkly beautiful: the foothills miles away at the horizon, in a checkered pattern of luminous golden sunlight and shadow that moved slowly across it, like brooding thoughts, cast by isolated clouds. Though the air at ground level was hot, hazy, humid as an expelled breath, the sky overhead was a crystalline blue.

I turned onto the graveled road and drove a half-mile. There was no mistaking Dr. Moses's house/museum for it seemed to be the only human habitation on the road, and the sign in the weedy front yard was prominent.

MUSEUM OF EDEN COUNTY MEDICAL ARTS
Proprietor Moses Hammacher, M.D.
Hours Daily Except Monday
10 AM—4:30 PM
Free Admission

There was something naive and touching about Dr. Moses's museum, I thought. The carefully posted visiting hours, the appeal implicit in *free admission*. For who would ever come to such a remote, dreary place? The house was tall, dignified, impressive; one of those gaunt stone houses built at the turn of the century, with steep roofs (because of the heavy, often damp snowfall south of Lake Ontario from November through early April); the grey fieldstone of which the house had been constructed looked bleak and stained. There were double bay windows and a narrow veranda. On the highest peak of the roof there was even a lightning rod, relic of a vanished rural past, only just slightly askew. (And there was a TV antenna.) I parked my car in the cinder driveway, conscious of being watched. (A movement at one of the downstairs windows?) Though I'd written to my mother telling her I would be coming, I couldn't be sure that she'd received the letter, and that anyone expected me. Or would wish to see me.

Judging from the waist-high grasses surrounding the house and by the quantity of weeds in the driveway, there were few visitors to Dr. Moses's museum.

As I climbed out of my car I thought I saw again, fleetingly, a movement at one of the windows. Dr. Moses? Or—Mother? Frightened at what I might find inside, I smiled, and called out shyly. "Hello? It's me, Ella." I felt it might be a mistake to step boldly onto the veranda and ring the doorbell, though visitors to the museum would be expected to do this. "Ella McIntyre." As if my

17

last name might be required! My hands were shaking badly by this time, and my throat was painfully dry.

After a moment the front door opened, and a figure appeared in the doorway. I smiled, and waved. "Hello! It's Ella." Dr. Moses stepped out onto the sunlit veranda and regarded me in silence. I was startled that the man, in person, so closely resembled the Dr. Moses I'd been envisioning. Except that he wasn't so tall as I remembered, and his hair, though still surprisingly thick, was no longer snowy white but a faded ivory. He wore a starched white shirt, sleeves rolled casually to his elbows, and dark, pressed slacks. At a distance of twelve or fifteen feet he seemed to me quite handsome, an individual of some distinction, though obviously elderly. And he'd put on his head, in a gesture of hasty gallantry, one of his straw hats. His right hand was held at a stiff, unnatural angle, however, pressed against a pocket of his slacks as if against—what? A weapon? Not a gun, it wouldn't have been large enough. A knife, or a small hammer. A scalpel?

Cicadas screamed out of nearby trees. The heat lifted from the earth into my face. I was reminded of that attack of wasps out of the sky. I smiled harder, as a flirtatious child might smile at her taciturn, frowning grandfather. "Dr. Moses? It's your daughter-in-law Ella."

Suddenly, Dr. Moses's face melted into a smile. His teeth were still shiny-white, and his eyes, behind winking bifocals, were appreciative, affectionate. "Ella, dear girl, hello! Your mother and I have been waiting for you."

It isn't possible, he remembers me? As a girl, years ago? Dr. Moses has been awaiting me, all this time?

Gentlemanly Dr. Moses left my mother and me alone to visit in the parlor. Though we were shy with each other, self-conscious and awkward. I kept wanting to touch Mother, as if to prove she was *here*, and I was *here*, this wasn't a dream. I kept saying, dazed, "You look so young, Mother. You look so pretty."

"And you, Ella. You've grown into a . . . beautiful young woman."

We gripped hands, and stared at each other. I was feeling faint and I believed that Mother was deeply moved as well. Her thin fingers were icy, I'd noticed a mild palsied tremor in both her hands. Tears brimmed in her eyes that seemed to me strangely exposed, and enlarged, as if lashless. Several times she wanted to say more, but stammered and fell silent. Was she frightened? Of me, or of her own emotion? Or—of her husband? After Dr. Moses's initial, courtly greeting of me, whom he referred to as his "prodigal stepdaughter," he'd retreated upstairs, meaning to be inconspicuous perhaps, but his slow, circling footsteps sounded directly overhead; the high ceiling above creaked; Mother glanced upward, distracted. I was asking her simple, innocuous questions about her wedding, her honeymoon, relatives, Strykersville neighbors and friends, and she answered in monosyllables; I told her about my teaching job, my semi-detached brownstone with its small rear garden, my regret that I hadn't seen her in so long. Some caution prevented me asking of more crucial matters. I sensed that my mother's mood was fragile. And a harshly medicinal, gingery odor pervaded the room, making my nostrils constrict; after only a few minutes I began to feel mildly nauseated. The parlor was furnished in period pieces of the late 19th century (not a single item anything I recognized of Mother's) and its two tall, narrow windows were shaded against the August heat; brass lamps with curiously leathery shades emitted a dim light. Truly I could not see Mother clearly, even at close range. *Ella! Help me.* I heard this appeal silently, as Mother squeezed my hands.

I whispered, "Mother? Is anything wrong?" but immediately she pressed her fingers against my lips and shook her head *no*.

Meaning *no*, there was nothing wrong? Or *no*, this wasn't the time to ask?

In her weak, eager voice Mother asked, "How long can you stay, Ella? We were hoping—a few days?"

A few days! I didn't believe I could bear more than a few more minutes, the smell made me so nauseated.

Yet I was smiling, nodding. "That would be lovely, Mother. If you and—" (I paused, for to call my stepfather "Dr. Moses" as we'd called him as schoolchildren seemed inappropriate), "—and he— wouldn't be inconvenienced?" In the airless heat of the parlor I was nearly shivering. I was desperate to flee this oppressive place, yet I would not leave without Mother, if she needed me.

"But Dr. Moses expects you to stay with us," Mother protested, "—he's had me prepare a guest room. I've made your favorite dessert for dinner tonight. Dr. Moses is very eager to get to know you, Ella. I've told him about you." Mother spoke wistfully. (What could she have told Dr. Moses about me that wouldn't have given her pain?) I noted that Mother too called her courtly husband "Dr. Moses." I wondered if such old-fashioned formality was a natural part of their relationship. For Mother was so much younger than Dr. Moses Hammacher, a girlish, indecisive personality clearly dependent upon him, it would have been difficult for her to call him "Moses," as if they were equals.

"I suppose I could stay. At least tonight . . ."

"Oh Ella, you *must*. Dr. Moses and I would be so disappointed if you didn't."

Dr. Moses and I. I didn't like the sound of that.

It was strange: I had not made any plans for the night. Vaguely I might have planned to return to Strykersville to stay with Brenda, or in a motel; next morning, I might have driven back to Oriskany to visit with my mother, if our first visit had gone well. But really I hadn't thought that far ahead, my mind was blank as a child's.

Overhead, the ceiling creaked. I glanced upward nervously.

"I was surprised to hear you'd married Dr. Moses, Mother. But of course I'm happy for you." I peered closely at her. *Should I be?* "Brenda has told me . . . you sold the house, and everything in it, and your car. It was a small 'private' wedding."

"Not a church wedding," Mother said, smiling regretfully. "Dr. Moses doesn't believe in superstitious religions, as he calls them. But he does believe in a *creator*."

"He seems very—" again I paused, desperate to think of the appropriate word, "—gentlemanly."

Mother laughed suddenly, and winced as if it hurt her to laugh. Tenderly she touched her face at her hairline. "Oh, yes. He *is*."

"And you seem so—happy. Together."

Was this true? I'd seen Mother and Dr. Moses for only a few minutes when I'd first arrived at the house. During that time, Dr. Moses had done most of the talking.

Again Mother laughed, and winced. The footsteps had ceased circling overhead. (Was Dr. Moses coming downstairs to join us?)

"I am happy, Ella. My life was empty and selfish before I met Dr. Moses. It was at the funeral of your great-aunt Helena May— you wouldn't remember her, she died at the age of ninety-seven. But Dr. Moses had known her. He claimed to have been a 'beau' of hers. This was just last fall! Since then . . ." Mother stared at me with her exposed, lashless eyes. *Ella, please. Don't judge me harshly. Help me.* Her hands were visibly trembling. There was a tremor in her left eyelid. She was clearly a woman in distress, in thrall to a tyrannical male. Yet it was typical of my mother, mad-deningly typical, that she would wish to defend him, in her weak, hopeful way, as for years she'd defended my father, and then my brother, as if she believed such loyalty was expected of her as a good woman. "I can help Dr. Moses, you see. With his work. He's such an idealist! And sometimes he isn't well. I don't mean in his soul, he has a strong, pure soul, but in his 'mortal coils' as he calls his body. For he will be eighty-five years old in December. Such a youthful eighty-five! Still, he needs me. And I didn't need that house, or those possessions, or even a car. Dr. Moses has a car, and a Land Rover. He will drive me anywhere I need to go, and my needs are few. In fact we've gone on several journeys together, and have new trips planned: to Alaska, next summer, where Dr. Moses has been years ago, which he describes as 'beautiful, and so pure.' Sometimes, in remote places, where medical help isn't readily available, Dr. Moses volunteers his services; and people are so *grateful*. They've given him gifts, mementos." Mother was speaking rapidly, almost feverishly. As if wanting to convince herself as well as me. "Dr. Moses is a special person, Ella. He isn't ordinary. People whisper about him behind his back—and about me, I know!—but they're just jealous. I've helped him with the Museum, you know. I'll be helping him when he expands it. I want to help him. He's so proud of the Museum. He'll be showing you through it, before dinner. The County Historical Society insulted him, Ella! Giving him such a small grant. A man of his accomplishments! Dr. Moses deserves more respect from the citizens of Eden County, and he will receive it."

"How have you helped Dr. Moses with the Museum, Mother?"

By giving him your money, obviously. What else?

Mother smiled mysteriously. The tremor in her eyelid was more visible. Her eyes brimmed with tears and, unexpectedly, she hid her face in her hands.

Earlier, when I'd first arrived, we'd embraced awkwardly, and shyly, scarcely touching. For Dr. Moses had been present. But now I hugged my mother hard, to comfort her, as she tried not to cry. I was shocked by how much weight she'd lost, I could feel her ribs through the filmy layers of her shirtwaist as she trembled in my arms. What most shocked me was that the medicinal, gingery smell lifted from her, like perfume.

"Mother, what is it? Tell me."

It was then that Dr. Moses entered the room, pushing open the door without knocking. Gently he said, "Ella, dear. You're upsetting your mother, you see. Which you don't want to do, if you value Virginia's health."

4. THE MUSEUM OF
DR. MOSES: FIRST VISIT

Dr. Moses was eager to show me the Museum. By this time, I was very curious what it might be.

On a table at the entrance was an open ledger for visitors to sign. Surreptitiously I saw that the last visitors were a couple from Troy, New York who'd been there on June 8, 1978. More than two months ago. Prior to that, someone had visited in April. "Not everyone signs the ledger," Dr. Moses said severely, seeing where I was looking. "Some visitors forget."

Immediately I took up the pen and signed.

Ellen McIntyre Bryn Mawr, PA August 1978

(Strange, how you wanted to please Dr. Moses! A childish wish to entice, out of that gaunt brooding face, the man's sudden approving, warm, fatherly smile.)

"Very good, Ella! Now 'Ella McIntyre' is part of the Museum's official history."

With the air of an impresario, Dr. Moses switched on lights and ushered me into a large, rectangular, cluttered room that had probably once been the formal living room of the old stone house. There were double bay windows, and an imposing marble fireplace. The twelve-foot ceiling was a filigree of cracks and the ornamental moldings at the top of the walls were outlined in grime. The space was airless and intense, as if most of its oxygen had been siphoned off. The medicial-gingery odor I had smelled on my mother prevailed here, but was challenged by a stronger, sharper odor— formaldehyde? And there was the underlying odor of dust, mice, time that belonged to such houses. I felt light-headed, thinking of my poor mother trapped in this place, deluded into imagining herself the beloved helper of a vain, eccentric husband. At once, I could see Mother's touch in the Museum: the dark crimson silk panels at the windows, which could be drawn over the venetian blinds by cords, made from the identical pattern of our living room drapes in the Iroquois Street house; several attractive hooked rugs of the kind Mother used to make to give to relatives and friends, like the one I'd had in my college dormitory room, of which I'd been proud; handsewn linen lampshades in that dignified hue called eggshell. "How ambitious this is," I heard myself say falteringly, for I felt that some immediate, positive response was required. "How—*interesting*." My nostrils constricted, I had to fight an impulse to gag. Dr. Moses took not the slightest notice of my discomfort, for clearly he was captivated by his own domain. Proudly he showed me a row of glass display cases that had obviously been dusted and cleaned very recently, perhaps that very day, for there were telltale lines of demarcation between grime and polished glass; I had a disagreeable vision of my mother, frail, unwell, hurriedly dusting and cleaning these cases under Dr. Moses's sharp-eyed supervision. In our house in Strykersville, Mother had kept things obsessively clean, in a perpetual anxiety of allowing dirt and disorder to intrude by the smallest degree; I'd had to resist such impulses in myself as an adult, understanding that they were insatiable, like addictions. Yet, I had to acknowledge, Mother had given this bleak, austere place a welcoming, even homey touch.

Dr. Moses said, "Some of these instruments are my own, and some I've acquired over the years. Decades! People may think that Dr. Moses is old as the Oriskany hills but of course there were predecessor physicians in Eden County, dating back to the late 1700's." We were staring at primitive medical instruments: stethoscopes, wooden tongue depressors, forceps, suction devices, rubber enemas, small handsaws. Saws! I laughed, pointing at these badly rusted things. "Is this why doctors used to be called 'sawbones,' Dr. Moses?" It was a sincere question, such as a bright child might ask. Dr. Moses chuckled, opening the display case and removing a ten-inch saw to show me. "Of course, the amputee would be strapped down onto a table. A limb would have to be removed if it became infected and gangrenous. If the patient was lucky, he or she would be rendered unconscious by a powerful dose of whiskey or laudanum." Dr. Moses indicated leather straps attached to an examining table, and hanging from a wall. I was feeling dangerously light-headed, but I tried to smile. The saw's teeth, stained by rust, or blood, or both, felt disconcertingly dull against my fingertips. "But you've never done such an amputation, Dr. Moses, have you? Not *you.*" My question was nervy, almost coquettish. Dr. Moses seemed to be brooding upon it as with finicky care he replaced the saw back inside the display case and shut the glass lid. Thoughtfully he said, "Not of any living person, I believe."

I'd been forgetting: Dr. Moses had been Eden County coroner for forty years.

On the wall before us were framed anatomical drawings, some primitive and crude, some finely rendered, and startlingly beautiful; among these were Leonardo's symmetrically ideal human being (male, of course) and several line drawings of Dürer. "Our ancestors believed that the immortal soul dwelled within 'mortal coils,' you see. But the question was: where?" Dr. Moses indicated a drawing of what appeared to be a dissected human brain, but I glanced quickly away. I pretended a greater interest in the miscellany of medical equipment Dr. Moses had assembled in his Museum. So much! More wooden tongue depressors, which reminded me of the popsicle sticks of my childhood, and tourniquet devices, and rubber contraptions resembling hot-water bottles; a rubber ball attached to a pronged hose—"To flush the wax out of your ears, dear." There were hypodermic needles of different sizes, one of them unnervingly long—"Nasty, yes. But death by rabies was nastier." There were thin transparent tubes suggestively coiled—"Early catheters. Nasty, yes, but death by uremic poisoning was nastier."

I found myself staring wordlessly into a large display case of metal specula, several of them mounted with tiny mirrors, which made the pit of my belly—or the mouth of my uterus—contract in an involuntary spasm. Dr. Moses may have noticed me wince, for he said, in his kindly, firm voice, "Again, Ella!—the alternative to a thorough pelvic examination was often, for females of all ages, much nastier than any examination." I staggered away, into another aisle, wiping at my eyes. An entire section of the Museum was devoted to childbirth but I wasn't in a mood to examine anatomical charts of pregnant bellies, embryos curled in the wombs of headless female bodies. Nor did I want to see close up the "birthing" table, with far-spread stirrups and gnawed-looking leather straps. A centuries'-old odor of urine, blood, female suffering wafted from it. I murmured, "Dr. Moses, shall I go help Mother prepare dinner? I always used to help her when I was a . . ." But Dr. Moses, intent upon leading me forward, didn't hear, or took no heed.

We were in a part of the Museum devoted, as Dr. Moses explained, to more personal items. He'd begun his practice in Eden County in 1922, nearly six decades were represented here, so he'd had to be highly selective. On an antique sideboard were more modern, stainless steel instruments, scalpels and such, which looked razor-sharp; I felt a shiver of dread, that Dr. Moses might lift one of these for me to touch, as I'd touched the saw, and I would cut myself badly. I felt relief coming upon an old-fashioned scale of the kind I recalled from childhood, and climbed up on it. Dr. Moses weighed me, frowning as he shifted the small lead weights back and forth on the rod. "What! Only one hundred eight pounds, Ella? Really, for your height, you should weigh twenty pounds more." Dr. Moses measured my height, bringing the steel rod gently down on the top of my head. "Yes. You're five feet nine. We'll have to fatten you up, dear, before you leave Oriskany!" Dr. Moses patted my head, my shoulder, my bare, slightly trembling arm. Close up, his handsome ruin of a face was a maze of miniature broken capillaries and his eyes, behind the bifocal lenses, were sharply alert, like darting fish.

Next we came to a vision chart, a display case of old-fashioned lenses and eyeglasses, and, to my delight, the gigantic eye. It was about the size of a large watermelon, lone and staring in a corner of the Museum. Excitedly I said, "I remember this, Dr. Moses! Your wonderful talk at our school. We were all so—impressed." Dr. Moses had some difficulty opening the eye, parts of which seemed to have stuck together; the veiny interior was laced with cobwebs, which Dr. Moses brushed at irritably. (Whoever had cleaned the Museum had not thought to clean the interior of the eye, obviously!)

"But do you remember the lesson, Ella? Can you recite for me—?" He pointed at the parts of the eye and with schoolgirl solemnity I recited: "The pupil—the cornea—the lens—the iris—the retina—the sclera—the aqueous humor—the vitreous humor—the optic nerve—the blind spot." Dr. Moses was genuinely surprised. He mimed applause. "*Very* good, Ella. No one else from that school assembly, examined at this time, would do so well, I'm certain." My face smarted pleasantly. I'd surprised myself, in fact. "Your mother has told me you were an honors student, and I can see she wasn't exaggerating, as Virginia sometimes does. A pity, though, you hadn't gone on to medical school. We might be a team, Ella."

I laughed, feeling my face burn. Truly, I was flattered.

But you're retired, Dr. Moses. Aren't you?

The rest of the Museum visit wasn't so pleasant.

At the farther end of the room were shelves of bottles containing rubbery semi-floating shapes: some were human organs, including eyeballs; some were human fetuses. These, Dr. Moses called his "specimens"—"mementos." Clearly, each bottle had a personal meaning to him; shelves were labeled according to dates, bottles were yet more meticulously labeled. The stench of formaldehyde was almost overwhelming here, but Dr. Moses took no notice. He was smiling, tapping at bottles. I'd averted my eyes, feeling faint, but soon found myself staring at a quart-sized bottle containing a shriveled, darkly discolored fishlike thing floating in murky liquid, apparently headless, with rudimentary arms and legs and something—a head? a heart?—pushing out of its chest cavity. "This poor creature, I delivered on Christmas night, 1939," Dr. Moses said, tapping at the bottle. I felt faint, and looked away. *Not a fetus. An actual baby.* I wanted to ask Dr. Moses what had happened to the poor mother, but he was moving on. You could see that the Museum was Dr. Moses's life and that a visitor was privileged to be a witness to it, but in no way a participant.

It was then that Dr. Moses muttered, "What! What are these doing *here?*" I had a glimpse of what appeared to be human hands. Embalmed hands. Several were appallingly small, child-sized. Dr. Moses blocked my vision, frowning severely; he gripped my elbow and led me firmly onward. I made no sign that I'd noticed the hands, or Dr. Moses's agitation. I was hoping that, if there'd been a mistake of some kind in the Museum, Mother wasn't responsible.

The Museum tour was ending. I was exhausted, yet strangely exhilarated. Almost, I felt giddy; drunken. The powerful smells had gone to my head. And Dr. Moses's mesmerizing nearness. *This man is my stepfather.*

Slyly Dr. Moses said, "Ella, dear: meet Cousin Sam."

With a snap of his fingers he'd set the skeleton to rattling and vibrating. I had to check the impulse to shudder, sympathetically. "Cousin Sam has been with me for a long time, haven't you, Sam?" Dr. Moses said. Naively I wondered if this was a commercial skeleton of the kind sold to medical schools or if Dr. Moses had constructed it himself, meticulously wiring and bolting bones together. It appeared to be the skeleton of a man of moderate height; its bones discolored with age and its skull dented; the eye sockets were enormous. The skull seemed to be listening to us with a monkeyish air of mock severity. Strands of cobweb drifted between the skeleton's ribs; something scuttled inside one of the eye sockets: a spider? I looked away, unnerved. Dr. Moses chuckled. "And these, Sam's relatives." Close by, on a fireplace mantel, was a row of silently staring skulls. These too appeared to be listening to us with mock severity. "Skulls resemble one another to the untrained eye," Dr. Moses said, "but to the trained eye, distinctions abound." He picked up one of the smaller skulls and turned it over so that I could observe its badly cracked cranium. I had to suppress the instinct to hide my eyes, as if I were looking at something obscene. "This is the skull of a young girl of about thirteen. She died, very likely, by a severe blow to the head. A hammer, or the blunt edge of an ax." I wanted to ask when the girl had died, but could not speak. "She died before your time, Ella," Dr. Moses said.

I managed to ask, "Where did you get these skulls, Dr. Moses?" *From the county morgue. From the county graveyard.*

Dr. Moses smiled mysteriously. "Death is plentiful, Ella. There is no lack of specimens of the genus *Death*."

The tour was over. It was time to leave the Museum.

But I'd noticed double carved-oak doors at the rear of the room, and asked what was behind them? Dr. Moses said, "A new wing of the Museum, 'The Red Room'—not yet ready for visitors. Another time, Ella."

5. THE REVELATION

If I can endure this meal, I can endure anything.

And yet: I surprised myself at dinner, I was so hungry for my mother's food. I had not eaten since breakfast that morning, twelve hours before, and my hand shook as I lifted my fork. "Mother, this is *delicious*." Despite the heat, and her apparent infirmity, Mother had prepared one of her heroic meals. Thinly sliced roast beef, delicately whipped potatoes, several kinds of vegetables, fresh-baked whole grain bread. For dessert, my childhood favorite: cherry pie with a "braided" crust. Dr. Moses had an elderly man's finicky appetite but it was clear that he liked to be presented with a full complement of carefully prepared food. And though he drank sparingly, he also served red wine in fine crystal glasses.

A bamboo fan whirred and hummed over the dining room table, stirring the languid air and diluting the pungent medicinal odor. There were freshly cut crimson roses (from Mother's small, meticulously tended rose garden at the side of the house), scented candles burning in silver candlestick holders. The dining room was furnished in an early 20th-century style but on the windows were flounced white silk drapes my mother had hand sewn and I recognized the crocheted place mats as her handiwork. The thought occurred to me: *Wherever my mother goes, she brings herself. It was wrong of me to leave her.* Through dinner Mother sat wanly smiling at me, and at her husband, but was virtually silent, as if she were very tired, unconsciously touching her hairline and jaw where it appeared to be slightly swollen. She'd put on lipstick, but no other makeup. She'd forgotten to remove her apron. Her silvery-white hair had gone limp in the humidity. She ate and drank little, while Dr. Moses, fresh-shaven and handsome in a taffy-colored seersucker coat and yellow striped tie, turned his attention to me. It was "Ella"— "Ella, dear"—"dear Ella!" until I began to feel uncomfortable.

Dr. Moses told me he'd been born in Düsseldorf, Germany, in 1893. His parents had brought him to the United States, to the port of Boston, when he was seven years old; he'd gotten his medical degree from Boston University; in 1920, an adventurous young man, he'd emigrated to the wilds of upstate New York. Initially, he settled in Port Oriskany. He married the daughter of fellow German emigrants. He moved to Eden County, to the town of Rockland, and then to Strykersville, where he would maintain his medical practice while buying this stone house in the Oriskany hills, and living here happily ever since. "Solitude and beauty, in Oriskany," Dr. Moses said, lifting his glass to me. He paused. "We were not blessed with children."

"I'm sorry," I said uncertainly.

"Dear Ella, you shouldn't be! There have been many children in my life, children I've loved, and who have loved me."

For some reason, this statement, not boastful but matter-of-fact, made me very uneasy.

And what became of your first wife, Dr. Moses?

In the parlor, I'd noticed a stiffly posed sepia-toned photograph of a young, dashing, dark-haired Moses Hammacher seated in a Model-T beside a plump, stern-browed young woman with a look of being tightly corseted; this woman, I assumed, was Dr. Moses's first wife. Naively I asked her name, and Dr. Moses said with surprising sharpness, "It isn't good manners, Ella, is it, to discuss a previous spouse in the presence of—" He indicated Mother, whose cheeks flushed with embarassment at being so singled out.

Mother protested weakly, "Oh, I don't mind, dear! Her name was—"

"*I* mind." Dr. Moses struck his fist on the table. Our wine glasses shuddered, the lighted candles flickered in alarm. "She is not Mrs. Moses Hammacher *now.*"

Dr. Moses was breathing audibly. His eyes lurched behind his shiny glasses. Like guilty children Mother and I lowered our gazes to our plates. I wanted badly to reach over to Mother beneath the table, and take her hand; I knew her fingers would be thin, chill, limp. Yet she would grip my hand, hard. *Help me, Ella! Take me from this terrible place.*

The remainder of the dinner hour passed in a haze of strain and apprehension, though Dr. Moses didn't lash out at Mother again, or at me. He resumed his cordial, courtly manner, telling me at length of his plans to expand the Museum and to advertise—"Statewide, beyond the narrow parameters of Eden County. Perhaps, in the preparation of a brochure, you might help me, Ella?" Startled, I may have smiled; I said nothing. As if to impress me, while Mother sat silent, looking very tired, Dr. Moses told me of his travels—his "frontier adventures"—in Mexico, the American Southwest, and Alaska, "among indigenous peoples." He'd retired as county coroner in 1964, and for several years following he traveled extensively every summer—"Following the horizon. The lure of the mountains. The very sky called to me." How lyric Dr. Moses's voice, how yearning! Though I feared and distrusted Dr. Moses, knowing him now to be a domestic tyrant, and possibly a dangerous one, I found myself charmed by him, as I'd been in the Museum. His sensual, powerful will. His sexual will. *Women have been captivated by him. And men.* A man who has exerted his will over others never relinquishes that will, or the wish to exert it, as he ages; his victims understand this, and succumb. The strength of the one draws the weakness of the others, as in a perverse magic. "On my travels, I've met many people, including young girls and women," Dr. Moses said, smiling wistfully. "I was a Pied Piper to them, bringing medical attention and care where there'd been little— but, of course, I never took advantage of their trust. Did I, Virginia?"

Mother woke from her mild, melancholy trance to smile quickly. "Oh, yes. Dr. Moses. I mean—no."

"Your mother has aided me invaluably in my Museum, Ella. Since last fall. Did you know that, Ella, dear?"

Was there some secret message being conveyed to me, in these words? Dr. Moses spoke with such certainty, fixing me with his singular, intense gaze. Was he suggesting that, one day, I too might aid him?

But how?

A strange, original character! After a glass or two of wine it didn't seem to me far-fetched to believe that Dr. Moses was more than an ordinary man. If circumstances had been slightly different he might have been an individual of public renown; a medical educator, a health official in the federal government, a TV personality. *He might have been my father.*

Seeing my stricken expression, Dr. Moses asked playfully, "Have you any questions, Ella?"

That question! Put to us junior high school students, with the effect of silencing us all.

Now, however, I asked a question I might have wished to ask at that time, if I'd had the vocabulary and the courage. "What compelled you to become a doctor and a coroner, Dr. Moses?"

Dr. Moses stared at me, brooding. " 'Compelled'—? Why do you say 'compelled'?" His white, wiry eyebrows frowned. "It has always been my own free choice, dear Ella. As it was your mother's free choice to become my beloved wife and helpmate, and yours to come here."

It wasn't that the kitchen of Dr. Moses's old stone house was brightly, or even adequately, lighted; but the overhead light was strong enough to allow me to see clearly, for the first time since I'd arrived, Mother.

She hadn't wanted me to help her with the dishes, of course. She'd protested feebly. But I'd insisted, carrying plates into the kitchen, stacking them in the sink. It was then I saw that Mother wasn't at all well. Her face was swollen and discolored at the jawline; she walked slowly, favoring her left side; she appeared to be in pain. I took the dishes she'd been carrying from her, set them in the sink, and placed my hands firmly on her narrow shoulders. I was several inches taller than Mother, who'd certainly shrunk in the past decade. In a lowered voice, I asked, "Mother, what is it? What has he done to you? *Tell me.*"

Mother was trembling, and could not speak. Her eyes pleaded with me. I touched her face with my fingertips as gently as I could, yet she flinched with pain. Though Mother tried to ease out of my grip, I managed to examine her face, and discovered, at her hairline and behind her ears, scabby scarred incisions and ugly black stitching. A face-lift? *Mother had had a face-lift?*

"It will heal, in time," Mother said quickly. "Dr. Moses wanted simply to 'restore my youth' to me. He'd seen me and remembered me, he said, from years ago, when I was younger, and—well, he wanted that woman as his wife. Ella, don't frown so, I agreed, of course! And it hasn't been terribly painful, really. Dr. Moses gives me pills. I've been able to sleep, most nights. And I do look younger, I think? Don't I?"

I was incredulous, appalled. "Dr. Moses gave you a face-lift? Here? In this house? But—it looks infected."

"It isn't infected, I'm sure," Mother said. "Dr. Moses examines it frequently. When the incisions have healed a little more, he'll remove the stitches. And the staples." She laughed, apologetically. She took my hand to guide it, and allowed me to feel rows of staples in her scalp, embedded in her very scalp like nails. Staples!

"Mother, this is terrible. This is barbaric."

"Ella, no. If I'm not healing well, it's my own fault. This lumpiness by my ears, I should be massaging it, Dr. Moses says. I'm not a very good healer, I never have been. After having my babies, I was weak, sick for months." Mother was pleading with me, standing close so that she could speak quietly, urgently. "I never did recover, I guess! But I love you, Ella, and I love Walter, and I—I don't regret having my babies, I *don't*. And I don't regret marrying Dr. Moses except I'm afraid of—" She paused, breathing hard. She was leaning against me, a frail tremulous weight.

"Afraid of what, Mother?"

Mother shook her head wordlessly. *Afraid.*

The strange thing was: the barbaric face-lift had worked, to a degree. Mother's face had been tightened, the droopy jowls and

35

flaccid flesh of late middle age were gone; in the more flattering light of the parlor, she'd seemed quite attractive, pretty. I'd reacted in the most predictable and banal of ways, seeing her: I'd complimented her on looking "young"—"pretty." As if such attributes were of high value, worth the agony of a face-lift; as if youth and feminine prettiness were unconditionally superior to the dignity of age. Unknowingly, I'd reinforced Dr. Moses's selfish act. And I was this woman's daughter. "Let me take you out of here, Mother," I whispered. "Right now!" I would take Mother to the emergency room of the Strykersville hospital, I would have her wounds examined at once. I would protect her against her tyrannical husband. . . .

But Mother resisted. In her weak, stubborn way.

Pleading, "Ella, please don't speak of this to Dr. Moses. *Please.*"

"Mother, of course I'm going to—"

She pressed her fingertips against my mouth. *No.*

"Dear, I beg you, *please.* Just for now. I do love Dr. Moses, you see. He has made me feel worthy, and desired. He has allowed me to help him in his work. His mission. He isn't always strong, at his age. Don't judge us harshly, Ella, as you are always judging others! I'm your mother."

I'm your mother.

But that was why I'd come to help her, wasn't it?

Mother said, in her anxious lowered voice, now gripping my hands in hers, "Dr. Moses calls me his 'helpmate.' Oh, I was afraid at first, but he gave me a potion to drink, and my fears dropped away—or almost. His first wife, he said, disappointed him. She had no *imagination,* and she had no *courage.*"

Mother was speaking wildly, desperately. I saw that I could not convince her to come away with me immediately; I would have had to carry her bodily, and fight off Dr. Moses. Tomorrow, I would reassert myself. If Mother remained stubborn, I would confront Dr. Moses in person.

I relented, "Mother, all right. I'll wait until tomorrow."

Yet still Mother clutched anxiously at me. "Ella, you do promise? You won't speak to Dr. Moses tonight?"

Suddenly I was very tired, my head ached from the several glasses of rich, inky-dark wine my new stepfather had pressed upon me. "Yes, I promise! Not tonight."

I knew, that night, I would dream of ugly black stitches in my own flesh, and rows of staples in my scalp.

6. THE MUSEUM OF
DR. MOSES: THE RED ROOM

I am in the Museum of Dr. Moses. I too am a specimen.

In the middle of the night I was wakened by the end of a dream that, as it vanished, cracked and stung me like a whip. I sat up, heart pounding alertly, and switched on a lamp.

Silence. The old stone house, the steep-slanted roof above my head. In the night sky a pale, opalescent moon was partly shrouded by clouds.

I hadn't undressed, I'd only taken off my shoes. Lying on an unfamiliar bed in my damp, rumpled clothes. I had not intended to sleep but to lie awake vigilant through the night.

The guest room to which Mother had brought me, on the second floor, front, of Dr. Moses's stone house, had a single bay window framed by yellow chintz draw curtains; I'd recognized the design at once, and felt comforted. As a girl, I'd had similar chintz curtains in my room. In fact, I'd helped my mother make these curtains, laying out material on the living room carpet, measuring and scissoring. *My little helper!* Mother had called me.

Though I'd been uneasy about spending the night in Dr.

Moses's house, when Mother brought me into this room and I saw the curtains, the matching bedspread and pillows, and, on the floor, a hook rug like the one I'd had in my college room, I felt a stab of happiness. "Mother, thank you." I'd wanted to hug her, but resisted the impulse for Mother was in pain. She smiled almost shyly, touching her swollen jaw. "I thought you might like this room, Ella. You'll be the first guest, since I've come here to live."

In the hall outside, Dr. Moses stood uncertainly, wanting to say goodnight. He extended a hand to shake mine, an awkward, formal gesture, but I pretended not to notice, for I couldn't bear to touch him. "Goodnight, dear Ella!" I only murmured in response, and did not smile. His eyes lingered on my face wistfully.

Since Mother's shocking revelation, I looked upon Dr. Moses with distaste, and fury. In his presence I'd been very quiet.

He knows. We are aware of each other now.

It was a childish gesture, I'd pulled a heavy mahogany rocking chair in front of my door. As if, if Dr. Moses wanted to enter in the night, this could keep him out. (The door had no lock.) But, I reasoned, if the door were pushed open, there would be sufficient noise to rouse me.

Now I myself dragged the rocking chair away from the door.

There was no bathroom in this guest room, I would have to use a bathroom in the hall Mother had shown me. "It will be yours, Ella. No one else will use it." Barefoot, I walked stealthily. In my rumpled shirt and slacks, hair disheveled, I would have been embarrassed to be seen by my hosts.

I'd brought with me an eight-inch flashlight, which I always carried in my duffel bag.

In the antiquated, poorly lighted bathroom, I examined my face in the mirror; gingerly I touched my forehead, cheeks, jaws, for I looked strangely puffy, especially beneath the eyes. And my eyelids were reddened. Had I been crying? In my sleep? I ran my fingers quickly through my hair, drew my nails across my scalp, searching apprehensively for—what? Staples? Small nails? Behind my ears, where I couldn't see, the skin was tender as if inflamed, but there were no stitches.

My mother's voice murmured *Ella, help me! Don't judge me.*

Boldly then I left the bathroom, and stood for a brief while in the darkened corridor. I knew what I must do, but hesitated before taking action.

The house remained silent. Except for the wind, and a thrumming rhythmic sound of late-summer insects in the tall grasses and foliage close outside the house. The long corridor, running the width of the house, faded into darkness at its farther end. I didn't know which was the master bedroom, but I believed it was some distance from my room. *He would not have wished me closer to Mother, to hear her cries in the night.*

I made my decision. I descended the stairs, which were covered in a threadbare carpet.

On the first floor, I made my way quietly and unerringly to the Museum. Adrenaline flooded my veins! The heavy outer door was unlocked. Inside, I shut the door, and switched on my little flashlight, which provided a narrow, intense beam of about fifteen feet, and made my way along the center aisle, past the glass display cases, past Cousin Sam dangling motionless before me like a mock-proprietor of the Museum of Dr. Moses, and at the double oak doors at the rear of the room I paused, and swallowed hard. *The Red Room. Not yet ready for visitors.*

It had been a warning, I knew. Dr. Moses had warned me.

Still, I pushed inside. I had come so far, and would not turn back.

The Red Room: so called because the walls were covered in crimson silk wallpaper. Once it had been elegant, now it was rather tacky, yet still striking, attractive. The elaborately molded ceiling had been recently painted white, there was even a chandelier, antique, once beautiful but now somewhat tarnished, its cut-glass ornaments glazed with grime. This room was smaller than the other part of the Museum and the exhibits were crowded together, most of them not yet labeled. I found myself staring, at first without comprehension, into a glass display case containing human skulls; except, when I looked more closely, these were heads; human heads; somewhat shrunken, and the faces shriveled; they had swarthy, coarse complexions and straight lustreless black hair, their eyes still intact, though half-closed, sullen and unfocussed. They were, or had been, the heads of aboriginal peoples—Indians, Mexicans, Eskimos. Adults, adolescents, children. Atop one of the cases, set down in apparent haste, was the miscellany of hands I'd glimpsed yesterday evening in the Museum, whose presence had so offended Dr. Moses. The hands were clawlike, some of them blackened and missing fingers and nails, but otherwise perfectly preserved. Some were still wearing rings. I heard my small, naive voice—"These can't be real." In fascinated revulsion I touched the smallest hand, which must have belonged to a girl of about eleven. The fingers were utterly motionless yet seemed warm with life. As I nudged against the hand, the hand naturally moved.

"No!"

Unknowing, I'd begun to speak aloud. The shock must have been so profound.

The flashlight beam seemed to be moving of its own volition, jerkily. My hand had begun to sweat and I could barely hold it. I was staring at a large, rectangular Plexiglass case in which luxuriant coils of lustrous, glossy hair were displayed. There must have been a dozen hair samples: ash-blond, russet-red, dark brown, dark

blond, wheat-colored, silvery-gray, black threaded with gray. . . .
Unlike the embalmed heads and hands, these hair samples were
beautiful to contemplate. The flashlight beam lingered on them.
There did not appear to be remnants of scalp attached to the roots.
Several of the samples were prettily braided with satin ribbons.
Others were bow-tied with ribbons. The effect was festive, mesmerizing, as Christmas decorations. I wondered: Did these locks of
hair belong to girls I'd once known in Strykersville? Was it possible, two of the matched braids had been *mine*?

He is a murderer. A demon. These are his victims.

Glass jars in which appalling things floated. Eyeballs that stared
without rancor at me, and through me. Organs I did not wish to
identify: fleshy, fist-sized hearts, livers, female and male genitalia.
Each jar was marked in a cryptic code, neatly inked on white adhe-
sive labels: rq 4 19 211; ox 8 32 399. *Yet a code can be cracked like
any riddle.* In my numbed state my mind worked rapidly as a
machine: the numerals might refer to letters of the alphabet, the letters might be reversed. There was a logical intelligence here, a scientist's methodology.

The flashlight beam led me on. I was very tired and wanted
only to crawl somewhere and shut my eyes and sleep and yet my
eyes were opened staring at fresh-skinned skulls mounted on poles,
whose bones glistened wetly; lampshades of fine, fair human skin,
meticulously hand sewn; the facial mask of an attractive woman,
skin peeled carefully from her bones, attached to a mannequin's
egg-smooth, featureless face; sawed skulls, painted like bowls, displayed on shelves; dangling things that stirred with my breath, a
Calder-like mobile of fingers, toes, noses, lips, female labia; what
appeared to be a belt of linked female breasts, with protuberant
rosy nipples. On a dressmaker's dummy was the skin of a big-
breasted female torso, flayed and made into a kind of vest, sewn

onto a durable material like felt. Appalled, yet fascinated, I turned over the hem of the vest. . . .

"Ella!"

The whisper came from behind me. Yet my heart was beating so powerfully, I wasn't sure I'd heard. The flashlight slipped in my sweaty hand and fell loudly to the floor. I turned, panting, and crouched, but could not see clearly. An indistinct figure stood at the threshold between the two rooms. "Ella, no." I drew breath to scream, but could not. My legs lost all strength. The floor beneath me opened suddenly and I fell, fainting.

7. MORNING

He is a murderer. A demon.

Morning! A shaft of sunshine fell across my dreaming face like a laser ray. My eyes opened, I found myself lying on an unfamiliar bed, in rumpled clothing. My head was twisted at a painful angle as if in my sleep I'd been trying to scream. The soles of my bare feet were sticky.

Quickly I got up. I could barely stand, I was dazed with exhaustion. I saw that I was in the room to which Mother had brought me with the yellow chintz draw curtains—the "guest room." Except the curtains had not been drawn, morning sun flooded hotly through the windows. Confused, I saw that the heavy rocking chair had been dragged back in front of the door.

I fumbled, checking my bag: my little flashlight was missing.

It was 7:20 AM, I saw by my watch. I could not believe that I'd slept the remainder of the night, after the horrors of the Red Room. And so heavy, stuporous a sleep, my head ached violently and my mouth tasted of ashes.

I began to panic. I threw my things into my bag, and prepared to escape. In the corridor outside my room I heard voices downstairs. My heart flooded with adrenaline. I knew of only one way out, down those stairs. As I descended, I heard Dr. Moses's voice grow louder, scolding. My mother's voice was faint, nearly inaudible.

They were in the kitchen at the rear of the house. I wondered if they were arguing over me.

I thought I heard Dr. Moses say, "You will *not*"—or maybe he said, "She will *not*."

I heard a screen door slam. Through a side window I saw Dr. Moses walking swiftly past, I saw just the top of his bare head, his thin stained-ivory hair. I recalled a small barn to the rear of the house, converted to a garage, and hoped that Dr. Moses was headed there.

I went into the kitchen where Mother was seated numbly at a table, in a dressing gown and slippers. The dressing gown was one I'd never seen before, champagne-colored, made of a gossamer fabric and decorated with lace; the satin slippers were a match. *Her new husband bought that for her. For their honeymoon.* I felt a stab of revulsion at such knowledge. Mother's swollen eyes, lifting to me, were stricken with guilt.

"Mother, we're leaving here! I'm taking you out of this terrible place."

"Ella, no. I can't—"

"Mother, you *can*. We're leaving *now*. He can't stop us."

Yet I spoke angrily, desperately. I pulled Mother to her feet. She clutched at my arms. She said, pleading. "Ella, I can't. He would never let me leave. 'Whither thou goest, I will go.' He made me pledge these words when we were married. He meant them—'for eternity.'" In the bright sunshine I could see the ugly staples and stitches in Mother's scalp, above her hairline, through her limp, silvery-gray hair, that had pulled her forehead taut, smoothing out the wrinkles to make her look "young"—"pretty."

"He's a demented, evil old man. You know what he is."

"He would follow us, and hurt us both. You don't know, Ella—"

"I know. I saw."

"You saw—what?"

"The Red Room."

Mother hid her face in her hands and began to cry silently.

"You judge us too harshly, Ella. You don't *know*."

"I know what I need to know, Mother!"

My mind was working rapidly but not clearly. I knew I should escape Dr. Moses's house—if I could—and notify police—and return to get Mother. But—what if he hurt her in the interim? What if he fled with her, took her hostage? Killed her? Like the others? I was too distraught to speak with him and pretend that nothing was wrong. He would see through any subterfuge, he was far too shrewd.

"Ella, what are you looking for?"

"Something—to help me."

I was rummaging through drawers. My fingers closed about a sharp blade, a steak knife; I saw that I'd cut myself.

"He's a murderer, Mother. He's crazy. He has killed people for his museum. We have to protect ourselves." I took the knife and hid it in my bag. My hand was trembling badly, smarting with pain. Mother stared at me. Her swollen face had taken on a passive, childlike expression. She was stroking nervously at the underside of her jaw. "Come on, Mother. *Please*."

At last she allowed me to lead her through the house, to the front door. It was a desperate flight, no time for her to pack. No time to take anything! I'd hoped that Dr. Moses had driven out in one of his vehicles, but I hadn't heard the sound of any motor. My own car was parked in the driveway where I'd left it. I had to trust that Dr. Moses had done nothing to it, that the ignition would start.

"Ella, where are you taking my wife?"

Dr. Moses was waiting for us on the front porch. He'd circled the house as if guessing my intentions. His voice was coldly furious, threatening. He possessed little of his courtly charm: he'd become an old, ravaged, truculent man with glaring eyes who hadn't yet shaved, stubble glittered like mica on his jaws. He wasn't wearing his starched white cotton shirt, or his dapper straw hat. Instead he wore work clothes, gardener's clothes, soiled. On the trouser cuffs were earth stains, or blood stains. *His butcher's uniform. And now he has come for you.*

Suddenly I lost all control. I pushed blindly at him. The astonished old man could not have been prepared for my ferocity, my desperation. "Murderer! Demon!" I shoved both my hands against his chest, I pushed him backward off the porch, and he fell heavily down the stone steps, his expression stunned, bifocals flying. He fell hard against the front walk, striking his head, and groaned, and twitched, and convulsed, and made no more sound. I had a fleeting impression of blood at his nose, outlining his gaping mouth. Mother was whimpering, yet docile. I half-carried, half-walked her to my car. "You're safe, Mother! He can't hurt you now."

I hadn't had to use the knife, for which I would always be grateful.

8. ESCAPE

He has died. He can't follow.
  An old man, his skull eggshell-thin.

Was it true? I wanted so badly to believe so.

I drove south toward Strykersville, but would not stop there. I would not stop for hours, fleeing south out of the Oriskany hills, and out of Eden County, and into Pennsylvania. Mother in her dressing gown curled up beside me as I drove, drew her slippered feet up beneath her on the seat, like a child so exhausted by fear and strain that, at last, she has become relaxed, and sleeps innocently, not knowing what it is she flees, and whether it will follow.

WORSE THAN BONES

by Ramsey Campbell

As Hammond unpicked the staples of the padded envelope he'd been handed on his way to work, Mrs. Middler arrived at her desk. "You'll break your nails if you aren't careful," she informed him, and frowned at the grey stuffing the envelope had begun to shed. "The cleaners won't thank you for that."

"What's someone sent you in a plain brown wrapper, Mr. Hammond?" Charl expected to learn, though she wasn't even close to half his age.

"Maybe it's something to make you blush, Charl," Denny said, despite being younger still.

"I know you'd love to see that but you're never going to."

"Let's be polite," Mrs. Middler said, Hammond wasn't sure to whom. "So may we see what all the fuss was about?"

Hammond refrained from pointing out that he'd made none of it. He lingered over relinquishing the book once he'd stripped it of its cerements of newspaper. Just enough of the dust jacket remained to show the title, *Tales of the Ghostly*, and the top of a wisp that might have been mist or a bit of a ghost. Mrs. Middler's scent, which always led him to expect her to be wearing more makeup, met him as he handed her the book. She lowered her plump smug middle-aged face, presenting him with more of a display of her severely curled blond hair. "I hope you didn't pay much for this," she said. "Why, it's been scribbled in."

"That's half the charm of old books for me. It makes a book seem lived in if whoever had it before leaves their mark."

Denny poked his thin permanently disappointed face at the book. Three small red spots led like the end of an unfinished sentence from the right-hand corner of his mouth. "Died in, more like," he remarked.

This book belongs to Hettie Close; so, if you've found it, please, return it to—Hammond read that and glimpsed an address down in Cornwall followed by a series of dates, and then Mrs. Middler turned the page. "I won't pretend I'm a book person," she said, "but I wouldn't give you tuppence for this one."

Each title on the contents page was accompanied by a handwritten comment. "It's very rare," Hammond felt bound to protest. "The catalog said it was only a reading copy."

Charl rested a hand on Denny's shoulder. Her hair was nearly the color of her winter tan, and almost as short as his, both of them seeming eager for baldness. A grimace drew her small face tight. "I wouldn't be seen dead reading that," she declared.

Hammond had never seen her or her colleagues read anything but magazines composed mostly of advertisements. Mrs. Middler shut the book and passed it to him, and he tried not to recoil from the sensation of inadvertently touching her hand. He had just grasped that he'd touched only the wrinkled cover when Charl said, "Anyway, you can't call it that."

"Why can't I?"

"Not you," she told Hammond with a fragment of a giggle. "You can't just say tales of the ghostly. Tales of the ghostly what?"

Denny emitted a desiccated laugh of agreement and squeezed her arm until she pulled away from him. "It's a perfectly decent title," Hammond was saying meanwhile. "Back then they knew their grammar."

"I believe Charlotte's right," Mrs. Middler said and stared past him at the clock beyond the dozens of occupied desks. "Put it away now, Mr. Hammond. It's past time to start work."

He was being blamed for an argument of which he'd been simply the victim. He laid the book to rest among the paper clips and rubber bands in his desk drawer, and didn't look up until his face had stopped burning. He often felt like a schoolboy who'd been given a desk near the teacher's for being unable to spell. More people knew the name of his condition now than anyone had when he was at school, which meant that fewer thought he must be able to spell if he could read, but nobody had found a cure that worked for him. That was why he only checked arithmetic he would have been capable of doing, and fetched files so that people younger or much younger than himself could send out yet more correspondence about tax, and replaced files and sorted them into the alphabetical order they seemed unable to retain.

The smell of the files made him hungry for his book long before Mrs. Middler sent him to brew tea for the mid-morning break. As soon as he'd dropped the sodden tea bag in his metal bin he resurrected *Tales of the Ghostly* from the drawer. All by itself the contents page made up for the morning so far. Each title allowed him a glimpse of an era when people had the leisure to see ghosts, as did Hettie Close's comments and the painstaking script in which they were expressed. *The Gay Dancers* was judged to be "A-glitter with memories," *The Song in the Church* "Uplifting," *The Plea of a Child* "Good and tearful," *The Mummy's Voice* "Exotic and eerie," *The Phantom Railway Signal* "An up-to-date ghost" . . . He was savoring the prospect of so many unfamiliar tales—*A Distant Melody* as well and *The Keeper of the Light* and *The Padlocked Door*—when Charl, having taken a daintier sip than her coiffure would have led him to predict, blinked at him. "Are you just going to read what they're called, Mr. Hammond?"

"Read us a story," Denny presumably joked.

"I liked being read to when I was little," Charl said. "Will you, Mr. Hammond?"

He and his parents had read to each other almost as long as he'd had any parents. The thought of reawakening Charl's love of books made him indifferent to Mrs. Middler's frown. He was turning to the first tale when he grasped how inadvisable it would be to tell his present audience that a story was called "The Gay Dancers." He leafed through the warm withered pages to the tale Hettie Close found "Haunting as only true ghosts can be." "This is called *The Path by the Churchyard*," he announced and, resting his hand on the blank page opposite, read:

"In the twilight of a winter's afternoon of the year 18—, a traveler encountered a countryman on approaching a village in the southeast of our island, where the trees stoop close to the flat land while the winds constantly moan. 'Well met,' says J—to the countryman. 'Pray tell, who is being mourned in yonder churchyard?'

" 'None as I knows of,' responds the countryman.

" 'Then how comes it,' J— inquires, 'that I hear sighs beyond the hedge that bounds it?'

" 'Naught but wind in the trees,' returns the countryman. ' 'Tis thirteen years since yon churchyard was chained and locked.'

"Taking his leave of him, the traveler advanced and saw that it was so. . . ."

Hammond became aware that everyone within earshot had hushed to listen to him. He felt as if he'd been discovered at last. He was drawing a breath to do justice to the next sentence when a phone rang, and Denny was the first to laugh. Meanwhile Hammond's flattened hand jerked so nervously he might have thought the page had grown restless beneath it. "They didn't know much about writing in the olden days, did they?" Denny said. "Didn't know what year it was or the poor twat's name."

Charl dealt him a reproachful blink, only to add "Excuse me, Mr. Hammond, but I think you mixed up your tenses a bit."

"I never mix up what I read. Come and look if you don't believe me."

Mrs. Middler cleared her throat with a sound shriller than the phones. "We've had our break now. Lots of work to be done."

Hammond kept his hot face low for some moments after the book was shut up, then trudged to kneel by Charl. The left-hand drawer of every desk but his contained boxfuls of cards twice the size of a page of a notebook, each card representing a taxpayer. Hammond carried the first of the boxes to his desk and set about checking the latest column of arithmetic on every card. Charl started at Abel and finished at Bogle, but Hammond had only reached Aycliffe when it was time for lunch.

He went out for as prolonged a walk as he could stand, among buildings much like the squat five-story concrete office block, except that people lived in them. Plastic cartons dripping red, egged on by lidded cups that sprouted straws for antennae, pursued him through the wasteland relieved only by the twitching remains of young trees. He wished he were on a heath or a hill, where the wind could find something old to enliven. Before long it and its scuttling companions drove him back to the office.

He was about to sit down when his body stiffened, wakening all its aches. The drawer with the book in it, which he'd shut flush with the desk, was open at least an inch. The front cover of *Tales of the Ghostly* was no longer closed but held ajar by a ballpoint pen. "Who's been in my drawer?" he demanded.

Everyone seemed to have agreed to meet him with silence until Charl admitted "I borrowed a paper clip. I didn't think you'd mind."

"You didn't need to touch my book."

"I didn't," she said, looking hurt. "I was careful not to."

"Well, somebody did. There's a pen in it now."

"Maybe it wants more scribbling in," Denny said.

Hammond confined his response to examining the book for damage. After less of this than he felt entitled to, Mrs. Middler said, "I'm sure Charlotte would never have interfered with your property, and anyway I don't see anything to make a fuss about. There isn't much that could be done to it that hasn't been."

Hammond shut his lips and the drawer tight, and didn't speak to anyone for hours, even when Mrs. Middler told him to make the tea. He was planting Charl's Majorca mug on her Ibiza beer mat when Charl said "It ought to be called *Tales of Ghostly Things*."

Mrs. Middler clearly thought that deserved more than the grunt he gave it. "Why do you want a book like that?" she apparently needed to know.

He could have said he would rather hold a book than a hand any day. Instead he told her "Most books are ghosts" as he opened his drawer to reassure himself that nothing else had befallen the book. He must have closed the drawer too hard last time; the pen was back under the cover. He transferred the pen to the top of the desk and eased the drawer shut, and would have apologized to Charl if there hadn't been an audience.

When it was time to go home he found that the cleaner had disposed of the padded bag. He slipped the book into a large brown Confidential envelope, challenging Mrs. Middler to do more than frown at the use, and buttoned his coat over it. On the dwarfish bus he clung to a metal bar crowded with hands and clutched the package to his bosom with his other arm, much as a woman was holding her child on the seat below him. He couldn't help wondering if the little girl would ever read a book for pleasure. If he'd had both hands free he might have read to her from his book.

The wind rushed him from the bus stop by the park patrolled by litter and stray dogs to his house, a thin red-brick slice of a terrace. A smell of aged paper greeted him as he shut out all but the roar of the wind. He laid his prize on the balding carpet on the stairs while he draped his coat over the post at the foot of the rickety banisters, then shied the crumpled envelope into the splintered wicker wastepaper basket in the front room and sat the book erect in his father's sagging armchair.

Apart from the kitchen and the toilet, which was equally a bathroom, every room was rendered cosier by shelves of books. All his books were secondhand, and he hadn't bought an uninscribed one for years. He took down a few at random to remind himself how inscriptions brought them alive. Here was a volume of Grimm presented as a school prize in 1923, here was an Edwardian Everyday Reciter whose previous owner had indicated all the points at which he should take a breath; an espionage omnibus from a wife to her husband "so you'll remember I've got my eye on you"; a dictionary of seashells from a father to his daughter "to answer all those questions you used to ask" . . . Hammond shelved the books and cooked himself two poached eggs on toast to accompany a bowl of cereal, quite enough of a dinner for him these days, especially when more would consume money better spent on books. Having washed up and dried the dinner things with the least tattered of the kitchen towels, he settled himself in the front room.

There must be a draught, and no wonder with the wind flinging its huge soft icy self against the house. *Tales of the Ghostly* had stooped forward on the armchair, propping itself on its open front cover. He glanced at the flyleaf as he retrieved the book. Hettie Close seemed to have needed to reconfirm her ownership every few years; the last date was nine years ago. He scanned the paragraphs he'd read aloud and leafed onward, each page trying to cling to his fingertips like another skin.

As J— walked through the village it began to look familiar, the buildings and the people too, though he had a sense that they were older than they should be. The only innkeeper told him there was no room and gave the impression of being afraid to have J— under his roof. As the night closed in, anyone J— approached fled inside and barred the door against him. Sounds of mourning led him back to the churchyard, where he found a gap in the hedge through which he was able to pass. He followed the sounds to a gravestone, and as the sighs faded into silence, the apparition of the moon through tattered clouds showed him the plot. Carved on the memorial was his own name.

Hammond had thought as much, but the confirmation was a pleasure in itself. It wasn't why he emitted a startled grunt, muffled by the books around him. On the contents page Hettie Close had described the story as "Haunting as only true ghosts can be," yet beneath its final paragraph she had written much less neatly "Falsehood and foolishness." She must have turned against the tale in her old age.

In *The Gay Dancers* a young woman on a visit to friends in a
remote part of France was drawn by sounds of revelry to a château,
where she danced with a mysterious aristocratic youth who promised that their dance and the night would never end. At the height
of their waltz she cried out to him to keep her always, and was
never seen again. In an epilogue her friends searched for her near a
château that had been in ruins for a hundred years. Apparently
Hettie Close had ceased to find the story "A-glitter with memories";
across the blank half of its last page she'd scrawled "Lies the living
want to believe."

Hammond had bought the anthology because the bookseller's
catalog had listed it as extensively annotated by the previous owner,
but he was starting to find the annotations disconcerting. He riffled
through the book and saw that every tale was followed by a comment, which he might have read if that wouldn't have involved
glimpsing the conclusions of the stories. Each final page looked
faded, both the print and the progressively effortful scrawl. He'd
had enough of Hettie Close's bitter afterthoughts for one night. He
turned to the shelves for companionship.

His favorite books proved less congenial than usual, perhaps
because he couldn't help wondering how the people who had written in them or been addressed had ended up. Before long the smell
of old paper grew oppressive, almost cloying, so that for the first
time in his life he was close to wishing he had a television. When a
collection of Shelley kept drooping in his hands, he took himself
upstairs.

Since all the shelves except those in his room were full, *Tales of
the Ghostly* accompanied him. As he lay in the dimness thick as dust
he imagined the book had perceptibly added to the smell of old
paper. In the depths of the night he was wakened by sounds he put
down to a mouse—less than a scratching, just a faint buried rest-

55

lessness all the more annoying because indefinable. He slapped the bed until the activity ceased or at any rate passed beyond audibility. He had to tell himself it had rendered not the smell more intense but his perception of it before he was able to sleep.

Was his memory as exhausted as he was? In the morning he saw the new book was half out of the shelf, though he seemed to remember pushing it all the way in. He lined it up with its neighbors and got hastily ready for work, having overslept for the first time in his life despite his parents' alarm clock that he'd transferred to his room, never needing it while they were present to waken him.

He was three sweaty panting minutes late for work. Mrs. Middler said nothing to him until it was time for tea, and not much then. As he stood her Union Jack mug on the mat depicting a minute map of Britain she relented sufficiently to ask, "Did you sort out the business with your book?"

He felt as though she'd noticed something he had overlooked. "What business?"

"Weren't you going to get some money back at least for the condition it was in?"

"I told you yesterday," he said, and was disconcerted to realize he was about to lie. "It was what I expected."

"You'll have to forgive me for being surprised, Mr. Hammond. Do you ever write in your books?"

It had never struck him before, but he didn't. "Not yet," he said.

"I hope you never reach that state."

"Pretty soon nobody will read books," Denny told Charl. "Everything worth having will be on the Internet. You'll just need to know how to use it."

"Just because it gives you a big head doesn't mean there's more in there."

Hammond had no wish to become entangled in their flirtation. It wasn't until the afternoon break that he asked Denny, "Can you really find anything you want to on your computer?"

"Print it out as well. Go ahead, tell me something to bring you. If it's something Charl shouldn't see, just whisper."

Hammond would have liked to make his distaste clear, but couldn't risk offending Denny. "I'd like to know who lives at an address. I'll give you it tomorrow."

That was one reason why as soon as he reached home he tramped upstairs and took *Tales of the Ghostly* off the shelf. It came so readily it might have been waiting for him. He was sure the smell in the room was stronger. The book wasn't staying where he slept if it smelled that strong. In the kitchen he copied Hettie Close's address onto the message pad for which he never seemed to have any messages, then wrote his name and address on the flyleaf under hers and her trail of dates. He left the book in the front room while he fed himself his eggs and toast and cereal, wondering what second thoughts she might have in store for him. Once upon a time she'd found *The Song in the Church* "Uplifting," but how much had she changed her mind?

In the story a mother returned to churchgoing after the loss of her only child and came to believe that the highest voice in the choir was her daughter's. Having secreted herself in the church overnight, she heard the child alone. Next morning the woman was found dead, lying on a pew, smiling peacefully. "Smile while you can," Hettie Close had scrawled in ink almost as faded as the print above it. "Smile like the skull you'll be, you fool, before you're worse than bones."

Not only the sentiment dismayed Hammond. His memory must be succumbing to age, because he'd been convinced that each story was followed by far fewer handwritten words. Perhaps this one was the exception; he wasn't yielding to the urge to find out. He took down a shaky tome about ancient Greece, replacing it with *Tales of the Ghostly*, and tried to immerse himself in legends he'd loved to hear and then read as a child.

Tonight he found them too concerned with the underworld, with people who wouldn't stay dead. The idea struck him as both childish and distressing. He nodded over the book and jerked awake, convinced he'd heard restlessness somewhere near. He left the book on the couch and climbed the stairs under the bulb that had taken on some of the color of old paper. He tried to read himself to sleep with Dickens, and then just to sleep, but kept being roused by an impression that there was movement downstairs he couldn't quite hear. Even if only the smell of books was looming over him, in the dark that felt close to solid.

Next morning it was mostly the prospect of speaking to Denny that urged him out of bed and to the office. But Denny was late, and hid his face from Mrs. Middler with a heap of files he tried to pretend he'd spent time selecting. Hammond barely waited until her scowl at Denny subsided. "Did you find out what I asked you?" he said low.

"Are you after an old girl, Mr. Hammond?" Charl suggested.

"Close," Denny said.

Hammond forgot to keep his voice down. "What are you getting at? What do you mean?"

"The woman who lives there," Denny told him, "she's called Margaret Close."

Charl gave Hammond a secret grin while Mrs. Middler's disapproval threatened not to remain mute. Once he was on his knees by Denny, Hammond risked whispering "Did you get a phone number?"

"Obviously," Denny muttered, yanking a folded slip of paper

out of a pocket of his jeans along with a bony cigarette he quickly hid.

Nobody was supposed to make personal phone calls from the office, let alone long distance, and nobody as menial as Hammond had a phone at all. The nearest public phone was at least a mile away and unlikely to be intact. He willed Mrs. Middler not to stay in the office at lunchtime, and almost sighed aloud when he saw her don her coat. He gave her five minutes away from the building and sat at her desk, ignoring Denny and Charl. As he dialed he feared Margaret Close would be out at work, but the distant bell was stilled before it had finished ringing thrice. "Hello?" a woman's voice said.

He had to take a deliberate breath. "Is that Mrs. Close, or is it Ms.?"

"I'm the only one there is. It's Ms."

She sounded far too young to have written any of the comments in the book. "Someone else of that name used to live there, didn't they?"

"Were you a friend of my mother's?"

"In, well, I suppose you might say in a kind of a sense," Hammond said, and immediately thought he shouldn't have.

"Are you the man she was always hoping would come back?"

"I never knew her."

"Not you, then. She carried on hoping to the end. Someone she thought she should have spent her life with. Maybe she found him waiting if that's possible. We can't know, can we?"

Hammond felt he wasn't expected to respond, but the next question was sharper. "So what's your interest in her?"

"I've got a book of hers."

"Which book is that? Don't tell me. She's in it, isn't she?"

"You could say that."

"All over it. I know the one. I sold all her books at the market. How much did you pay for it?" the daughter said, and interrupted any answer. "Forget it. I don't want to know."

He had no idea what else to say. After a pause the daughter said, "I'm still not getting why you called."

"I suppose I just wondered if you could tell me anything about her or the book. As you say, it seems so full of her."

"That's how she was. You always knew when she was about or even on her way. She'd make sure you did."

"Knew," Hammond ventured to ask, "or know?"

"She's gone. She isn't here, anyway." With some briskness the daughter said, "You wanted me to tell you about the book."

"If there's anything to tell."

"She died with it by her bed, if that's what you mean." Presumably realizing he hardly could, Ms. Close said, "She thought the writers back then knew how it was going to be when you were dead, the Victorians with all their spirit stuff, you understand. I tried to make her see once they were just stories, and we had a bad argument even for us."

Hammond had thought of nothing he could say when the daughter admitted, "I hope she found what she expected if there's any finding to be done."

"She didn't."

He hardly knew he'd spoken, the thought was so immediate. "I beg your pardon?" Ms. Close said, not begging at all.

"Sorry, I shouldn't have—I've got to go," Hammond said and did, not soon enough. Mrs. Middler had sailed into view under the clock, carrying a bag of lunch from a salad bar. He retreated to his desk and tried to look as if he'd been there all the time. As she dumped her lunch on her desk, however, her stare provoked him to say "Just borrowing a paper clip."

Only her stare answered him, and could be avoided by lowering his head. He didn't speak to anyone throughout the afternoon—he was trying to decide whether he wanted to rush home or delay that as long as possible. The end of work was bearing down on him when Mrs. Middler tapped on her desk with a pen. "Mr. Hammond."

"I'm here."

"Better be over here unless you want everybody knowing what I have to say."

He watched her jab a stubby silver-varnished fingernail at a column of figures, then at another. "You passed these, Mr. Hammond, and they're wrong. You'd have had this lady getting a refund she wasn't entitled to and this gentleman paying hundreds of pounds too much back tax. I hope you aren't too old to keep your mind on your job."

He might have kept his peace except for that. "There are more important things than money," he blurted.

"Perhaps you wouldn't think so if you weren't earning any." Apparently in case that wasn't enough of a threat, she added, "And don't let me see you sniffing round my desk for stationery again without asking, never mind taking any home."

Another retort found its way to his lips. "I can think of a lot better uses for paper."

Denny had to snort and Charl to giggle under cover of her hand before he realized what he might have seemed to say. He no longer cared. He turned his back on Mrs. Middler's incredulous glare and, having retrieved his coat from the hook by the tea urn, marched out of the office.

At least she'd made him eager to go home. In the act of opening the front door he almost called "Hello." He wasn't surprised to find *Tales of the Ghostly* sprawled facedown on the front-room carpet as though exhausted by its latest effort—it was more unexpected that the pages on which it lay open had nothing extra written on them. He was examining the book when it seemed to waken in his hand. As he dropped it on the table and tried to rub off his fingertips the sensation of having touched flesh that ought not to have stirred, the front cover fell open. Unlike Hettie Close, he hadn't written a date after his name and address, but one was there now, in a script so large and clumsy as to suggest that the writer was no longer able to see or the writer's hand, if it was one still, to control the scrawl. The date was today's.

He stared until it appeared to writhe, and then he turned the pages with a fingernail. Soon he sucked in a breath and did his best to expel its musty rotten taste. The comment following *The Gay Dancers* had been expanded. After "Lies the living want to believe" words in a larger looser version of the handwriting occupied the rest of the page. "Lies you do, Thomas Hammond."

That was too personal, too aggressive, too close. He tugged the cuffs of his coat over his hands so as to carry the book to the kitchen table, where he used an old redundant knife and fork to turn the pages. The comment at the end of *The Path by the Churchyard* was no longer just "Falsehood and foolishness." The scribble that almost spilled over the margins added "The path leads to me, Tommy boy."

"Good luck to it," Hammond muttered, flicking pages over. Every tale was followed by an extra message now, and even those that didn't include a version of his name seemed aimed at him. The ink on those pages was faded as though drained in order to compose the scrawl. The message at the end of the last story was the most uncontrolled in both handwriting and content. "Don't keep me waiting here in the dark long, old Tom."

He slammed the book shut and stared at its tattered back cover.

He didn't know if he was challenging some movement to take place or doing his best to prevent it. When his eyes began to twitch he saw to his dinner while continuing to watch the book. As he ate he grew aware that Hettie Close no longer could. A sense of her hunger sickened him, so that he scraped half his dinner into the bin and abandoned the utensils in the sink.

He'd forgotten to remove his coat, but the house felt too cold for him to do without. He trapped *Tales of the Ghostly* between his cuffs again to transfer the book to his father's armchair, where he could keep an eye on it while he read something else—except that all the favorites he attempted to read, and the inscriptions in them, seemed unreachably remote. Before long he returned to staring at the book propped on the chair.

As the hours passed he began to suspect it of restraining itself until it was unobserved. Once he lurched at it and thumbed through it, but nothing appeared to have changed, except that when he slumped back into his chair he thought the smell of more than aging followed him. Did that herald another transformation? By the time he wondered that, he was as disinclined to stir as the book seemed to be. Only his eyelids could move, and only to droop. He tried to keep them up until he forgot to keep trying.

A secretive movement wakened him. *Tales of the Ghostly* had fallen on its face, and the back cover was wide open. As he wobbled to his feet he saw writing on the rear flyleaf. He was stumbling around his father's chair when the ungainly ill-proportioned scrawl grew clear. "Come to me now, old Hammy, or I'll come to you."

"No you won't," Hammond retorted, "and don't call me Hammy either." Nobody ever had. He seized the book by its rear board and snatched it up, its pages flapping. He was about to thrust it into the space on the shelf when he thought he felt it writhe like some part of a withered body not quite dead. "You won't do that to me again," he yelled, ripping the pages loose from the spine, crumpling them into a wad he pitched into the dusty fireplace. "Let's see you get up to any tricks now," he said, hurling the boards into the fireplace. When there was no response beyond a feeble restlessness of paper that subsided as he watched, he stumped upstairs to bed.

He left the bedroom door ajar in case he heard any mischief downstairs. He almost kept the light on until fury at his own childishness made him tug the cord. He lay listening for indications of stealth in the dark until sleep found him. He dreamed that far too old a woman—so old that she was doing without most of her face—had set about crawling up the stairs to him without employing any limbs. As he saw the ragged brownish lump of a head waver above the edge of a stair, then over the next higher, he struggled to waken before he could see it in more detail. He managed to produce a strangled cry, and the object, as misshapen as it was determined, vanished from within his eyelids. When he opened them, however, it was beside him on the pillow.

Even if it was composed of crumpled paper, it had a crooked tongueless grin that gaped wide as he shrank back in the tangle of blankets. He wasn't trying to escape only the mockery of a head. In the twilight before dawn he could just distinguish that the print was fading from the pages while a mist as dark as ink seeped out of them. He hadn't disentangled himself from the bedclothes when the mist rushed into his eyes, filling them with blackness.

He'd hardly begun to cry out with the stinging of his eyes when it ceased. In another moment they cleared, and he tasted ink. On the pillow was nothing but a shapeless wad of paper. Its smell was in his nostrils and then deeper in him. He felt his hands tighten into claws and drag him upright against the headboard. He felt his lips part as the gap in the wad of paper had. "I'm alive," he said, or his mouth did, in a voice delighted to rediscover itself. "I'm alive."

KING OF OUTER SPACE

by Peter Atkins

1

She'd been crying herself to sleep for nearly a year now but it still didn't feel like a habit. It still felt new and raw.

Here's how it went: She'd do the bathroom stuff, get into bed, read for a while, remote some late-night host into TV life, kill the light, and close her eyes. And somewhere between the last sentences from the chat show and the first whispers from the dream country she'd be jerked awake by a body-racking sob and find her eyes were full of tears.

Her name was Marion Marshall, she was twenty-eight years old, and her fiancé was dead.

FADE IN
EXT. DEEP SPACE

Against a field of stars, a ROCKETSHIP hurtles
through the void. Flames shimmer from its boost-
ers, their majestic roar telling the laws of
physics to go fuck themselves.

The ship is a retro-futurist dream. Fins, chrome,
and streamlined splendor. Like the child of some
1958 jam session between Werner Von Braun and a
hotshot from the design team at Cadillac.

No. Screw that. You know what it's like? It's
like the Legion Of Super-Heroes clubhouse from a
1963 issue of Adventure Comics. Turned on its
ass, fitted with a nose cone and a bunch of
thrusters, and sent blasting through the inter-
galactic ether as if Imagination had grabbed
Science in the schoolyard and slapped the little
geek around some till it knew its place.

DISSOLVE TO INT.
ROCKETSHIP COCKPIT

A big curved window offers an unobstructed view
of the cosmos and the walls are studded with
pieces of equipment picked up from a yard sale
thrown by the guys who designed The Quatermass
Experiment.

Sitting in the single chair is JONATHAN KING,
astronaut. Mid-30s. Ruggedly handsome. Spacesuit
from the racks of the tailor who dressed Adam
Strange and Steve Zodiac. Skin-tight and colorful.
Heroic and decorative. Stopping just short of the

point at which you'd question the wearer's sexual
preference.

CLOSE on King's eyes. Fixed on the window.
Flicking steadily from side to side, systematical-
ly scanning the galactic vistas through which he
rides.

CLOSE on King's left hand. The fingers are
wrapped in sensor-tape, fiber-optic cables trailing from them into a computer-input in the
chair's armrest. Pulses of light throb down the
cables.

CLOSE on the ship's monitor screens—across which
streams of data play as the information from his
scanning eyes is electronically stored.

WIDE—as King unhooks the sensors from his fingers
and walks over to the radio. He grabs the hand-
set—which looks suspiciously like the bulky RCA
mike Elvis used on Ed Sullivan—and talks into it.

KING
Hello? Hello? Can you hear me? Can . . .

CUT

3

Marion wasn't sure what woke her up. Groggy and confused, she
rolled over to blink her bedside clock's LCD into focus.

4:02 AM.

After four. The little girl in her was relieved. She hated waking
at night to get up and pee or whatever because she was never quite

sure that something supernatural wasn't waiting for her in the dark. But some long-forgotten Counsellor at some long-forgotten Summer Camp had once told her that it was only the four hours after midnight that were the dangerous ones and she'd lived by that wisdom ever since.

She was about to push the covers aside, ready to head to the bathroom, when she realized that it wasn't her bladder that had pulled her from sleep after all. It was a noise; low and barely heard, a continuous stream of crackle and hiss like an AM station failing in a desert midnight. Marion padded her hand in a blind arc across her quilt and found the remote. She'd already hit the power button before registering that the TV hadn't been on until she'd done so. She killed it again before the infomercial had a chance to pitch itself into the darkness of her room and propped herself up on one elbow to try and locate the source of the sound.

It was coming from the drawer of her bedside table. Her hand was braver than her heart, reaching instinctively to pull the drawer open before she stopped it, suddenly convinced that she was misreading the sound. She heard it transform in her imagination, moving from the electronic to the animal, becoming chitinous and agitated, the sound of some multilimbed insect monstrosity, a huge lightning bug trapped and furious and eager to be free. A panicked revulsion swept through her and, clicking on the reading lamp, she swung her legs around to sit on the edge of the bed, staring helplessly at the drawer.

Then she got it. Maybe it was the light, maybe it was taking a breath, maybe it was just the resurgent reason that came with a fuller wakefulness, but she suddenly knew precisely what the noise was. With a self-deprecating groan she pulled the drawer open.

Her Earthquake-Preparedness Kit wasn't much by Los Angeles standards and its components were all but hidden by the various unfiled receipts and other detritus of daily life that Marion regularly threw in the drawer to keep her surfaces tidy but some quick scrabbling revealed the flashlight, the first-aid box, and—finally—the tiny transistor radio.

She pulled it from the drawer, wondering how it had somehow turned itself on, and listened to the strange atonal music of its stationless signal as it seemed to strain for clarity and connection. An unbidden image came to her, straight from the World War II movies her father had loved and had tried in vain to make her love also; a soldier, lost behind enemy lines, trying desperately to find a frequency that would bring him nearer to home.

Her eyes had just registered the curious fact that the radio's power switch was firmly in the off position when the signal suddenly locked in. A voice, tiny and distant, emerged through the whistle and whine.

" . . . you hear me? Marion? Marion, it's me. It's Jonathan."

She dropped it like she'd been bitten, her hand flying to her gasping mouth and tears filling her eyes as the old wounds opened again.

4

"And the radio shut off when you dropped it?"

"As soon as it hit the floor."

"Or as soon as you allowed the grief to flower properly?"

The therapist allowed herself a small smile. Gentle. Not smug at all. But Marion didn't like it anyway.

"My grief has no problem flowering. I water it every night," she said, and instantly regretted it. Juliana was particularly fond of extended metaphor and could often take these weekly sessions

into such convolutions of figurative overlay that Marion sometimes wondered whether her eighty dollars was being spent on
therapy or on an unacknowledged prep course for some bad creative writing class. She jumped back in before the other woman
could run with it.

"But that's not the point," she said, "Yes, his voice went away.
But I heard it."

"It was four in the morning," Juliana said. "You'd just woken
up."

"I wasn't dreaming."

"No. I'm not suggesting you were." Juliana's eloquent hands
moved in a symmetrical semaphore, placatory and soothing. "And
I don't doubt that white noise from the radio is what woke you up.
But . . ."

Marion interrupted. "What then?" she said. "I was still in a hyp-
nagogic state and the voice was in my head?"

"Do you think?" Juliana said, crossing her perfect legs and
cocking her head as if the thought had never occurred to her.

5

I resent her, Marion thought as she made the left onto Olive too
sharply, the Chevy's ten-year-old engine giving a rattle of complaint.

I resent her trim little figure and her soft little voice. I resent her
precise little hands and the way they weave their subtitles for the
emotionally hard of hearing.

I resent her black stockings and her high heels. I bet all her
male clients want to fuck her and I resent that too. I . . .

"Shit," Marion said out loud, glancing into her rear-view mirror.
She'd been so busy bitching that she'd missed the right on Buena

Vista. Now she was screwed. Burbank always confused her and she knew there wasn't another road that would deposit her on the freeway for a couple of miles. She wondered if one of these side roads would at least take her down as far as Riverside. She could take that through the park and come out on Los Feliz.

Staring out the right to try and judge the streets, she found herself looking at a store window. The sadness overwhelmed her before she realized why it was. HOUSE OF SECRETS, the sign said. She knew it well and had been there many times. Not recently, though—no reason to, not now—and she hadn't realized it was this close to Juliana's office. It had always been Jonathan who drove when they made those Saturday morning trips to let him browse excitedly through the old comic books in which the store specialized while she hovered near a rackful of action figures trying to pretend she had the slightest interest in being there.

For a crazy moment, she considered parking the car and going in. Thought about peeling open one of those stupid plastic bags that the geeks cherished (*Museum-quality! Acid-free!*) and breathing in the mustiness of an old issue of *Mystery in Space* the way he used to do. And then she thought about the fresh bullets of pain such a sensory trigger would fire into her and she jumped the light, ignoring the honking horn of the Accord she'd cut off, and headed south.

On Riverside, she switched from NPR to an oldies station and was rewarded with The Penguins singing "Earth Angel." The record was older than she was—her parents had still been in junior high when it was made—but she loved it. She knew enough about music to understand that its chord sequence was banal and its melody simplistic, but she knew enough about magic to understand that none of that mattered. Her mouth creased into something that felt unfamiliar and a little forced but was still undeniably a smile. She began to hum along as the road took her through Griffith Park.

By the time the Chevy was climbing the elevation that let the road look down on the concrete slash that called itself the Los Angeles River, The Penguins had been replaced by The Stones and their white-boy wannabe swagger. How come Eminem's a wigger, Marion thought, and Mick Jagger isn't? The static that was starting to break up Mick's little fantasy about a New York divorcée she put down to the altitude and then realized it wasn't meant to work that way. Puzzled, she looked down at the dial as if it were going to explain itself to her. Her finger was reaching out, ready to punch in another station, when the static overwhelmed the song completely. Its cacophony crescen-doed and then cut off. There was a beat of utter silence—Marion heard a dog barking distantly somewhere in the park—and then a voice, a little out of phase in each of the car's four speakers:

"Marion, are you receiving me? Over."

6

Once upon a time, there was a little boy who lived in the forest. A kindly old woodsman had taken a shine to the boy, who looked to him often for answers to the questions that his wicked stepmother was too busy to consider.

"I was at the stream this morning," the boy said one day while the woodsman was sharpening his axe, "and there was a horse drinking. After a moment, it looked up at me, flicked its tail, and said 'How many miles to Babylon?'"

"There's no need to be embarrassed," the woodsman said. "You're young. You can't be expected to know the answers to every esoteric question some horse wants to ask you."

"That's not the point," the boy said excitedly. "People will think it strange. Everyone knows that horses don't talk."

"Was this horse wearing a saddle?" the woodsman asked.

"No. I think it was a wild horse," the boy said.

"Then what does it care for the opinions of men?" the woodsman said and turned his attention back to his whetstone.

7

Here's what Marion did. She did all that stuff you do. She talked to people. She made phone calls. She examined all the relevant paperwork. She pushed and she prodded and she made herself unpopular, kneading at history to try and make a new shape of it. She doubted her sanity often and regretted it hardly at all. And eventually all this doing led her to the complex of buildings where Jonathan had worked and where he had died.

CosmoTech Research had its own grounds on the outskirts of Simi Valley. It had a big rectangular building with very few windows. It had a parking lot and a guard who checked out your legs as you left your car. It had a nifty corporate logo and potted plants in its lobby. What it didn't have was a metal detector. Which was extremely handy because Marion had a gun.

8

"Jonathan's alive."

Krevitz blinked, which was a fairly big reaction for him. Marion wasn't sure if she'd in fact ever seen the lids lower on those pale blue eyes before. He preferred to blink when people weren't looking, she'd figured, lest it allow some reading of what he was thinking or feeling. Jonathan and he had known each other since college and they'd already been partnered on their research work when Marion and Jonathan had met. Tidy little man. She'd never liked him, and she liked him less now.

His office, surprisingly, wasn't neat and precise—papers and shit were piled everywhere—though there was a completely clear semi-circular area on his desk immediately in front of him as if he was somehow Canuting the tides of chaos and getting a kick out of it. He still hadn't answered her.

"He's alive," she said again. "And you're going to tell me where he is."

"Marion," Krevitz said, "we were both at the funeral."

"Memorial service," Marion said. "You can't have a funeral when there's no body."

"And you can't have a body when a laboratory blows up and everything in it is reduced to ashes."

His voice was as calm as if he were debating a sports scholarship student in a logic class. But then she hadn't shown him the gun yet.

"I have a theory," she said. He smiled a little—as if theories weren't really available to pretty girls who worked in insurance—but she didn't let that put her off. "I think the explosion was a cover. I think your research went further than you ever told anyone. I think you . . . you sent him . . . somewhere. Somewhere out there."

She was furious with herself for faltering at the end, but she couldn't help it. She couldn't say out loud in a sunlit office on an October afternoon in a California suburb what her midnight thoughts had led her to believe: that this privately financed space research company had somehow built a rocket, launched it in secret, and sent her boyfriend into space.

Krevitz laughed at her, which was all she needed. Her hand was in her purse as he began to speak.

"God almighty, Marion," he said. "Do you honestly think . . ."

He broke off to stare at the gun.

"Fine," she said. "Fuck what I think. Tell me what happened. Or I swear to Christ I'll shoot you in the face."

9

She'd made sure they'd walked close together as he led her down to one of the labs, close enough for Krevitz to never stop considering how much damage a bullet could do from such proximity. They'd gone through several levels of security, but Krevitz's card had opened every automated door without a problem, despite the satisfying trembling of his hand. By the time he opened the final door they were several stories below ground and hadn't passed another human for quite some time.

The laboratory was probably impressive if you knew anything about laboratories, but, despite her life with Jonathan, Marion had always remained happily ignorant of such things. It was a big room full of science shit. She had no idea of the specific functions of most of the equipment with which the place was packed to overflowing—monitors, data screens, dish receivers, and a thousand annoyingly untidy wires—but the centerpiece of the whole operation, the thing from which many of those wires originated, was appallingly clear.

An image from a hundred bad movies, it surprised her only in its familiarity: a large vat filled to within a few inches of its glass lip by a salmon-pink translucent substance and, floating in the center of that amniotic jelly, a human brain.

10

Krevitz's hand was still shaking but the Marlboro seemed to be helping. He was perched on a lab stool beside a workbench and was taking long greedy drags of the cigarette as if he still couldn't believe she'd allowed him to light up and might at any moment rescind her permission. As if she cared. As if she cared about anything anymore.

He also wouldn't shut up. Marion doubted he'd ever talked so much in his life. He hadn't actually admitted that he'd killed Jonathan, but his ramblings were making it clear that their relationship had changed in a somewhat fundamental way once Krevitz had realized he needed a guinea pig.

"He was asleep when it happened," he said. "He didn't feel a thing."

He gestured expansively with his cigarette-free hand at the various data-recording devices.

"He's sending so much stuff," he said, a tiny hint of pride creeping back into his nervous voice, "Stuff a machine just wouldn't get. Guiding intelligence, you see. I knew that was what was needed."

Marion had already started tuning out the specifics. The essence was clear. She'd not really been wrong. Jonathan *was* in space, in a manner of speaking, his mind hardwired into some kind of radio-telescope system and transmitted out into the ether to explore the universe on behalf of this contemptible little shit.

"Does he *know*?" she asked.

Krevitz shook his head.

"We weren't sure," he said, "Until we started getting the pictures."

11

There was nothing wrong with the VCR or the monitor, but the images were distorted and grainy, like a warped kinescope of a weak broadcast of old monochrome nitrate.

"Imagination," said Krevitz. "I hadn't figured on that surviving. But it's allowed him a construct, as you see." He paused, as if puzzled not by the inexplicable presence of the images but by their provenance. "Curious choices."

Of *course* his ship would look like that, Marion thought, Of *course* that's how he'd be dressed. She didn't realize she was weeping until the salt stung her lip.

She let the tears keep coming, crying not for herself but for Jonathan's orphaned consciousness, lost out there in the galaxy and dressing its voyage in half-remembered dreams of space heroes to comfort its lonely and endless flight.

Her sobbing seemed to increase Krevitz's anxiety. She wasn't surprised. Distraught woman with a gun. Make anyone nervous. She swung to face him, lifting her weapon.

"I can turn it off," he begged, the cigarette dropping from his fingers, "Turn it all off. Give him peace."

Marion let him sweat for a moment, then shook her head.

"That's not what I want," she said.

12

FADE IN EXT.
DEEP SPACE

The ship blasts through the void. Ridiculous.
Magnificent.

DISSOLVE TO
INT. ROCKETSHIP COCKPIT ARTIFICIAL DAY

The cabin is identical to when last we saw it,
except that there are now two chairs in the cen-
ter.

Jonathan King, astronaut, is in one of them. In
the other, dressed in form-hugging space-girl
gear, is his fellow crew member. Dale Arden to
his Flash Gordon, Alanna to his Adam Strange,
Dejah Thoris to his John Carter.

Marion looks around the cabin. She blinks . . .

. . . and the cabin MORPHS in a shimmer of
becoming . . .

A THRONE ROOM IN BYZANTIUM—

A royal peacock walks unselfconsciously behind the
enthroned lovers as Marion's bejewelled hand
reaches for Jonathan's.

Jonathan cocks his head, as if learning the rules
of a new game. He blinks. . . .

A BRIDGE OF A PIRATE'S GALLEON—

The Buccaneer Captain smiles at his Pirate
Princess and lifts his hand to meet hers. . . .

DISSOLVE TO
EXT. DEEP SPACE

*The full-rigged galleon holds its course among
the stars, sails billowing in impossible winds.*

*MORPHING in and out of new avatars—a gothic
cathedral, a huge white swan—the ship sails on,
disappearing into the distance.*

FADE OUT

PIANO BAR BLUES

by Melanie Tem

She liked to introduce herself by saying that Melody was her real name although it wasn't the name she'd started out with. She liked that to be the first thing people learned about her. She said it now into the microphone. "Hi, there, everybody. My name is Melody. Melody wasn't my given name. It's a *taken* name."

She paused for audience reaction, smiles and nods, people wistfully gazing down into their drinks. Nobody was paying the slightest attention to her except the regulars, who, although they'd heard it a thousand times before, were her friends, her family. They cared about her. They understood her. So they did smile and nod, and Charlene clapped.

At the piano, Fiona was smiling at her, too. High cheekbones and an aquiline nose caught by the dim yellow light gave her a witchlike look, ugly in a magical sort of way, repulsive and alluring. Melody wondered in passing what she would look like under other circumstances, but really didn't care to know. Right here, right now was enough. Or, if not enough, was all she had the energy to think about.

Moving things along, Fiona was already into the intro to "Misty," Melody's signature first song. Melody, however, pressed on, determined to say what she came here to say. "Melody is the name I chose for myself because music is so important in my life. This is one of my very favorite tunes, going out tonight especially for you. I hope you enjoy it."

Ever the pro, Fiona showed no impatience. She'd been filling in with something bluesy, probably of her own composition. Melody told herself to save enough money to buy one of Fiona's new CDs that were stacked on the corner of the piano. She could listen to it while she rode the bus all night. Maybe she'd sing.

She finished her drink and in the same motion signaled Bonnie for another. Fiona had gone off on a musical tangent, one thing leading to another; the tune to "Misty" was in there somewhere, but she'd made it her own. Anxious that she might have already missed her cue, Melody waited and listened intently. This was her song. Charlene never could restrain herself from singing along even though it was against what Melody understood to be the rules, and Vince considered it his song, too, because Sinatra had sung "Misty"—never mind that virtually everybody had sung "Misty" and Sinatra had sung virtually everything.

Once in a great while there'd be somebody else in the bar singing along, and Fiona was always on the lookout to recruit. "Join us," she'd offer, and Melody would feel her own heart rise as if she were being invited again for the first time, her own throat constrict with eagerness and jealousy. Sometimes such people had obviously only been waiting for an invitation and would readily sing, even solos, even songs no one but Fiona knew. Sometimes they had to be coaxed over time; this was how Fiona had snagged Charlene. Sometimes they never came back.

Tonight nobody but the regulars was paying any attention. The college kids shooting pool were talking and laughing among themselves. The fiftyish man and much younger woman holding hands in the back booth weren't noticing anything but each other; Melody envied them, not so much because they had each other—she'd never had any trouble finding partners for clandestine meetings in bars—but because both of them doubtless had homes to let themselves back into when they parted, homes to sneak out of for their next rendezvous.

Envy was pointless, and misplaced. She sang and they didn't. She knew Fiona, and they didn't. So absorbed were they in the reality they were weaving around themselves—false as it was; fragile and doomed as it was—that they were totally unaware of the music going on in the same time and space. She bet neither of them even sang in the shower. She, who didn't have a shower to sing in, was about to sing "Misty" while Fiona played for her.

Fiona paused, watching Melody, the two of them holding hands and poised on the brink of a musical cliff. Melody allowed two beats while the anticipation of music hovered palpably in the air, and then, when she couldn't bear it any longer, she half-whispered, half-sang a cappella the first three words of the wonderful old song: "Look . . . at . . . me." Fiona waited an unmeasured time, and then the piano came in. Melody shivered and closed her eyes so she could wrap herself in the exquisite tune and the lyrics that both warmed and chilled. "I'm as helpless . . ."

With songs like "Misty" to sing, it didn't matter that there was nobody waiting for her at home. That, in fact, she didn't have a home, but stayed with friends until they couldn't stand her anymore and then moved on; that she was moving on now, another bridge spectacularly burned, and had no idea to where. That she'd never been in love, and never would be. That she hadn't spoken to her only son in almost a year. Her loneliness was, in fact, an advantage for singing songs like "Misty."

She was in good voice tonight. When she went flawlessly from the clear, true high note of "following you" to "on my own" lower and lower in the back of her throat, it was as if the temperature had swooped upward a hundred degrees; cold sweat broke out on her brow and the backs of her hands, but she kept herself from shivering so as not to distort her voice.

Vince, naturally, was doing it Sinatra-style, with the hand gestures and the head bobs and the little struts and the God's-gift-to-women little smile. The crown of his soft tan hat was creased just so; the brim made his neck and shoulders look scrawny and his ears stick out, but she'd never seen him without the hat. Something about Vince was especially touching tonight, and if Melody looked at him much she wouldn't be able to sing with Fiona. Singing with Fiona was the point. She looked away, but not soon enough. Flustered, she screwed up the phrasing; probably nobody else would notice, but she and Fiona did.

Fiona sent the strong, silky, sticky filament of her concentrated music precisely toward Melody. Melody had seen her do that for the others, too, but this was for her, and she grabbed on, feeling captured, feeling safe.

When Melody had first started singing and following Fiona around to various piano bars, there'd been a regular who'd kept moving closer and closer to Fiona until he was finally on the inside of the horseshoe-shaped bar, leaning against the piano as if to take in through his pores the vibrations of the hammers on the strings created by Fiona's fingers on the keys. Maybe twenty-five years old, he'd favored Streisand tunes, although the range was way beyond him on both the high and low ends. For a while there, Melody had been thinking of him tenderly, like a little brother or a son; now she couldn't remember his name.

More recently there'd been a dear old lady, Belle or Bella, maternal in a quavery sort of way, who chain-drank "wodka vit no ice and just a smidgen tonic." At first she'd only mouthed the words. Then she'd whispered. Wordlessly, musically, Fiona had drawn her out until eventually she would sing full-out in a heart-breaking contralto that seemed to have nothing to do with her speaking voice. Melody had adored Bella. It crossed her mind now to wonder what had become of her.

Fiona was not playing "Misty" now but a riff of her own, variations on the themes of formlessness and formative love. Grateful to be in her thrall, Melody willingly let herself go, and both she and the music became something beautiful and clear and of Fiona's creation. When it was time she sang the last three words very softly, "Look. At. Me," three separate pleas, clutching the mic in both hands close to her lips. Fiona played a chord that took a while to merge, promised to resolve and didn't, slid-ing the after-chord like a mandible under Melody's skin. Melody felt something leave her and go to Fiona. This was what she came here for. This was what she lived for. She could hardly breathe, and hardly needed to.

After a long quiet moment, Charlene gave a little whoop of appreciation. Vince tipped his hat. Fiona growled, "Not too bad, honey. You actually hit a few notes."

Stung, Melody made herself giggle. "Hey, you be nice to me, girl. I'm feeling tender tonight."

Over her wine glass, Fiona raised heavy brows. "Tender?"

"Yes. Tender."

Charlene launched into "Tender Is the Night," and Fiona picked it up. They all sang. Sinatra having, naturally, done this one, too, Vince was in his element. Melody hadn't expected them to ask her what was wrong, and she couldn't have told them anyway, really, but she hadn't been kidding and now she felt mocked. She finished her drink, waved at Bonnie, lost herself in the song, and felt better.

"Sorry I'm late, but I was drunk." This was Byron's standard entrance line, and indeed he was drunk; Melody had never seen him any other way. His gray hair was further grizzled by snow, and the shoulders of his topcoat sparkled until the gray wool absorbed the moisture and darkened. Bonnie had a gin and tonic at his place before he'd even sat down. He beamed and gave her a courtly little bow, and Melody thought how homey it was not even to have to say "the usual" for someone to know what you wanted.

Byron claimed to have once made his living singing in San Francisco nightclubs. He'd also been a member of the Olympic bobsled team, a big game hunter in Africa, and a Hollywood producer. Some of that might be true. In his seventies now, he somehow gave the impression of being both hearty and frail, and Melody loved him like a father. "Good evening, Miss Melody," he greeted her in his usual way. "You're looking lovely tonight."

"Why, thank you, sir. I bet you say that to all the girls."

Indeed, he'd turned his attention elsewhere. "Good evening, Miss Fiona. Good evening, Miss Charlene. How wonderful to be in the company of such beautiful ladies. Nice to see you, too, Frank." Vince gave a Sinatra-esque salute.

"We missed you last night at Millie's, Byron," Melody said.

Byron sighed, "Ah, yes," and for a dreadful moment seemed about to disclose something about his outside life. But he recovered. "Here's a little tune I wrote while I was gone," he announced, and Melody thought that could be true. But it wasn't; the music he handed to Fiona, at which she barely glanced before she started to play it, was "You're Nobody Till Somebody Loves You." Holding on to the padded edge of the bar with both hands, Byron hit almost all the notes.

How true it was, Melody thought as she bowed her head and listened to him. She would be nobody at all if she didn't have piano bars to go to, where Fiona could play in your key every song ever written and people loved you in tried-and-true lyrics not for who you were but for who you presented yourself to be.

During Byron's solo Charlene had gone to the restroom, which meant it was her turn next. She came back now visibly agitated. "I can't find my lipstick," she wailed. "How can I sing if I can't find my lipstick?"

Grinning and trying for a light tone, she was genuinely upset. Byron and Vince muttered chivalrously. Melody assured her she looked fine, although the truth was that without lipstick Charlene's face suggested a torn mask, eyes ringed with deep blue shadow on top and deeper blue shadows of fatigue and sadness underneath, makeup imperfectly blended under her jawline.

Fiona said Charlene's name and tossed her a shiny gold metal cylinder, a tube of her own lipstick. Moved by the generosity of the gesture and both jealous of and put off by its intimacy, Melody readied herself to take an extra turn while Charlene was back in the restroom. But once Charlene realized what Fiona wanted her to do, she fished a compact out of her purse, snapped it open on the bar, leaned close over the tiny mirror as if she were snorting a line of coke, and quickly finished her makeup. The lipstick was purple. She was still folding her lips in and pressing them together to smooth the color when Fiona started her song, and she slid hastily off the bar stool with the microphone caressed in both hands Judy Garland–style. Charlene was just now learning how to carry a tune. For her and for the rest of them, Melody was glad.

Her mind wandered, though, while Charlene was singing, and she found herself thinking dangerously about Josh, in college not thirty miles away but as distant from her as if he weren't her son, as if he'd never been born, as if he'd died or she had. She didn't deserve to be treated like this. She'd done her best with him. Maybe she hadn't always been very together as a mother, but she'd loved him. She still loved him. Surely she loved him as best she could. But he didn't seem very real, and if she thought about that her heart would break.

Fiona was always behind the piano well before anyone else arrived, and she stayed after they all left, so that it was impossible to imagine her in any other setting. She could play anything, jazz and classical, standards and show tunes and pop and blues, folk and heavy metal, Gilbert and Sullivan and rap, original compositions she'd revised and performed many times and on-the-spot extemporizations lovely and wild that she might never repeat. Rarely did she look at the keys. Her hands moved constantly, as if sub- or supra-consciously; when she reached for her drink, the other hand kept playing. When she bantered with the folks around the piano or told jokes, many of them vaguely racist and/or off-color in an oddly juvenile way, the words were accompaniment to the music and not the other way around.

She was playing something jazzy when Melody decided to stop thinking about Josh by asking, "What ever happened to Bella?"

"Who?" both Charlene and Byron asked, but Fiona knew.

"Ah, Bella died."

"Oh, dear." The sorrow was real, real as anything in any song.

"She was a sweet old dame," Vince declared, and gazed off as if into the twilight, as if with baby blue eyes.

"Did she have family?"

"She had me," Fiona snapped.

"Well, that's true. She had us."

"She had me. I was her family. This is the etude for her. I was playing it at the moment of her passing."

What a wonderful loving thing, Melody thought, a trifle uneasily. Fiona's music swelled and held, then grew quieter and quieter, inviting, suggesting it could indeed carry a person off somewhere beautiful and peaceful if it had a mind to.

Melody demanded, "And what about that kid that always wanted to sing Streisand? What ever happened to him?"

Fiona let loose with the opening chord sequence from "People," the phrasing so heartfelt it bordered on parody. "Bobby. He came to me for private lessons for quite a while. Then one day he didn't come. He was passionate about music, although I'm sorry to say he had very little talent. It wasn't like him to miss a lesson. I called his house again and again and there was no answer. Finally I went over, and there was a lady going through his things. His mother. He hated his mother. Going through his things and crying."

"He died?" Charlene pressed her plump fingers to her plump cheeks, stubby red nails looking nearly black against her pale skin. Speaking or singing, her voice was thin.

Disgusted, Byron drained his drink and thumped the empty glass onto the bar. Bonnie was right there with a fresh one. "Good God in Heaven, enough already. I come here to *sing*."

"It's my turn," Vince pointed out, and Charlene echoed, "It's Vince's turn."

"Suicide," Fiona finished.

"Did he have any family besides his mother?" Melody felt compelled to ask. "Any real family?"

"He had me."

Fiona segued into "That's Life," the song Vince had flashed her from his huge black binder of laminated Sinatra scores. Vince readied himself. He adjusted his tie and vest, took several seconds to arrange his hat. Above the rolled-up sleeves of his checked shirt, his raised elbows were sharp, white, childlike. Every few weeks he'd pass around his songbook so they could admire the new photos he'd downloaded from yet another Sinatra website or had the librarian copy from microfiche, and now, for just a moment, he rested his hand on the publicity still on the page facing this anthem, as if to receive guidance or gain strength. Vince was acutely shy. Performing like this was a supreme act of self-sacrifice and love.

He didn't quite hit the first note, but it was closer than usual, and after that he was okay. Melody let out her breath in relief. His reedy voice could not do justice to his obvious strong emotion. It crossed her mind to wonder what personal experiences Vince drew on when he sang, whether he'd ever been "ridin' high in April" or, for that matter, "shot down in May."

This was not a train of thought she wished to pursue. So she didn't. Thoughts of Josh were not so easy to banish, though; before she could stop herself, she'd remembered from beginning to end two or three little defeats and triumphs from his growing-up years. They were all a long time ago, and she wasn't even sure she had them right. Had he really scored the winning soccer goal when he was seven or eight? Had a girl broken his heart in about sixth grade? Was it true that he'd earned Boy Scout badges for horse-manship and service?

"You all right, honey?"

She was about to say, "No. No, I'm not all right. I miss my son. I don't have any place to go," when she realized Bonnie was asking about the status of her drink. She was down to nothing but faintly flavored ice; Bonnie had known what she needed before she had, and gratefully she let herself be tended to.

As the evening worn on, Byron started telling jokes that Melody found offensive not because they were dirty but because they were callow and dumb, tortured narratives building to utterly flat punch lines about bathroom habits and women's body parts. After a certain point, the more Byron drank the more like a tiresome and truculent pre-adolescent he became. It was time for him to go home. He made allusions to having a wife; his wife, in fact, figured prominently in his jokes. No matter how he really felt about her, it was time for him to go home to her.

He called for another drink. Fiona shook her head and Bonnie didn't come. Fiona leaned toward him, white hair undulating as it moved through yellow light and yellowish shadow. "No more for you, Byron. It's time to call it a night."

"I have another song," he protested.

"Save it. We'll hear it tomorrow at Millie's."

"Fiona—"

"Good *night,* Byron."

Surly, he gathered up his music, drained the dregs from his glass, slid unsteadily off his stool, and left without saying good-bye to any of them. He'd be at Millie's tomorrow, and at The Saguaro on Sunday, and at Kit Marlowe's on Monday, and back here next week. What kind of woman was this wife of his to put up with this, to make him want to leave her four nights or more a week, to let him come back home? When he opened the door, cold punched through the close, warm, smoky air of the bar; when he shut the door behind him, the stream was cut off at its source, leaving the chill to swim around like a lost live creature until it wore itself out.

Charlene left next, of her own volition. "Tomorrow's a work day," she always said, no matter what day it was. Melody had no curiosity about what Charlene did for a living, though she sometimes enjoyed speculating to herself whether her co-workers had any clue about Charlene's secret life as a piano bar singer.

Charlene patted her shoulder as she passed behind her, and Melody, in a rush of sisterly affection, called after her, "See you tomorrow!" Charlene didn't always show up, though; apparently there were nights when she had something else to occupy her time. The cold made itself felt again, but Charlene was quicker than Byron had been and it didn't last long.

Vince had mellowed throughout the evening almost as if he were drunk, too. Fiona gave him a hard time about his ginger ale, teasing with a sharp edge to it, but for all his nerdy appearance and demeanor he never wavered about that. Actually, when you thought about it, Vince didn't waver about anything; the Sinatra obsession was certainly weird, the persona laughable, but that's what he *did*, three or four nights a week, not counting preparation time, not counting immersion time. He knew who he was, even if it wasn't real. Melody admired that. Now he sang "It Was a Very Good Year," his standard finale, as if he himself had never had a very good year but Frank Sinatra had and that was enough for him.

Melody applauded for him. He took a little bow. Then he carefully gathered his numerous annotated Sinatra songbooks, tipped his hat to Fiona, and delivered his exit lines: "Thank you. You've been a great audience. I'm sorry to have to leave you, but it's almost my dad's bedtime and he'll be waiting. Good night, ladies and gentlemen. Good night."

Melody blew him a kiss. "Good night, Vince." She'd almost said "Frank." Tomorrow night she would. He'd like that.

"See you tomorrow," Fiona told him. "We'll have a martini ready and waiting. Somehow I can't see Frank Sinatra drinking ginger ale, you know?" Vince laughed uncomfortably and took his leave. Melody braced herself for the outside air; it seemed more frigid with every opening of the door.

Fiona played for a few minutes, irritably, and Melody traced designs with her index finger on the slightly sticky bar. Bonnie came around for last call. Fiona ordered another glass of red wine, Melody brandy. Melody had no place to go. "I have no place to go," she said.

Fiona nodded rhythmically and said without missing a beat, "Come home with me."

"Really? Oh, Fiona, I don't know—" Neither the surprise nor the reluctance was feigned. Fiona had never occurred to her as a friend who might take her in, and something about the invitation— delivered, characteristically, as a command—made her nervous.

"Sure. Why not?"

Melody didn't understand why this sounded like a challenge, or why she'd be insulting Fiona if she didn't go home with her. She also didn't understand the cold, disconnected fear that floated through her mind. She loved Fiona. She had no place to go. Fiona was gazing at her and evidently composing at this very moment the beautiful, slightly atonal melody just for her. She accepted the invitation. She grabbed on and was pulled in. She had no place else to go.

At Millie's the next night, Fiona was already behind the piano when Vince and Charlene came in. They hadn't arrived together, only at the same time, and they were a little embarrassed by the coincidence, a little shy. Both shivering and stamping their feet, they didn't look at each other.

The piano at Millie's was on a sort of dais in the middle of the room, looking down on the tables and the dance floor that was empty on this one night of the week unless somebody wanted to dance to Fiona's music. The regulars never danced. They came to sing.

Tonight Charlene was going to sing "The Sound of Music"

straight through. Vince sang Sinatra. They took turns, back and forth, Fiona's transitions more and more organic until the disparate songs became a kind of call-and-response, a kind of duet. Charlene and Vince met and held each other's eyes. They felt very close, like sister and brother, like lovers.

"Sorry I'm late," Byron declared when he showed up. "I was drunk," and he was, but apparently not enough; he finished the gin and tonic the waiter brought him before he tried his first song of the night. The waiter, a jovial guy named Guy, joined them on his break to sing a medley from *The Pirates of Penzance*; he had a trained voice, and he said tomorrow was his night off and he'd come to The Saguaro to sing with them.

It wasn't until Fiona started playing "Misty" that anybody thought to ask about Melody. Fiona shook her head, drank some wine, kept on playing. After a while she told them. "Melody died last night."

Charlene gasped and covered her face with her plump, maroon-nailed fingers. Vince shoved his hands in his pockets and ducked his head as Sinatra might have. Byron exclaimed, "Good God in Heaven!"

"What happened?" Charlene asked through tears.

Fiona kept playing. Under her hands the lovely old tune was a symphony. When she told them the story she was almost singing. "She must have followed me home. When I woke up this morning I found her on my front steps, curled up, blue with cold and not breathing. She must have died of exposure. Or maybe her heart was weak and just stopped. We don't know yet."

"She was a swell dame," Vince declared. "Things won't be the same around here."

Charlene wiped her eyes with a bar napkin and took a shaky breath. "She used to talk about her son."

"Josh." Fiona nodded. "Nobody knows where he is."

"I guess we were her family." Byron raised his glass in salute.

Fiona frowned but didn't contradict him. She played those first three heartbreaking notes, and they all sang "Misty" together in memory of the woman they'd loved like a sister or a mother or a daughter. Although he hadn't known her at all, Guy sang, too, and Fiona sent her music out to find him and bring him in.

THOSE VANISHED
I RECOGNIZE

by Tom Piccirilli

Clay had heard about this sort of thing before, and he would have believed this was a sign of Obsessive-Compulsive Disorder if it had affected any area of his life but the driving.

But there was none of the repetitive hand washing or twisting of hair, no facial tics or other preoccupation. Only the impulse and need to ride. A sleek '68 Mustang Fastback, sky blue with one of the last 289 V-8 engines off the line, and the seat now perfectly adjusted, his legs finally long enough after all these years, so that he didn't even have to press down on the pedal, it all came naturally.

A steady 60 mph could take him anywhere if he could just get west of the Robert Moses Causeway. Hit the Long Island Expressway, cruise into Midtown, squirm through the ice-slick streets and past the dying, pale whores waiting at the mouth of the

Lincoln Tunnel. Hopefully get by them without incident, no dealings with the big poppa pimps and the wide-eyed stable of chicks who run the gamut from crackheads with the herpes flair to ones who looked like Hedy Lamarr out of *Samson and Delilah*. Buzz beyond them and keep it going straight through Jersey, then slip out into the rest of the moist, flustered world.

Except he couldn't get west of the Robert Moses Causeway. That gave him a route heading two hours to the end of Long Island, only stopping when he came to a historic park called Montauk Point, where he'd pull into the lot at the base of the lighthouse, sit for a moment listening to the waves slash against the stone, and then head back again, right to the starting line.

Clay had been at it for fourteen hours straight, since noon yesterday. He felt wide awake and only a bit stiff. The six-packs and burgers held him over fine, and so long as it didn't take him more than two or three minutes to fuel up, he didn't get jittery at the gas stations. Still, he had begun to question himself over exactly why he had the urge and where it had come from. He had the uneasy notion this was starting to get a little unreasonable.

That was all right, though. He drilled along on Sunrise Highway heading east, past the Pine Barrens and farther until the island forked. For some reason he hadn't been able to take the North Fork yet and go out to Orient Point. Instead, every time he got to the end of Sunrise, with his hands growing sweaty, and his knuckles—even the pinkies—crackling, he swung south and continued to gun toward Montauk.

It had something to do with his father, Clay thought, and he decided to let it come to him in its own time. That kept his pulse down as moonlight swept over the road, breeze hurling leaves against the grille and spinning across the hood. The burned remnants of the Pine Barrens came into view, his headlights illuminating the unnatural stance of scorched trees along the shadowed terrain. It had been five years since the largest fire in the island's history cut through this area, and still there had been scarcely any regrowth.

He kept heading toward Route 27 and on to the Hamptons, where the New York elite resided. His father used to point out celebrity homes whenever they came here to fish and spend an afternoon at the beach: Joseph Heller, Kurt Vonnegut, Jackson Pollock, and dozens of others. Clay never understood where Dad got his information.

A tightness seized him, maybe a touch of nausea. The heater softly hummed. This was where the pain would come. He waited and started the countdown, each car length left behind being another lost part of him. The rearview mirror had been removed for this reason. He couldn't stand to watch all that continued receding behind him. He watched the mileage gauge, knowing what would happen on the next tick of a tenth of a mile. There, almost there, almost—

The Hamptons, as always, invaded Clay as he entered town, mansions whirling by in a haze of jealousy, respect, love and wanting. The solidity of riches he would never own pressed him from all sides, dropping off his shoulders and into the back seat, where he could hear the vinyl groan beneath its weight. He gritted his teeth and fought not to let out a yelp. The Mustang slowed, and he had to stamp his foot down in order to get past. There were hardly any streetlights here, but the few he hit were already yellow and waiting for him, holding out the extra couple seconds, and just barely letting him slide by.

The road curved and kept coiling as if it would never finish going through this spiral. His odometer shot up insanely, engine squealing as the back end fishtailed on black ice. He struggled to regain control, letting the edges of his mouth hitch into a grin, fighting the wheel. At last he felt the smooth catch of the tires on the pavement as he came out of the corkscrew stretch and maneuvered past the saw grass of Southampton College.

That salty scent of the ocean clung to him, thriving everywhere in the car. He enjoyed watching the rising mounds and bluffs of the golf course on the other side, and he perked at the monolithic structures rising to the south. Jutting arcane shapes sloped against the roiling clouds. They might be homes or something more—trawlers dry-docked, or machinery to repair the damaged shoreline and bulldoze tons of sand back into place. Radio towers or high-voltage steeples, or maybe it was only his vision failing. No matter how many times he went past he could never be sure.

Twenty minutes later he wheeled through the fishing town of Montauk again, past the seafood restaurants where his parents would take him and his sister Jamie on the way to the park.

"The abstract expressionist Jackson Pollock painted in a barn, did you know that?" Dad had asked.

Jamie, beaming, twelve at the time, answered gleefully because she always had the answers. "Jack the Dripper! His studio was right there"—pointing, the index finger a little crooked, but knowing exactly where everything was as they drove—"in East Hampton, back in the late Forties and early Fifties, after he and Lee Krasner got married and moved out of the city."

"Correct!"

Clay would keep silent, uncertain if these were particulars he was truly supposed to know or if this was a private diversion, a personal game between his father and sister. A series of meaningless questions and trivia, or maybe they were making it up as they went along. Dad had once claimed that three atomic bombs had been dropped on Japan: Nagasaki, Hiroshima and *Tokyo*. Jamie, intent in either salving their father's conceit or only wishing to be loved the best, curled lithely into the crook of Dad's arm and cooed, "Yes, I know."

Perhaps the rotten, weak son, the living disappointment, Clay had searched a dozen books and asked all three history teachers in school, searching for his father's fact.

The Mustang's engine had a nice thrum and rumble now, the oil beginning to break down after gunning a thousand frosty miles in fourteen hours. Clay didn't let the pressure of the night close in as he sped toward the park, headlights digging channels through the dark that let him cleanly pass through. He slowed until the sound of the splashing surf could be heard over the engine.

On the last circuit, four hours ago, there had been a dozen cars in the lot, mostly teenagers making out parked behind the storm fences or middle-aged couples bundled in sweaters taking a stroll up the beach. Now he was alone and wasn't sure how much he liked it. The lighthouse, which hadn't been lit in years, loomed above.

Clay pulled in and waited. He wondered if he could last longer than a couple of minutes this time. He hoped so, though he still wasn't afraid of this need for a bizarre, redundant journey. It would work itself out. He turned the key but wasn't convinced he'd broken the cycle yet. There was the strong impression that he hadn't been able to shut the car off the last time he was here—or the time before, or the time before, or—

He sat back and let this interim carry him, with enough moonlight funneling into the interior so that he could read his watch. Five minutes passed, then ten. It wasn't until his breath fogged up the windshield that he realized he was cold. His brow furrowed until he remembered it was January.

"Do you know who ordered that the lighthouse be built over two hundred years ago?" Dad asked.

"The lighthouse was authorized by the Second Congress, under President George Washington," Jamie said. Clay thought it could be true.

"When?"

"In 1792."

When they got back home that day, sunburned and with the sea salt drying to a thick powder on their skin, Clay immediately noticed the stench. Jamie didn't, heading off to shower. Knowledgeable yet indifferent. The light in the living room was all wrong—dim, with a haze of smoke drifting past.

Dad leaned over the couch, peering. Mother's legs were folded behind her, one hand flat, palm down on the throw pillows, the other fist positioned differently. Dark, and growing darker as Clay watched, not bloody but blistered and cracking, lying atop the exposed light bulb of the overturned reading lamp, skin charred and growing blacker. Her shoulders had slumped so far forward that her head hung over the far side of the couch where he couldn't see her face. Blue and yellow pills lay scattered across the carpet. Dad picked one up and tried studying it in the dim light. He had a rough time, squinting, holding the pill this way and that, and moved closer to the lamp with the fumes of frying meat rising from it. The billowing smoke broke against Dad's face. And Mother not moving her hand, and still not getting up.

By the time Clay walked the dirt path down to the water he realized somebody was watching him.

It took a while for his eyes to adjust, even with the vibrant moon and silver mercury clouds. The ocean splashed and churned, clawing up the beach. The other person's presence tugged at him like fishhooks, so that he let himself go and followed into darkness.

He found her within a hundred yards, sitting back in the sand surrounded by half-buried stones. She gestured but he couldn't make out what the motion might be. He picked his way carefully to her as the breakers clapped and roared around them.

From the midst of an enveloping blanket, with only the suggestion of something actually alive in there, she looked up. "Hello. Care for a swim?"

He let out a barking laugh, and the sound startled him. He could hardly make out her long hair swaying and flopping in the wind, murkiness braided into shadow. The white of her eyes came through. "I'll take a rain check until July."

"I suppose you're right." He saw the glow of her teeth. "This might sound crude, depending on what you do for relaxation, and seeing as how we've only just met, but I figured I'd ask anyway. Do you have any weed?"

"Some beer in my car."

There was an odd, lethargic trait to her voice. She spoke in sluggishly unwinding whispers. "I don't feel like walking back to the parking lot."

"Neither do I."

He got closer and really focused, staring until she took a more precise form. The eyes came and went as she blinked. He thought she was a couple of years younger than he, maybe seventeen or eighteen at the outside. She sat near enough to the water that shards of moonlight swept up against her, illuminating her only in fragments.

Yet there was an extra quality to her that came through. She was at ease inside her body, even with him moving in now, cautiously taking another step, and one more, until he sat beside her. She contained the gentle sexuality of someone who lost her virginity long ago, and had never been burdened with any of the obsessions, fears and confusion that everyone else had to suffer through.

Dad had asked, "Are you a man yet?"

Clay, astounded and drawing away, grunted as if kidney-punched. His father had spoken with a kind of reverent tenderness, inquiring but embarrassed, yet desperately needing the truth. Clay remained silent, watching Dad gape and trying to say more, mouthing words or names, reaching to touch Clay on the shoulder but never quite getting there. Dad turned to Jamie, expecting an answer and, as always, getting one. She told him, "Clay's made it with that Felecia McAlester, down by the docks, in the front seat of your Mustang."

That got reality moving again. Clay didn't mind that his sister had told, or that she somehow knew what she couldn't have known. It made its own sense, which was a relief of sorts.

"Let's build a fire," the girl said so quietly that he almost didn't catch it. There was an odd clacking noise coming from nearby.

"There's not enough driftwood."

"You haven't even looked."

"I don't need to. There are folks who clear it out every day, not that there's ever much to begin with. The coast is too rocky."

"So what shows up gets turned into lamps and shit?"

"Pretty much."

They watched the foam dashing against the rocks, spattering and reforming into plumes. He thought he saw clothing floating out there, rising on the crests and retreating. The lighthouse stood silhouetted, perfectly centered before the blaze of the moon.

"My mother is out there," she said.

"Your mother?"

She started to yawn but didn't seem to have the energy for it. It took her a long time to talk, even with that intensity, everything coming out so languidly. "We lived in Queens. Forest Hills. She went out to buy fresh tomatoes and a week later they found her floating here."

"Yeah?"

"No marks on her." Slower still, her sentences almost solidifying in the air. "Everybody tried to believe she was kidnapped but I think she killed herself. It's the nicer thought, really, if you've got to dwell on it."

"And you do."

"Yes, of course."

She shrugged and the blanket slid off her shoulders, showing that she wore something too thin and pink beneath. He leaned forward and realized he was wrong; she was naked. Soft angles and outlines wove into one intimation. She must have been turning to ice but didn't bother to pull the blanket back up into place.

Jamie had held tightly to their father's hand at Mother's funeral. It was allowed, even expected, though there remained a crass edge about it. She was fifteen then, dressed in black chiffon and appearing too adult, as if she had advanced into a new role. She never let Dad's hand go for a moment, not even while the priest droned on and the neighbors wept, and the roses were given out. They approached the grave together, his father and sister, pausing to pray as the seconds coagulated into a clot of unbearable time, until Clay, so miserably alone and lonely, joined them, and they moved away from him.

He stood there trying to say good-bye, but couldn't even recall what his mother had looked like. He wanted them to open the casket once more, so that he could see and remember. He must have asked this aloud, and repeatedly, because Jamie, from the far side of the grave, made excuses for him, smiling at the crowd and still not letting Dad go. "He was very close to her, and he's been running a high fever. You can't blame him his ways. None of us can blame him."

"The water has a draw," the girl said. The clacking continued until he realized it was her teeth chattering.

"I know," Jamie would have told them, "tidal forces. It's called the gravitational and centrifugal gradients theory of the Earth-Moon system."

He looked at her naked breasts, uncertain if he was feeling lust or not. Seashells prodded him, the rising wind slithering under his collar and swabbing his forehead, like his mother's compresses when the fevers got too high.

"I'm waiting," she said.

"For what?"

"The nerve to follow in after my mother. I thought it would be easy, but I'm too afraid. I don't want to die."

She tried getting to her feet, but she was already hypothermic. She must have gone through the heavy shaking period before he got here, and was now experiencing the onset of serious cramping and muscle lock. She fell over and lay feebly trembling in the sand. He stood and took a step back.

"Will you take me home now?" she whimpered.

"To Forest Hills? No, I can only go so far."

"Home with you."

"I'm not going there."

Her lips barely moved. "I'll freeze to death. I threw my clothes away."

"I saw them. In the surf."

"Home." She tried gathering herself again, but could only turn over in the moonlight, revealing herself completely to him. A powerful gust caught the blanket and threw it at his feet—a deliberate action deserving another in response, where he kicked it into the waves. "Please, I want to go home."

"So do I."

"I was wrong. I don't want to die. Don't leave me here. Please."

Clay turned and walked back up the path to the parking lot, got in the car and started it.

He hoped the next time he got back he would see his father and sister well-defined in the foam, rearing and casually tumbling against the jagged rocks, hand in hand with each question and every answer. He could almost recall having watched them here in the tide before—perhaps swimming, laughing, begging or gasping. It would take hardly any effort to do what the girl had done, and roll among the whitecaps until his loneliness was at an end, when at last he joined them and the others like them.

As he came out of the park his mother was there, breaking from the darkness at the side of the road, awash in the headlights. With her one good hand held out before her, she urged him not to go on, to finally rest and find peace as she had, by the strength of one's own will, but he could only do what he had grown accomplished at, catching her sorrowful, black-rimmed gaze as he now, and forever, continued to drive by.

INLAND, SHORELINE

by Darren O. Godfrey

1. INLAND

An antler gripped in one gloved hand, Gavin smashed the skull against a boulder. Pieces flew.

"Who gets to keep the rack?" I asked him, watching as he raised the deer's head above his own, preparatory to another blow. Perspiration ran down his pale thirteen-year-old face, mist plumed from his mouth and nose, rising up through the falling snow.

"Maybe we can split 'em, cousin," he said. He smashed the skull again; bone chips rained down on our boots.

"Split 'em how?"

"Well, we get a hacksaw from Aunt Madeline's shed and cut right here"— he indicated the point where skull became horn—"and you keep one side and I'll keep the other." He grinned at me, then peered into what little was left of the skull cavity. Having first spotted the buck's decaying head lying in the weeds, Gavin received the privilege of deciding its fate.

He'd apparently determined enough had been accomplished with the smash-and-bash method because he turned, then, and started down the hill. I followed.

"Won't just one side of a rack look kinda funny on a wall?"

"Probably. But you and I look kinda funny, too, so that's all right. *Comprende?*"

"No, not really." We emerged from a stand of evergreens into a shale-littered clearing where the hill began to slope more steeply. The snow wasn't sticking, but it was doing a pretty fair job of making everything slick and uncertain.

About half a mile down the valley, our Aunt Madeline's house sat, gray smoke curling from its leaning chimney. Cars and trucks belonging to other aunts, uncles, cousins, grandparents, mothers and fathers lined the gravel driveway like a stalled funeral procession.

The Thanksgiving feast would commence soon, and my stomach told me it was primed, and I had to remind my boot-heavy feet to step carefully—one wrong move and a kid could find himself at the bottom of this hill in a hurry and in a cast by the end of the day.

"We don't have to go back right now, Danny," Gavin said abruptly. He came to a halt, and I nearly put my face into his back.

"What?" I came around him, peered into his flushed face and asked again, *"What?"*

"We have time. We don't need to go down just yet." His dark-ish eyes were directed at Aunt Madeline's house, but it seemed to me that the house wasn't at all what he was looking at.

"What do you mean?" I asked. "I'm starved, aren't you?"

He turned to me, his face moving into the strangest expression I'd ever seen him do, and I'd seen him do some mighty strange ones. He began: "I want . . ."

A pause. His head tilted as if wondering just what it was he *did* want, and then there came a loud crack. Gavin's face turned a bright, liquid red. It disappeared. There was an echo.

"What . . . ?"

All was quiet.

I turned. The cars and trucks were gone. My aunt's house stood silent, no smoke wafting from its chimney. Its innards were undoubtedly as cold and empty as . . . as that of an old deer skull. It was not Thanksgiving 1977.

It was October of 2000.

I stepped carefully over the weather-beaten antlers, where, unbelievably, they still lay among the loose rock. I descended the hill.

Alone.

2. SHORELINE

The boardwalk is moderately crowded. I am the only one here who is not watching the water. The wind whips dirty hair into my eyes as I stare at the dull, flat face of the West Wind Hotel. Half an hour ago, I found my father's olive-green Oldsmobile in the hotel parking lot, just as the private detective told me I would. It was identifiable (again, via the private dick) not only by make, model, and color, but by the bound-and-gagged Garfield doll suction-cupped to the rear window: a gift from his latest bimbo, I guessed.

I'm gazing up at the West Wind's dirty windows and I wonder if he is looking back, perhaps wondering a thing or two himself. Perhaps not. We've not seen each other for over twenty-one years— would he know me? Would I know him?

A few days ago the mental slide-show, incredibly detailed replays of November 1977, began and I've slept little since. They happen often, and without warning. Now, with a little perseverance and a lot of money, I have found him. My father. The source, I believe, of my mind's weird hiccups.

Kathy, my wife, is home and no doubt thinks I've lost my mind, but I hope that's not what she's decided to tell our children.

I turn slowly, taking in the rest of the town. This is my first visit to Harper Cove, my first visit to the west coast. I find it quite beautiful, though not exactly what I expected. The people are cordial, not closed off. They talk to me.

"Hey, Danny," I say, almost beneath my breath. "Clap your hands if you believe in fairies."

Then, louder, "You're a funny guy, Dad. By the way, do you remember me?"

3. INLAND

From the doorway of the master bedroom I watched as my Uncle David tried to bring his son back to life. Most of the women were crying. Aunt Nell, Gavin's mother, screamed repeatedly until someone dragged her to one of the back bedrooms. Uncle Ray gave a lot of orders to which no one paid any attention. From behind me, I heard Grandpa Marsh mutter something about how tough it was going to be getting the bloodstains out of those blankets.

"Emery!" Grandma scolded. "Such a thing to say!"

There was a lot of blood.

My mother sat in a chair in one corner of the living room and said nothing. She watched me. She knew I was stunned—fair understatement—but she also seemed to know much more. It was her eyes, I realized later, which made me think that. Her eyes knew everything.

There was a rough whisper of, " . . . *hunting accident* . . ." and Aunt Madeline's wrinkled hand fell on my shoulder, her wrinkled voice fell on my ear: "Danny, I really think you should go outside and keep the little ones company, don't you, dear?"

I agreed.

Heading out, I wondered where my father was. I could not see our car among the others parked along the lane, though I admit I didn't try very hard to find it.

I somehow managed to get the kids interested in a game of hide and seek, but when little Joey, all of three years old, tripped, skinned his knees, and began to scream . . . it all vanished. I was on my hotel bed, with tears in my eyes.

It doesn't matter. It's all gone. My mother died of cancer in 1978, but Dad had already skipped out by then. I grew up alone. I learned.

4. SHORELINE

October 19. Afternoon.

Cloudy in Harper Cove. I wonder if, had I grown up here, would anything have been different? If I'd been raised in a place where the horizon was so boundless, so open, might it have mattered?

Stupid, to wonder such things. Pain is here, same as anyplace else.

I'm sitting at a table in the Pacific Coast Restaurant, just in sight of the West Wind. The main attraction for me this time is not the hotel, however, nor its inhabitants. It is the water. The steady, uncaring motion of all that water.

"What'll it be?"

Mmm. Good question, that.

"Pardon me, sir, but can I get you something?"

The waitress is standing at my elbow with a pinned gray bun on her head, tapping her pencil on her order pad. She regards me with a polite smile.

"Yes, I'd like that."

After taking my order and answering a private query, she hurries off. I consider calling Kathy, assuring my children their father is still among the sane. I consider forgetting my father, as he has forgotten me, and returning home. I consider a normal life.

I remember my mother, who, to me, was a little like one of those shadowy characters in the background of a '40s film noir: forever present, but barely visible beneath a soft fedora . . . observing all, but rarely speaking. The one who sometimes fills in the story gaps for you at the end of the movie. I waited a long time, though I didn't realize it then, for the gaps to be filled in, for some explanations of my father and his hateful, ignorant ways. Maybe some guidance as to my place in the scheme of things, funny as that seems now.

But if Mom had any answers, she died before she could reveal them, fading away silently, back into the shadows.

Gradually, my attention is pulled back to the mass of moving gray water. So powerful.

5. INLAND

By the time he'd arrived, there was little need for Dr. Mullins. His station wagon, however, was useful in transporting Gavin's body into town where it could be, in the doctor's slowly drawling words, "examined good 'n proper." Almost everyone went along, following the doc in their cars and trucks. Our car was not among them.

Where's Dad? I wondered again. It was a question, for whatever reason, I didn't ask aloud. Instead, it was this: "What do they need all those people for?"

I stood at the kitchen window watching the many pairs of tail-lights recede into the cold darkness. Snowflakes passed through Aunt Madeline's reflection in the glass. She smiled oddly, then set about fixing me a plate of turkey, ham, bread stuffing, cranberries, the works. I heard Grandpa Marsh's snores coming from the living room. Grandma Marsh was relieving herself, probably thinking herself unhearable, in the bathroom.

My mother lay down with a headache in one of the bedrooms.

I sat and nibbled at Aunt Madeline's feast, idly wondering why I wasn't crying.

Dad finally stomped in through the door around nine. He didn't say where he'd been, and no one asked. He wouldn't look at me. The pungent smell of whiskey followed him like a cloud. Mom came out of hiding, announced, "It's time to go home," but by then Grandma Marsh and Aunt Madeline were sleeping, too, so there was no need for good-byes.

Dad told me to get in the car.

I did.

End of another installment of Danny Remembers.

6. SHORELINE

October 21. Night.

I have never owned a gun before. It's a Harrington & Richardson .22-caliber revolver. The man at Sam's Sport Shop, where the waitress from the Pacific Coast Restaurant referred me, called it a "good plinker." He also said that $75.50 was a damn good deal, but I suspect that doesn't matter.

What matters is that my father and his bimbo are just down the hall in room 210 at this very moment. And I am lying here fully clothed on an unmade bed at five minutes to midnight, my tired eyes tracking the pattern of cracks in the ceiling of room 206. I wonder if their ceiling has this many cracks, and are they looking at them? Perhaps while sharing a post-fuck cigarette?

I know if I stare at my ceiling's cracks long enough I will begin to see things in them. Words, perhaps. REVENGE. FAGGOT, maybe. It would be easy to see these things if only I set my mind to it.

Ah, there's one. FATHERHOOD, it says. Great. I wonder what his ceiling might be saying to *him*?

I sit up, peer out the window where a string of yellow lights tries vainly to illuminate the boardwalk. Beyond that lies the undulating water of the bay, felt more than seen at this hour. I think of cold, of Thanksgiving, of taillights dwindling, and of the heavy odor of liquor.

I think of the first time my father referred to my cousin as a "fucking faggot." Gavin was only twelve at the time. I was nearly that. I didn't even know what "faggot" meant, and had only an adolescent, giggling idea of what "fucking" was. Gavin, though, seemed to be deeply troubled by my father's words . . . by my father in general.

Clap your hands if you believe in fairies. . . .

I'd always been a little bit afraid of Dad, though he rarely hit me. But what seems strange to me is that it wasn't until I'd reached the age of fifteen that I realized the man was a complete idiot. A simpleton.

At the tender age of seven, I had idolized him, naturally. He'd held the sole image in my mind of what a father is, does, acts and smells like. He was *Dad.* Dads know everything. Dads are there to help you.

Certain things, the events surrounding Gavin's death chiefly among them, eventually led me to the conclusion that my father was an imbecilic, bigoted, self-centered asshole, not to mention a cold-blooded murderer.

And *that* is what he *should* be reading in the cracks.

Time to go. My watch tells me so. I rise, tuck the loaded revolver down the front of my pants, cover it with a jacket, quickly comb my hair, and there is nothing wrong with what I am about to do.

I step out into the corridor. Except for the two plastic ferns in plastic pots, it is deserted. I am calm, my thoughts together and at peace as I approach their door. I knock with little hesitation.

I hear muffled talk, a cough, a girlish giggle . . . and . . . well, I'm not sure how to explain this sufficiently, but with that giggle, that goddamn childish rippling noise, something somehow *changes* . . .

shifts . . .

inside me.

My father is not worth killing.

I'd known that . . . but I hadn't really grasped the *simplicity* of it. It is not cowardice (which is what *he* would think, I'm certain), not at all. It is a basic realization: He's not worth it.

As I turn my back on the door, prepared to walk away forever, I hear the shallow squeak of its hinges.

"Yeah?"

His voice. It hasn't changed.

7. INLAND

The drive home that night was silent but for the whistling in the crack of the passenger side window and the occasional whispered curse from my father as fat snowflakes swept into his headlight's beams. Mom said nothing. The dashboard's green glow threw an eerie light over both their faces—Dad's, a goblin mask; Mom's, a neutral caul.

Dad punched the radio on, tilted an ear toward it as it spoke of politics and the ongoing war in some faraway place. He punched other stations, grunted dissatisfaction with each. He snapped it off.

"Will we be going to Aunt Madeline's again next year?" I asked when we'd finally reached the driveway of our home. I knew the question was foolish even as I asked it. I didn't care. Perhaps I was in shock. It didn't matter, no one answered it.

Dad backed the car into the driveway, something he normally did not do, put it in park, then sat there, staring at his hands, his *fists*, which didn't seem to want to ease their grip on the steering wheel. He didn't move. Mom, too, seemed frozen.

Abruptly, then, Dad got out, keys jingling, and slammed the door. Mom and I sat there as he walked to the back of the car, opened the trunk. I felt more than heard him take something from it. The garage door rattled up and he thumped his way inside.

Mom's mask broke, then. "Get ready for bed, dear," she said, attempting a smile. She failed. We went inside.

8. SHORELINE

I turn and face him.

He wears only a towel around his ample middle.

"Whatcha need?" he says, and there is not so much as a spark of recognition in his eyes. His bristled face hangs on his skull like peppered dough, his breath stinks of whiskey, and, sure enough, cigarettes. Post-fuck variety. Only that voice is the same, and from far inland I hear a crack and see liquid red, and I hear anger, " . . . *fucking faggot . . .*" and disbelieving whispers, " . . . *hunting accident? . . .*" and harsh laughter, " . . . *clap your hands if you believe in fairies. . . .*"

From behind him: "Who is it, honeycheeks?"

Honeycheeks?

The whole upper half of his face tightens in a squint. "Do I know you?" he mutters, then burps.

"It was your hunting rifle, wasn't it, Dad? The one you said could drop a moose from three hundred yards? More than just a good plinker for you, eh? A *fuck* of a lot more."

"What in the . . ."

"I've got to admit, Dad, it was one hell of a shot."

"*What?*"

"But who was it you were trying to help? Who the Christ were you trying to protect? Me?"

His eyes grow wide. His mouth, now a sagging hole, moves greasily. It's beginning to sink in, I think.

"I didn't need your help, Dad. You never understood that. You never understood that I could take care of myself if I had to. I didn't need you . . . at least . . . at least not then. Not for that." I feel a flutter of dim hope, hope of a little understanding, on his part as well as my own. "But now . . ."

"*Who* did you say—?"

"I could use your help now, Dad. I really could, because my life is . . . it's not right. It's shit, Dad. I need help now."

His unbelieving gaze moves from my face down the front of my jacket to my arm. My hand. His eyes widen further and he takes a quick step backward.

"Here." I extend the hand bearing the revolver. My fingers now clench not the gun's grip but its barrel.

"Go away," he croaks. "You're not my son. You can't be. I haven't gotta son."

Laughter behind him again. Not a girlish giggle now, but a harsh, nicotine-stained snort.

Dad takes another step back and slams the door.

Too little, I understand, *too late*.

9. INLAND

November returns and so do I.

The gray lateness of the day infects Gavin's headstone and all those surrounding it. It taints the grass, the air, the cemetery gates with a dullness numbing to the spirit. It will be dark soon.

"It's funny," I whisper, the vapor of my breath misting my vision, "Neither one of us got the rack. After all this time, it's still up there."

No response from the grave. Cold stone. Cold earth.

"'You keep one side and I'll keep the other,' you said. Remember? But half a rack *would* have looked funny."

A chill gust hits me; snowflakes swirl, touch down around me. My left hand is tucked deeply into the left pocket of my coat, where it is warm. My right hand is in the right pocket of my coat, where it touches cold steel.

A few feet of earth, a bare whisper of time. But the actual distance between Gavin and me is really just an illusion. A crack in the air, somewhere far away, followed by its echo. I'd told Dad it was a good shot, but I was wrong.

He missed.

I hope I don't.

THE WINDOW

by Joel Lane

It wasn't until their third date that the boy asked Richard to behead him. He'd been asked for similar things in the past, but had never taken it literally. What people tended to want was to hear themselves ask, and then to go through some kind of ritual that took them close. So close that a careless or vicious twist of the garrotte or jerk of the harness could end it. Edge games. But somehow, he was sure Ian didn't want to play a game. The boy had probably been born in role.

It had started a fortnight earlier, in Subway City. Richard had been window-shopping. He was too old to stand a chance with that crowd, but the images helped to renew his desire for the other things he did. Imagination couldn't run without fuel. He watched the pale, speed-driven teenagers shiver around the dance floor. Droplets of light sprayed onto their faces and T-shirts. In alcoves, couples were frozen in the trance of foreplay. The beat was too quick to dance to, almost too deep to hear. It was like the roar of water in an underground cavern.

Wearing a black T-shirt and matching jeans, Richard crept from bar to bar. Frequent body contact was unavoidable, but nobody gave him a second glance. That was fine. He sipped chilled vodka, the ache in his side barely noticeable. For now. He began to imagine some of the lithe bodies twisting in pain, their mouths open in a silent awestruck grimace. He'd seen enough. Any later and taxis would be hard to come by. A friend of his had been half-killed outside here; it wasn't a good street for hanging around.

First, he needed a piss. Bypassing the club's famous paired urinals, he made his way to the main toilets on the ground floor. Various shattered youngsters were slumped against the wall, shirts dark with sweat, hair reduced to thorns of chaos. The petals of their skin. He stumbled inside, wincing at the scent of violets, and relieved himself. As he was rinsing his hands, a face appeared in the mirror beside him. A teenager, brown spiky hair, eyes so dark they were like holes. The face rang a faint bell, but he couldn't place it. He rubbed his hands under the dryer, which wasn't working. Then the boy's pale hands took hold of his and stroked the water from them. He could feel the tension under the skin.

"Batman." The boy's face was low, breathy. His mouth twisted into a question.

"Shh. I'm here incognito. What do you want?"

"I've been watching you. At the Basement. And the Nightingale. You punished me in a chatroom, last Friday."

Richard laughed. What on Earth had the boy's messages been like? *Bruise me. Cut me in half with your sword.* A blur of one-handed typing. "Ian, yes? If I'd known you were a local boy, maybe we could have . . ."

Ian nodded. His eyes were fixed on Richard's. There was a bleak stillness in his face. Now he thought about it, Richard did recall seeing him in the shadows of the Basement. But he'd been otherwise engaged at the time. He touched the boy's neck, gently but with a firm hand. "Look, that Internet stuff is just daydreaming, OK? The things I do for real, they don't just happen. I have to get to know someone. Train them. I can't do it overnight."

The boy leaned against him. "So what *can* you do overnight?"

"This." He took Ian's arm and drew him out into the dim hallway that led to the cloakroom, then pushed him to the wall and pressed their mouths obliquely together. They kissed desperately. Richard filled his lungs with air and blew it into the boy's open mouth. He drew a finger across the back of Ian's neck. His other hand traced the outline of a stiff cock through denim.

"Taxi. Come on." They joined the cloakroom queue. Richard had his trademark leather jacket with the Bacardi bat logo; Ian had a white ski jacket that made him look even younger. Instead of waiting outside the club, they walked together up Snow Hill to the city center. It was surprisingly warm for an October night. Maybe autumn was a thing of the past now. Cars and lorries raced along the expressway; on the other side, yellow lights shimmered on patches of canal glimpsed through Victorian stone arches. For a moment, Richard didn't feel like Batman, an invisible creature of the night, or a master about to initiate a new servant. He just felt like a middle-aged man who was grateful for some company.

Back at the house, he poured Ian a Cointreau and himself a Bacardi, unobtrusively necking a couple of paracetamol and codeine as he did so. Ian admired the somber living room: black leather sofa, prints of Symbolist paintings, wooden masks. He told Richard he was seventeen and worked in an electrical goods shop.

They shared a joint. Then Richard undressed Ian on the sofa and fucked him slowly in front of the coal-effect gas fire.

Afterward, they lay tangled together on the rug. Richard kept his face in shadow, so Ian wouldn't see how tired he was. Sex seemed to put years on him these days. He was about to suggest they move to the bedroom when Ian started putting his clothes on. "I'd better go, mister."

"You're welcome to stay for breakfast."

"It's OK. Sorry. I don't like to stay over. Feel strange in the mornings."

"If I'm going to be your master, that'll have to change."

"Then, yes. But not now." Ian's face was blank, masklike in the fire's orange glow.

"Shame. I love the smell of melted KY in the morning." Richard struggled back into his tight jeans with as much dignity as possible. "I'll call you a cab. Don't want you to come to harm, do we?"

"When can I see you again?" The boy's tone was low, deferential. But he seemed oddly sure of himself. That was Richard's cue to be difficult. But he wasn't in the mood.

"Give me a call on Wednesday night," he said. "Seven o'clock. Five minutes late, and you've blown it."

When the cab arrived, they kissed slowly in the dark hallway. Then Richard opened the door and let the teenager out into the quiet suburban street. "Take care." Fine wires of rain slashed through the yellow light. He shut the door, poured himself a final drink and stood in the kitchen, watching the rain scar the full moon and disappear into the black undergrowth of his hopelessly neglected garden.

Their first date was a week later. They met at Boots, a new leather and denim bar on the edge of a Digbeth housing estate. As the dimly lit bar area filled up with skinheads and ugly trade whose only hope of intimacy was the back room, Richard explained what the duties of a servant were. Talking through the details was important: it established the relationship. Ian was quiet, attentive, a quick learner. But hopefully not so quick that he wouldn't need the occasional correction.

When the bar became too crowded for talking, they went on to the Nightingale. Richard made Ian stand motionless and silent, holding Richard's glass while he chatted with his friends in the members' bar. As a reward, he was given a sip of beer every half hour. He seemed to find it easy to switch off. Maybe he didn't know anyone here. Eventually they caught a taxi to Richard's place in Solihull, Ian maintaining the required silence. It was colder than the previous week. There was hardly anyone out on the streets.

Back at the house, Richard poured them both a large whisky. Then he told Ian to undress and led him into the black room. It was a spare bedroom upstairs, overlooking the garden. The walls and ceiling were painted black; there were black velvet curtains. Richard dimmed the light until Ian was only just visible. He directed the boy to lie down on the table, face against the wood. "What do you want me to do?"

The reply was almost a whisper. "Whatever you desire."

"What's your name?" He began fastening the clamps to the boy's tense arms and legs.

"Whatever you choose to call me." Ian winced silently as Richard tightened a wrist clamp.

"Listen carefully. From now on, you call me only Master. If you call me Richard, this will stop. But it won't start again until it suits me. Is that clear?"

"Yes, Master." Richard applied the neck brace and tied the chain around Ian's ankles, so that he was bent back from the table. Then he went and poured himself a drink, took it into the black room, and stood by the window. He drew back the curtain. The garden looked alien in the bleached light: broken flagstones, rotting shrubs, patches of spiky grass. A cat darted across the muddy path, paused and leapt. He didn't see what it caught. When he turned back, Ian's eyes were closed; he was sweating. Richard unlocked the trunk he kept under the table and took out a bamboo cane.

An hour later, he rubbed Savlon into the boy's wounds and carried him into the bedroom. They made love with a tenderness that was almost unbearable. Richard always tried not to get involved in ways that could undermine his control. But somehow, Ian was different. There was a kind of purity in him, a distance in his thin face that made him hard to possess. Richard had been careful not to mark that face.

While Ian lay asleep, Richard went back downstairs and finished off the whisky bottle with some ice. The pain in his right side was sharper now, as if a rib had broken free and was tearing something. It was only justice. If you stole the fire of the gods, they'd send an eagle to peck at your liver. He tried to be a good boy most of the time. But sometimes he'd rather have the fire.

Something flickered outside the kitchen window. Surely it couldn't be snowing this early? He looked out at the ruined garden. For a moment, something pale and bright seemed to cover the ground like frost. Then there was nothing. He blinked, drained the glass, and rubbed the stiffness from the back of his neck. Still nothing, except the first grey hint of dawn over the built-up skyline.

He spent the week attending to business. He was a landlord with a dozen tenement houses in the Shirley area, and an investor in several bars and nightclubs. His actual income wasn't huge: he'd only be rich if he liquidated his assets. All through the week, images of

Ian hung at the edge of his vision and confused him. The still, intense face; the pale, curved back; the scarred buttocks and thin cock. He was so wrapped up in Ian that, one evening when he ran into a similar-looking boy in the Nightingale, he'd bought him a drink and was about to kiss him when he realized it wasn't Ian.

Night after night, he told himself he should finish it. There were too many risks, legal and emotional. But even as a part of him mechanically added up the dangers, another part knew that he needed something like this. It gave him a window onto humanity. Maybe just for a few weeks, until the feeling wore off and he could go back to what he knew.

On the second date, he insisted that they go back to Ian's place. "It's too easy to command you on my own ground," he said. For a moment Ian seemed reluctant, but he was in no position to refuse Richard anything. They left the Jester's claustrophobic, over-lit basement bar and caught a taxi to Northfield. It was on the south edge of the city, a cluttered overspill district of steel-grey housing estates and shops fenced in with wire netting. They stopped in the concrete triangle between three tower blocks that shut out the moon and the city's light. A few windows shone high up in a wall of nothing.

The lift stank of ammonia. Ian unlocked his door and switched on the light, then held the door open for Richard to go in first. The flat looked surprisingly comfortable: a new red sofa, black rugs, a small TV and computer. A shelf of videos; framed photos of film actors. Where had he got all this stuff from? It didn't seem to go with Ian's stark, empty character. Maybe a legacy, or some gifts. Richard felt a blackness wavering in the air. He closed his eyes. The chemicals in the lift must have got to him. Feeling less than masterful, he stumbled to the toilet and knelt over it. Nothing came up.

Ian touched his shoulder. "Is there anything I can do for you?"

Richard wiped his mouth and stood up. "Would you like something to drink?"

"You have vodka?" The boy nodded. "And I'm cold. Put the fire on." While Ian sorted out the drinks, Richard stared into the gas fire. Behind the blue sparks of flame, the ceramic grid was cracked and grimy.

The vodkas were large, triple measures at least. They drank quickly, together on the sofa. Ian's face flushed. He knelt before Richard and sucked him off with heartbreaking skill. Richard's climax reminded him of the convulsions of nausea.

"Have you got a balcony?" he asked. "I need some fresh air." Flecks of darkness were swirling in the light, like ashes in the heat haze over a bonfire. They wouldn't go away. Ian opened the left-hand curtain, revealing a small door and a black-railed section of balcony. "Stay here," Richard said.

The city's lights hung like a firework that had stalled. Richard zipped up his leather jacket. He could smell traffic fumes in the damp air, and vomit in the back of his own throat. So many separate lights. So many bars, restaurants, bedrooms, vehicles. And the pattern they all made. This was his garden. From this vantage point, all of it was close enough to touch. The frames of stone and metal, the bodies they held, and the cave of night that surrounded them. Smiling, Richard turned back to the window, and stopped.

The inner surface of the glass was streaked with dust. Through it, the moonlight caught on blank floorboards and scraps of rubble. The two halves of a shapeless piece of furniture were joined by some kind of pale stuffing. Where Ian had been, there was nothing. Just some clothes pulled out of shape. The window had no curtain.

Richard stood with his hand on the door for several minutes. Finally, he pulled it open. At once, the room was full of electric light and fluid, pulsing music. He drew the curtain shut and felt the sense of dereliction fade, settle behind the walls. "Ian?" The boy was nowhere in sight.

The bedroom door swung open. Ian was wearing a green rugby shirt, white shorts and plimsolls. "Are you OK?" Richard said.

"Yes, sir. Just twisted my ankle. I thought I'd get an early shower."

"Let me see you do some exercises first. You don't get off that easily."

They ended up in the shower, Ian's face pressed against the immaculate white tiles. Clouds of steam filled the room like dust. As his fingers gripped the pale flesh of his pupil's shoulders, Richard felt sure of who he was and where he was. Nothing else mattered.

The next night, he stayed in and drank his way through a bottle of dry Martini. Some phrases from a song kept drifting through his head. A student party in Leeds in the late seventies. They'd been sitting in a circle on the carpet, passing round a huge joint that probably wasn't just hash. Leonard Cohen was singing about a man standing by the window, weighed down by pain and remorse. Then something about kissing the moon. Leaving the ruin for a new holy city. The word becoming flesh. He sounded so tired, so uncertain, so desperate to lose himself. Outside, dawn was rising between the thin houses.

He couldn't remember the words. At nineteen, he'd found the voice impossibly old and bleak. Now, it felt like a comfort. But he'd left all his records behind when he'd left Leeds, gone to Frankfurt, then den Haag, then Birmingham. A trail of empty bottles and empty boys. Looking for something to take away the feeling of powerlessness. He'd never got close. . . . The phone rang, blocking the thought.

Ian. "Master. How are you?"

"Tired, boy. I wore myself out correcting you."

"I've been bad. You don't know how bad." He could almost feel those lips whispering in his ear.

"Do you need to be punished again?"

"I need to see you." There was a pause. "I need you to do something. Please."

"What is it? What do you want?" Another pause.

"I want you to cut my head off."

Richard put the phone down. Then he picked it up and dialed back. "You've got to be fucking kidding."

"No." The voice in his ear came from darkness, from a cold outside the city. "I need it."

He put the phone down again. Filled a tall glass with ice and vodka. Gazed down over the unlit garden. Now he was thinking back past university. The house in Stockport, with its roses and hollyhocks. The red books, hardbacks, tales of adventure and magic. The bedside lamp.

Where had he read it? The rose elf. The jealous madman who killed his sister's lover, buried the head in a flower pot. The rose bush that grew with its roots in the dead man's skull. The elf in the rose who told the bees, so they flew into the murderer's chamber and stung him to death. Jesus, why did they give this stuff to children?

Why did they give this stuff to children? Why wasn't it on the top shelf, out of reach? Along with the drugs and the dirty books and the truth.

Maybe he and Ian could start again. Get to know each other as people. Talk through all this shit. Come through the night. Richard stood with one hand pressed against the damp window, and the other gripping his right side in a posture that was becoming habitual. It was too late, he realized. They couldn't get out of role. The safety words didn't exist.

Their third date was on Friday night, in the Basement. A petrified forest of leather. Ian was perfectly obedient, fetching drinks, speaking only when spoken to. He was shivering a little—from tension rather than cold, as the crowd of black-clad bodies kept the Basement sweaty and airless. His eyes were lowered, searching the floor. There was nothing there but cigarette butts and fragments of glass.

"Tell me something," Richard said. "Were you a happy child?"

"Think so. Don't remember it much."

"Nothing you hold on to? A perfect time?"

Ian's mouth twisted. "Before I was born. You know how, when you're a kid playing in the park, you want to hit the ball so hard it's never seen again? So it ends up somewhere that nobody ever goes? I wanted to be the ball."

Richard's hands began to explore Ian's torso. He could feel the heartbeat, the slow breathing. "How did you get to like pain? How did you get used to it?"

Ian shrugged. "I don't remember. There wasn't like an abusive stepfather or something. I'm not a professional victim."

You're more than that, he thought. "Tell me about the first time."

Ian bent his neck, looking rather like James Dean. "I'd rather not," he muttered. "Please don't make me."

The music was industrial techno, a pulsing echo that made the room seem vast and empty. Vodka was smearing the lights across the black walls. Richard slipped a hand inside the boy's shirt and teased his nipple ring. Ian gasped silently.

"What do you want?" Richard said. "Are you trying to get back to something, or become something new? What would make you happy?"

The boy's face was a pale, damp mask with holes for eyes. His teeth caught the molten light. "Just imagine, Master. Imagine a moment so perfect that you'd spend the rest of your life reliving it. So true it would never end."

"What you asked me to do. I can't."

Ian looked back at the ground. He let Richard pull him close and kiss him. They stumbled together through the webbed curtain that enclosed the back room. "Don't move," Richard said. They stood for a while, listening to the sounds of pleasure in the dark. Richard fended off other men's hands from them both. Gradually, his eyes adjusted until he could make out the contorted figures. Or perhaps he was imagining them, building images from the sounds. He and Ian were silhouettes a few inches apart, not touching. The air was thick with the odors of sweat, amyl nitrite and semen.

Eventually he touched the boy's arm, then pushed his way out through the webbing. The main bar wasn't much brighter, though a blue strip gleamed above the optics like the nightlight in a hospital ward. Ian followed him to the cloakroom. "Hang on," Richard said. "I need a piss. Wait here."

There was a queue at the urinal, which stank of bleach. It took him a long time to empty his bladder; he was aware of being drunk. Instead of washbasins, this place had holes in the wall that dispensed soap, water and heat. The chipped mirror had a crack in it. No, not a crack. There was a mark across his throat. He lifted one wet hand and felt a ridged scar. He rubbed it, but it didn't go away.

When he got back to the cloakroom, Ian hadn't moved an inch. Probably hadn't even breathed. They walked out into the dim backstreet, overshadowed by defunct warehouses, and up to the pale vomit-spattered pavements of Paradise Circus. Unsteady teenagers were emerging from the clubs: boys with their shirts open, girls with white bellies and thighs exposed.

Back in Solihull, the air was tinged by the bonfires of early November. There was no one about. Richard made two cups of black coffee. When he opened the kitchen drawer to find a teaspoon, he let his fingers slip over the edged knives. The steel was as cold as the air. They drank their coffee in silence. Then he took Ian's hand and led him up to the black room. "Time for a change, boy wonder." Ian stripped and lay on the bare table, facedown. Richard tied him in place: first the ankles, then the wrists, then the neck.

He stood like that for a while, then reached out and touched the hair at the back of Ian's head. "How many times?" he asked. There was no response in the dark eyes. Richard began to shiver.

In the kitchen, he poured himself another vodka with the last of the ice. His right hand nervously massaged the pain in his side. A mouth opening, dark with blood. He thought about locking the door and never going back in. An end to the black room and all that happened there. It was like the old joke: the masochist saying *Beat me* and the sadist saying *No.* An end to roles, an end to the moment of forever. Perhaps, much later, a burial. It was all he could do.

As he turned back to the fridge for the last of the vodka, a glitter of fragile white caught his eye. He stared at the window. The garden was nearly covered with rose petals. They were scattered evenly, as if they had fallen from invisible shrubs. The wind made them rise and fall. They had no trace of color. He stood there, watching, as condensation dripped from the glass onto his hand.

The only implement he had for digging was a rusty trowel. He'd expected the ground to be hard, but it wasn't. Not the first time, anyway.

AUTHOR, AUTHOR

by Gordon Linzner

The gray wood facade of the house hadn't been painted in years, and the architecture was an uneasy mix of gothic, Victorian, and federalist. It stood at the end of an isolated road; Catherine MacGowan could have driven nowhere else without turning around. If she needed further confirmation that this was her destination, six or seven cats lounged on the weathered porch.

Roberta's directions had been letter-perfect.

This did not improve Catherine's mood, however. She still didn't understand why she'd had to drive here on her own, while her publicist fetched the photographer. Catherine would have torn Roberta a new one if she'd actually been able to talk to the girl, instead of getting that too-chipper message on her voice mail. If the author who signed her paycheck could find her way here by herself, why couldn't the damned photographer?

She shook her head. The things she did to sell a few more books.

In fact, Catherine had been growing increasingly disenchanted with Roberta's work over the past few months. This morning's signing at the mall had attracted all of four people, of whom only one actually bought her new hardcover, *Nine Lives to Baldpate*. The paperback copy of *Dial M for Meow* that had been thrust in her face was so ratty she'd been loathe to touch it, let alone sign the thing. And what the hell was that vet's office opening about the day before? She should have made Roberta put on the dark glasses and wig again for that one. As long as the publicist didn't speak or sign anything, the substitution seemed to work.

This afternoon promised to be the topper, though. *Mistress of cat mysteries meets greatest fan*. Plus a couple of dozen felines, which was why the woman couldn't meet her at the bookstore for the photo op. Forewarned, Catherine had worn her dark brown pantsuit, which would show the least amount of cat hair. She could almost smell the overflowing litter boxes from the driveway, with her car windows rolled all the way up.

She saw no other vehicles. How did the old woman get around? Never mind that: where the hell were Roberta and the press hack? Maybe he *was* an idiot, as Roberta claimed, and had gotten lost even with the publicist riding shotgun. So now she had to sit here for god knows how long, with the sun beating down. And she really had to pee. Why did bookstores always offer coffee at signings?

Catherine climbed out of her car. I'll make a game of it, she thought. For every five minutes I have to spend inside alone, I'll deduct an hour from Roberta's check. After half an hour, I'll deduct Roberta.

Visions of the publicist smeared with honey and staked naked to a red anthill helped.

Porch boards creaked as Catherine climbed the steps. Two of the cats looked up curiously, then dropped back into their siestas.

At least they're not rubbing against my ankles, she thought. Yet. Her palms itched with the urge to wring one or two of their tiny little necks, just for the experience.

Only after she had knocked on the door and heard the soft shuffle of footsteps on the other side did she realize she did not know the name of the little old woman she was calling on. It was with Roberta's directions, which she'd copied down and which now, of course, were on her dashboard. She turned her head, as if she could read the name from the porch. Or, better yet, slink away as if this had never happened.

Then the door opened.

"Yes?" The matronly woman was neither as little nor as old as Catherine had imagined. Something about her watery blue eyes made it difficult for Catherine to focus on her face more than a minute. The author took an immediate dislike to her.

"Ah," said Catherine. "Um. I'm Catherine MacGowan. The author? I believe I'm expected?"

"Well, of course you are, dear. I'm Sylvia Nimms. Won't you come in, please?"

"Thank you." Catherine sniffed. The tang of cat urine was acceptably faint, but only just. "May I use the facilities?"

"Beg pardon?"

"I need to freshen up."

"I don't understand."

With a determinedly grim smile, Catherine said, "Where's your bathroom?"

"Oh, you need the toilet! Right off the kitchen, dear. Follow me. I'll make you a nice cup of tea. Or do you prefer coffee?"

"No coffee. Please."

"The tea's only herbal, I'm afraid."

"Fine. Thank you."

"Peppermint, chamomile, or . . . ?"

"Anything," she said quickly, trying to avoid hobbling. "Thank you."

Catherine slipped into the tiny bathroom. A hidden fan hummed into life when she switched on the light; the house was not as antiquated as it appeared. This afternoon session might be tolerable, after all. Perhaps she wouldn't kill anyone today, after all.

She still resolved to dismiss Roberta at the earliest opportunity.

When she entered the kitchen, hands reeking from oily perfumed soap, two cups of fragrant tea were already poured. Between them sat a dubious yellow slab on a serving plate. Four cats rested in full view about the floor; parts of several others dangled from cabinets or stuck out from behind the refrigerator, twitching occasionally as proof of life. Pity.

"Ah, there you are, Cat. I can call you that? And you must call me Sylvia. None of this Miss Nimms nonsense."

I'd rather call you a hearse, Catherine thought. "Cat. Fine." Never Margaret, or Maggie, or even, for god's sake, Peg, she thought sourly. That would've been too much to expect, to achieve fame under her own name. If Catherine had realized just what she was getting into, she'd never have let her publisher talk her into the pseudonym. Or maybe she would. Those had been pretty lean times for her, though murderous thoughts had been less frequent then. "The photographer seems to be late, Sylvia. Please accept my apologies. My publicist promised they'd meet me here at one. . . . "

Sylvia patted the back of Catherine's hand. The author flinched, but resisted the urge to pull away. "Don't worry about it, Cat. Gives us a chance for a nice chat, girl to girl. Talk about whatever you want."

Peachy, thought Catherine. She wants to bond.

Catherine took a sip of tea, repressed a sudden pucker that reached all the way to the back of her throat. This was the bitterest cup of chamomile she'd ever tasted. She shot a hand out for the bowl of lumpy sugar, dropped in two heaping spoonfuls, paused, added a third, sipped again.

Poison, she reflected. There's a possibility for dealing with Roberta. Not as satisfying as slow dismemberment, but just as effective in limiting her unemployment insurance payments.

After a moment of silence, Sylvia offered, "I've read all your books."

"Now why doesn't that surprise me?" Catherine bit her lower lip; she hadn't meant to speak the thought aloud. She must be more tired than she'd thought. Sylvia, though, seemed not to notice.

"My favorite, Cat, was *The Adventure of the Dancing Cats*."

"The second book in the Fluffy and Tiger series," Catherine pointed out. If she stuck to basic statements of fact, there should be little risk of further incivility. If she keeps calling me Cat, though, I just might shove a cat toy down her throat and feed her to her precious brood.

Not a bad publicity angle, at that. *Mystery author discovers body, vows to solve crime.* That might be just the extra boost she needed to finally break away from her genre trap. They'd never suspect her, of course. No author in her right mind would kill a fan!

"I know. I didn't care for *The Giant Cat of Sumatra* as much. Too unrealistic."

"As if cats solving crimes and talking to each other were realistic," Catherine muttered. *Oops.*

"I didn't quite catch that, Cat."

"Oh, nothing. Nothing a fan should hear."

"Are you working on something new?" Sylvia continued. "Roberta tells me writers are always working on the next book."

"Nothing right now, thank god. I just turned in *Fluffy's Last Case*. He gets eaten by raccoons. My editor will probably change that, though. I'd like to try something different. Like a dog detective," she mused bitterly. "Wouldn't *that* be a stretch for my readers!" She glanced up at Sylvia, who again seemed oblivious to the sharp comment. Catherine shook her head and took another sip of tea. She rarely spoke so freely; in fact, she never did, except to Roberta. Bluntness was bad for sales.

"Perhaps a crime that doesn't involve murder?" Sylvia suggested. "It's so nasty, killing people. And almost never necessary."

"There are always exceptions." She glared at Sylvia, then sipped more tea. "No one was killed in *Katzapoppin*."

"The tabby was."

"Offstage."

"Still. Cats are people, too."

"Right. And I'm the Queen of Siam."

A calico kitten leapt into Catherine's lap, stared into her eyes. "Heavy little bastard," she said.

"No canned food for them. All fresh. That's why they're so healthy."

Catherine raised a hand to shoo the animal off, then changed her mind. Too much effort. Another sip of tea, that's what she wanted, but that, too, seemed too much trouble. It had been a long day, though it couldn't be past two now.

"You seem unhappy in your work," Sylvia observed.

" 'Course I'm not." She heard the slurring in her voice, but didn't care. "Neither would you be, if you had two brain cells to rub together in that dried-up skull of yours. Same cutesy crap every day. Won't let me do anything else. 'You do it so well,' they say. 'The sales staff wouldn't know how to handle something different.' Meaning promotion would be zero, despite my best-sellers." She leaned forward slightly. The motion made her dizzy. "Tell you a secret. I didn't much care for cats to begin with. Now I'm starting to hate them."

The kitten sniffed at her lips, wrinkled its nose.

"You, too, you little bastard," Catherine muttered. "Like to put you in a sack and drop it in the lake."

Sylvia stiffened, reacting at last. "That's what Roberta told me. I didn't believe her. Not then."

"Great publicist, huh? Telling people stuff like that. Kill my career. You had a nice long conversation with Miss Incompetence, then? Got on a first-name basis and everything? Maybe she can room with you."

Sylvia smiled thinly. "I ought to know my own great-niece's name."

Catherine blinked, slowly; her eyelids felt so heavy. "Should've known. So goddamn eager for this stunt. Get auntie in the papers. Hell with that. You can both rot."

Catherine lurched forward in her chair. Her legs didn't respond.

"I wouldn't try standing, Cat. The dosage was quite strong. It had to be, to act so quickly."

"Drugs?" Catherine scowled. "You drugged me?"

"Some kind of truth serum. I can't pronounce it. Roberta found out about it, doing your research."

Catherine's left hand flopped onto the table, swung out. The tea cup crashed to the floor. "Bitch. I'm leaving. Tell Roberta when she gets here, she's fired."

She pulled herself up, using the edge of the table. The kitten hissed as it lost its purchase on her lap, tumbling roughly to the floor.

As one, the rest of the cats in the kitchen looked up and growled. More slunk into the room, to sit and glare at her.

"Now you've made them mad," Sylvia said. "But I suppose that's inevitable, considering your nature."

Catherine stood for about five seconds before the floorboards rose to slap against the back of her head. Her fingers wriggled in slow-motion frenzy as she lay under the table, dust tickling her nostrils. "So what're you and Roberta gonna do now? Expose my hideous secret? Ruin my career? Hell, go ahead. I can live off the interest in my account. Never have to write another damn cat book again. Never want to see another cat as long as I live."

Sylvia tsked. "I can't promise that, Cat, but if it's a consolation, the rest of your life won't be very long."

Suddenly Catherine felt very cold. "Sounds like a threat."

"Oh no. Threats are something that *might* happen. You've already condemned yourself."

More cats entered the kitchen, surrounding Catherine as she lay on her back, hissing, prodding her exposed flesh with razor-sharp claws. Catherine licked her lips. "Whatever you're planning won't work, Sylvia. People know I'm here, Sylvia. Roberta . . ."

"Roberta, who had you sign a power of attorney yesterday?"

"That was a photographer's release form."

"Did you read it?"

No, she hadn't. Catherine's eyes began to water.

"*She* was your biggest fan, you know. Not me. I enjoyed reading them, but that was it. Working for you was her dream job. So disappointed she was, seeing your true colors, hearing your petty carping. So devastated to learn you *only rented* that Persian you pose with."

"The photographer . . ."

"What photographer?"

"The one . . ."—Catherine's voice faltered with sick realization—"I never met. Or knew his name."

"Because he doesn't exist. Exactly. Your money will go to a good cause, though, maintaining the Nimms Home for Stray Cats. Just the sort of charity the suddenly reclusive Cat MacGowan, author of the Fluffy trilogy, would donate all future royalties to."

"Won't . . . work."

"Of course it will, dear. As long as Roberta doesn't have to talk or sign anything. You've given her ample opportunity to practice. Oh, don't look so pathetic. You've plotted this kind of thing a thousand times."

"There's a difference between thinking and doing."

"Yes, there is. And the world belongs to the doers."

"You're . . . insane," Catherine managed before her lips went completely numb. Her vision started to grow dark at the edges, narrowing to pinpoints.

"I may well be," Sylvia said cheerily. "But at the end of today I'll be alive, while you . . . well, Roberta assured me you wouldn't feel any pain. Or wouldn't care. I forget which." She gestured to the ever-increasing number of cats filling the kitchen, closing in around Catherine, blocking off what little light she could still see.

"Come, darlings. Num nums."

HAMMERHEAD

by Richard Laymon

One thing about a hammer . . . it's quiet.

It's not *silent*. God, no.

In fact, I love the sounds of it. Each blow, like a snowflake, is different. Everything from the soft *pap!* when the hammerhead hits a breast or blubbery buttock to a *bok!* when it strikes a skull. And there is an infinite variety of sounds in between.

All luscious. All fairly quiet. Not at all like the sharp blast of a firearm.

Of course, I *can* make a gunlike sound by striking hard surfaces such as wood.

I can make *very* loud sounds with my hammer.

But I only do so when necessity calls for it, such as the occasions when I must smash through a door or window. Normally, I prefer the quiet music of my hammer striking flesh and bone.

Frankly, it is beyond my comprehension why *anyone* would ever want to use a gun. They're so incredibly boisterous! They announce your presence to the world, wake people up, give them a chance to flee.

Not only that, but a gun is so . . . distant. The bullet leaves you behind, travels on its merry way to the target and smashes through your person all by itself. *You* don't feel the impact. *You* don't feel the skin break, the bursting of the tissues underneath, the breaking bones. The blood doesn't leap out over your hand (unless you fire at *very* close range). With the gunshot ringing in your ears, you may not even be able to *hear* the impact of your bullet.

Wielding a hammer, however, you're at the very heart of the experience, being flooded with wonderful sensations that simply can't be yours if you use a firearm.

Now you might be asking yourself how I came to discover the splendors of hammer attack.

I'll tell you.

You won't want to hear it, though.

Try this on for size. At the age of seven, I was busy one fine summer morning in my backyard nailing some boards together when an intruder came along: my three-year-old sister, Angela. She grabbed for the hammer, whining, "Gimme, gimme! I wanna! I wanna!" So I gave her hammer all right, smack on top of her little blond head with all my might. The hammerhead caved in the top of her skull and blood flew up like a pretty red fountain and little Angela keeled over, probably dead before she hit the grass.

Are you shocked?

Quite possibly not.

Now let me whisper you a small secret. The intruder that morning wasn't my little sister Angela. It was her kitten, Tabby.

Ha!

God, you should've seen it!

Now you probably *are* shocked.

How dare he hammer a sweet little kittycat?

Worse than giving my sister a taste of the steel, right?

I know, I'm awful.

Tabby *was* the first to fall beneath my hammer. Its little head virtually disintegrated under the blow. As I heard the crackling sound and felt my hammer sink in, the kitty let out one quick *ROW!* and flopped dead.

Then I licked my bloody hammer clean.

From that moment on, I was hooked. I spent much of my childhood romping through the parks and woods and alleys near my house, clandestinely whomping this creature and that: spiders, ants, caterpillars, ladybugs, butterflies . . . often tasting the mashed results of my mayhem but usually being disappointed by the flavor.

Whenever the opportunities arose, I hunted cats and dogs. One blow, smack on the noggin, and down they went.

I not only relished the killing blow, but also the clean-up job: licking the cool steel head of my hammer, sucking on it. Fur and bits of bone always found their way into my mouth, but they were small prices to pay—fishbones in trout—for the pleasures of my sanguine snack.

Then one summer morning when I was ten years old, my six-year-old sister, Angela, came upon me in the woods only moments after I'd found a robin on the ground. It had a broken wing and couldn't fly away, so I picked it up and carried it over to a fair-sized boulder. I lay the robin down on top of the boulder. As I raised my hammer high, Angela cried out, "Simon! Don't you dare!"

I dared.

As the robin's small head exploded under my hammer, she screamed.

"Oh, knock it off," I told her. "It's just a stupid bird."

Tears rushing down her cheeks, Angela whined, *"I'm telling!"*

Then she whirled around and ran. As she raced off through the woods, she threatened, *"You're gonna be in soooo much trouble!"*

"If you tell on me," I shouted, "I'll tell on you!"

A tried-and-true tactic where siblings are concerned.

It stopped her.

She turned around and watched me.

I walked toward her with my left hand behind my back.

"I didn't *do* nothing," she protested, but she didn't sound terribly certain of it.

"You did, too," I told her.

"What'd *I* do?"

"I'll tell Mom and Dad *you* killed the bird."

"That'd be lying."

"But you'll have *this* all over you." With that, I swung my left hand out from behind my back and rubbed the bloody remains of the robin in her face.

She squealed in disgust and horror and tried to shove my hand away. But I was bigger and stronger. I shoved the bird into her mouth. Choking, she got away from me and started running again.

I chased her. Her golden ponytail flipped and bounced. I considered giving it a yank to stop her. Instead, I swung my hammer and caught her in the ear.

She dropped.

Still very much alive, she clutched her bloody ear and writhed on the ground. She'd plucked or spat the bird from her mouth by then, so she was free to bawl and sputter out, "Lee me alone!" and "Don't" and so on.

I should perhaps explain that, though cute as a button, Angela had been a thorn in my side for years.

Now, she was at my mercy.

I had none.

Instead, I had fun. I found the bird (somewhat the worse for wear by then), stuffed it into her mouth again as something of a makeshift gag, then went at her with the hammer. Somewhat gently, but not *that* gently.

Not to bore or appall you with the details, let me simply say that I began by bruising her almost everywhere. Then I commenced with smashing bones—the smaller ones first. Toes and fingers, then kneecaps. Staying away from her head until the very last.

I know. I'm terrible. Sue me.

Though I'd often tasted the blood and brains of felines and canines and various other critters, none compared to the sweet, tangy flavor of Angela. For a long time, I lay on the forest floor near my beloved sister, dipping my hammerhead into the open bowl of her skull and lapping it, sucking it clean. Angela fondue.

By far, the finest day of my young life.

Unfortunately, it was followed by quite a few years of unpleasantness.

Though they kept me away from hammers and all forms of instruments that might serve as bludgeons, they could not keep my thoughts away from that day in my woods with Angela. I relived it countless times in my mind, savoring it, even embellishing on it . . . while keeping my nose clean, so to speak . . . until the day at last came when they allowed me to leave the institution.

At the time of my release, I was eighteen years old and completely cured of my various mental aberrations.

Most certainly.

Two weeks later, I walked into a True Value hardware store, stood in front of a tool display and gazed in awe, beholding hammers.

Claw hammers. Ball-peens. Sledgehammers of various sizes and weights.

Picks. Hatchets. Axes.

Oh, my.

But a simple claw hammer of the sort I'd used as a child was my weapon of choice. I chose one. Lifted it off the display wall. Felt its heft. Admired the gleam of its steel, the bright blue paint on its claws, the grain of its sleek wooden handle.

Struggling to conceal my delight, I carried it to the checkout counter and bought it with cash—$14.95 plus tax.

So much cheaper than a handgun.

And so much more sweet.

And no tests to take. No forms to fill out. No background check. No waiting period.

I left the hardware store with my hammer heavy in the bottom of a bag. As I walked, it made the bag swing and gently bump the side of my leg.

That night, I tested out my new purchase in the "stacks" on the second floor of the public library. Coincidentally, the girl was stacked. I crept up behind her and thunked the back of her head so hard that she slammed forward and almost knocked over a section of shelves. After lowering her to the floor, I sat on her back and popped the hammerhead into my mouth.

Delicious.

The taste of her filled me with memories of Angela.

I made my escape from the library undetected, of course. Had I been caught at that early stage of my career, the rampages for which I've become so famous might never had occurred.

But they did occur, as everyone knows.

For years and years, I traveled throughout the country, visiting small towns and metropolises, roaming forests and mountains, dropping in on our great universities and shopping malls, convenience stores and parking lots.

And homes.

Oh, so many homes and apartments and condos and townhouses.

I could go on for hundreds of pages, pestering and disgusting you with the glorious details of my depredations. I don't, of course, have time for that.

So let me simply cut to my encounter with Trisha Cooper.

I didn't, of course, know her name at the time.

I knew only that she was luscious, irresistible.

In my own defense, I must say that I was not at my best that morning. Otherwise, matters would've turned out quite differently.

I'd had a spree the night before, you see. Drawn by the beauty of a young woman who stopped beside my car at a traffic light, I'd followed her through the streets of Tucson and into a residential neighborhood where she pulled into the driveway of a modest stucco house.

I parked my car a couple of blocks away. Then, attaché case in hand, I walked back toward her house. Along the way, I kept my eyes open.

A house across the street had a FOR SALE sign on its front lawn.

I continued on to the woman's home and rang her doorbell. She opened the door for me. They nearly always do.

Women find me adorable.

I'm not only slender and devastatingly handsome, but I have gentle, hopeful eyes and a boyish smile. I keep my hair short and neatly groomed. I have no mustache, no beard, no piercings or tattoos. I dress myself to look as if I might be on my way to a business luncheon.

In short, I'm clean-cut, gorgeous and irresistible.

When this woman opened her door, she seemed pleased to see me, but cautious. "Oh, hello," she said. "May I help you?"

Her screen door remained shut and no doubt locked.

"Hi," I said. "I'm sorry to bother you."

"That's all right." She sounded slightly wary—probably expecting me to begin a sales pitch.

"I'm thinking about moving into the neighborhood," I told her, and nodded over my shoulder toward the house with the FOR SALE sign. "I thought I might ask around a little. You know, try to find out if it's a nice neighborhood . . . if there's something I'd better *know* before I make my offer."

"Oh," said the woman, "we've been very happy here." She opened the screen door. Being neighborly, smiling, she offered her hand. "I'm Peggy Wright."

"Wilbur Curtis," I introduced myself. I set down my attaché case and shook her hand. "Very nice to meet you, Peggy."

She appeared to be in her late twenties or early thirties. Flowing, dark brown hair. A perfectly delightful face with unusually large lips. A figure that was slender, but not skinny, with a full bosom and a blouse that allowed me to admire her cleavage.

Before she could withdraw her hand, I jerked it toward me. She gasped and tilted out over the threshold. I stepped closer, swinging up my left elbow, clobbering her in the cheek so hard her head turned sideways. Her hair flew. Her lips wobbled. Her spit flew. And down she went, backward into her foyer.

I took a moment to grab my attaché case, then joined her in the house.

At that point, it was nearly four in the afternoon of the day before my encounter with Trisha Cooper.

While Peggy Wright lay dazed on the floor of her foyer, I removed ropes from my attaché case and tied her up. I gagged her with a broad strip of tape. Leaving her on the floor, I picked up my hammer and explored the house.

Empty except for the two of us.

A relief, but also a disappointment. I'd rather hoped to find children, perhaps in the care of a nanny or babysitter. At her age, she ought to have had at least one or two kids. But no such luck.

I returned to Peggy, untied her feet, then forced her to walk ahead of me into the bedroom. I placed her on the king-sized bed. She looked rather terrified. Her beautiful eyes were bulging and she fought for breath, air hissing through her nostrils, her chest heaving, straining at the buttons of her blouse.

I stayed in the room, watching her. After a while, I unbuttoned her blouse and used a handy pair of scissors to remove her brassiere. Without the constrictions, her breathing may or may not have improved. But my view did.

Eventually, I heard a car pull into the driveway. A car door thudded shut.

"Sounds like the hubby is home," I said.

Peggy shook her head and pleaded with her eyes.

"I'll explain you're indisposed," I said, and left the bedroom. I shut the bedroom door, then hurried through the house.

By the time the front door opened, I was cleverly stationed behind it.

"Hi ho!" the hubby called out—rather like one of the Seven Dwarfs. But the dwarfs weren't women, and "hubby" was.

As she swung the door shut, I said, "Hi ho yourself."

I'd intended to cave in the husband's skull with a single blow (I may have my faults, but I'm not queer), but the sound of the house-mate's voice had changed my mind.

With the door out of my way, I saw that she was a slim and elegant blonde with a beautiful face.

I hammered her shoulder and she went to her knees in agony.

Her name, I later found out, was Ella.

And, once again, we arrive at a place in my narrative where a detailed account of my activities might unnecessarily appall and repel you, dear reader.

I wouldn't want to drive you away at this late stage, so near to the end.

So allow me to gloss over the "gory details." I'll simply say that Ella, Peggy, and Simon spent a very fulfilling afternoon and night together. By the judicious use of my hammer, my darlings remained conscious until almost the very end, which came at about seven the next morning.

By then, their bedroom was quite the mess and so was I.

In a full-length mirror, I found my naked self so befouled with blood and semen and other assorted fluids and bits of tissue that I barely resembled a human being at all.

I took a long, hot shower.

Then I packed up my ropes and hammer and pliers and spoons and other tools of my pastime (I had expanded my repertoire some-what since the early days), packed up my camera, and set the timer on my incendiary device for ten o'clock. I placed the fire-bomb on the bed between their bodies. It would do a fine job of tampering with the crime scene.

Eventually, all dressed and spiffy but weary to my very bones, I exited the house and returned to my car. In the driver's seat, I hardly had the strength to insert my key into the ignition.

Fighting to hold up my head, I eased away from the curb and drove out of the neighborhood. My eyelids felt like sand-bags. I rolled down my window and breathed deeply of the fresh morning air.

Hang in there, Simon, I told myself.

Though somewhat confused about my exact location, I felt cer-tain that I would be able to find the way back shortly to my motel. It was probably no more than ten minutes away. Surely, I could remain awake that much longer.

I turned the radio on, then pushed buttons trying to find a station that was playing something other than Mexican music.

I got Howard Stern, but listened for only a few moments before growing disgusted by his filthy talk. Too weary to go on seeking a satisfactory station, I silenced my radio.

Something was wrong. Somehow, I'd left most of Tucson behind. I seemed to be somewhere on the outskirts. There were houses around, but not many. Mostly, aside from the road, there was only desert and the desert looked scattered with frightened green people, their arms thrown high in alarm.

Just saguaro, I told myself. Nothing to worry about.

But I'd better turn around.

No traffic was in sight, so I made a U-turn and began heading back.

Soon, I would be back in town and well on the way back to my motel.

Just a few more minutes, I told myself.

My eyelids began drifting down.

With great effort, I lifted them. . . .

And saw the most glorious vision.

Had I fallen asleep? Was I dreaming? No, I was awake and the vision was real . . . a lovely blond girl crossing the street ahead of me, her golden ponytail swishing behind her. She wore a white T-shirt, faded denim overalls with short legs, clean white socks and dirty white sneakers. She carried a book bag on her back.

She looked to be about seven or eight years old.

She might've been the identical twin of my darling sister, Angela.

And she was alone, deliciously alone.

What kind of mother, I thought, would let such a darling walk by herself to school . . . or to the school bus stop, which seemed more likely?

Ha! MY kind of mother!

I stopped my car and watched the girl walk by in front of me, a bounce in her stride.

No other cars were in sight.

I called out, "Excuse me, young lady?"

She halted and turned her head. Her cute little face frowned at me. "Huh?" she asked.

"I know you're probably not supposed to talk with strangers, but I just wanted to ask if you've seen my little girl anywhere? She's about your age. Her name is Angela." (It was the first name to enter my head, for obvious reasons.)

The girl (named Trisha Cooper, I later learned) shrugged her cute little shoulders.

I imagined her left shoulder bare and how it would jump when I struck it with my hammer. And how she would cry out.

"If you see her," I called, "would you tell her that her daddy is . . ."

The girl whirled around and ran.

"No wait!"

Over her shoulder, she yelled, *"I'm telling on you!"*

I went after her.

Had I not been weary and disoriented from my night of passion with Peggy and Ella, I'm certain I would've kept my wits about me and driven away.

But I was half out of my mind and Trisha was the very essence of Angela.

So I swung across the road, hit the brakes, pulled out the ignition key, leaped out of my car and gave chase.

I'm a fast runner. In seconds, I was bearing down on her.

"Leave me alone!" she yelled.

Having left my hammer in the car, I snatched her by the ponytail, swung her and sent her tumbling over the asphalt. I hurried over to her. As I hunkered down, the saguaros beyond the road seemed to watch, their green arms high with alarm.

I picked Trisha up. Leaving her book bag on the road, I flung her over my shoulder and raced for my car. She hardly felt heavy at all.

Though she squirmed, I kept her in place with my arm clamped tightly across the backs of her thighs.

She kicked her feet and blubbered, "Lemme down! I'm gonna tell!"

"You're mine, darling!"

With my free right hand, I dug my keys out of my pocket.

"Please! Lemme go! Please!"

"Oh, we'll sure have fun! I will, anyway!"

I slowed to a jog as I neared my car. At its rear, I crouched and unlocked the trunk. Watching its lid rise, I wondered if I would have any luck finding Peggy and Ella's house. Nobody lived there anymore. I could easily de-activate my incendiary device. Then Trisha and I could live happily in the house ever after . . . or at least for a few days.

"What're you doing there, mister?" someone asked.

Oh, my.

I leaned forward, unloaded Trisha into the trunk and slammed the lid. Then I turned around.

She was a beaut. Nineteen or twenty, perhaps. Hair the color of sunlight, skin the color of dry sand. She wore jeans and one of those blue chambray work shirts. The shirt was pulled up, baring her midriff, and tied just at about her sternum. She wore a straw cowboy hat and snakeskin boots.

A real Arizona girl—up to and including the western-style

revolver in her hand.

Grimacing in a way that showed me her straight white teeth, she said, "Let's have you open the trunk back up."

"It's all right," I said. "She's a runaway. I'm a private investigator hired by her parents to retrieve her."

"I don't care if you're Sam Fucking Spade, bud, open the fucking trunk."

"Are you an officer of the law?" I asked.

"Just a gal on a walk. And it looks like I walked into a pervert in action."

"If you're not an officer of the law," I said, "this is none of your business."

"Me and Sam Colt have a different view on that."

I had a decision to make.

I figured, Arizona or not, this was only a girl. More than likely, she wasn't much of a shot.

This was another failure on the part of my weary mind. It was neglecting to remind me that a host of world-class shooters were females. And it neglected to mention Annie Oakley.

I broke for the driver's door.

Something hit me in the back. It felt like a hammer blow and was followed half an instant later by an ear-crashing blast.

Firearms! So incredibly boisterous!

But, oh my.

According to the doctors, I'll never walk again. The bitch (her name was Staci Hickok, of all things—no relation), had caught me in the thoracic area of my spine with a .45-caliber hollow point. Now they say I'll be spending the rest of my life in a wheelchair in a facility for the criminally insane.

A victim of gun violence.

I am being kept away from hammers.

But they can't keep my mind away from Angela. And all the others. So many others.

I often regret the loss of Trisha, of course. I feel as if she'd been sent to me as the *pièce de résistance* of my career. And yet I was unable to partake. . . .

I like to sit in my wheelchair and think about what I would've done with Trisha if only the bitch Staci Hickok hadn't happened along just when she did.

Staci and her handgun.

Her fucking Colt.

(Arizona, I found out too late, is a ghastly and primitive state that allows civilians to walk around *armed* like gangsters!)

I would *love* to lay my hammer on Staci. Smash her trigger finger. Break out those big white teeth. Pound in her eyeballs. Turn my hammer over and rip off her breasts with its claws . . .

Maybe someday.

They're having breakthroughs all the time in the treatment of spinal cord injuries. Before you know it, maybe I'll be up on my feet again. After that, I might soon be out of here.

I *was* out of my mind when I hammered those people.

The courts have said so.

Presently, I'm well on the road toward robust mental health, and I'm exceedingly contrite. Just ask anyone.

imbroglio

by conrad williams

I send sweets to my mother at the weekend.

She's fond of buttery caramels, or eclairs, or mint lumps that take forever to tame with the teeth. In this way I think I prove my love for her, more so than what a letter or a phone call might achieve. I remember the flare of joy I felt in childhood when she came home from her shift at the hospital and planted a white paper bag in my hands, a kiss on my forehead. I spent so much time sitting on our peeling wooden gate waiting for her that my dad swore he could see grooves developing in my backside.

Mum was easy to spot. She'd round the corner in those late summer evenings—a tall, broad-shouldered woman with wheat-blond hair and big eyes—and my jaws would squirt with the thought of aniseed and sherbet and toffee. Mum's neck was soft, a heaven of smells. Sometimes, before I grew too big, she'd whisk me off the gate and ask me how I was; what I'd done that day. She listened to me even though her eyes ached for sleep.

Our ritual: I loosen the twists in the bag. I peek to see what she's bought me. Always, I offer the first one to her.

These days I live by the sea. Nothing grand. Just a pleasant terraced house that takes a battering every once in a while by arctic winds channeling down through the North Sea. This town is a winding-down town. Old people come here to die. I'm maybe a third of the age of some of the characters who drift and stagger through these streets. Sometimes, on the beach, you'll see them moving across the sand, mouths agape, limbs wheeling as they take in the sea view for what might be the last time. Seeing so many of the old struggling like this, it seems to congeal the air with pain. They're like solid ghosts, infected by the grey of the ocean. Slowing down. Seizing up. I look at the horizon and see great swathes of black cloud closing in and it's hard not to believe that the dying aren't contributing to the confusion up there, even just a little bit. There's a sense of waiting among them. It's as though something is gravitating toward this town. Coming home.

But not just them. No, not just them.

When I was young, we lived in a police house that backed on to a school field full of bent and broken goalposts. Dad had been in the police force for fifteen years and bought the house when I was one year old. Back then, police houses could be acquired through the constabulary; Dad had applied and won the right to purchase it. Twelve Lodge Lane. It had a pleasant sound about it. Police houses are no different from ordinary houses, really. Apart from an extension at the front, which served as an office, in lieu of a proper station. Such offices were now defunct. There weren't the resources.

It was nice to live so close to a school. When I was old enough to attend, I used to roll out of bed at ten to nine and be first into the classroom for registration on the hour. But by then I was suffering from stomachaches. And I had a stammer. I could hardly speak sometimes. Drawing in a sketch book helped relax me, when I felt myself tying up in knots. I drew feverishly, layering bits of memory upon fragments of observed shapes, upon the form that I imagined my parents' speech might take if it could be turned into a visual thing. All sorts of things, really. I never finished anything, it simply trailed off, or formed the basis for something else. I had pages that, to the untutored eye, showed little more than a frenzied scrawl. But to me, each page was like a series of cels from an animation, albeit compiled arbitrarily. It was similar to staring at the branches of a winter tree, or the shapes in a fire; before long, order would suggest itself. You might see faces in there. You might see anything you wanted, or dreaded, to see.

I loved drawing. It was a place for me to retreat when my inarticulateness threatened to render me insubstantial; I felt as though I were shrinking from sight, as though my stammering was a bubble of invisibility being blown from my lips, encompassing me. I couldn't understand how the things I wanted to say, that formed so clearly in my mind, were being translated to gibberish by my mouth. I kissed my mum and dad with that mouth; I smiled at them with it. How could it not allow me to tell them that I loved them?

When I didn't have any paper, I drew on the walls. When my pencils or crayons ran out, I scratched patterns on the pavement with a piece of stone. The pictures in my head flew from me in this way. If they hadn't, I think my head might well have burst apart.

I wish I could say that my unhappiness as a child was because of bullying, or night terrors or even an allergy to food. We weren't well off financially, as I understand it now, but both my mum and dad worked and they were climbing out of debt; they were getting there. I loved my parents and I believe they loved me. I was unhappy. Maybe that's all there is to it. Don't you always need a reason to be happy too?

It's November 12, 1977. I'm not well, I'm never well. It's Dad's birthday. He's out at the pub with his friends. Mum's looking after me. We're sitting on our PVC sofa in front of the TV. It's dark outside. There are small explosions of rain on the window, like someone scattering shot against the glass. I'm eight years old. I want to be sick but it won't come. I love sitting next to Mum. She has a comfortable way about her that is infectious. She sits with her legs tucked under her, one hand in her hair, twirling it through her fingers. I do this for her too. She smells like . . . well, like Mum, a secret scent that mums are no doubt provided with when they are young and being taught the intricacies of what it means to be a mother. It's a smell to make you dizzy with love.

On the screen: NEWS FLASH.

A body has been found on the embankment under the train line that connects Liverpool to all points east. Mum leaps in her chair, knocking the bottle of juice out of my mouth. She swears and I laugh because I've never heard Mum bark like that. She swears again and now she's crying. I pull her hair gently. Her big, hazel eyes are wet through.

"What's up?"

She hugs me for an age, until the television reverts to a game show. Questions and answers and audience applause. Everyone's face looks rubberized. As though you could pick it away with your nails and there wouldn't be anything underneath but rotten air.

I fell asleep, I remember. Then Mum's renewed sobbing wakened me, what, a minute, an hour, a night-time later? Dad was back. I could smell him on the tails of the air that he pushed into the house ahead of him: alcohol, smoke, fried food. I heard his mackintosh crumpling as he embraced my mum.

I got out of bed and crept downstairs to the landing, making a cartoonish step over the riser that creaked when you trod on it. From here I sometimes watched television when Mum and Dad thought I was in bed. Late night films in black and white. Women with immaculate hair. Men who smoked and hunkered in the shadows wearing hats and raincoats.

Mum and Dad were in the kitchen. I saw their shadows on the wall as they talked in murmurs over cups of coffee. I heard words I didn't understand but which sounded awful. *Murder . . . ripped . . . stabbed . . . gutted . . .*

"In our town," my mum kept saying. "In our town."

Johnny Roughsedge was my best friend. He lived at 63 Lodge Lane. He came round to play the next morning, a Saturday. Sitting in the garden, chewing bubble gum, flipping through our collections of football cards, we talked about what we had both learned since last night, which was probably more than my mum and dad knew by then. Apparently, a woman's body had been found by a bunch of kids playing knick-knack. One of them was Johnny's cousin. They had knocked on someone's front door and legged it into the mound of vegetation that separated the main road from the steep mass of land leading up to the railway tracks. A lad bringing up the rear had tripped over something that felt too spongy to be bindweed or brambles.

"All of her tits were scooped out," Johnny said, eyes as big as the jawbreakers with which we were ruining our teeth. "And she was so jammed up with little pieces of glass, she lit up when they put a light on her, just like a Christmas tree. Every hole in her was filled with ash. Imagine that. Eye sockets, filled with ash. Her mouth. Her bloody mouth!"

Dad was coming home late from work. He was helping out with the inquiries, going door-to-door, asking people what and where and when. It was getting cold. Our town, a northern town, was nestled in a little bowl of land between the Irish Sea on one side and the Pennines on the other. We were visited by all kinds of weather, in any and every shade of bad. Dad's face turned weird. It had this blustery redness about it, spanked alive by the chill winds, but shivering underneath the color was a permanent mask, in pale cement. It was lean and hard. It was like he had two faces. I never knew which one of them he wore when he looked at me. But then, at that time, he rarely looked at me. He was either looking out of the window or staring into a small, chunky glass filled with whisky. Mum too.

It got so that Mum was scared to walk home. She worked all hours at the geriatric ward of the hospital. It was ten minutes away. But to get home, she had to walk under the railway bridge. Nettles and broad dock leaves grew wild up the sides of the bridge and threatened the gravel stretch of the railway. Four o'clock in the afternoon, it was already dark. The streetlamps had been bricked out by kids. Mist often hung about the roads here, ghosting in from the canal. There wasn't enough money for her to take a taxi and she always turned down lifts from the other members of staff.

"You just don't know, do you?" she said. "How can you tell?"

The body was that of a hairdresser called Elaine Dicker. She had gone to the secondary school for which my primary was a feeder; she had been one of the prefects. Elaine had cut Mum's hair. Elaine had stopped some bullies from pushing in front of me at the queue for ice cream. She had gently impinged upon any number of lives in the neighborhood. The ordinariness of her and the extraordinary manner of her death plunged the town into a torpor. There wasn't so much panic in the streets as a slow kind of awe that shifted through them.

Women gathered on the pavements to talk about the murder. I watched them from my parents' bedroom. Some appeared to revel in the fact that a killer had come to our town. There was the hushed admiration of celebrity in it. They used his shadow as they might currency, handing over a few coins of gossip, snapping their lips shut on suspicions of his identity like the cruel clasps of an ancient purse. As the daylight slunk away, so did they, seeking the sanctity of a locked door, a roof.

I continued to sit on the gate, waiting for Mum to come home. She took to taking the bus, which meant she couldn't stop by at the sweet shop for a quarter of something for me. No kola kubes or midget gems. No peanut brittle. No raspberry laces. No fudge. Her face was drawn when I rushed to greet her, stepping from the bus with her uniform in a Co-op carrier bag. I saw in her features how death might one day settle in them. I was afraid for her and saddened by my disappointment in her fragility. When I hugged her she seemed thinner and she smelled of disinfectant. I did not know it then, but to be surrounded by the dying at work and to be shadowed too on her way home by death's specter took a lot out of her. Her little boy wasn't enough to reset the balance.

Things didn't get any better for her. One night she was assaulted by a drunk who tried to put his hand up her skirt while she waited at the bus stop. From then on, she resolutely marched home, willing to take her chances. Only later in my life did I realize how brave she was. And how foolhardy.

One night I thought I would help Mum. I left our house at four AM, while Dad was slumped against his desk, and walked Lodge Lane to the traffic lights at the top of the road. It wasn't so cold that night, but moisture hung in the air, teasing out the bulbs of the red, amber and green lights so that they resembled miniature explosions. In my front pocket I carried my penknife. I also had my catapult in my back pocket and a length of string, to tie the murderer up with. I had dressed in black clothes and rubbed black boot polish into my face to camouflage me against the night. I was a wraith. Nobody saw me as I drifted through the streets. I even moved like a commando. Johnny had told me that soldiers marched for twenty paces and jogged for twenty paces. In this way you could cover enormous distances quickly without ever becoming tired. Whenever I jogged, my voice kept time with this mantra: *I will kill you mis-ter mur-der-er/I will chop your bloo-dy head off/I will kill you mis-ter mur-der-er/I will chop your bloo-dy head off*. . . .

On Lovely Lane, I tried not to falter as I approached the railway bridge over the road, but I had to stop. There was a figure standing underneath it, spoiling the geometric pattern of the bridge's shadow with his hunched shoulders and bobbing head as he stalked around, the cleats on his heels skittering and scratching against the concrete.

I argued with myself. He couldn't be the murderer. Murderers hid in the dark waiting for someone to walk past. This man was openly showing himself to the world. But what if he was the murderer and he was simply pretending to be normal? The police, I knew, were having difficulty trying to find any clues to make their job of narrowing their search easier. The killer was a clever man.

I nipped across the road and down a side street that would bring me on to the cobbled alleyway near Toucher's bowling club, a drinking den that seemed to have been constructed for the sole use of fat men with mutton-chop whiskers and their wives, who sported tall nests of hair and left glossy, plum-red lip-prints on their cigarette ends.

The alleyway was jammed with Ford Cortinas and Austin Allegros in various shades of beige. A scabby sign above an archway read: FRANKS MOTOR-FIX. Through the archway, cairns of automobile parts gleamed. I hurried past, holding my nose against the soft breaths of burnt oil. Ahead, rising above a diamond link fence, lay the embankment. On the other side was the vast expanse of the hospital car park.

The fence was not as secure as it might be. I ripped and tore at a hole that had been begun by a dog or a rabbit and pushed my body through. I froze half way up the embankment as the killer whispered to me.

"Shall I show you the shadows of the soul?" he hissed.

But it wasn't him. It was the tracks, spitting and sizzling with the promise of a train. I edged farther up the embankment, thinking that I might beat the train and get to the other side before it chuntered past; it would be slowing by now anyway, the station only a quarter of a mile farther along. At the top, I could just see the soft lights on the platform stuttering in the mist. Behind me, however, the train was already upon me. I slunk back into the shadows as it clattered by, lifting the hair off my scalp and farting diesel fumes. I saw my face, a grey orb, in the dirtied steel of its flank, warped, streaming into a featureless smear by the speed of the engine and the tears filling my eyes.

The taste of the scorched diesel stuck in my throat. I palmed away the grit from my face and hurried over the sleepers, careful not to make too much noise in the gravel bed of the track, even though the thunder of the engine would no doubt be sufficient to mask any sound that I made. The car park was white with frost. Black rectangles hinted at recently departed vehicles. From here, they resembled freshly dug graves awaiting the coffin. I slithered down the other side of the embankment in time to see Mum striding across the road, her head down, a plastic bag shining under the lights of a florist's. I started running toward her and glanced to my right, at the railway bridge. The man was gone.

I saw Mum falter as she approached the span across the road. At the last moment, she stopped and turned back, disappearing down a side street running parallel to the track. I called to her, but my voice was small in the whipping wind. I still had some grit in my eyes. I hoped the shadow that bobbed and jerked after her was her own, but surely it must have been too long.

I ran after her, my legs failing to cover the ground as quickly as I would have liked, and plunged into the side street after her. Terraced houses rose above me on either side, leeched of color by the poor street lighting. I could hear the click of Mum's heels and the clip of something sharper. The echo, I hoped, although my doubts were growing. I saw shadows leap and shudder on the wall of the end house of a lane adjoining this street. By the time I reached the same spot, I was breathing hard and little black spots were exploding behind my eyes. The cold had sealed my lips shut. An intense stitch had replaced my heart.

At the foot of the street, a car park stretched into darkness. Garages lolled like a row of rotten Hollywood facades. There was an industrial skip brimming with timber and rusted scaffolding, a tarpaulin cover failing to protect the contents from the inquisitive wind. It flapped and fluttered like the wings of some crippled prehistoric bird. To the right, another railway arch created a dreadful frame for the school field and the sky beyond. I saw how Mum was thinking. If she took the route that was too obviously a dangerous route, how could the murderer possibly be lying in wait for her? Nobody would be stupid enough to take this path with a killer at large.

I watched her move through the arch, her head still bowed as if in deference to the enormity of the silence, the almost religious blackness of the place. I tried to keep pace with her, but she was hurrying now and I was very tired, my arms and legs filling with cold. The wind was enjoying its directionless game and ripped at me from all sides. I staggered across the fields in the direction that I hoped was my home. The thought of my bed and the hot water bottle, Mum bringing me some warm milk and shutting the curtains made my stomach lurch.

A woman screamed. I don't know where the scream originated, but at once it seemed as though her voice was assailing me from all angles. I continued to run, sobbing now, certain that I would trip on the steaming shell of my mother's remains. But it didn't happen. I found the path alongside the school and followed it to the end where our house stood. In the upstairs window, I saw Dad with his hands resting on the sill, looking out at the night. I didn't see much else until I got inside. I was crying hard. It was the first time I had been outside and separated from my mother. Though she had not heard or seen me, it felt terribly as though she had abandoned me.

They called him The Breakfast Man.

Both Elaine Dicker and Hannah Childs, the second victim, were killed around 5 AM, a time, in our town, when the hardcore workers turned out of bed to scrape a wedge for the family and the roof that sheltered them. Wire was our key industry back then; the town was noted for it. If you were up early enough, you could watch scores of men in black donkey jackets warming their fingers on the nipped coals of roll-ups, or hunched over the handlebars of their sit-up-and-beg bicycles. They drifted toward the wire factory like fleshed-out Lowry sketches. None of them had any straightness in them; they looked defeated, primitive. Yet they moved resolutely through the dawn mist as though sucked in by the opening of the factory gates.

The police believed The Breakfast Man was one of these workers. Someone with a grudge, someone whose frustrations and failure had manifested themselves in brutal violence.

Dad said: "Five'll give you ten the killer was divorced in the last six months." He said: "The killer lives alone and he can't cope. With anything."

I didn't know Hannah Childs, but plenty did. They pulled her broken body off the mangled wood and iron teeth of the skip I had scurried past that morning. I didn't tell anyone where I had been. I didn't tell anyone about the scream. I didn't need to: they had found the body anyway.

Hannah worked at the hospital too. She was a clerical assistant. In her spare time she showed pedigree dogs at competitions across the northwest. She had a prize cocker spaniel. Its name was Skip.

A week later Mum told her superiors at the hospital that she would no longer work the graveyard shift. If she can't work afternoons, she told them, she won't work at all. Goodbye, they told her. There were plenty of women who weren't knocked back by the deaths as much as Mum. Plenty of hungry women in our town.

Dad's bottle was half-empty. He was snoring slightly in his chair, an envelope in his hands. He had taken to falling asleep in the office during the evenings and those days when he wasn't required at the station. Photographs fanned from the envelope's mouth but I couldn't make out what they depicted. When I disturbed him, he opened a drawer and dropped the envelope into it. Then he lifted me onto his lap and hugged me. He smelled sour and sickly. He smelled of sleeplessness.

"Danny," he said, "what are your five most favorite places in the whole world?"

"Here," I said. "The field and the sandpit. Nana's place. And in my head."

"In your head?" Dad mulled this over, his eyebrows raised, before nodding slowly. "I know what you mean. Good answer. As good a place to be as any."

"Safe," I said.

Me and Johnny could no longer go out to play on the field at the back of our house. The weather was deteriorating rapidly. Five or six days out of the week there'd be a caul of frost on the grass, or fog loitered among the goalposts, turning them into exposed bones on a fossil dig. But on the first day of December, a hole appeared in the sky and through it came a few weak, watery rays of late afternoon sunshine.

Coincidentally, my stomachaches retreated. I felt better than I had for a long time. I badgered my mother for an hour's play on the field and although she did not relent, she agreed to let me go up there, as long as she could come too. We collected Johnny and set off through Tower's Court, a little maze of houses that abutted the field.

The cricket pavilion was the first thing I saw, picked out by the sunlight. A fence had been erected around it because it was rotting and in need of demolition. That didn't stop kids from climbing over and using it for a den. Walking by it now, we saw a boy and a girl kissing in the shadows, their faces moving in a way that reminded me of how a dog watches a washing machine work. Another boy was spray-painting his name in red on the boarded windows.

Johnny had brought his ball, and we kicked it about in the mud. Mum looked better in the sunlight. She laughed at us as we slid about in the dirt. I let the ball bounce on my head and shrieked when about half a ton of slime spattered my face. Mum had brought a few pieces of lardy cake with her. And some Tizer. We ate and drank. Johnny showed us how he could gargle the first verse of the national anthem without stopping, but it went wrong and he ended up snorting pop through his nose. Mum and me laughed till I wet myself. I think Mum wet herself too, just a little bit. It was a good day.

The next morning, the milkman found Mum nailed to a lamp-post with a cat's head stuffed so hard into her mouth that the surgeons had to break the lower jaw to get it out. I couldn't get through to Dad for days. Even with the light on, he seemed to attract darkness to his face. He didn't reflect any light at all, he absorbed it. He was dark matter. He was a black hole.

One thing my dad said that I remember, when he wasn't drunk or unconscious:

"It's as if she willed it upon herself. She was convinced she was on his unwritten list. She was a line and his arc bisected it."

At least she survived. Dad thought it would have been better if she had not.

Mum came home from the hospital a few days before New Year's. Christmas might as well have never happened at all in our house. There were no presents or cards, no decorations. A cake, awaiting its toppings of marzipan and icing, sat in the kitchen, the only signifier.

Early in the morning, Mum had been disturbed by the sound of a cat yowling in the street. She went outside and saw a thickset tabby with its back arched, its tail swollen to the size of a draught excluder. She had tried to comfort the cat and was looking into the street to see what had frightened it when The Breakfast Man attacked her from behind. Knocking her out, he pinned her to the lamppost and did for the cat. He was readying to chisel Mum open when the chink of bottles and the whine of the little electric engine on the milk float sent him running for cover.

The police wanted to know what he looked like. Mum couldn't remember. He wore one of those snorkel jackets, with the hood pulled up over his face. She said he was probably wearing a stocking over his head too; she just couldn't see anything behind the oval of grainy darkness that contained his face. She remembered how he smelled of lead, like rusty pipes, she said. His breath was like rusty pipes.

How could we expect her to revert to her normal ways after that? She grew distant and yet, to me, she seemed closer than ever. Perhaps it was because she was inhabiting the same regions of isolation that I had been traveling for so long. We understood each other's dislocation. Precious little connected with us; people seemed to operate on a different level, as though something fundamental had been omitted from our make-up, a vital element of the human blueprint that was out of stock at the moment we were rammed into being.

That said, Mum recoiled from me whenever I came into the bedroom to be near her. Her eyes flitted around, seeing things that weren't there, or that were there and she had been granted the privilege of witnessing. *It's okay, Mum*, I wanted to tell her. *I see them too. You won't be harmed.* But I couldn't say it and even if I could, she wouldn't have heard me. In me, she had focused all of her fears and apprehensions. I hoped that it was coincidence. That it was as likely she zeroed in on a bunch of flowers or an old slipper to help pin down her neuroses, but I couldn't help feeling that her resentment of me had long been there, buried within her, and now, as her health gradually declined and she became less linked with what was real, she could give it full rein without remorse or self-consciousness.

Dad too was diminishing, a kite whose guy had broken free. His drinking had increased; he was getting through a bottle and a half of whisky every day. I remember how he used to wince when he gulped it. Now he was swigging away as though it were water.

His superiors had allowed him unlimited compassionate leave, but he spent most of his time in the study working anyway. He had built up a deep folder of newspaper cuttings. Whenever I went to see if he wanted to kick a ball around in the garden, he would stare at me with his bruised eyes as if I were a stranger who had wandered into his house. Then some ember of recognition would pulse deep within and he might try on a smile, or ruffle my hair. But it was to his dossiers that he then turned; never to the comics, or the Meccano, or *The Three Stooges*, stuff that we had huddled over together in the past.

He didn't tell me what to do anymore, or how to behave. He let me play with Johnny pretty much when and where I liked. Most of the time we wandered down to the canal that ran along the end of our road. Its towpath led to a stile at the mouth of a dense wood. Not too far in was a mulchy clearing dominated by a tree trunk felled either by lightning or the rot that had consumed much of it. Mum and Dad used to come here when I was a toddler. I'd play near the tree while they filled a wheelbarrow with leaf mold for our garden. In October, we'd visit with black refuse sacks stuffed into our coat pockets. There was a clutch of chestnut trees at the wood's eastern edge. If you timed it right, you could arrive with the sound of chestnuts falling to earth like strange rain. The vibrations went through your wellington boots and you'd have to shield your head to make sure the spiny cases didn't clout you. We'd eat as many as we picked, it seemed. Under the pith, the chestnuts were pale and creamy with a crunch and a sweet taste far more enticing than that to be found when they were roasted. I write that with a jolt of surprise; I have yet to eat a roasted chestnut. I trusted my dad when he told me they were inferior.

Johnny and me, ghosting through the silver birch, the copper beech. We didn't have any jam jars with us to go sticklebacking. It was too late for chestnuts. We walked. Johnny apologized for the description of Elaine Dicker's mutilated body, in the light of what had happened to Mum.

"How d-d-did you know abuh-about her in-injuries?" I asked. In my pocket, my fingers rubbed against one of the textured pages in my sketchbook. I had a brand new, freshly sharpened Lakeland by Cumberland 3B pencil behind my ear. I was aching to use it.

"I made it up," Johnny said, sheepishly. "Well, I didn't exactly. Not on my own. Dave Cathersides made most of it up. Him and Callum Fisher. It was just a laugh."

I saw tangles in everything I looked at; in the pattern of the leaves against the sky, in the fruiting loam, in the collapsed cobwebs hanging from the massed ranks of rhododendron. There were signs in the spiral wormcasts, messages in the glittering frogspit wadded in the exposed roots of the hawthorn bushes. Even on Johnny. I peered at him, the whorls of fair hair under his ears, the minuscule patchwork of diamonds that made up the skin on his face, the pores ranged across his chin, gleaming in the wintry sunshine. What was so different from him, from all of this, to the stuff I created in my drawing pads? Just a nudging toward convention, a fluke of geometry.

I didn't say anything. We dug around in the humus and tossed pinecones at each other. Johnny spotted a fox. We watched it jogging through the undergrowth like magical fire, coloring in the uniform grey and black of its surroundings. The vortices it created in the mist dragged more through the boughs until it wreathed our legs. We couldn't see our feet. We pretended that we were blinded by the mist, and ranged around in the undergrowth, arms outstretched, eyes closed. Every time we bumped into a tree, we apologized profusely. I was in tears, laughing.

When I opened my eyes, the mist had risen to my throat and I jerked my head up reflexively, as though if I didn't, I might drown. I couldn't see Johnny, but I could hear him, still excusing himself and laughing, mad as a satchel of badgers. Looking up at the canopy, I managed to pick a way through the trees toward Johnny's laughter. Suddenly I saw him. The mist had somehow caused him to look elongated. It was like viewing someone from afar on a hot day, an instance of *fata morgana*; Johnny's head appeared as two or three disconnected bands linked tenuously to an etiolated body. He moved ponderously. You might believe that the mist had infected him and the dampness in his bones was now grinding him to a halt.

I took out my sketch pad and translated the shocking sight into my comfortable scrawl. Then I remembered the way a teacher had lost her temper and screamed at somebody to be quiet and the sketch took off in a new direction. And again: the train on the tracks and my face staring back at me without any eyes. And again: Dad's lips pressing together on another mouthful of pain relief. And. And. And . . .

Johnny found me a little later slumped on the ground, my head ricked back against a tree, spittle oozing from the corner of my mouth. My eyes had rolled back into their sockets and I had gone into spasm.

My hand moved independently of the body's trauma, filling the page with graphite jags and curlicues and cross-hatchings.

The following morning, a woman was discovered facedown in a water barrel. He had tried to peel her skin off in one piece, as one might do with an apple, but had given up on the task and split her in half, vertically, instead with a series of heavy blows from an ax they found wrapped in newspaper and dumped in a litter bin. Her name was Michelle Paget, a nineteen-year-old veterinarian's assistant.

She was the last of The Breakfast Man's victims.

I still have those old sketchbooks with me now.

This morning, I flicked through them, trying to pinpoint some madness in the method. I suppose I was hoping such a study would prevent me from thinking about what came next. But of course, rather than distract me, the sketches, ostensibly vague, served only to crystallize that time in my thoughts.

I took the sketchbooks with me down to the beach. It's a nice beach, if a little exposed. Raw winds tear into the coast during winter. There's a good mix of pebbles and sand and, if you know what you're looking for, you can find little nuggets of amber among the stones.

There was a shag on one of the outermost groynes, wings outstretched, bill agape. An old couple walking a dog far in the distance. And the waves, sprinting in to shore, their tops disintegrating to mist as they met the ferocious winds.

The sketches seem to have been imbued with fresh meaning. It was a bit like looking at one of those 3-D pictures that were popular a couple of years ago. The ones where you have to stare *beyond* the hectic patterns until something solid pops into view so forcefully, you wonder how you could not have seen it immediately.

I saw things I don't want to talk about. I saw suggestions in the confusion. I saw faces that are no longer around.

Dad committed suicide. I found him slumped across his desk. He had a tumbler next to him, but it hadn't seen any whisky at all. I guess he used it to trick himself into believing his drinking remained civilized; he was necking the Scotch straight from the bottle. There were pills. White dust clung to his lips.

I reached across him, my arm brushing against his cold forehead, and pulled open the top drawer. The envelope was still there, with its glossy, awful cargo.

And all I could think, as I shuffled through this unconscionable deck, was how alike The Breakfast Man and I were. Only, his canvases were flesh, his pencil a fifteen-inch boning knife.

The police closed the case. They believed my dad was the killer. Mum made half-hearted protests from her bed in the psychiatric ward at Winwick hospital. But the police were vindicated. There were no further deaths. I wonder . . . I half-wonder whether my mum suspected Dad. I quarter wonder.

I went to stay with Nana until she died and then for years I was volleyed around the care system. I lost my appetite for sketching. I lost my appetite for everything. In my teenage years I got into trouble with the police for fighting, shoplifting, drunk and disorderly. I didn't see Mum in all that time. Then they told me she had had a stroke and would not live for much longer. That was ten years ago. I tried to end my life that night. I hanged myself with an old school tie from the lamp flex in my bedroom, but the light was frail and half the ceiling fell to the floor along with me.

"Want one?" A nurse who smelled of Daz and nutmeg offered me a bag of caramels. She couldn't understand why I collapsed in tears.

I burned all of the sketches under the pier. I might have been kidding myself but the smoke smelled, I'm sure of it, of growing up. Of Johnny's bubblegum and Mum's warm neck and Dad's cardigan when he pulled me in close for a hug or a wrestle. The last sketch in the batch I couldn't fathom for a long time, but then I saw how the swirls parted and allowed me to see myself. A vague profile. I think I'm smiling. But not for much longer. I think after tonight, the police might re-open their files on The Breakfast Man.

A last wrap of sweets for my mother, then. I love the way the shopkeeper will lick his thumb and rub away a white paper bag from the sheaf hanging from a piece of string on the wall. How he flaps it open and pours in the quarter measure of boiled sugar from the deep metal dish on the scales. Taking the ends, he twists the bag shut with a few flurries of movement.

I wish I could do the same with my own thoughts. Twist them shut, seal them in. Offer them to no one.

TRANSORBITAL
LOVE PROBE

by Th. Metzger

Again, Georgie stabbed the Kuhli loach in the head; it stopped wriggling. Pinned to his corkboard, it was pretty: red and black and yellow stripes around its eelish body.

"Georgie!"

He ignored his mother's wit's-end wail.

"Georgie!" She scuffed down the hall in her bathrobe and fluffy slippers, but didn't enter his room. She only came in once a week—on Thursday mornings—to clean. That was part of their agreement.

"Georgie, you put those nails in the oven again."

"I know."

"Didn't I ask you not to do that anymore?"

"I explained this all before. Sometimes they need heat."

His mother remained in the doorway.

Sighing loudly, Georgie got up from his work and followed her into the kitchen. By the oval clock on the back of the range, he saw that it was well past midnight. But for the clock and the oven door window, the kitchen was dark. Inside the Hotpoint, his nails were glowing: seventeen common roughing nails on a cookie sheet.

"They're done anyway," he said, opening the door and using an asbestos mitt to take them out. He dumped the nails on the souvenir ceramic platter his Aunt Bernice had brought back from Queen Elizabeth's coronation a few years before. She had red red lips, a sash over her bosom, a crown, and a pointy scepter.

"I don't want you doing this anymore," his mother said.

"I told you already. They need heat sometimes, like we need food and water. That's just the way it is." He carried the platter back to his room and laid it carefully on the brick platform he'd made there earlier in the week, soon after the nails had come into his life.

He closed the door and put on his pajamas. The nails were still glowing, though very faintly now. He fell asleep as the last traces of light faded from the air.

The next day, Georgie's mother found the nails imbedded in the garage wall, an inch deep: seventeen steel darts aligned in a perfect triangle.

This time she crossed the line. She came into his room, angry, though trying not to let it show. Usually that made matters worse. Georgie could smell anger like a dog smells fear.

"Georgie, I think we need to have a little talk."

"Fine."

"Did Dr. Freeman upset you?"

Their consultation the week before had been brief. Dr. Freeman had barely made eye contact with Georgie as he pronounced his diagnosis.

"No, nothing is bothering me." He had a jewel darter and a neon tetra on his drying board. They'd lost most of their color already. The smell was gone too. Georgie brandished a sticking pin like a tiny sword. "I didn't do it."

"You didn't do what?"

"Whatever you're going to accuse me of."

"Then who did it?"

"They did it themselves. I explained that already. Sometimes they just disappear and show up later in another place. I don't have any control over that." Georgie held the pin against the plush of his thumb, readying to push it in.

"You're sure there's nothing you want to tell me?"

"No." They'd let him graduate from high school even though everybody knew he didn't have the credits. They just wanted to get rid of him. It wasn't that Georgie was stupid. No, he knew more about the British royal family, about tropical fish and space travel than anyone he'd ever met. It was just that he'd have his moods and then nothing went right. Since June, he'd had a few part-time jobs, but they hadn't worked out.

"Everything is fine." He jabbed the pin into the corkboard. He heard the infinitesimally faint squeak as the silver point slid through the cork fibers. No one else in the entire world could hear that sound. "Everything is wonderful, A-OK, shipshape, copacetic, A-1, el perfecto, fine and dandy."

A week passed before his mother brought up the subject again. She'd found the nails in the attic, spaced evenly around the outline of her wedding dress, holding it flat to the flakeboard wall. They looked like the pattern of daggers he'd seen once at a sideshow: a silhouette created by the knife-thrower, marking clearly the arms and legs and torso of the pretty blond assistant.

Georgie's mother took the dress down and locked it again in the battered black steamer trunk by the chimney. "I've asked Chuck to come and have a talk with you," she said. Chuck was Georgie's sister's husband, a big beefy man with a poorly concealed bald spot and a brand new Plymouth.

Georgie didn't bother to argue.

Chuck showed up the next day "to have a little man-to-man talk." Georgie's mother disappeared, leaving them alone in the parlor.

"Well, your mother tells me you've been a little upset lately."

"No, I haven't been upset. Everything is just fine, peachy keen, excellent, boffo, couldn't be better, tip-top."

"Then why are you causing her so much trouble?" Chuck was a guidance counselor at the high school. He was using his sincere and helpful voice. Georgie didn't answer. He stared down at the floor, concentrating on the individual threads in the braided rug.

"I want to help you. Why don't you tell me what's on your mind?"

Chuck now wore the same expression as when he'd explained the facts of life to Georgie.

"Do you believe in aliens?" Georgie said at last.

Now it was Chuck's turn to sit uncomfortably in silence.

"From another world. Do you think it's possible that creatures from another world could come here and we wouldn't suspect a thing?"

"You mean from outer space?"

"I don't know. Visitors, or maybe invaders."

Chuck was not a psychiatrist like Dr. Freeman. His strength was in career counseling, making sure kids fit the right electives into their schedules. Georgie had figured out a long time ago the best way to get rid of him.

"What if a transorbital creature came to our world but nobody knew it was really an alien? What if it looked like seventeen common nails I bought at Stollmeier's last week? What if it was an iron-based life-form which established partnerships with certain humans, giving them great powers in exchange for providing a few simple needs, like putting them in the oven every few days or rubbing them for exactly eleven minutes with a piece of Number Four steel wool dipped in mineral spirits? What if that was true?"

Chuck did as Georgie expected: nodded, made a few comments about buckling down and keeping his nose to the grindstone, and went to look for his mother-in-law.

Later, when the two of them came into his room, he couldn't tell which one was angrier.

"This is too much. I've been lenient. I've indulged you, given you what you want. But this is too much."

"Too much what?"

"And don't play dumb with me, young man. Your nails are sticking in Chuck's tires. Fours nails in each one."

Actually, the right rear had five.

"Do you know how much those tires cost?" Chuck's face was red. His bald spot, too, like a warning light on top of his head.

"How much?"

They both left, flushed and fuming. A few minutes later, Georgie heard his mother talking quietly on the phone, probably to Dr. Freeman.

Chuck's car sat in the driveway overnight. When the tow truck came the next morning, the nails had vanished.

He kept out of sight. They knew where he was but pretended that he was gone, or never existed. He had a little hiding place behind the knee wall on the third floor. He'd insulated it with rockwool scraps and carpeted the floor with old burlap.

The nails were in a clear plastic bag, though he left the opening undone to let them breathe. There were times when he'd buy cunners and monk guppies and midget shad from the pet shop and bring them home in a bag like the one now holding the nails. Usually he'd put them in one of the holding tanks until he was ready to stick them on the board. Once, he'd performed timed trials using a stopwatch to find out which breed flopped and gasped the longest.

Georgie lay in the narrow cubbyhole all day, falling in and out of sleep. Lying on his back, he tracked the movement of the sun across the sky, though all he could see were the sap-stained two-by-eights and batts of pink insulation. He knew exactly where the sun was by the focal point of its heat. It rose slowly, went beyond the roof's ridgepole, and descended at dinner time.

He was hungry, hot, cramped, and his bladder had been near to bursting for hours. But he stayed hidden until he heard the radio shut off and the creaking of his mother's bed cease.

He snuck out just as the moon was making its appearance: a sac filled with yellowish liquid. A rocket probe would burst it like a dart. Seventeen spearlike rockets could puncture it and pin it to the surface of the sky like an old rag.

Chuck's Plymouth was gone, though there were faint splotches on the driveway, pools of tears cried by the big car as the nails had penetrated the soft rubber of the tires.

The house was totally dark; he passed through like a ghost. Outside, he thought he saw Sputnik, a tiny fleck of light gliding among the unmoving stars. It had only been up a week. Everybody was talking about it: the first man-made thing to escape from the Earth.

But compared to the nails—how far had they traveled to be with him?—it was nothing. A little toy. It would go round the Earth a few times and then get sucked back in by gravity and burn up. The nails, compared to Sputnik, were like Chuck's car next to Georgie's Schwinn: infinitely more sophisticated. They'd come from way out beyond—transorbital visitors.

At the halfway point on his trek—the ruins of Mrs. Engwald's silo—he stopped briefly to check on the nails. They were aligned perfectly in the bag, the points all facing the same direction. There was no trace of rust or dirt on them. The imperceptible—to everyone but Georgie—fluting around the necks was still sharp and distinct. They were clearly now one, rather than seventeen: one entity with seventeen component parts. He knew that even if he dropped them one at a time half a mile apart all the way to town, they'd still have the same essential unity. In an instant they could be together again, ready for action. If they could travel to earth, to Stollmeier's hardware store, from some infinitely distant world, then there was nothing that he could do, nothing Chuck or his mother or the off-duty cop at the all-night store could do to prevent them from reaching their ultimate goal.

He stood a long time at the big cooler in the rear of the store trying to decide what would be best. Coke or Orange Crush, Juiceroo or Joy-Pop. He could take the bottle outside, fill the plastic bag and let the nails float around in the sweet colored water like stiff little fish.

The off-duty cop—Georgie could tell he was a cop by the shape of his belly and the web of white foam in the corners of his mouth—was watching him carefully. Georgie waited at the cooler, his nose only inches from the frosty glass. Finally the cop came down the pretzel and potato chip aisle and asked him if something was wrong. Georgie didn't answer.

"Boy, I'm talking to you. You got a problem tonight?"

Still Georgie remained mute, concentrating on a single bottle of root beer with a blindfolded unicycling polar bear on the label.

"I think you better come with me," the cop said, touching Georgie on the shoulder.

Instantly he spun around, like a discus thrower, once, twice, then let go of the bag. The nails flew out like seventeen spears in wedge formation, aimed at the cashier's face. It took them less than a second to fly from one end of the store to the other, but as they sailed through the air Georgie was suddenly inside them, the pilot. He saw the clerk's face looming up ahead, the way space commanders would see the surface of the moon growing and growing, blotting out the sky. Georgie was the captain, the navigator, the bombardier, the warhead, the detonator and the thrusting jets of flame roaring out behind.

The clerk opened her mouth, a vast crater. Her skin was pitted with volcanic acne.

Inches from impact, a minuscule fraction of a second before slamming into the clerk's face, Georgie veered the squadron upward at a right angle. They swooped in a tight curve and then headed downward again, this time aiming for the boiling surface of the deep fryer. The hot fat called to him, to the nails: a seething greasy siren song. Taking a deep breath, he let go of the joy-stick and rode the nails down into the fryer, a crash landing in the boiling seas of some unknown world.

Instantly he was overcome by pain. The heat was huge, cooking him in a flash like the French fries and onion rings that more often than tiny alien spacecraft writhed in the hot fat.

He felt pain, but elation, too. In a flash he was replenished, his energy and his faith completely restored.

His mother came to pick him up at the sheriff's station. Chuck and Georgie's sister were there too, looking just as worried. Ruthie didn't have a glowing bald spot like her husband, but in most other ways looked just like him.

Apparently there was no bail or bond to post. His mother had Dr. Freeman call the sheriff and explain the situation.

Georgie went with them silently, sitting in the back of the Plymouth with his mother.

It wasn't until he saw the house that he realized the nails were gone. The sheriff had confiscated them after the clerk had fished them out of the fryer with a long-handled sieve.

Chuck helped Georgie up to his room. The other two stood in the doorway, observing the "no girls allowed except on Thursday mornings" rule.

His entire collection was gone. And all his equipment too: pins, drying boards, steel racks, gro-lights, fungicidal cremes, dyes and paint brushes.

They'd even taken his signed picture of the Queen and Prince Phillip.

A week or two before he would have started screaming, throwing things, cursing and banging his head against the doorknob.

"The doctor thought it would be best," his mother said, in a voice like a squeaky cat toy. "He thought you needed a break. Overstimulation is a bad thing. Maybe when you're feeling better you can have your things back. But for the time being you need a change of pace."

"Where are my specimens?"

No one answered.

"Where are they?"

Chuck cleared his throat. "Everything is at our house. We packed it carefully. It's all in the basement. When things settle down a little you can have it all back."

They were lying. Georgie knew that his collection had been

thrown out. Years of work, important scientific research, were piled in a dump somewhere, buried under shriveled orange peels, steak bones, Kleenex, newspapers, balls of tinfoil and corncobs.

"Get out," Georgie whispered. "And close the door."

That night he sat on the edge of his bed looking out the window for hours. He had a good view of the road, the farm across the way, and the place on the horizon where the moon came up. It was even bigger that night, a membrane stretched near to bursting.

He concentrated on the moon, a vast pockmarked bag hanging above the corn fields. He knew that if he climbed to the roof, detached the lightning rod and held it up like a sword, the moon would soon pass by and snag on the sharp point. The enormous pent-up volume of yellow water would explode onto the Earth. Like Noah's flood, the deluge would come. And only Georgie would be safe, up on the roof, as the entire world was covered.

He must have fallen asleep, though he was still sitting upright with his eyes open when he discovered the nails were back. They lay on the bedspread, bright and flawless, perfectly aligned.

"Body heat," Georgie said, realizing that the nails didn't need to be cooked in the oven. They could absorb warmth from a source much lower in temperature. Georgie saw them now as seventeen thermometers, sleek silver probes. Except they wouldn't burst—squirting mercury like metallic blood—when they reached their peak.

He divided them into two handfuls and placed them gently in his armpits. Cold and hard, but reassuring. They warmed, but not enough. They needed more heat than he could give them.

As he opened the bedroom door and stepped into the hallway, the nails began to purr. He paused only a moment before entering his mother's room. The nails were singing now, as though they'd already been released, flying through the air as seventeen arrows of desire.

It seemed strange that the nails' wailing didn't wake his mother. Usually she was a light sleeper.

She had on a dimpled rubber sleeping cap. In the feeble moonlight, everything in the room seemed gritty, granular. Her face was pocked by hundreds of tiny holes. Her mouth was an ocean, her eyes lakes, her pores craters. The sound of her snoring was enormous, an entire world shivering and groaning, trying to bring itself awake. Her dentures shifted: vast tectonic plates realigning themselves.

"Mom." She stirred but didn't wake. "Mom." He had to shout to hear himself above the scream of the nails. "Momma!"

She jerked awake, sitting up. Her nightgown hung open. Georgie tried not to look at the hugeness of her bosom, but his eyes wouldn't obey. He was shrinking, moving backward in time, becoming Captain Baby Missile Commander again.

"What are you doing here? Why aren't you in bed?" Her voice filled the room, filled the expanse of lightless space.

As she leaned toward him, glowering, her gown covering almost nothing, his hand flew forward and the nails took flight. Seventeen jets of flame shot out the tails; seventeen shrieks fought to be the loudest, the fastest. Which would be the first to reach the target zone? Which would be the one and only?

Again, Georgie was inside them as the pilot, the wing commander, the soul of their flight. In an instant, everything was blotted out by her form. She was not a planet but a sun, a vast sphere of roaring atomic fire. Her eyes shot geysers of flame miles into the sky. Black clouds roiled from her nostrils. And her voice, the furious bellow demanding obedience, filled all the dead space between the worlds.

He couldn't turn back now even if he wanted to. Gravity was already too much, doubling, tripling, quadrupling his momentum.

Ahead of him pulsed the bloated sac of fire. He was ready. His seventeen little lethal fish were ready. The warheads were all armed. The navigation systems were locked on target. The homing instinct, which had drawn the seventeen specks of life—like fish drawn thousands of miles to mate—had overcome all obstacles.

He needed merely to let go, to relax into the irresistable pull and ride those last few miles, meters, microns into the living ball of fire.

"Did you ever hear of Ja-el and Sisera?"

"What?" the nurse said.

Ja-el sounded like somebody in the League of Superheroes: "Ja-el, Science Lad of Krypton." But Ja-el was a she. "In the Bible. She's in Judges, chapter four." Georgie recited the verses: "Then Ja-el, Heber's wife, took a nail of the tent and took a hammer in her hand and went softly unto Sisera and smote the nail into his temple and fastened it to the ground. For he was fast asleep and weary. So he died. Behold, Sisera lay dead and the nail was in his temple."

Georgie looked up at the nurse. She was pretty; why were all nurses pretty? Ja-el must have been pretty, too, for Sisera to let her do that to him. "I'm not going to die, am I?"

"No, no, of course not."

Georgie's mother appeared—Band-Aids on her face and arms and hands. She was worried and afraid, and it showed.

"You're not going to die," she said. "You're going to feel better. The doctor is going to make it all better."

The nurse gave Georgie a rag of flannel to bite down on, then held his hands. They were warm and soft and he liked that.

Then Dr. Freeman appeared with his portable electroshock machine. It was squarish, roughly the size of a cigar box, with a transformer to step down the wall current. The doctor wore a goatee, like the old-fashioned, old-world neurologists. But he was no fusty old man. Tall, tanned, stripped to a sleeveless white gown that left his muscular arms exposed, he was all business.

He brought the electroshock wand—a silvery steel wishbone—close to Georgie's skull. "You'll feel a slight discomfort," he said. He wore no surgical mask, no gloves. He hadn't even washed his hands.

With a quick nod to the nurse, he turned on the toggle switch and a blast of current ripped through Georgie's skull. It hurt; it hurt a lot. He writhed and squirmed and bit down hard on the rag. The doctor gave him a quick inspection, decided one more jolt was needed and fit the twin prongs around his head again. Again he hit the switch. This time, after the blast exploded in Georgie's head, he was—as far as the others knew—unconscious. But they weren't inside his head; they couldn't guess what was really going on.

He felt the doctor's fingers plucking at his eyelid, a deft pinching between thumb and forefinger to pull the eye open. Georgie saw it all: the doctor's fierce glare, the nurse placid as a plaster saint, and his mother far in the background, sick with guilt.

The doctor lifted an eight-inch-long steel spike from a special case and Georgie felt a wave of relief. The nails—or nail now, fused into one grand, glittering transorbital probe—had returned.

Dr. Freeman carefully inserted the point of the spike into Georgie's tear duct. It didn't hurt now. It was right, good, perfect, excellent, all for the best, exactly as it should be. The rocketship was going home.

Taking a deep breath, the doctor dropped to one knee, aimed the spike along the ridge of Georgie's nose. It all looked so crazy from that angle: everybody looming like giants, everything twisted, out of proportion.

The surgical mallet rose, fell on the blunt end of the spike and it broke through to the other side: three inches of healing steel into his brain. But it might have been three million light-years. The spaceship, the leucotome as the medical people called it, the spike which had come to save him, the nail, passed round the orbit of his eye, through the boney vault of his skull and into his prefrontal lobe.

The probe went in and Georgie felt the warhead explode in his brain. Light and heat erupted inside him, though not pain. The brain tissue can't feel pain.

The doctor moved his leucotome from left to right, then up and down, a silvery lever cutting through his gray matter.

Then he pulled the probe out and did the other side. The spike broke through, entered him, cut the offending tissue, raked up and down, back and forth, and it was over. Five minutes at the most.

"You'll notice the difference immediately," Dr. Freeman said, turning away with a flourish.

That night Georgie lay awake for hours, a sheet draped lightly over him. Chuck had brought him home, helped him up the stairs. "That's right, big boy, you're doing fine." Chuck put him in bed. Georgie's mother made him a peanut butter and banana sandwich with lots of shiny white mayonnaise just the way he liked it. But he didn't eat much.

He waited patiently, first for Chuck to leave, then for his mother to go to sleep, then for the world to get quiet and dark.

A long time past midnight, Georgie sat up on the edge of his bed and looked out the window. Yes, it was there: Sputnik, sailing like a red hot cinder across the sky.

Georgie opened his fist and found that the nails too had

returned. They remained in their final form: fused into one spike, an eight-inch space probe, heavy and warm, damp from his grasp, throbbing, eager. The probe had gone inside him and touched the core of his brain, the inner secret place that no one knew about. He'd read in *LIFE* magazine how some people called the operation "soul surgery." He'd been going to the library, looking up articles— they even had a book by Dr. Freeman—about the operation. Ever since he went for his first appointment, he'd been getting ready.

Now the probe was back, ready for action.

Georgie stared awhile at Sputnik. It disappeared and Georgie waited for it to come back from the other direction. Round the world, slowly being pulled in by gravity. Georgie opened his window, careful, quiet. No, he'd have to do this outside.

He tiptoed downstairs, holding up his pajama bottoms because the elastic was worn out. He went out the kitchen door and stood in the backyard. Quiet, peaceful. No dogs barking, no traffic, no voices. Just the far-off hum of Sputnik, a tiny fly buzzing across the sky.

He cocked his arm back, like a javelin-hurler, and aimed.

He threw, his pants fell to his knees, the probe went up swift and sleek. It flew. A jet of flame squirted out the back and then grew to a powerful thruster. The rocket rose, fighting gravity. In a second or two it had reached the moment of truth: the point where the Earth's pull would say "no, come back here," and make it arc downward. Georgie felt it: the exact point where it should have tumbled back, defeated.

He raised both hands, pointed his fingers like a wizard casting a spell. The probe hit the breakthrough point and kept going. Georgie took a few steps, tangled in his pajamas, kicked them free and ran, following the probe.

Panic, a cold stab of depair: it was going to leave without him.

Like the last man on a sinking boat, reaching for the dangling rescue ladder, Georgie reached for the rapidly dwindling probe. He stretched; he clawed at the air.

And made it.

In the cockpit now, wearing his test pilot helmet, looking out through the tiny windshield, Georgie drove the space probe upward. Through the stratosphere, the mesosphere, the ionosphere. He chanted the names like a prayer. Out past the Van Allen Belts and into the cold, bleak emptiness of space.

As he zoomed out beyond the last traces of earth's atmosphere—a few molecules of oxygen, a wisp of hydrogen, the delicate aftertaste of nitrogen—he saw Sputnik. It was a weak-looking thing: a shiny aluminium globe only two feet across, four antenna-rods sticking out the back like stiff legs. The newspapers had made Sputnik seem like a huge, hulking monster. This was a bug, a silvery virus, an outer-space germ that would fall to the Earth in a few weeks and burn up to nothing.

As Georgie roared past, strapped securely into the driver's seat of the transorbital probe, he waved a friendly good-bye to Sputnik, and then to everything else: to tropical fish, to the British royal family, to Chuck and Ruthie, and then to his mother. He saw her turning restlessly in bed, dreaming of her one and only, now gone, lost to her forever.

He gave a smart salute and then grasped the joystick with both hands, aiming the nails back where they'd come from.

THE IMPRESSIONISTS
IN WINTER

by Susan Fry

"I know where we'll paint tomorrow," said René, picking at the carcass of the roast chicken on the table between us.

"Tomorrow?" I asked. We'd spent the three days since arriving at Rochebleu tromping around snowy meadows, scouting for views. I'd been hoping to spend tomorrow at the inn with a pipe and a good fire. "It may snow."

"You're a lazy dog, Emile," René said. He grinned. "What would Monet say if he knew what a lazy dog you were? I don't think he would invite you into the exhibition."

I frowned. René's jokes often cut too close.

The kitchen door opened, and Madame Moreau came in with a peach-preserves tart. She smiled, sat at the table, and cut it into four pieces, even though there were only three of us. One piece was much larger than the others. René reached for it.

Madame Moreau slapped his hand away. "No, you don't," she said. "That's the ghouls' share."

"The what?" René asked. He raised his eyebrows at me.

Madame Moreau slipped the fourth piece onto a plate. "The ghouls. The dead. So they won't come for us," she said, quite seriously.

"Ah," said René. He looked quite serious, too. I smothered a smile. Madame Moreau was so pretty I often forgot she was just a peasant.

Madame Moreau frowned at me. "You smile. But in the winter, the dead are even colder and hungrier than usual. You cannot blame them for being angry. They hate us because we are warm, and alive."

She stood up and opened the door of the inn, letting in a frigid blast of winter air. The fire flickered. I shivered. Madame Moreau bent down and placed the plate outside the threshold then shut the door quickly. Even with the draft gone, the room seemed colder.

René shrugged and helped himself to a smaller piece of tart. He dug into it. With his mouth full, he said, "Pissarro told me the secret to painting snow so it glows. You . . ."

"Don't you ever talk about anything besides painting, Monsieur Saint-Jean?" Madame Moreau asked.

"What else is there to talk about?" René said.

I could think of many things. That the room at the inn was pleasant. That everything in it—the long oak table, the chairs, the dishes—was rough-hewn and sturdy, except Madame Moreau, who was slender and lively. She was twenty-four and a widow. She seemed to have no regrets about her husband's death six months before. I was understandably curious about this. He had been much older than she, I supposed. I wondered whether it was his spirit she was placating with the offers of food.

"Well, you haven't opened your mail." Madame Moreau point-ed at the pile of letters by the fireplace. It was the first mail we'd gotten since we'd arrived. We were truly in the country if it took let-ters three days to reach us from Paris.

I was nervous as I opened my letters. I was hoping for one from Monet about the exhibition.

I had three, one from my mother complaining about the way I was wasting my inheritance, one from my brother complaining about my mother, and one from the manager of our weaving facto-ry about the sale of some land I'd arranged to pay for my winter of painting. They were all dated three days before.

There was no letter from Monet. At least René didn't have one, either.

René's four letters were from women in Paris who were upset he was spending winter in what they called "barbarous Burgundy." He opened the first letter, read a few lines, and laughed. The firelight made his handsome face look devilish, despite his angelic blond curls.

"What's so funny?" asked Madame Moreau, cutting into her peach tart.

"She says," René said, adopting a high, squeaking voice like a woman's, " 'It's the coldest, cruelest winter in Paris in ten years. Without the warmth of your love, the streets are like ice.'"

He sounded so much like a woman that Madame Moreau and I laughed. René enjoyed our laughter. He continued the imitations, reading lines out of that letter and the next. For the third letter, he even got up and flounced around the room with the tablecloth tied around his waist like a skirt.

I laughed until my sides ached. Then I noticed that Madame Moreau was looking at René with warm appreciation. Until now, she had been friendly but distant with both of us. But I could tell she was beginning to prefer René. It destroyed my pleasure in the evening.

René picked up his final letter. This one was on thin, cheap, onionskin paper. When he held it up to the firelight, I could see the fine, spidery handwriting on the other side. He read a few lines silently. He frowned.

"What does it say?" Madame Moreau said, a laugh in her voice.

René didn't answer. He scanned the letter to the bottom, and with one of his quick changes of temper went from charming to furious.

"That woman!" he spat. "She wants my money. She wants to marry me. She wants me to give up painting. Selfish!" He cursed, wadded the paper up, and tossed it into the fire. "I hope the bitch rots in hell," he said.

Madame Moreau lifted her hand and made a sign against the evil eye. We sat in an uncomfortable silence for a few minutes.

I was surprised about the money. René's family was no wealthier than mine. I knew he'd sold some of his family's silver—silver from before the Revolution—to finance his part of our stay in Rochebleu.

Finally, Madame Moreau dusted the crumbs from her bodice and rose. "I'm going to bed," she said. "Good night." She shook each of our hands with a solemnity so quaint it was nearly noble. I thought she lingered a moment longer over René's hand than mine.

René and I watched her slender figure mount the stairs. René hummed in appreciation. Then he winked at me, got up, opened the front door again, letting in another blast of air, and returned with the large piece of tart. He picked up his fork and began to eat.

"No point letting the cat have it," he said. "Ghouls, my arse."

He offered some to me, but I shook my head. I knew, of course, that there was nothing wrong with what he was doing. I was not a superstitious peasant, like Madame Moreau. But I felt a faint shiver of uneasiness all the same. I was tempted to make the sign of the evil eye myself. But of course I didn't.

After René had finished the tart, he went up to bed, too. I heard his footsteps creaking around his room, then the squeak of his bed, then silence. I sat and smoked in front of the fire. René's letter had long since burned to ash, and I wondered what had been in it.

Then I put out my pipe and went to bed.

"Here it is," René said.

My heart sank. There were kilometers of beautiful meadows surrounding Rochebleu. But the site that René had chosen was not beautiful.

It was the lane that led to the village. In the summer it probably would have been very pretty, but in the winter the trees that lined it were bare of leaves and skeletal. The lane was industrial in its regularity, like a railroad in Paris—the white, straight lines of the snow-covered road, the black, straight lines of the trees, the iron-gray sky overhead. It was so stark and bare it unnerved me.

But of course I couldn't say this to René. The whole trip had been his idea. He was the one who had told Monet and Pissarro that we were going to follow in their footsteps. Instead of moving indoors the way most painters did during the winter, René had told them, he and I would continue to follow the Impressionist philosophy of capturing natural light and natural settings. Without René's proposal, Monet would never have even considered us for the exhibition.

The thought that Monet, right now, might be looking at my paintings in Paris sent a shiver down my back that had nothing to do with the cold. He might accept both of us, I thought. He might accept only one.

So I sighed, watching a gust of white billow up from my scarf-covered mouth, and set up my three-legged easel, my folding stool, and my little brazier by one side of the lane. René set up on the other side.

"I think the light's only good here until one o'clock," he said, "so we've only got an hour and a half to paint."

An hour and a half. I sighed again. Until several years ago, of course, painting outside during the winter at all would have been impossible. That's when paint was stored and carried in pigs' bladders, which froze and chipped in cold weather. Now that we had paints in little metal tubes, even cold couldn't prevent us from coaxing them out onto the palette in the most freezing storm. Of course, we still needed the little braziers nearby as a source of heat. I lit mine. Its flame was the brightest thing in the landscape. It barely warmed my hands.

The brush felt stiff and unwieldy through my fur-lined gloves. The paint was truculent, congealing from the cold as soon as I got it onto the canvas. I was tempted to paint exactly what I saw: straight lines, black, white, gray. But I knew that a painting like that wouldn't get me into Monet's exhibition. Even if it did, I'd probably be banned from the Academy for life. So instead I began to dab little spots of stiff paint onto the canvas, hoping they would resolve into something recognizable.

Time passed. My painting grew. The scene got more and more ugly. I felt shivers run up the backs of my legs and my spine, as if someone were watching us. My feet, even in their knee-length boots, had somehow gotten wet. I stomped each one to bring life back into my frozen toes. I pulled my hat lower over my forehead and my scarf higher across my nose.

I wasn't going to be the first one to say that we should go

back. René had called me a "lazy dog" the day before, and I wasn't going to give him the satisfaction of seeing me admit to being cold.

Finally, René said, with apparent regret, "The light's changing. We should come back tomorrow." He stood up, stretched, and looked over at me.

Some stubborn streak in my personality made me say, "You go ahead. I want to finish one last thing."

He grinned as if he knew exactly what I was doing, but he packed up and went back to the inn. I counted a hundred frozen puffs of breath before I finally allowed myself to pack up as well. By then the shadows had lengthened. The trees looked as if they had feet and could walk after me. And as I left, I felt more shivers up my back, as if something was indeed following me.

It's just an ordinary lane, I told myself, but I was relieved to get back to the warmth of the inn.

We warmed ourselves at the fire, ate lunch with Madame Moreau, and then finally, in the afternoon, painted one of the beautiful meadows. When the light changed again we came back in. By the time we'd warmed ourselves up this time it was dark.

I hated the winter. I could tell Madame Moreau shared my feelings because that morning on her trip to the village she'd brought back not one, but two round-bellied bottles of wine. We drank one over a lamb cassoulet. We opened our letters.

Neither of us had letters from Monet.

René again imitated two of his lady friends from Paris. I wondered how he had time to find them, with all the painting he did. He was twice as prolific as I was, another reason I worried he would get into the exhibition and I wouldn't. He was even funnier than he'd been the night before, and I laughed, forgetting my earlier disputes with him.

Then I noticed Madame Moreau shift closer to René's side of the table. My good humor vanished.

René opened his third letter, another onionskin one. He barely glanced at it this time before throwing it into the fire. There was something so savage in his expression that he frightened me. Madame Moreau also fell silent, and after a minute René got up, said he was going to the privy, and walked out the back of the inn. René only needed to go off by himself when he was very, very angry. It looked like he would be gone for a while.

Eager to take advantage of being alone with Madame Moreau, I poured her another glass of wine. We finished it, then a second, and soon we were just as merry as before. I let my hand rest over hers on the table, and she let me do it. But when I pressed it more strongly, she drew back.

"No, don't," she said.

"Why not?" I asked.

She said nothing, but her eyes slid toward the vacant seat where René had sat only moments before.

I frowned. "You can't be serious," I said. "Haven't you been listening to him? In another month, he'll be reading your letters to someone else."

She raised her little, pointed chin proudly. "He's twice the man you are," she said.

I sat back. "Perhaps," I said.

Deep down, I believed it was true. A better painter, a better lover, a better man, I thought.

"But it is cruel of you to say so," I said.

She shrugged. The shadows over her collarbones were enchanting, and her eyes looked black in the firelight.

René came back into the room. He didn't notice the silence.

"I'm going to bed," Madame Moreau said. She rose. "Oh! The food for the ghouls . . ."

"Don't worry," René said. He winked at me. "I'll take care of it."

She went upstairs. I didn't watch her go.

The next morning we went upstairs to fetch our half-finished canvases. We stored them in an empty bedroom in the inn, a bright, cheerful room with several windows. Madame Moreau followed us up. She said she wanted to dust. I thought she wanted to see what we had painted.

My painting of the meadow was much prettier than René's, but I gasped when I saw what he'd done with the lane. Madame Moreau went straight up to it and put her fingers out as if she wanted to touch it. I couldn't blame her. He'd slapped the paint on thick, like frosting on a cake. Up close, the paint swirled and squirmed across the canvas in violent colors—yellows, blues, and purples—that I certainly hadn't seen in the lane myself. But ten paces back, the colors coalesced into a frighteningly accurate picture of the snow-covered lane. He'd captured all the eeriness I'd felt the day before. Next to his painting, mine was dull and geometrical. Monet would never have chosen mine.

But René had also added something to his picture that was not in mine—the figure of a woman walking down the lane toward the viewer. That human figure in the center of such bleakness rounded out the picture and made it complete.

I stared at the woman, and I envied René. He'd used only a few splotches of paint, and yet the figure was, unmistakably, a woman, her skirt gray and black, her walk purposeful. A smear of paint indicated a veil over impossibly lovely features.

I stood back. "You cheated," I said.

"What?" The cold yesterday had brought a bloom to René's face.

His blue eyes were bright, his cheeks red. I couldn't blame Madame Moreau for looking at him with such admiration.

"The woman," I said. "You made her up. Monet says Impressionists paint only what they see."

"Don't be ridiculous! She was there yesterday. You saw her yourself."

I shook my head.

"Stop it," René said. "You know you did. About half an hour after we started painting. She walked down the road toward us, then turned off and went between the trees." His lips tightened. "Perhaps I'm just more perceptive than you are, Emile."

I frowned.

"She's not wearing a winter coat," Madame Moreau said softly.

René glared at her. I could tell he was furious that she would take my side and not his.

"Come on, Emile," he said, "I'll prove it to you. We can find her footprints."

We went out, carrying our paintings, easels, and braziers. But it had snowed the night before, and the road was as smooth as an empty canvas. There were no footprints.

"I tell you, I saw her!" he said.

I shrugged. "We may as well finish our paintings while we're here." I felt a strong satisfaction in having caught him out in a lie.

So we again set up on either side of the lane. I could hear René muttering and grumbling to himself.

After about half an hour, René lifted his head and said, "There, I told you so!"

"What?"

"She's there," he said. "I told you."

I looked down the lane. It was the same lane I'd seen moments before. White snow, black trees, gray sky. Empty.

"I don't see anything," I said.

The small slice of his face visible between his hat and scarf turned red with anger. I was angry with him, too, for trying to trick me.

"You missed her," he said. "She just turned off between the trees. She came closer than she did yesterday. She must be some village woman, on the same errand every morning. Come on!"

He jumped up and ran down the lane. I followed him, reluctantly, certain he was lying. My frozen feet were heavy, and I became angrier with him by the step. He stopped so abruptly I ran into him.

"There!" he said in triumph. He pointed at the ground.

Sure enough, something now marred the perfect smoothness of the snow. It wasn't a set of footprints, though. It was a trail a half-meter wide, an indentation in the snow that reminded me of the slime a snail leaves as it passes.

"It does look like something came this way," I said. I remembered Madame Moreau's ghouls—the spirits of the dead, walking in anger. I shivered.

René and I followed the trail. It led us between two trees on the side of the lane and out into the meadow on the other side. It ended a few meters later, and the meadow stretched before us, empty and sparkling. The dark clots of trees on the other side were very far away. It would have been a much better scene to paint than the lane.

"She's gone," he said. "Where did she go?" He looked so frightened I felt sorry for my earlier accusations.

"It's probably just a village woman," I said, "playing a trick on us."

He nodded. Then his face brightened. "I know what the trail is," he said. "It's her skirt."

I nodded, too. A skirt dragging in the snow could have left tracks exactly like that.

Heartened, we went back to our work. It was only as we were

packing up that I realized that, even if her skirt had left a trail, we should still have seen the pointed marks of her boots. And what woman, I thought, wears a long skirt over snow?

That evening René only had two letters. One, on onionskin paper, he threw into the fire unread. The other was from Monet, inviting him to participate in the exhibition. Madame Moreau was so excited for René she kissed him on both cheeks. I tried to be happy for him as well and shook his hand, three times, over the table.

"I'm sure yours will come tomorrow," René said. Even in the midst of his happiness, he looked worried for me.

He is twice the man I am, I thought.

Madame Moreau went to bed first. René ate the ghouls' share of food and then followed her upstairs. I sat in front of the fire, thinking about the woman René had or hadn't seen. I realized he hadn't asked Madame Moreau if there was a woman in the village who walked down the lane every day. I decided to ask Madame Moreau myself. But when I went upstairs to her door, I heard René's voice inside, then Madame Moreau's soft laughter.

I didn't sleep until dawn.

The next day, René insisted on going back to the lane.

"I don't see why you pretend this woman exists," I said, though in fact just the day before I'd believed in her, too—or nearly.

René started to get upset, then stopped. "Look here," he said. "I know you're not really arguing about her. It's about the exhibition, isn't it? I promise I'll put in a good word with Monet."

My face flushed in shame under my scarves.

René smiled, slowly. "Or is it about Madame Moreau?"

I turned away.

He laughed. "You can have her," he said. "I just don't want you to be angry with me."

I looked back at him and realized he meant everything he said. He did want me to be his friend. He believed that he had the power to make me happy, with a word to Monet, a word to Madame Moreau. He was absolutely confident of this. His confidence made me furious.

I shook my head. "She doesn't want me," I said.

He looked hurt, as if I'd rejected him by not taking advantage of his generosity. Then he shrugged and started to paint.

I didn't even try to work. I stared at the ugly canvas I had painted. I stared at the ugly, snow-covered lane. I wished I had never left Paris. I imagined burning my painting, to finally get some decent color into it.

"There she is again," René said.

His voice was low, as if he were trying not to startle her. I looked up. Again, I saw nothing. René's eyes twitched, as if watching something I couldn't see. I couldn't feel my hands or my feet. My brazier went out.

"She's coming closer this time," René said. "She's past the spot where she turned off yesterday."

He turned to me, pulling the scarf off his mouth in his eagerness. "This time we can catch her," he said. He sprang to his feet. "Come on!"

I looked at him. I was cold, and I remembered the voices in Madame Moreau's bedroom the night before. I remembered Monet's letter. I remembered René's other jokes at my expense. I could have stopped him. I could have gone with him. But I just shook my head.

His chin came up in a proud gesture that reminded me of Madame Moreau, a gesture that rejected me as utterly as I had just rejected him. At that moment, our friendship was over.

He turned and walked down the lane. From the square, masculine set of his shoulders I knew he was afraid.

"Hello, mademoiselle!" he called out to the blank air. "Excuse me for a moment. Mademoiselle?" He walked on a few paces more.

"She's coming closer," he called out.

I knew he was calling to me. I knew he wanted me to join him. But I didn't move.

"She's lifting her veil!"

Then René screamed. It was a high-pitched scream, more like a cat than a man. He stiffened, as if he'd been struck. "No! Not you!" he shouted. A strange blur rippled across his back. It reminded me of the paint smear of the veil covering the mysterious woman's face on his painting. Then the blur separated, like two arms wrapped around him, and his body crumpled to the ground.

When I reached René, stumbling on my frozen feet, the lane was silent again. I fell to my knees in the snow next to him. I could feel the cold seeping into the knees of my trousers. I rolled René over. His body was a dead weight. His blue eyes were still bright, but his lips were black, as if they'd been brushed with poison.

I looked around. My heart pounded, and my breath steamed in the air. But I was the only living thing in the landscape

The wide-brushed trail on the snow ended at René's body.

The doctor we got in from the village said it had been a seizure of some sort. He couldn't explain the black lips, except to say that strange things happened to bodies in the cold. None of this comforted Madame Moreau, who glared at me as if I had murdered René. In a way, I felt I had.

René's family sent someone down on the train to take his body back to Paris. I was supposed to pack his things and leave the next day. Madame Moreau and I ignored each other in the evening, and the house was silent that night.

I slept late the morning of my departure. I came down at noon to find her sitting at the kitchen table where she and René and I had laughed so much just a few nights before. She'd been to the village, and a pool of letters lay in her lap. One of them, written on onion-skin paper, lay open on the table in front of her.

She looked up as I came in. Her cheeks were red and her eyes starry. She'd been crying. "I was wrong," she said. "You were the better man." She pushed the letter toward me. "And I hate you for it." The proud, pointed chin trembled. She ran past me and up the stairs.

I looked at the piece of fragile, yellowish paper. There were two notes written on it. The top one was in the familiar, spidery hand-writing, addressing René and asking—no, begging—for a hundred francs. It was signed simply, "Your true love, Sandrine."

The sentences at the bottom of the page were in a stronger, firmer hand. Even the ink was darker. A Dr. Langmuir wished to inform Mr. Saint-Jean that Mademoiselle Chambord had died the day before at noon, in childbirth. "Mademoiselle," the doctor added, "had been suffering from severe malnutrition and cold." The letter was dated three days before.

I sat in front of the fire. I thought about how cold Paris had been that winter—the coldest winter in ten years. I thought about how much money René had spent to come to Rochebleu to paint. I thought about the woman in the lane yesterday, and that she had appeared three days ago, around noon. The same day and time Mademoiselle Chambord had died.

Then I went upstairs and packed René's things and my own. I waited until I was finished with everything else before going into the spare bedroom to fetch our paintings. There were four. Just four. We'd planned to spend the entire winter painting, and to come back to Paris with at least a hundred. For once, Rene's plans had not worked out.

I missed him terribly.

On impulse, I uncovered René's painting of the lane. Monet would love the painting. I was tempted to sign my own name to it. Who would know? An innkeeper's wife in the countryside? The ghouls?

The woman without a winter coat looked desolate and alone in the dead landscape. But there was something terrible in her desolation. I looked at the smear of veil over her face. I put my face up to the painting until she dissolved into dots. I could have sworn she was smiling.

I covered up the painting.

I carried the paintings downstairs. The cart had arrived to take me to the train station, and I loaded my things. I went back into the kitchen, hoping that Madame Moreau would come down. I waited, watching the driver outside stamp his feet as he got colder. I thought that if she came down, somehow something good would have come of the winter. I wanted to go upstairs and knock on her door, but I didn't.

She didn't come down. Finally, I went outside and jumped up into the cart. The driver glared at me from between his layers of scarves, cracked his whip in the air, and drove me away.

WHOSE GHOSTS
THESE ARE

by Charles L. Grant

The street does not change morning to night. Shops open, shops close; pedestrians walk the crooked sidewalks, with or without burden, peering in the store windows, wishing, coveting, moving on; vans and trucks make their deliveries and leave, while automobiles avoid it because it curves so sharply, so often. To walk from one end to the other is like following the dry bed of a long-dead stream that snakes from no place to nowhere.

None of the buildings here are more than four stories high, though they seem much taller because the street itself is so narrow. They are old, these buildings, but they are not frail. They are well-kept, mostly, almost equally divided between brick and granite facades with occasional wood trim of various colors. Nothing special about them; nothing to draw a camera lens or a sketchpad, a commemorative plaque, a footnote in a tourist guide. Stores, a few offices, at ground level on both ends, apartments and offices above; in the middle, apartment buildings with stone stairs and stoops, aged white medallions of mythical creatures over each lintel. Gateless iron-spear fences, small plots of grass, flower boxes, trees at the curb.

Nothing changes, and Hank Cabot liked it that way.

He walked this tree-lined block and the surrounding neighborhood for close to fifteen years, his uniform so familiar that in his civilian clothes people he saw every day sometimes had to look at him twice just to be sure he was who they thought he was. An almost comical look as well, as if he had shaved off a mustache and they weren't quite able to make out what was different about him.

It was a partial anonymity that he had never been able to decide was good or bad.

Retirement, on the other hand, was, in the beginning, good.

He had loved his blue tunic and the brass buttons and the polished belt with its gleaming attachments, refusing promotions once he reached sergeant because he'd wanted nothing to do with the politics of being an officer, nothing to do with other parts of the city, nothing to do with anything but his job as he eventually defined and refined it.

He was a beat cop, nothing more, nothing less.

He wrote parking tickets and scolded kids who taunted other kids and old folks; he investigated minor break-ins and petty theft; he had heart-to-hearts with shoplifters and angry spouses; he broke up fights and arrested drunks and gossiped and swapped jokes and had once spent an hour on a damp stoop with a little girl, trying to reattach the head of her doll.

He was a beat cop.

And now, at long last in his mid-fifties, he was something else, and he wasn't sure yet what that was.

That was the bad part.

In a way, it was kind of funny, that first day away from the job. He had slept in, a sinful luxury whose guilt he had cheerfully grinned away; he had made a slow breakfast and read the paper and did a little cleaning of his second-floor apartment; and when at last habit grabbed him by the scruff, he had taken out a new denim jacket and gone for a walk. The street first, of course, then several others north and south. Not too far afield, but far enough. Restraining himself from checking closed shop doors, the timing on parking meters, the alleys between buildings, the empty lots.

It had been an effort.

It had nearly worn him out.

It hadn't been until that evening, while he ate a sandwich in front of his living room window and watched the street put itself to bed, that he'd realized no one had greeted him with anything more than a polite nod, or complained to him and whined about how the injustices of the city had settled upon their shoulders and why the hell couldn't he do something about it.

The good part was, he didn't have to answer them anymore, didn't have to lie or be a confessor or a teacher or a parent who happened to have a gun on his hip.

The bad part was . . . nights when he couldn't sleep because he was supposed to be on shift, nights when he slept and didn't dream and woke up feeling as if he'd walked a hundred miles with a hundred-pound pack on his back, nights when nightmares of horribly distorted and twisted faces pressing close to his sat him up and made him scream—except the scream was only a hoarse croaking, and the nightmare itself eventually began to lose some of its terror when he figured they were the faces of the angry victims he couldn't help and the angry culprits he had apprehended over the course of thirty years.

A year later, he and the nightmares had become old friends, but his friends on the street still looked at him oddly.

"It'll take some getting used to, you know," said Lana Hynes for at least the hundredth time, dropping into the chair opposite him at the Caulberg Luncheonette. She fanned an order pad at her neck as if it were muggy July instead of the cool middle of October. "For them too, I mean. All this time, they don't know what you look like."

"Oh, yeah, sure. I've lived here forever, right? I didn't have the uniform on all the time."

But he thought he knew what she meant. He was, in or out of the Blue, nothing special. Not tall, a slight paunch, a face faintly ruddy, red hair fading much too swiftly to gray. An ordinary voice. Cops hated people like him—no one ever knew what they really looked like.

She grinned then, more like a smirk, and he felt a blush work its way toward his cheeks. This time he knew exactly what she meant. They had been lovers once, before he jilted her for the Job, and now, for better or worse, they were friends. So much so, it seemed, that lately she had taken to ignoring him when he came in, just to tick him off so she could tease him about it later.

"Knock it off," he muttered at that grin, grabbing his burger quickly, taking a bite.

"Why, Mr. Cabot, I am sure I do not know what you mean." A laugh soft in her throat, and she leaned forward, crinkling the front of her red-and-white uniform blouse, the one that matched the checkered floor, the tablecloths, the pattern around the edge of the menu. It drove her crazy, and frankly he was getting a little tired of hearing about it.

"The bill," was all he said.

She scowled. "Screw you, Cabot."

His turn to grin: "Been there, done that."

A close thing, then: would she slap him or laugh?

It startled him to realize that he had, at some imprecise moment on some non-momentous day, stopped caring very much. Startled him, then saddened him, then angered him that she didn't realize it herself. Maybe it was time to start eating somewhere else.

All this in the space of a second, maybe two.

Damn, he thought; what the hell's the matter with you, pal?

She neither slapped nor laughed. She tapped a pencil against her pad and said, "So, you been to that museum yet?"

Curtly: "No."

"Well, why not?" Her own red hair fell in carefully arranged curls over one eye. "I'd've thought you'd like something like that. All those bad-guy exhibits. You know, like that Ghost guy."

"That Ghost guy," he said, knowing he sounded stuffy, "is a killer, Lana. Nothing interesting about him, not at all. And I had enough of that on the Job, thank you."

A hand reached out and slapped his arm lightly. "Oh, please, give me a break, okay? No offense, but it's not like you were a detective. You didn't work with dead bodies every day, you know?"

"Yeah, maybe, but still . . ."

An impatient call from the counter brought her to her feet. She dropped his bill on the table, leaned over to kiss his cheek. And whispered in his ear: "It's been over a year, Hank. Do something different for a change, before you turn into an old woman."

He nodded automatically, gave her an automatic "Yes, dear," and laughed silently when she slapped him across the back of his head. Not so lightly. Another laugh, and he looked out at the street while he finished his lunch. The trees had turned, and sweaters and lined jackets had been rescued from storage. A puff of autumn cold surged against his ankles each time the door opened. A pleasant shiver, a comfortable reminder how of miserable the previous summer had been and how far away the next one was.

He spent the afternoon at a high school football game. He didn't know the teams, didn't know the schools, just enjoyed the hot dogs and the soda and the cheerleaders who made him feel exceedingly old. A fair-to-middling dinner at a small Italian restaurant took him past nightfall, and he decided to walk off all the wine he had drunk.

With his collar snapped up and his hands deep in his pockets, he moved through the fleeting clouds of his breath, instinctively watching the dark that hid behind all the lights. The shadows he made as he passed under streetlamps swung around him, fascinated him for a while so that he wondered if, like fingerprints, everyone's shadow was different. When the angle was right, the light just so, his shadow took to a low brick wall and paced him a few strides, and he decided they weren't like fingerprints at all. They were like ghosts who gave you an idea of what it would be like to be dead.

Damn, he thought, and cast his attention out to the city instead. Where he glowered at a young couple arguing under the canopy of a luxury apartment building, whistled softly at a cat watching him narrow-eyed from a garbage can lid. A taxi nearly ran him down when it took a corner too tightly; his footsteps sounded too sharp, and for half a block he tried to walk on his toes.

Halloween decorations everywhere, here and there mixed in with cardboard turkeys and cartoonlike Pilgrims. One damn store even had its Christmas lights up.

He felt his temper, so long with him it was like an old comfortable coat, beginning to wear thin at the edges. A shift of his shoulders, a brief massage to the back of his neck and he quickened his pace, anxious to get to the three rooms that were his. The second-hand furniture, the old-fashioned kitchen, the rust-ring around the tub's drain that had been there when he'd moved in. It wasn't the warmth or the comfort; he just wanted to be away from the streets, the people, the traffic . . . the city.

Breathing hard. Watching his shadow. Following his shadow until he blinked and found himself at the living room window, staring down at the trees that smothered most of the night's artificial light, leaving specks of it on the pavement, shimmering as an autumn wind rose while the moon set unseen.

A deep breath, a sigh for all the wine that had stolen some of his time, and he slept most of the day away. It felt good. It made him smile. Another habit broken, and he treated himself to dinner and a movie, and walked home again. He liked it so much he did it again a few nights later, and again the night after that, and a few nights after that, taking a childlike pleasure in once in a while losing track of the hour. No schedules, no meetings; just him and the street that never changes, morning to night.

A week after Halloween he finally returned to Caulberg's for an early supper. His usual table was already occupied, so he took a stool at the counter, waiting patiently for Lana to acknowledge him. When at last she did, with a look he knew well—*it's about time, you son of a bitch*—he felt a momentary crush of guilt for ignoring her for so long. She was a good friend, after all; probably . . . no, absolutely his only friend. But his temper came instantly to attention when she slapped a cup and saucer in front of him, poured coffee and said, "Well, look who's here. The Lone Stranger."

"Sorry," he said flatly. "Been busy."

"Too busy to stick your head in, say hi or something?"

He shrugged a weak apology. "Been busy."

"Yeah, right."

He tried a smile. "Hey, I'm retired, remember? Things to do, places to see. I'm going to the Riviera next weekend."

Her expression suggested his eyes had changed to a none-too-subtle brown, and she moved away to place his order, take care of the only other customer at the counter, slip into the kitchen without looking his way again. She didn't return until his hamburger was ready, and she delivered it as if she were slapping his face with a glove.

He leaned back and gave her a look; she stepped back and folded her arms across her chest and gave him a look.

They stared at each other for several seconds before her lips twitched, and he pulled his lips in between his teeth.

"Laugh and you die, Cabot," she said.

He nodded; the tension vanished.

She stepped back to the counter and leaned over it, forearms braced on the surface, her face only a few inches from his. "The thing is, Cabot," she said, keeping her voice down, checking to be sure no one could eavesdrop, "we don't like it when you disappear, okay? I know what you think, but we depend on having you here all the time, just in case."

"But I'm not a cop any—"

She shook her head. "It doesn't make any difference."

"And they barely—"

"It doesn't make any difference."

"But—"

She grabbed his chin and held it tightly. "Listen to me, you old creep, and none of your false modesty or any of that other crap, okay? We're worried about you." She nodded sharply, once. "You are, whether you know it or not, kind of important to us. God knows why, but you are. When you go off like that without telling anybody, it makes us nervous. I mean, that damn Ghost freak did it again last week. What, the fifth? The sixth time? Since July? They still don't know who the body belongs to." Her hand slipped away as she straightened, lay flat against her stomach. "We thought it was you, you son of a bitch. We thought he'd gotten you."

He almost said, *we, or you?* but for a change he kept silent. Instead he looked at his meal, tilted his head to one side in a brief shrug, not knowing what to say. All his complaining, and he had had no idea. None at all.

She pointed at his plate. "Eat," she ordered. "Then get a god-damn hobby."

"Oh, right, like Dutch?"

Dutch Heinrich owned the butcher shop around the corner. This week, on top of his window display case, was a three-foot-tall cathedral fashioned entirely out of toothpicks, none of which were immediately visible because of the way the man had painted the model. It looked carved from stone.

Finally she smiled. "You could do worse. He sells those stupid things for a fortune." A wink, then; an eyebrow cocked; a gentle smile. "Just do it, Hank. Stop lying to yourself, you're bored as hell. Make us all happy, just do it."

A promise to think about it, a command from her that just thinking about it wasn't an option, and she left him alone to eat. As he did, he wondered; when he left, he headed for the small park a few blocks up, and it wasn't until he realized he had spent a full hour watching two very nearsighted old men playing a truly bad game of chess that he finally understood his yearlong vacation was over. Fifty-something, with probably another thirty to go.

Good God, he thought, I'll probably shoot myself next Christmas, and won't Lana be pissed.

He laughed aloud, and the old men glared without really see-ing him. He gave them a jaunty salute and whistled himself back home, and to a vow that tomorrow he would either find himself a part-time job or a time-gobbling hobby.

Which might be, he thought when he saw the next morning's newspaper, filing the necessary applications for an investigator's license. Job or hobby, it would give him an official-sounding excuse to be nosy. To poke around, uncover the true identity of the man they called the Ghost.

He had killed again.

The sixth time since the end of July, the second time in a week. There wasn't much in the article, aside from recycled quotes from psychologists and criminal experts about the mind of such a man, but the police vowed they were on it with promising leads in an intense investigation. He snorted. He had heard that story before—it meant the victims had no common ground, no links; the cops hadn't a clue and weren't about to get one. The worst kind of killer—completely random. He also knew there had to be more; something had been held back from the public so the nuts and habitual confessers could be weeded out. He leaned back in his chair, stared blindly at the kitchen ceiling. He could call in a favor or two, find out what the missing information was, and take it from there.

"Sure," he said to the ceiling light. "Take it where?"

He had a better question: "Why?"

Because it was interesting? Fascinating? A puzzle that wanted solving? A chance for a little action? An opportunity to do something valuable with his time? A way to get himself involved with the public again?

A way to justify the block's belief in him? Concern for him?

He made a derisive noise deep in his throat, folded the paper to put the sports section on top—to read whenever he returned from wherever he would go to pass the daylight hours—and pushed his chair back. Flattened his palms on the small table and pushed himself to his feet.

Why?

Because Lana was right. He was goddamned bored out of his goddamn mind, that's why.

Which wasn't the real reason, and he knew it, but it would do for now. It would have to.

He walked.

He window-shopped.

He spent some time in a showroom, pretending he was thinking about buying a car.

He had lunch in a place he had never been to before; he spent a couple of hours on a tourist bus, seeing things he had never seen before; he watched the sunset from a bench in a park he had never been to, and when the sun's reflection slid out of the windows and let in the dark, he flipped up his collar and made his way to a bus stop, where a trio of kids cut in front of him so they could get on first. When he said, "Hey, damnit," only one looked back, gave him a sorry-didn't-see-you shrug; the others played push-and-shove until they found their seats.

Hank didn't get on.

He let the bus go, turned away from the exhaust wash, let his temper subside to a more manageable level. It wasn't easy. His jaw was so taut it trembled, and heat behind his eyes made him slightly dizzy until he closed them tightly. It wasn't easy. If he had had the uniform, they wouldn't have done it. Maybe they would have been just as smartass, just as rude, but they wouldn't have done it.

Uniform or no, they never did it to him on the block.

A step back from the curb, head lowered, throat working to

swallow, he stared at the tips of his shoes until the night's chill and the traffic's clamor forced him to move.

He found the museum a few minutes later.

There was nothing special about it that he could see—a single door in a narrow building that could have used renovation a decade or two ago. Lana hadn't been here herself; it was one of those heard-about-it-from-a-friend things, but she figured he would be interested, being a cop and all.

He hadn't been, and had avoided actively searching for it since she first brought it up.

He was a beat cop, for God's sake. Didn't she understand that? An ordinary beat cop. He saw bodies, he saw blood, he saw the instruments that had drawn one from the other, but he wasn't the one who hunted the killers down. No, he was the one who found what was left of their prey.

On the other hand, he thought as he glanced up and down the avenue, feeling vaguely uneasy, as if he were about to walk into a porn shop or something, maybe this was a sign. What the hell. At the very least, it would keep her off his back for a while.

He grunted, shook his head quickly, scolded himself for being unfair. She meant well. She cared.

The museum door opened, and he looked down in surprise at the hand, his hand, that had turned the dull brass knob.

Okay, it was a sign.

A half-smile took him over the threshold and out of the cold. A brief unsettling sensation of déjà vu before he noticed a tiny wood table on his left that held an untidy stack of pamphlets—*The Museum of Horror Presents*. He took one, opened it, and realized the light was so dim he practically had to put his nose through the thin paper in order to read it. A simple diagram of the interior, a few words, not much else. The main premise seemed to be that he had to discover for himself the details of the exhibits. Which were sealed upright cases ranged along narrow aisles, glass cases touched with dust and annoying flared reflections of small caged bulbs hanging from the ceiling, cases whose contents startled him when he walked past, only glancing in until he finally understood what he had seen.

"You're kidding me," he said quietly.

The preserved bodies, or damn fine replicas, purportedly those of murderers of the first rank, criminals of the mind, villains of the body. Supposed personal items tucked around their feet and on small glass shelves. He recognized none of the names, none of the crimes, but it didn't make any difference; it was bad enough looking at the corpses, real or not; it was worse reading what they were supposed to have done.

Soft voices and whispers from other parts of the large room.

Soft footsteps and whispering soles.

The impulse to giggle in such a solemn place became an urge, and he rubbed a hard hand across his lips. A second time, harder, for a shot of pain to kill the laugh. Sniffing, grabbing a handkerchief to blow his nose and wincing at the explosive sound of it; wandering the aisles, reading the legends now, thinking the curator or whatever he was called had one hell of an imagination. In spite of himself, stopping now and then to examine a body, the clothes, flicking dust away to peer more closely at a face.

Soft voice.

Soft footsteps.

A check over his shoulder now and then, but he saw no one else. Only heard them, felt them, had almost convinced himself he was in here with ghosts when, rounding a corner, he nearly collided with a woman, a teenager really, whose eyes widened as large as her mouth when it opened to scream.

"Jesus, where the hell did you come from?"

He grinned. "I'm haunting the place."

Too much makeup, hair cropped unevenly, she sneered thick lips at him and huffed away. "Stupid creep," she muttered.

He scowled at her back, half tempted to call after her and demand . . . what? What the hell was he getting so pissed about? They had startled each other, they were mad because they'd been scared, what's the big deal, Hank?

He scratched the back of his neck, pulled at his nose, and looked at the case immediately to his left.

It was empty; a little hazy because of the light dust, but still, it was empty.

Yet there was a card, just like all the others, and this one claimed that what he saw, or didn't see, was the mortal remains of the recent serial killer known as the Ghost. It took him a few seconds of frowning before he caught the joke and smiled. Nodded his appreciation. Looked around, wishing there were someone nearby with whom he could share the curator's bizarre sense of humor.

No one.

He was alone.

And being alone, he checked again to be sure he was right, then reached out a finger and drew it gently along the case's seams, stretching to reach to the top, bending over to reach the bottom. The glass felt warm, but comfortably so, and there was a faint vibration, the traffic outside, footsteps in here. It would be cozy inside, he figured, and almost laughed again. Cozy. Snug. The Ghost making faces at those whose peered in, trying to make sense of what they weren't seeing.

This time he couldn't stop the laugh, and didn't want to.

"Boo!" he said to his reflection in the glass, and feigned stark terror, clamping a hand to his heart, staggering backward, nearly colliding with the exhibit behind him.

"Boo!" he said through a deep rippling laugh, and wiped a tear from one eye, pressed a hand to his side where a stitch had stabbed him.

He was coming apart, he knew it, and he didn't give a damn.

"Boo!" one last time, and he made his way to the exit, giggling, shaking his head and chuckling, on the street laughing so loudly he embarrassed himself even though he was alone.

He felt . . . great.

In front of Dutch's closed butcher shop he applauded when he saw that the cathedral was gone. Another sale. Bravo. Bravo.

He patrolled the neighborhood, just like the old days, and like the old days saved his street for last. He didn't mind the damp November cold that seeped up his sleeves and down his collar, the way the few remaining leaves hustled after him on the wind, the way his footsteps sounded flat, not October sharp.

He didn't mind at all.

He patrolled until near sunrise, then slept the sun to bed, no nightmares, no croaking screams.

Just before Thanksgiving, Lana commented on his attitude as she served him his steak and potatoes dinner. "Jesus, Cabot," she said, "it's like you're almost cheerful for a change."

And he repaid her by leaning over the counter, taking hold of her arm, and planting a big one on her lips. "Why, thank you, my dear," he said as he sat back on his stool, picked up his knife and fork, and gave his meal a smile.

Lana, startled into silence, could only swallow, and touch her lips with a finger as if to test them. A dreamy smile, a scowl at her reaction, and when he finished she said, "Hank, you all right? You're not . . . I mean, like, on drugs or something?" A finger pointed. "And don't you dare say you're just high on life."

"My hobby," he told her, dropping the price of his supper on the counter.

"You're joking, right?"

"Nope." He struck a pose. "You want to hear one?"

"One what?"

"Poem."

Her mouth opened, closed, and he said, "Whose ghosts these are I think I know/ Their graves are in my dreams, you know."

She waited.

He watched her.

She said, "Is that it?"

He shrugged as he zipped up his jacket. "I'm still working on it."

"It . . . kind of sounds familiar."

"Maybe," he said as he walked toward the door, a wave over his shoulder. "Maybe not."

Maybe, he thought as he caught the next bus uptown; maybe not.

He returned to the museum and gave himself five minutes before he made his way to the Ghost case, touched the seams and found them cold. His eyes closed briefly. His stomach lurched. He held one arm away from his body, for balance. He made his way carefully to the sidewalk where he looked up at a sky the city's lights robbed of stars and moon. He didn't move until a gust of wind nudged him; he didn't choose a direction until he reached a corner and turned it; he told himself he didn't know what he was doing until he recognized his home, and saw a man in a topcoat and felt hat urinating against one of the iron-spear fences.

"Hey," he said, his voice quiet but mildly angry. "Kids play there, you know."

The man zippered himself and buttoned his coat. "You a cop?"

"Nope."

"Then screw you, pal," and he walked away.

Hank watched him go, looked at the windows above him, across the street, saw shades glow and dark curtains, and imagined he could hear the sounds of sleep and making love and television shows and stereos and children dreaming and old folks dying.

I'm a beat cop, for God's sake.

Stop lying to yourself, Lana had told him.

So he did.

He followed the man in the expensive topcoat for several blocks, out of the neighborhood and into a street where there was more night than nightlights. He moved swiftly without seeming to, and when the man turned around, glaring at the intrusion, Hank took him by the throat with one hand and held him, knowing now, aware now, what the published reports did not say—that the bodies were somehow thinner. Older. Maybe drained, but not of blood or bone or muscle.

Hank held the topcoat man until he crumpled into the gutter, his hat rolling into the center of the street, stopping upside down. A sigh, but no regrets, and he took a bus uptown for the second time that night, and did not marvel that the museum was still open. He went straight to the Ghost's case and ran his fingertips along the seams, feeling the cold eventually, slowly, become warm, watching the haze inside thicken . . . just a little. Placed a palm against the front and felt that faint vibration—not traffic or footsteps, it was the reverberation of faint screams.

If he looked closely enough, hard enough, he might even see his nightmare, not a nightmare any longer.

A quick smile, a ghost of a smile, and he left for home and slept the sun to bed.

Comforted in knowing that outside the street never changes from morning to night.

Comforted too in knowing that at night the street is haunted.

PERDIDO
A Fragment from a Work in Progress

by Peter Straub

PART ONE: GETTING THERE

1

Margie flew up the narrow trail as if climbing a mountain in a tight skirt and two-inch heels was like walking around the block. The ivory rectangle of the pet carrier swung beside her legs. Through the mesh at its back end now and then flashed Pillow's platinum coat. Carver had resisted bringing the cat to Perdido, but he had also resisted Perdido. Now Margie, burdened only by the pet carrier and a knapsack the size of a Filofax, scampered into shimmering grey haze while he trudged sweating after, strapped into two hanging bags and pulling a wheeled carry-on with each hand. He was thirty yards behind and losing ground with every step. If Silsbee had been obliged to describe his sojourn at the odd resort still half an hour distant, which of course he had been, Silsbee being a great reveler in descriptions of the pleasures beyond the reach of his friend, Carver wished he had chosen to revel when Margie was out of earshot.

Yet who would have imagined that the description should have intrigued Margie, who had always taken Silsbee with a generous spoonful of disdain? She had once called him "that lunatic friend of yours, the dentist." It was no use protesting that Silsbee was neither insane nor, technically speaking, a dentist. He was a periodontist. No periodontist, especially one so spectacularly successful, could be crazy, even if he carried on like Silsbee.

"Amazing place, utterly . . ." Silsbee had leaned back, on the fatal evening, in his lounge chair and gestured at the rank of lighted windows arrayed below, at the river and the horizon of neon and tumbling clouds. He had interrupted his revel to insert into his mouth a massive cigar of Cuban provenance. The desire for nicotine had banished them to the Carver terrace. Silsbee's lighter hissed and flared, and a fragrant exhalation accompanied the strategic adjective: " . . . astonishing."

Carver emitted gouts of smoke recycled from a Marlboro Light.

"Perdido never advertises. It's never written up in the usual magazines. They don't want publicity. The right people will hear about it for themselves."

"People like you," Carver had said.

"How many people like me do you know?" asked the amused Silsbee. "It isn't *that* particular. They just have to be right for the place. People who don't mind dealing with the unexpected. You could say, people who *prefer* the unexpected. Who want more from a vacation than a good beach, decent meals, and a steady supply of rum. Mind you, I'm not saying it isn't comfortable. Perdido can beat any resort hotel you've ever seen for blind staggering opulence, if that's what you're after."

Silsbee may have smiled. He released a luxuriant plume of smoke. "By comparison, the places whose entire point is opulence are unforgivably boring. You think you'd enjoy that, Bobby, I know, but let me tell you what happens. Two days of unadulterated luxury, and you're not just sated, you're stifled. Doesn't matter where you are, Bali, Mustique, wherever, doesn't matter that beautiful women cater to your every whim, that your clothes are laundered and pressed every night, that every step you take is enveloped in a sacred hush of privilege and gratification, you're sound asleep with your eyes open. I've had enough of that. Never again. Not after Perdido. And the other ones, if I can swing it."

Margie, who seldom participated in her husband's evenings with Silsbee, surprised Carver by sliding into the adjacent chair. "This resort is part of a chain?"

"My dear," Silsbee said, "you grace us with your company, how delightful. No, the other ones are part of the same facility, except for being separate."

"Separate," Margie said. "But equal."

"Not at all," said Silsbee. "That's why they're separate. The other two are farther up the mountain."

"Ah," Margie said. "Where is this mountain? Nowhere in America, I bet."

Silsbee revolved the tip of his cigar in the ashtray and amputated two inches of cylindrical gray ash. In the twilight, his skin was smoothly, handsomely dark. His black hair gleamed. "Norway, actually."

"A Norwegian mountain," said Margie. "What's the name of this mountain?"

Silsbee's expression lost a degree of self-satisfaction. "The name doesn't matter. Would you like to know what does?"

"You're dying to tell me. All right, what matters?"

"The process of application and acceptance, to begin with," Silsbee said. "The way you let them know *you* know. How you find out you've made the grade. What happens when you do. There might be other ways of being admitted to Perdido, but this is the method that was described to me. You place a personal ad in the Friday *Times*. 'If invited, will accept.' You give your name and address. I gather they do some research. If they decide to take you, two weeks later a messenger delivers an envelope. Inside the envelope is a letter. Someone named E. Bantling welcomes you to an unprecedented experience and explains the next few steps. There's also a first-class ticket from JFK to Oslo on an airline you never heard of. The flight leaves at noon the next day."

"What airline?" Margie asked. "Why 'someone named' E. Bantling?"

"Chariot Air," said Silsbee. He laughed. "I suspect that 'E. Bantling' doesn't exist."

"I suspect Chariot Air doesn't, either," Margie said. "I've been to JFK a thousand times, but I never saw Chariot listed on any of those signs."

"Margie," Silsbee said. "Please. Does it sound as though you go out to the street and hail a cab? A limousine picks you up at eight forty-five on Saturday morning. Before the exit for JFK, the driver gets on an unmarked road leading to a long, low brick building. You're nowhere near the other terminals. Inside, it looks like the lobby of a London hotel catering to Agatha Christie characters. Club chairs and leather sofas, fellows in swallow-tailed coats who serve tea and whisper that the management discourages conversation between guests not previously acquainted. When I went, there were only two couples besides me, and I wasn't tempted to talk to them, anyhow."

"Why not?" Carver asked. "You're a talkative guy."

"Instinct. You know how you're supposed to act. About fifteen minutes after I arrived, we were led on board a plane like a corporate jet divided into compartments. *Extraordinarily* comfortable. Good food and great wines. Choice of a movie—*any* movie. You have your own monitor. I asked for *The Fountainhead*, Gary Cooper and Patricia Neal. Beautiful film, a masterpiece, but I didn't think for a second that they'd have it. The steward went away and came back with the tape. Ate my Dover sole, enjoyed my Meursault, watched the movie, dozed off and woke up just before landing. In Oslo, we were whisked through Customs and driven to the Grand Palace Hotel. Room service produces what seems to be breakfast for six. You enjoy a nap. A fellow directs you to the roof and a waiting helicopter. For two, two and a half hours, you fly north. I suppose it's north. The pilot doesn't utter a word. All you see are lakes and forests. Deep, deep green, deep, deep blue, the way the world must have looked before human beings loused it up. So beautiful you damn near weep. The helicopter lands in a meadow at the base of a mountain. The pilot unloads your bags and points at the mountain. You pick up your bags and start walking. Then you see a trail going up the mountain, and you carry your shit up the path."

"That's a nice touch," Margie said.

Silsbee chuckled. "Oh, you entertain some doubts, I'll grant you that. But an hour later, there it is, Perdido, right in front of you. Breathtaking. Looks so much like Shangri-La, you can almost hear the soundtrack."

"I don't get the part about the other two," Margie said. "The ones that aren't equal."

Silsbee released another fragrant cloud. "Mordido's another

hour up the mountain. Endido's close to the summit, but we're talking about a *Norwegian* mountain, not an Alp. Margie, with your legs? You could walk up there in maybe three-four hours, never break a sweat."

Margie had not responded to this provocation. "If you're so much in love with this place, why aren't you talking about making a return visit farther up the mountain? Can't swing it? Too expensive, even for you?"

Silsbee frowned less at Carver's wife than at what appeared a breach in his self-esteem. "No, money doesn't come into it." The tip of the cigar traced a wavering red line in the darkening air. "Perdido isn't like that."

"Of course not," Margie said. "Still. All these limousines and private jets, these hotel suites, these helicopters, doesn't that add up? Joe Schmoe and his wife aren't going to be drinking champagne and gobbling caviar in your mysterious terminal."

"True," said Silsbee. "Perdido isn't for Mr. and Mrs. Joe Schmoe. But you're charged no more than you can afford, whatever that is. Sliding scale. Within reason, naturally."

"Within some people's idea of reason."

"Within yours and Bobby's, certainly. Money is not the issue."

"Ah, we're back to acceptance, then," Margie said.

"You're saying *we* could afford this place?" Carver asked.

Silsbee had ignored him. He was looking at Margie in appreciative contemplation. "You're right—*exactly* right. Everyone who visits Perdido wants to go back, but everyone doesn't make the cut. They only select those whom they've decided are ready for the next step."

"In other words, Mordido," Margie said. "Where you can go only if you've already been to Perdido and used the right forks at the dinner table. And remembered to put your napkin back in the napkin-ring. Or whatever they judge you on."

"I don't suppose table manners would be their primary concern. It's whether or not you seem right for them. Pass muster, you move up to the next level."

"How many Perdido-ites make it to Mordido?"

"About a third, say, at a guess. They never talk about this, you understand, you have to figure it out for yourself. One afternoon while you're strolling through the gardens, you notice a group wandering across the lawn. They look completely at home. Three nights later, you spot them at the edge of a fancy-dress party. They seem set apart, enjoying themselves without quite participating. The group drifts out onto the terrace, and you trail along behind them. By the time you reach the terrace, they're already moving through the gardens. You turn to one of the staff and say, 'Who are those people?' He says, 'Our Mordido guests often like to pop back in for a visit, sir.' "

"And the guests from Endido? Do they ever drop in?"

"Not as far as I know," Silsbee said. "But they must be extraordinary."

"It's a cruise ship," Margie said. "People in first class wander wherever they please, but if you're anywhere else, you can only wander down."

"It's nothing like a cruise ship," said Silsbee. "I grant the point about mobility."

"Poor Silsbee," Margie said. "After passing all the tests to get into this place, you discover you're in steerage."

"Oh, everyone begins in steerage," Silsbee said. "You start with Perdido, no matter who you are. Next summer, I have hopes of spending two weeks farther up the mountain. If you can forgive this blatant immodesty, I think my chances are pretty good."

"Immodesty?" Margie asked. "Bobby and I are shocked."

"Then let me be immodest on your behalf. Bobby, you and

239

Margie could get into Perdido. Why not treat yourselves to an experience you'll never forget?"

Carver said, "You're kidding."

"Our friendship would count in your favor, of course."

Margie snickered. "Bad, *bad* Silsbee."

"But what happens at this place?" Carver had asked. "Once you spend an hour humping your bags up the mountainside and get to Shangri-La, do you play golf and tennis and take yoga lessons? Or is it mud baths and aerobics classes? What makes it so great, anyhow?"

"The activities are up to you," Silsbee said. "No two people come away with the same experience. That's what makes it extraordinary. You get what you want, even if you didn't know you wanted it."

Margie had gazed at Silsbee with an expression at once impish and thoughtful. Carver pressed for details, which his friend allusively supplied. Margie asked how much, approximately, the management might charge them for two weeks of desire-gratification. After drawing upon his cigar, Silsbee uttered a figure Carver knew to be at, but not beyond, the far boundary of the affordable. Margie also knew that Silsbee's figure had struck, like a dart on a dartboard, within their limits. Carver saw her make up her mind on the spot. Her next question was as good as an announcement: "Do they allow pets?"

Silsbee smiled. "Every afternoon at five, a tall, red-haired woman used to walk a pet jaguar through the garden they call the Memory Terrace. The jaguar was on one of those leashes that spool off a reel."

An hour or two later, Silsbee had glided through the door and slipped from view for a number of months. His disappearance was partially answered by a smug postcard from Lisbon: *Poking around this haunted city. Question is, who's haunting it? Question #2: Have you two been thinking about Perdido?*

During his absence, the Carvers now and again had found themselves discussing Silsbee's tale. The discussions began as jokes in which the resort served as marital code for Silsbee-ish self-dramatization, then expanded into speculations upon the ratio of truth to fantasy in the recital. Silsbee returned from his travels and summoned his friend to lunch at an obscure *boite* on Ninth Avenue. During the meal, Carver asked if he had received an invitation to Mordido. "Bobby," Silsbee had said, "even you should know better than that."

At the end of May, Carver placed an advertisement in the personals of Friday's *New York Times*. "If invited, will accept. Marjorie and Robert Carver, 195 East End Avenue, Apt. 35B, NY, NY 10128." He expected the matter to go no further.

Two weeks later, when a messenger failed to appear at 195 East End Avenue, the Carvers understood their suspicions to have been validated. Silsbee had invented every detail.

At 7:00 on a Friday evening at the end of June, the messenger arrived, wearing tight, black leather and a visored helmet. The envelope he passed into the hands of a dismayed Carver contained a letter signed by E. Bantling, two tickets on a Chariot Air flight to Oslo, and three single-spaced pages of instructions.

2

Sorry, *sorry,* I don't want to do this, but I see no way around it. Unless I break in and say what I have to say—which feels as intrusive on this end as it must on yours—everything from here on out will sound like a fever dream. It probably will anyhow, no matter what I do.

I have lived with this story most of my life, and although its meaning keeps changing shape, I have come to understand that it does at least make sense. If it doesn't make some kind of sense to you, too, there is no point in going on. So I have to go into the following.

For the past three decades I have been one of those thoroughly marginalized creatures, a contemporary composer. Like most of my middle aged, prize-certified, not altogether infrequently performed peers, I enjoy the security of a professorship in the Music department of a large university, in my case an excellent university. Last year, the Cleveland Symphony commisioned a concerto for orchestra from me. Half a dozen of my pieces have been recorded on respectable labels, and before the end of this year some gifted young people are going to fill a double-CD set with my works for string quartet and percussion. In the minuscule world of modern composers, I am, if not a towering eminence, at least a minor grandee, the custodian of a burgeoning reputation, a frequent guest at one of our most distinguished arts colonies, the recipient of numerous grants and awards, and—twenty years ago—an invitee to a dinner and concert at the White House. I was seated between Lauren Bacall and the soprano Mireille Freni, who was saving her throat for later in the evening, when she was to sing arias from *Manon Lescaut*. I can be nothing but grateful for the way my life has gone, but when I began my career, it was on an entirely different path.

Throughout childhood and early adolescence, I was a working musician. Although I detest the term, a child prodigy. I started violin lessons at five. At the age of eight, I performed the Brahms Violin Concerto with the Milwaukee Symphony at the Civic Auditorium under the baton of Zdenek Prohaska. The following year, I appeared with the Chicago Symphony in a performance of the Berg Violin Concerto conducted by Fritz Reiner. I was taken out of school and educated by tutors—you can't stay in elementary school and maintain a concert schedule.

We lived in various countries, serially, like gypsies, whisked here and there by the violin gurus who captured my parents' attention, also by certain passionate, non-musical interests of their own. In the first of the two years we spent in Buenos Aires, I did a recital at the Teatro Colón with a twitchy, incomprehensible fourteen-year-old pianist named Leonid Encardo, a fellow prodigy of Russian-Chilean parentage who came unglued shortly thereafter and as far as I know has never emerged from the shadows. During rehearsals, Leonid sometimes became too overheated to speak English and burst into gabble I took for Russian but turned out to be a private language governed by an elaborate tonal system. (As a rule, musical prodigies have dreadful lives.) At the end of our stay in Argentina, I returned to the Teatro Colón to perform Bach's Sonatas and Partitas for solo violin, the apogee of my career as a boy musician. In those days, there were only two serious music critics in Buenos Aires. Both of them attended my concert. One confidently predicted a great international career; the other remarked the absurdity of any child's having been given a solo recital at the great theater, especially if the child were as talentless as I.

The next year, a mild but incapacitating tremor in the fingers of my left hand led to our relocation to Berlin, where the treatments provided by a famous specialist, in my opinion an absolute fraud, failed to correct or even reduce the disorder, thus putting an end to my life as a celebrated boy fiddle player.

Less comprehensively than Leonid Encardo, I fell apart. What I did was, I cut school—the tutors having vanished for good—and broke into the houses and apartments of my classmates' parents. I learned whose parents worked during the day, took the bus or the underground to their houses, smashed a window or climbed down from the roof, and broke in. You can't imagine how embarrassing this is: I look back at the thirteen-year-old me and see a sizzling, pint-sized monster. When music was stolen from me, I turned into a walking toxin. I *loved* breaking into those cushy pads. Witless as a monkey, I stole whatever snagged my eye, anything that glittered or sparkled. Watches, tie-clasps, jeweled pins and brooches, military medals, snuff-boxes, porcelain dogs and dopey porcelain shepherdesses holding crooks the size of candy canes. Mind abuzz, heart booming, I knocked over lamps and peed on the carpets.

Violation was the point, *damage.* If I had a goal, it was the expression of a demonic outrage. Because I could not take my stolen baubles back to our apartment, I pushed the watches and snuff-boxes into storm drains. Later on, I abandoned thievery and concentrated on the outrage. I *trashed* those comfortable interiors, I turned them into moonscape devastations. This lunacy occupied me for three months, and I quit only because I feared that someone would notice the correlation between the dates of the break-ins and my absences from school.

Though we lived frugally, our savings dwindled, and my parents began to panic. In hopes the famous quack would restore me to the concert stage in short order, they had transported the household to Germany without bothering to secure employment there. Employment was not an issue for my parents. After my cure, I'd be performing again, spinning off money in the usual way. The concert fees had been paying our bills for years. My mother sometimes worked in art galleries, and my father wrote occasional columns published in the Milwaukee *Journal*. My parents worked because work relieved their boredom. They yearned for more stimulation than the obligations of my career permitted. While I fiddled, they sat around in hotel rooms and waited through sound checks in unheated halls.

The quack's failure to effect a cure changed all of that. Weeks dragged by, and the money kept shrinking. My mother landed a job in an art gallery peddling strips of felt and piles of bricks to Swiss millionaires, and my father sent a few columns of ironic commentary to Milwaukee, but it wasn't nearly enough. We moved to a cheaper apartment, we sold some furniture, we moved again, this time to a single room in an area where whispering Turkish men sidled up to my mother when she went to the market. My symptoms continued to ignore the expensive treatments. After endless late-night discussions, my parents cut their losses, packed a couple of trunks and skipped out of the apartment. We took third-class passage on a night train to Amsterdam, where my father had booked the tickets on a charter flight to Chicago, then Milwaukee.

They returned to our native city in the role of sophisticated prodigals welcomed by the friends they had not seen in years. My father rejoined the staff of the Milwaukee *Journal*, to which he contributed a twice-weekly column of lazily charming "observations"; after a failed attempt to sell avant-garde art to the practical citizens of Milwaukee, my mother passed the required examinations and became a remarkably successful real-estate agent. I was enrolled at an Anglophile school for boys no less philistine than others of its kind, which was okay with me. The last thing I wanted to think about was music.

In June of 1961, four years after we had come back to Milwaukee and on the recommendation of an oral surgeon acquainted with my father, my parents spent two weeks at a Norwegian mountain resort called Perdido. A school friend had invited me along on a family trip, and no one could be found to care for our lumbering, hopelessly dependent white cat, so after suffering a battery of vaccinations, the unsuspecting Poodle, drugged unconscious within the pet carrier, flew to Norway with my parents.

3

Silsbee's fantastic account proved reliable at every turn. By means of an unmarked road winding through the warehouses and freight offices of the airport's westernmost district, a limousine delivered the Carvers to a red-brick terminal where they were deposited in leather armchairs, served tea by gentlemen in swallow-tailed coats and advised not to converse with their fellow travelers, in any case an assortment of couples and single persons of remote, unpromising aspect seated so distantly as to discourage even sociable glances. A Customs official wandered from chair to chair. Within twenty minutes, stewards approached the parties of one and two individually, accompanied them across the tarmac and conducted them to compartments inside the spacious airplane. The Carvers lolled into padded brocade, sipped champagne, ordered stupendous meals from handwritten menus, and requested their choice of in-flight films, *Gone With the Wind* for Margie and *The Fountainhead* for Carver, who experienced a mixture of boredom and loathing ten minutes after it started. Pillow gobbled up her meal, inspected the smoked glass door of the compartment, mewed, levered herself onto on a cashmere blanket strewn upon a convenient divan, and slept. After partaking of Bavarian chocolate cake and (for Carver) liberal helpings of cognac, they covered themselves with their own cashmere blankets and did the same.

Arrival in Oslo brought a collegial chat with a Customs officer, a pause on the tarmac as the parties were gathered into a series of waiting cars, and a swift passage to the splendid hotel and a handsome suite, to which room service delivered a lavish breakfast and a bottle of champagne. Pillow made use of a clever, odorless cat-box and a generous portion of raw fish. The Carvers dozed. After using their in-room sauna, showering, and dressing in what E. Bantling had called "cocktail attire," they were escorted to the roof. A pilot with a resemblance to the young Gary Cooper stowed their bags and pet carrier in the rear of the helicopter and assisted them into the cockpit.

"Two hours away, is it?" Carver asked. The pilot responded with a reassuring smile. ("He doesn't talk, remember?" said Margie.) Oslo petered out into suburban clusters, farmland, and roads skimming through sloping hills.

Soon the Carvers were floating above woodland sprinkled with villages that fell away before the great, expansive carpet of a single, unbroken forest stretching away to the horizon on all sides. Elongated, shaped like half-moons, some the size of tennis rackets, others no larger than an infant's fingernails, the lakes sparkled a cold, lacquered blue. Looking down in rapture, Carver felt as though suspended above a landscape never before known to exist but mysteriously always longed for, a world utterly apart from everything he knew and for which he now realized that he had forever yearned. A bright tendril of fear scorched his viscera. When Carver glanced over his shoulder, he was astonished to see tears gliding down Margie's face.

Hastily, he turned away and, in obedience to an impulse he could not have defined, closed his eyes. Senses he did not possess told him that the pilot was grinning. Carver chose not to verify or disprove this impression. If a peek through a cracked eyelid should actually find a grin on the pilot's face, the grin would have nothing to do with his passenger's cowardice, to use a wildly inaccurate word. The pilot smiled all the time anyhow.

Carver opened his eyes and peered sideways without moving his head. Unsmiling, the bored pilot was occupying himself with pilot details. Carver made a discreet show of looking down.

Foothills, some crowned with tiny lakes, rippled the fabric of the green carpet in their progress toward the two-dimensional silhouettes of white-peaked mountains. A spell of nausea forced Carver to shut his eyes again. Over the brute whir of the rotors, he imagined he heard the cat's despairing outcries echoing from the spaces behind. The next time he opened his eyes, the mountains had widened out into individual entities separated by grassy meadows and serpentine rivers. He glanced at the pilot, and the pilot pointed down.

With an ominous clank of gears, the helicopter drifted toward a barren-looking meadow, then halted and dropped straight down. The surface of the meadow flattened and rippled like brown water.

Margie said, "Did you see anything on the mountain? *I* didn't."

"I didn't really see the mountain," said Carver.

The helicopter patted the ground. In the silence that followed the last movement of the rotor blades, Pillow uttered a heartbroken lament. "Poor sweetie," Margie said, "Mommy promises it won't be long now, Pillow-baby." The pilot jumped out, trotted around to Carver, assisted his passengers out of the helicopter, and briskly tossed their luggage into the tall grass. Moaning Pillow was passed into Margie's hands. The pilot pointed a gloved finger at the far side of the meadow, where tumbled boulders lay at the foot of a mountain. The pilot raised his eyebrows. Carver nodded and aimed his own index finger at the boulders. Margie cooed to Pillow and began striding away. The pilot jumped back into the cockpit. Vaguely aware of Margie's progress across the field, Carver gathered up the bags and dragged them away from the helicopter. He ducked, flinching, when the blades began to spin. The roar deafened him, and the wind tore at his clothing. In seconds, the helicopter shrank to the size of a dragonfly, a mosquito.

Carver scanned the perimeter of the meadow and located his wife's retreating form. She had already passed between the first of the boulders and appeared to be moving up a kind of path too faint to make out. "Margie!" he shouted. "Wait for me!" She did not stop moving.

He strapped the hanging bags over his shoulders and pulled out the retractable handles of the carry-ons. "Hold on!"

Margie turned around. Platinum fur glimmered through the grate of the pet carrier. "I found the path!" she yelled.

Carver struggled forward. Margie scooped her hand through the air, telling him to stop being a slowpoke, turned her back, and danced off. Before Carver reached the border of the meadow, the path came into view. A narrow patch of beaten ground between two massive boulders widened out to perhaps three feet as it ascended. A good way up, he was going to have to negotiate the bags through passages narrowed by other, smaller boulders and piles of fallen rocks. Rough steps had been cut into the earth at the steepest inclines. Margie's doll-sized legs gleamed as she skipped around a boulder and vanished from sight. At what seemed an impossible distance above, a shimmering layer of silver-grey haze obscured the rest of the mountain.

Half an hour later, his shirt glued to his body, Carver watched Margie actually *break into a trot* and disappear within the shimmering haze. He wished that Silsbee had never boasted of his visit to Perdido, but that was pointless: Silsbee boasted the way monks in monasteries prayed, unceasingly. More reasonably, he wished that Margie had stayed inside. The sheer unlikeliness of her fascination with Silsbee's tale impressed itself upon him yet again. Margie did not merely distrust Silsbee, she *detested* him. He was "your lunatic friend, the dentist," a figure of chaotic excesses. She was right. Carver wished Silsbee had never been born.

Another fifteen minutes brought him to a plateau formed by a ledge of rock extending twenty feet outward from the now sparsely wooded mountainside. Silver haze enclosed this expanse like the walls of a room furnished with a long, flat slab the height and approximate dimensions of a CEO's desk. Seated atop the stone desk with her legs crossed, flanked by the pet carrier and her knapsack, Margie finished retouching her lip gloss and gave herself a last inspection in the mirror of her compact. "You're a mess. You should see yourself." She inserted the cosmetics into the knapsack and shook her head.

Pillow yawned, displaying a ribbed pink palate.

Carver propped the carry-ons upright and slid out of the straps, letting the hanging bags slump. His shoulders felt like raw meat. "This is the worst mistake we ever made. I don't understand why we're doing it, anyhow. You don't even like Silsbee." He mopped his face with his handkerchief and glowered at Pillow, who glowered back.

"This has nothing to do with *Silsbee*. Do you want me to tell you why you're upset? You packed too much, and now you're stuck with dragging it all up the mountain. You should have left your tuxedo at home. 'Black tie optional,' they said. I tried, honey, but you wouldn't listen."

"A tuxedo weighs about a pound and a half," Carver said.

"Don't forget those patent-leather shoes. And the shoe trees! There's another four pounds, right there. Plus the shirts, the studs, the cufflinks, and whatever. No wonder you're sweating like a pig."

"You packed three times as much as I did," Carver said. "I'm carrying your bags, too, in case you didn't notice."

"It isn't the same for men. A man takes off a necktie and puts on an ascot, he's wearing an entirely different outfit." She patted the top of the slab. "Don't get grumpy on me, now."

Carver moved across the shelf of rock and sat beside the pet carrier. "Silsbee wears ascots. I don't."

"Catch your breath. The place is fifteen minutes away." She stroked the back of his head. "Bobby, we're climbing up the side of a mountain! Isn't that *spectacular?*"

"Fifteen minutes is good," he said. "But let me ask you this: If we can't see more than twenty feet in front of us, how will we know when we get there?"

"Thank you for your negativity." Margie slid down, shouldered her knapsack, and grabbed Pillow's container. She was out of sight before Carver had reached their bags. Furious footsteps preceded him up the narrow trail, sometimes audible in the click of a heel against an obdurate stone, sometimes in the pat of leather soles on packed earth, but always furious.

"I didn't mean anything," he said.

"It was only a question," he said.

"Okay, run away," he said. "I don't give a damn, I just wonder how we're supposed to *see* the place."

Unfortunately, Carver said to himself, *we probably will see it.* He was unaware that he was mouthing the words as he trudged along. *We'll spend two weeks in that dump, and every day is going to be horrible because Margie, may she fall into a bottomless crevasse, will be angry the entire time. She'll pretend she isn't, she'll put on an act, but she'll be punishing me for trying to spoil her vacation. That's why she wanted to come here in the first place—to make my life miserable. How did I get talked into this? She'll flirt with some rich guy. His wife won't give a damn because she'll be boffing the tennis pro. Pretty soon, she and the rich guy are sneaking off to his room, and if I say anything—*

"Please, Bobby." He snapped his head up to find her, much

closer than he had imagined, gazing down from the entrance to a white gazebo or pavilion where the path ended in a series of broad wooden steps. Framed by gleaming columns beneath a ceiling arching into a dome, Margie was looking at him with a kind of expectant entreaty. "Don't act like that."

"Like what?"

"I don't know what you were saying to yourself, but it must have been terrible."

"I'm sick of hauling our luggage up this mountain, that's all."

"Weren't you fretting about being able to see Perdido when we got there?"

"That was a concern of mine, yes." Carver took his eyes from Margie and glared at the structure surrounding her. "Don't tell me *this* is Perdido."

"You have no idea." She stepped back and turned away. Her blond head moved beneath the arch of the dome and disappeared from view.

"You have no idea," Carver parroted, and shifted the luggage to the bottom of the steps. Margie was still out of sight. He mounted the first tread. "You can see something?"

"Uh huh."

Carver reached the top of the steps and moved between the columns. Across the expanse of the pavilion's floor, Margie stood with her hands on a railing, facing out into a flat sheet of silver.

"Sure," he said.

Margie spun around. She was radiant with pleasure. "Bobby, this is incredible." She turned back to the railing.

"Incredible would be nice." Margie did not respond. In the silence, Carver's footfalls rang on the white floor.

Each of his reluctant steps altered the flat, silver panel before the unmoving Margie. Its color became less uniform, thinning into an ivory band at its midpoint, speckling dark and light above and below. The stripe of ivory widened and paled to white gauze. The dark speckles retreated into suggestions of forest on a distant slope where patches of white resolved into snow. Alarmingly, some particle of self-hood embedded deep within stirred into life, a tiny corpse galvanized by a jolt of electricity. By the time Carver stood beneath the dome, he had again become aware of the inexplicable emotion before which he had closed his eyes in the helicopter. *All right,* he thought, *let it be.* He stepped forward, and turrets, spires, and parapets took form within the vagueness. Like a great shark that dives from sight the moment it is seen, the sense of a powerful yearning flashed along his nerve-endings, then subsided. Carver walked toward his wife, the railing, the gathering details.

Transparent northern sunlight streamed into a valley where a long castle-like structure commandeered the top of a grassy rise and extended its wings downward through a series of gentle terraces divided into formal gardens, ponds, and lawns. Flowers blazed in beds between gravel paths; tall hedges gleamed. In mullions, windows shone. A curving path cut through the meadowland between the pavilion and the castle, and up this dark ribbon advanced two uniformed men who clearly intended to welcome them to Perdido.

"This is a real place?" Carver said.

PART TWO: BEING THERE

4

The night before my parents were supposed to return, a man named Jay Silsbee telephoned me from Madison and said that he had just spoken to my father, who had asked him to drive the ninety miles to

Milwaukee and stay with me until he got home. Silsbee could not tell me what, if anything, had gone wrong, nor did he know if my parents' arrival was to be delayed. He just wanted to be sure I would stay up to let him in: At 73 or 74, however old he was, he had forgotten that 18-year-old boys, especially 18-year-old boys embarking on the summer between high school and college, considered 11:30, the hour he expected to turn up, far too early be in bed.

In the years before we had left for Europe, I had met Jay Silsbee two or three times when my father had taken me with him to Madison. Silsbee was a watchmaker and repairer of watches with an obsessive, lifelong interest in magic and the occult. When you entered his apartment, you wound through tables littered with watches and watch parts, display cases filled with magic memorabilia, metal files and file boxes in stacks and piles of books, to get to the clearing made up of a coffee table, a stained, dirty-looking sofa and two equally disreputable chairs. Posters and bookshelves covered the walls. Silsbee himself resembled a badger, squat and thick in the body, his downcast head crowned with silver fur and rimless glasses, his large, pale hands usually folded before his expansive stomach. He had a furtive, watchful air shot through with an odd theatricality. Silsbee, I gathered, seldom left his apartment, and then only under compulsion, when obliged to attend an auction for the purpose of acquiring a pair of handcuffs once used by Houdini. My father had met Silsbee in his youth and once or twice a year devoted a column to him, which is how I came to visit his apartment. Although I could tell that my father had a long-standing relationship with Silsbee, he was nothing like my father's younger friends, the jocular circle he had created for himself in Milwaukee. I thought Silsbee was a little creepy. On our first drive back home, I asked my father why he liked him, and my father said, "Jay Silsbee is the most remarkable man I've ever known."

The one time I asked my mother about Silsbee, she shuddered and said, "Please, I'm making lunch."

Around 11:45, a pair of headlights appeared on the hill at the top of our street. From my chair beside the living room window, I watched the headlights move slowly downhill as the driver checked out the numerals on the front doors. The car wavered from side to side, as if the driver swung the wheel wherever he turned his head. I jumped up and flicked on the light over the front door. Anxieties of several kinds pushed me outside to stand next to the driveway.

The headlights swerved toward me, and a vehicle of what seemed unbelievable antiquity rolled up the driveway and jerked to a halt. Dark green, vaguely like a Parker House roll in shape, it brought to mind photographs in the family album of my father posing beside his first car, a Hudson Hornet. The lights died, and the motor uttered several loud ticks after it had been shut off. The driver's door opened. I stepped forward and saw, ornately emblazoned across the top of the grille, the word Hudson. A thick white hand gripping a brown paper bag emerged, fastened two fingers on the top of the door, and pulled from the interior Jay Silsbee's head, shoulders, and trunk. His cap of silver fur gleamed in the light from our windows. His leg followed, and his foot met the running board. Laboriously, Silsbee grunted the whole of his body onto the running board, gave me a mystical smile, and stepped down. He wobbled for a moment and clutched the bag to his chest. "Made good time," he said, and slammed the door so hard the Hudson's body trembled. That it was the Hornet in the photograph suddenly seemed obvious—my father had given his first car to this man. "The last time I saw you, you were just a sprat," he said. "Remember coming to see me with your dad?"

"I remember," I said.

"Didn't know I drove all the way down to see you play at the

Auditorium, though, did you? Brahms. In my opinion, that Violin Concerto smells like fish, but you were okay. In spite of that poncy little stick-waver, Prohaska."

"I'm sorry you didn't like the piece," I said.

"And I saw you in Chicago, when you did the Berg with Reiner. You got lost for a couple of seconds during the Allegretto, but Reiner saved your can. You still have a problem with your hand?"

"I don't think about it anymore," I said. "What did my father tell you? Are they coming home tomorrow?"

"We'll find out tomorrow, won't we?" He reached into the bag, drew out a half-empty Smirnoff bottle, and unscrewed the cap. "Fritz Reiner was a hell of a conductor." Silsbee put the bottle to his mouth and tilted it up to drink in long, steady swallows, as if the vodka were water. "Did he treat you like a professional? I'm curious."

"I don't remember," I said, although I did remember, precisely. "It was a long time ago."

"Hell, kid," he said. "That was practically yesterday."

I led him into the garage and through the back door. Silsbee looked at the kitchen. "All the comforts of home." It sounded like an insult. "Got anything to eat in here, maybe?"

He rooted around in the refrigerator and found some tired vegetables from before my parents left, a couple of foil-wrapped pieces of meat I had forgotten about, and a few other things equally as unpromising. I pointed him toward the pots and pans and the spice cabinet, and he found the knives and the wine by himself. When I asked him to tell me my father's exact words, he repeated what he had said before: My father had asked him to drive to Milwaukee and stay with me until his arrival. Silsbee dropped ice cubes into a glass, poured half of his remaining vodka over the ice, and drank as he chopped up the stuff he had taken from the refrigerator. He smashed a peeled garlic clove with the flat of the knife. No, my father had not said anything about my mother. No, he had no reason to suspect that my father would be coming back alone. Nor did he know why my father had asked him to stay with me. Of course I did not need a baby-sitter, he knew that, he wouldn't be much of a baby-sitter anyhow. Then why was he in my house?

"Because your old man asked me." Silsbee slid the chopped-up leftovers into a big frying pan and poured a little wine over the mess. Then he took down two glasses and filled them halfway. "Go on," he said. "You're tense. This'll help you loosen up."

I took the glass into the living room and switched on the television. Our home had been invaded. This old jerk had barged in and taken over the kitchen. Next he would probably take over the whole house. How did I know he had really spoken to my father? Maybe Silsbee had made everything up and my parents would arrive on schedule, around noon the next day. I imagined a scuffle, a violent eviction. On television, Richard Widmark, attired in a black shirt and a white necktie, pushed an old woman in a wheelchair down a steep flight of stairs. I gulped wine, wishing I could give the same treatment to Jay Silsbee.

An odor of amazing richness that seemed nearly like a meal in itself drifted from the kitchen. I had wolfed down a hamburger six hours earlier, and the smell instantly made me ravenous. When I could hold out no longer, I went back into the kitchen. Silsbee was pouring the last of his vodka into his glass and keeping an eye on the stove, now occupied by two more frying pans and a small, bubbling pot. I asked him what he was making.

"You could call it a ragout with pretensions to being a *daube*," he said. "Get a couple of plates, will you?"

I took two plates from the shelf, two sets of silverware from the drawer, and arranged them on the table. Silsbee distributed the contents of the pans and the bubbling pot onto the plates, combining some things, keeping others separate. The smell rising from the plates almost made me pass out from hunger. He told me to dig in and turned away to put the pans in the sink. I raised a laden fork, closed my mouth around it, and groaned with pleasure. Whatever was on the fork tasted like nothing I had ever eaten before, not even the lavish meals to which European concert promoters and their rich hangers-on had sometimes treated the prodigy and his family. Silsbee sat down and watched me eat. He took a sip of vodka, then a small mouthful from the meal on his plate. Another sip from his glass, another bite of food. By the time I had finished inhaling my dinner, he had dispatched less than half of his. I asked why he had eaten so little and was informed that cooks never ate much of their own food. Did he make these astonishing meals every day? He supposed so. After all, once you knew what you were doing, it was pretty simple. Would I like to have the rest? I nodded, and he slid the remaining contents of his plate onto mine. I experienced the miracle yet again. Where had he learned to cook like this? Here and there. In his youth, he had been a great traveler. France, England, Italy, China, India, Greece, Morocco, Algeria, the Netherlands, Scandinavia. Did we have an extra bed, or should he sleep on the sofa in the living room?

"The guest room is the first door down the hall," I said. "Were you ever in Norway?"

"Certainly." He refilled his wine glass.

"Did you go to Perdido?"

He smiled at me and took a swallow of wine.

"So that's why you're here."

My guess was as good as his, he said.

"What happens there? What kind of place is it?"

258

"You can't really describe Perdido," he said. "But I'll tell you one thing, I wish your folks had left the cat at home."

Ten or fifteen minutes later, Jay Silsbee picked up his paper bag, located a fresh glass and an unopened bottle of Scotch, and disappeared with them into the guest room, having evaded or ignored all my questions but one. When pressed about the cat, he said he thought pets did not belong at Perdido. Sometimes they got lost, or other things happened to them. Politely, he had declined to go into the nature of these "other things." I heard the guest room door close behind him and glanced around at the kitchen. Every surface sparkled: Although I had seen him do little more than wander back and forth from the sink, Silsbee had managed to wash the dishes and wipe down the counters and stove top. The kitchen looked cleaner than it had in a week; in fact, it looked cleaner than I had ever seen it. Quiet music filtered in from the radio in the guest room, making me feel queasy and unsettled even before I recognized it as the Berg Violin Concerto. I turned off the television and went to bed. In my dreams, a man with silver hair and fat white hands was slicing Poodle into bloody rags.

Silsbee had gone out shopping and returned with bags full of groceries and a new supply of alcohol before I awakened, and when I came into the kitchen, he was throwing out most of the contents of the refrigerator and replacing them with fresh vegetables, fruit, and parcels of meat. Boxes of pasta, rice, flour, semolina, cans of tomatoes, and bottles of olive oil, sesame oil, vodka, Scotch whiskey, and French and Italian wine stood on the counters, along with two funny-looking loaves of bread and transparent baggies containing parsley, oregano, basil, and other herbs I couldn't identify. It was hard to find the right things in Milwaukee, he said. He had driven all around town. Would I help him put the groceries away, or did I want breakfast right away?

"I don't eat breakfast," I said. "Let's call the airport and see if their plane is coming in on time."

He had already called, but the man to whom he'd spoken had said that he was not permitted to release information concerning flights on Chariot Air. We could do nothing but wait. In the meantime, if I helped with the groceries Silsbee promised a breakfast impossible to resist. I told him I never got hungry until noon, put away the things he'd bought, and went into the living room to turn on the TV. A tour of the three available channels turned up *George of the Jungle*, a Johnny Weismuller Tarzan movie, and *Scooby-Doo*. I dialed back to the Tarzan movie and dropped into my father's chair. In a jungle clearing, Tarzan discovered the corpse of an elephant. He battered his chest and emitted a tremendous howl, summoning an agitated chimpanzee who pointed into the jungle. Tarzan shot up a tree, grabbed a convenient vine, and swung along until he reached an encampment. Sneering white hunters in bush hats and safari jackets strolled out of tents the size of quonset huts. One of them said, We've heard about you, Ape-Man, but you can't stop us. We're going to bag all the elephants we like. No, Tarzan protect elephants, the elephants Tarzan's friends. Haw haw haw, said the hunters, this guy's too much. An amazing smell floated in from the kitchen. Hunger practically lifted me out of the chair. A white hunter at the edge of the frame said, If Tarzan ever climb mountain in Norway, Tarzan learn about his friends, haw haw. I said, "What?," and the television burped and went dark. The odor from the kitchen wrapped itself around me and pulled me from the chair.

My father arrived home late the following night. The only reason I had not gone crazy with worry was that when it had become clear my father had missed his original flight, Silsbee told me that unfinished business often caused guests at Perdido to delay their departure, sometimes by as much as forty-eight hours. The unfinished business could be any one of a thousand things, depending on the individual. He had a hunch that we would be seeing my father late that night. Instead of fading into the guest room at 11:00, as he had the previous night, Silsbee stayed up with me, watching the Late Show and steadily putting away the whisky, to no more effect than if it had been spring water.

I kept glancing at the window. Shortly after midnight, headlights mounted the crest of the hill and swung down toward us. "He's coming," I said. "Did he tell you it would be tonight?"

Silsbee shook his head. I watched the taxi and its triangular roof ornament come into view behind the advancing beams of light.

"Let me give you some advice. Your father isn't going to be at his best. Don't press him. He'll be worn out, and he won't feel like answering a million questions."

"I hope my mom and Poodle are in that car," I said.

"We are in total agreement," Silsbee said.

The taxi turned into the driveway, rolled past Silsbee's antique, and halted a few feet from the garage door. The light over the garage illuminated the driver's impassive face. My father's arm and hand moved into the light, holding money. I ran to the front door and stepped out onto the raised concrete slab and the welcome mat. The driver pulled a suitcase from the trunk and thumped it on the driveway. My father was standing beside the taxi in a yellow windbreaker and khaki pants. His hair was rumpled, and the lines in his face made him look old. He was staring at our house as if he had never seen it before, or seen it only in photographs that had led him to expect something more to his taste. He did not appear to notice me.

"Dad," I said.

"Go inside."

I looked over my shoulder and saw Silsbee hunched in the doorway. He stepped down onto the lawn. My father picked up his suitcase and half-carried, half-dragged it up the flagstones. His eyes slid toward me, and I said, "Where's Mom?"

He jerked the suitcase onto the concrete slab. Silsbee took the case and carried it inside.

"Jay," my father said. "I'm glad you're here."

"Can I get you anything?" Silsbee asked.

My father said he wanted to go to bed. Silsbee carried the suitcase down the hall.

"Is Mom coming home?" I asked.

"Not now," my father said.

In the bedroom, Silsbee laid the suitcase on the carpet and ran the zipper from end to end. My father peeled off the windbreaker and threw it at a chair. When I looked at the place where Silsbee had been, he was there no longer.

"Well," my father said. He was talking to himself, not to me. "Here we are." He dropped onto the bed and shielded his eyes with one arm.

"Is Mom all right?" I asked.

"Your mother is perfectly fine," he said. "Ask Jay to come back in, will you?"

"What about Poodle?"

"Poodle should rot in hell."

Slumped into the sofa cushions, his eyes closed behind his glittering spectacles, Jay Silsbee looked more than ever like an aged badger. The television had been turned off. He opened his eyes. "Does he want to talk to me?"

"Isn't that why you're here?"

He pushed himself to his feet and grabbed the half-empty bottle off the coffee table. "Give us some time by ourselves, all right?"

"I don't give a shit what you do," I said.

Silsbee lumbered off.

I fell into my father's chair, hoping to break it. Down the hall, low voices droned on and on like music without pattern, variation, or rhythm. The droning ceased, and footsteps padded toward the guest room. A door opened and closed. Another kind of music, a late Beethoven string quartet, swam toward me. I switched off the lights and went to bed.

The next morning, I discovered that my socks and underwear, including the ones from the day before, had been neatly refolded and arranged in orderly stacks. The same was true of my shirts, T-shirts, and sweaters. My bathroom sparkled, and the towels smelled good. A new bar of soap filled the soap dish; a full tube of Crest lay beside a new toothbrush. The clothes I put on looked and felt fresh from the dry cleaner's. The entire house gleamed as if a squadron of maids had been at work since the moment I closed my bedroom door. I could smell lemon-scented furniture polish and what I thought was perfume until I noticed a vase crowded with freesias on the coffee table. The ancient Hudson Hornet was gone from the driveway, and I hurried to the guest room and saw an open door and an immaculately made bed with a white sheet of paper folded on the blanket.

In a calligraphic hand, Silsbee had written: *Take care of yourself and be good to your father. I'll always be in Madison, if you feel like talking. Best Wishes, JS.*

My father stayed in bed until 6:00, when hunger forced him to shuffle into the kitchen. Silsbee had packed the refrigerator with nine, ten, maybe a dozen Saran-wrapped meals, all calligraphically labeled. I warmed our food and put it on plates, and my father said enough to let me know that my mother had left him. Left us. Never to return. After dinner, he went back to bed and slept another twenty-four hours, straight through.

The rest of the story, or the fragment he was willing to communicate, emerged over the next couple of days, during which he roused himself for no longer than the few hours required to consume one of Silsbee's extraordinary meals while watching *Rawhide*, *Gunsmoke*, or some other twaddle, mumbling answers to a small number of my questions, and á la Silsbee, downing whiskey. My mother had chosen to spend an extra week at Perdido. This week represented a period of adjustment. My mother had decided that her life had become an unbearable confinement. One half of the former partnership, hers, had grown and evolved, while the other half, my father's, had hardened into place like a fossil. Her physical and spiritual well-being demanded the expansions to be attained by entering into a relationship with a man other than my father. This man had been a fellow guest at the resort, although not at Perdido itself, but farther up the mountain. He lived right here in Milwaukee, so I would be able to visit my mother and her new partner any time I wished. This evolved gentleman, the fellow with whom my mother would be returning to Milwaukee six days hence, was the very same supposed friend, the oral surgeon, who had recommended Perdido to my father in the first place.

Stationed before the television in his hours of wakefulness, my father was too exhausted, too wounded, and too self-absorbed for narrative coherence. Half of the time, he was talking to himself. It took two days of *Rawhide*, *Gunsmoke*, Silsbee's gourmet care packages, and whiskey-downing, for the above information to emerge far enough so that I could connect the dots.

Then, as if by the flick of a switch, my father pulled himself together. He started getting dressed in the mornings, and he made a few phone calls. Within days, he was driving downtown and churning out columns in the *Journal* building. One of the first pieces he wrote after returning from Perdido described daily life in our house from a cat's point of view, as though Poodle were still with us. The column did not mention my mother. Another column, which lovingly evoked the meals Jay Silsbee had left behind in our refrigerator, located them in various European restaurants, also lovingly evoked.

The day after she returned, my mother called to invite me for lunch at a restaurant on the east side of town. I said I'd be there, but I stayed out all night and failed to wake up in time. She called again. We had to talk. Didn't I understand that? She could not come to our house, I would feel uncomfortable coming to hers, so we should meet on neutral ground. Did that make sense? It made sense, yes. We made another lunch date, and I said I wanted her to tell me everything that had happened at Perdido. Astonishingly, she laughed. What did your father tell you? Practically nothing, but he doesn't make sense anyhow, all he does is sleep, eat, and watch television. How could you do this, Mom, how could you walk out on us and move in with some guy you never even liked? Remember telling Dad that guy was disgusting? What happened, did you all of a sudden decide you couldn't be happy without being rich? Honey, please, it wasn't like that at all, I don't expect you to understand this for a long time, but I saw how empty my life was, I was like a dead woman. You'll never know how much it hurt me to break away. I said, how much it hurt *you*? Forget lunch, I don't want to see you again. She astonished me all over again—she said, All right, let's wait. You need time. I hope you'll be ready before you leave for college, but if not, when you come back for Thanksgiving. Or Christmas. And don't worry about your father. He knows it's all for the best, it may not look that way, but he does, it's just hard for him to admit it. Besides, your father loved that cat, and he feels terribly guilty about what happened. What happened? She said, what happened? Your father went crazy and he killed Poodle, she said, that's what, at least that's what he thinks happened. Call me whenever you can. I love you.

Twice that summer I drove across town from our west-side suburb to the older, richer, more established, utterly unsuburban suburb on the east side where my mother was living with a man she had once found repulsive. In my suburb, small ranch houses and a few "contemporaries" like shrunken A-frames stood at wide intervals along treeless streets bordered with drainage ditches; in my mother's neighborhood, massive residences of an astonishing variety, Germanic piles of dark stone, Moorish castles, French chateaus, English country houses, a few Frank Lloyd Wright buildings, crowded together on streets shaded by giant oaks that loomed over cement sidewalks. Lake breezes kept it ten to fifteen degrees cooler than our part of town, and everybody dressed better and looked taller, blonder, more assured. My mother's new house was a big brick building located on a long bluff above Lake Michigan. I parked across the street and sat in the car, scarcely knowing what I was looking for or why I had come. As far as I was aware, I felt nothing. The house looked more like the administration building of a New England college than a single-family residence. In comparison, our house and neighborhood were barren and graceless—the comparison was humiliating. My mother had abandoned us for a world separated by far more than the twenty miles between Brookfield and Lake Drive. She had ascended altogether out of reach. Both of the times I sat in the car across the street from her humiliating mansion, a woman's figure eventually approached a mullioned ground-floor window, and I sped away, vowing that she would never, ever, no matter how she begged, get me inside that place.

In September, I went to the University of Wisconsin and burrowed into the classwork, getting drunk on the weekends and throwing myself back into my textbooks and lecture notes every Monday. I came home for Thanksgiving and spent most of the long weekend in bed reading Robert Heinlein and Isaac Asimov, authors in whom I had lost interest at the age of fifteen. My mother called and asked to speak to me, but I declined. That evening I went out with a school friend and got too drunk to drive home, so I spent the night at his house. My father said, Next time you intend to stay out all night, I'd appreciate a phone call. From unexplained absences of his own, also from seeing him engaged in secretive telephone conversations, I gathered that he had a new girlfriend, one I was not supposed to know about. The night before I took the bus back to Madison, I watched him fork warmed-over turkey into his mouth and thought, *How can this sap be my father?*

The only reason I agreed to have lunch with my mother during the Christmas break was that Jay Silsbee had told me to. One day in the first week of December, I had looked him up in the phone book and dialed his number on impulse. He invited me to his apartment and, with the effortlessness I remembered, produced a stupendous meal we ate off trays while seated on the disreputable chairs in the midst of the Silsbee-clutter. The apartment seemed smaller and darker, almost spooky. Dismembered watches lay scattered across the tables, and the mesmeric eyes of forgotten magicians floated out from their posters. Various clocks ticked and chimed, irregularly and out of synch. Silsbee himself looked as if he would have benefited from being taken apart and cleaned. His head drooped toward his chest, exposing a ring of grime around the top of his collar. The whites of his eyes were the yellow of old ivory. To the extent that I thought about his condition at all, I blamed it on the vodka he had parked beside his chair. Silsbee said that my father appeared to be back to his old self. More or less, I said, and added that he had never talked to me about Perdido.

"They never do," he said. "They can't. When you get what you didn't know you wanted, you need time to adjust."

Did he think my father wanted my mother to leave him?

"The only thing keeping them together was you, and you were about to leave the nest. They weren't interested in the same things anymore. Your mother wanted to make money and wander through big houses, and your father liked coasting along and writing the fluff he put in his columns. When you were traveling around playing the fiddle, the three of you lived in hotel suites, everything was taken care of, and everybody was satisfied. Then you couldn't play anymore, and you all moved back to Milwaukee. For years, your parents tried to ignore the conflict in their goals. That's perfectly understandable. They're going to be all right. The person you have to watch out for is you."

"Maybe I should go to Perdido," I said.

"Sorry, kid," Silsbee said. "They wouldn't let you in. Anyhow, you have your own Perdido, so to speak, you just don't know it yet."

I was disgusted by his filthy collar, his air of omniscience, his assumptions. "Where would that be, exactly?"

"You'll find out, if you're lucky," he said. "Let me give you some advice. The next time your mother calls you, get together with her."

"Why?"

"Because it might keep you from getting seriously loused up."

I sneered at him.

"For one thing," Silsbee said, "unless I'm wrong, isn't she sitting on top of a pile of loot as tall as the Empire State Building? You're young, and you're angry besides, but there's no reason to be stupid."

The protestation that I could not be angry with my mother because I felt nothing for her sounded unexpectedly wilful in the face of Silsbee's concluding "Uh huh."

I may have told myself that I had agreed to meet my mother during the Christmas break because of a grubby old man's remark about her fortune, but the complex of emotions that surged through me when I entered the sedate restaurant and saw her smiling at me from a banquette proved otherwise. They were almost too much for me, those emotions. They certainly had nothing to do with money. An untarnished love and absolute joy mingled, painfully, with the grief of having deliberately avoided her for so long; the overflowing, welcoming warmth that flooded into her face nearly cut me off at the knees. Before I had taken another step toward the banquette, the anger I had been unable to acknowledge until my conversation with Jay Silsbee had reasserted itself, allowing me to move through the tables. By then, I had also begun to adjust to the shock of the change in my mother's appearance. She looked younger, happier, more resolved than I had ever seen her. Above all, maybe, she looked rich—every aspect of the change in my mother's appearance unsettled me, this one most of all.

She kissed my cheek. I sat down and ordered a German beer because it was expensive. She asked about college, she asked about my father. After we had been given our menus, I looked at the tables in the middle of the room and saw men in suits and ties glancing at her. Instead of my polo shirt and khakis, I wished that I were wearing the adult armor of a dark suit, a white shirt, and a striped necktie. The positive things she told me about the oral surgeon vaporized the moment they were uttered. You used to think he was terrible, I said. That's because I didn't know how terrible my life was. I did what I had to do, and I'm happy. Odd as this might sound, I'd like you to be happy for me, too. I said, I suppose you and your buddy will be getting married one of these days, and you know what? It'll be like I was never born. Not at all, she said. When that happens, I want you to come to the wedding. I'll need you to be there. I still love you, you know.

"You don't need me at all," I said. "That's obvious."

She trembled; she started to talk. Sometimes she clutched my hand, and sometimes tears leaked from her eyes. The things she said were the right things, but I was as far beyond the reach of the right, honest things she said as I thought she was beyond my own reach. Instead of listening, I pretended to listen.

Okay, I said, tell me this: Did you know he was going to be there? No. She had not known. In fact, he had not really been where they were, but at another resort farther up the mountain. At times, the guests from the other resort came down for a visit. She had accidentally met him in the Memory Garden, and as they conversed she began to realize that her own unhappiness had caused her to take his self-assurance for arrogance and his humor for cynicism. Two days later, a second encounter on the veranda of the Image Collection, a kind of library, reinforced her sense of having misjudged him. My father had taken part in the production of a play called "Murder Among Friends" that occupied most of his mornings and all of his evenings. When not involved with the play, he disappeared for hours and returned sullen and distracted. He had refused at the last minute to accompany her to a formal-dress ball but urged her to go by herself. Annoyed, in fact infuriated, she went to the ball, where the sudden lightening of her spirits produced by being unaccompanied made her feel released from some imprisonment. At that moment, my mother told me, she realized that her marriage had begun to die during our stay in Berlin and that she herself had been dying since our return to the States. Soon, a group from the other resort appeared at the end of the ballroom;

her new friend detached himself from his friends and danced her away, and she understood instantly that what had been given her was what she most needed.

When she returned to their quarters, my father had vanished again, along with Poodle. He reappeared the following morning, exhausted, his arms covered with scratches and his shirt bloody. She could do as she pleased, he said, it was all the same to him. Good-bye and good riddance. If she wanted to know the truth, he could no longer stand the sight of her. She had no idea—no idea at all.

"No idea of what?" I asked.

"Of what he had been going through. Because of his play."

"What he was going through because of his play? Did you ever see it?"

"'Murder Among Friends' wasn't that kind of play. You couldn't see it—there weren't any performances. They were just *in* it."

"You mean, they were acting all the time?" As soon as I said the words, the situation they represented flared into vibrant life within me. "I want to go to Perdido some day."

She dropped her napkin beside her plate. "Forgive me, baby, but you've already spent more time in Perdido than I ever will."

5

Carver began to understand Silsbee's refusal to describe Perdido in the afternoon of his first full day as a guest. Upon arrival, he and Margie had been given lunch for two on the Pandora Terrace. Over the descending series of lawns below, people in summery clothing played croquet, ambled arm-in-arm, and stretched out on comfortable-looking chaises to read fat books. A number of the men wore

Panama hats. Carver, who had packed only an old Yankees cap for headgear, envied them this elegant protection from the intense sunlight. The Carvers had strolled along the gravel paths of the Memory Terrace, come to a sculpted, twelve-foot hedge with an arched opening and a small brass plaque reading THE HIDDEN FOUNTAIN, passed through to observe a mazelike arrangement of similar hedges, and decided to investigate the Hidden Fountain another day. They strolled back to a lower wing of the great structure and in growing wonder proceeded down baronial hallways hung with silken tapestries and guarded by suits of armor. Being New Yorkers, the Carvers concealed their wonder behind a mask of worldly boredom.

Huge polished doors stood open upon lounges and libraries. A wide staircase curved toward an underground chamber where rows of columns rose into the mist ascending from a vast swimming pool. A blond-haired nymph unencumbered by a bathing suit glided near and bestowed a smile upon the Carvers, or upon Carver, executed a racing turn and glided off. Another curving staircase led them back to the realm of baronial hallways and glimpses into luxurious interiors. At the rear of a book-lined chamber dense with tobacco smoke, Carver saw, or thought he saw, a hawk-faced man in a deerstalker hat and an Inverness cape drawing upon a Meerschaum pipe. When he turned away bemused, a young woman with a piquant, foxlike face and wearing a flapper's camisole and cloche hat seared him with a glance straight into his eyes. Margie pulled him through a door labeled THE IMAGE COLLECTION and into a long room hung with portraits, landscapes and interiors with people beached on articles of furniture. Margie pretended to admire these vapors. In the dim light, Carver had barely made them out. They had drifted across the lobby, taken the elevator to the fifth floor and padded the half-mile to their room,

546, where for the first time in perhaps a month, the Carvers fell into each other's arms and grappled, to mutually satisfying effect, across the firm but yielding surface of the largest, most sheerly accommodating bed either of them had ever known.

That the dimensions, imaginative as well as physical, of room 546 failed to match those of its bed had been Carver's only true disappointment. Two chairs and a rectangular table with a worn green leather surface inhabited the corner between a blunt wooden cabinet and a window onto a potting shed, a narrow cement path, and a rocky shelf where an ancient net drooped over a disused tennis court. Three feet of mud-colored carpet separated the right, or Carver's, side of the massive bed and its foot from the faded vertical pink and blue stripes of the wallpaper.

The next morning, a schedule of the day's options written in a nearly indecipherable hand and presented in a copy both faint and blurry, had been slipped under their door. Breakfast was available in three different dining rooms; there were aerobics classes and lessons in golf and tennis (though not on the shabby court visible from the Carvers' window); tours of the hotel and grounds; lunch, to be had from noon to 3:00 PM in locations indoors and out; seminars dealing with topics Carver could not quite make out, apart from "Transformation and Challenge," turgid to the core; screenings of unknown, probably foreign films that seemed to be entitled *The Dreams of the Newly Dead*, *Fingerprints Obliterated by Bruises*, and *Distant Molehills*. At 3:00, unless it was 5:00, those guests who wished to join a "participatory drama" called "Murder Among Friends" were asked to assemble in the Charter Room, unless it was Churton or Chartwell. When at 3:00, Margie having declared an interest in sitting through *Distant Molehills*, Carver's aimless mooching through corridors gave him the promising spectacle of the girl in the camisole and cloche hat slipping around the door of a room identified by its plaque as Charleton, he followed her inside and was greeted by another dazzling smile from the water-nymph, who was seated on the floor with her fetching knees drawn up before her. Instantly, Carver closed the door behind him.

Before he could approach the water-nymph, from the far end of the room an elderly man wearing an eyepatch asked everyone present to be seated for a general introduction to the concept of "participatory drama." Three rows of three padded armchairs had been set up in the middle of the room. The nymph gracefully pulled herself to her feet and took the last chair in the third row. She smiled again at Carver, then turned her attention to the front of the room, where the man in the eyepatch was waving him to the first chair in the first row. Carver obliged, and the other people in the room, whose number exactly equalled that of the chairs, seated themselves. The girl in the cloche hat perched on the chair beside Carver's.

"I like your outfit," he said.

She placed her finger to her lips. "Shhh."

"As you will see, this must be a *very* general introduction," said the theatrical figure before them. The strap of the eyepatch sent a black stripe across his silver hair. He was leaning on a black, military-looking cane with a silver knob for a handle. He wore a close-fitting black suit, and his face was deeply lined. "I am Colonel Graham French, the person to whom you should address your questions or problems during the course of our forthcoming adventure, although I cannot guarantee that I shall be able to assist you. Now I'd like each of you in turn, please, to share your name with the rest of our little band." An ice-blue eye found Carver. "If you would be so good, sir."

Carver spoke his name, and without being prompted, the girl beside him said, "Chloe Lovejoy." The grandmotherly, white-haired, ample woman at the end of the row gave her name as Mrs. Agnes Ford. Seated in the second row were Bix Morton, a preppy thirty-something with floppy blond hair, Marcia Tuttle, a gaunt specter dressed entirely in black whose pronunciation of her first name as "Maw-sher" declared her a native New Yorker, and Joan Holtz, who looked like a prison guard and uttered her name in a spondaic bark. Behind them sat Gloria Leeman, a stiff, dark-haired presence exuding efficiency in a pinstriped suit, and a man in his mid-fifties who wore rimless glasses on his drab, pockmarked face and sounded as though he wished his name were not Arnold Bax, though it was. Awaiting the turn of the water-nymph, Carver had turned halfway around in his chair. She lifted her chin, flicked back her hair with a charming shake of her head, sent a complicitous glance at Carver, and in a bright, musical voice said, "Amanda Lake." As he turned back to the Colonel, his eye was caught by Chloe Lovejoy's, glittering beneath a raised, ironic eyebrow.

"Congratulations," the Colonel said. "You have chosen what in my opinion is the most interesting and challenging option Perdido offers. Also its most exciting. Have any of you ever taken part in a mystery weekend or something similar?"

Mrs. Agnes Ford raised a tentative hand. "I have."

"Where was it? Did you find the experience enjoyable?"

"It was at Mohonk Mountain House, in New Paltz, over in New York. I went with my best friend, Tilly Mason. We had such a good time!" Mrs. Ford swiveled to look at the people arrayed behind her. "That was in 1985. We bought tickets for 1986, but Tilly came down with her tumor and passed away right after Thanksgiving, so I stayed at home."

"No doubt," said the Colonel. "For the benefit of those who have never participated in such an event, would you describe the procedure?"

"Oh, yes! We had to guess who killed a librarian in a castle owned by a count who was supposed to look like Dracula, only he was a bald man and too heavy for the part. There was a mad scientist with a hunchback assistant, and a girl in a coma, and a werewolf, and some other suspects. Most of them were well-known writers in real life, except for the mad scientist, who was a famous cartoonist named Graham Wilson. When they gave their speeches and read things, he was awfully funny. Tilly and I liked him best. And Stephen King was the werewolf, and they kept him in a cage, where he had a typewriter. We were in teams, and we went around and questioned all the suspects over and over, because we had to figure out the story and put on skits where we showed who murdered the librarian. Our team decided on Graham Wilson. Wait. His name wasn't Graham. What was that man's name? He was so *comical!* I remember, it was Gahan! He didn't do it, though, so we didn't win. And you know what? Stephen King was just a plain old everyday person, not a weirdo like you'd expect. So this is going to be like Mohonk?"

"A bit, yes," said the Colonel. "At this moment, beyond the doors of this delightful room, a story called 'Murder Among Friends' has already begun to simmer, to take form and float through our salons, galleries, and gardens. It already saturates the air, already it drifts throughout the width and breadth of this extraordinary resort. From the moment you pass through those doors, all of you will be participants in that ongoing story. It is you who will bend it to its final shape and give it meaning, for this story, the drama called 'Murder Among Friends,' will be the creation of its cast, the people in this room. Although the plot will be common to all, each of you will adapt it to your own unique purposes. Some of you may lose sight of each other altogether. If that happens, do not be alarmed, keep concentrating on your role and your relationships with the cast members remaining on your particular stage."

Mrs. Agnes Ford raised her hand again. "That isn't anything like Mohonk. How do we know what our roles *are*? Who are the suspects?"

"Presently, you are all suspects," the Colonel said. "Detectives, too. Your individual roles will depend on your responses to whatever you see and whatever happens once you walk onstage."

"How can we walk onstage without scripts?" Bix Morton asked from behind Carver. "I don't want to sound stupid, but what about rehearsals?"

"Your life has been your rehearsal," the Colonel said. "In participatory drama, the script is made up of the words spoken from moment to moment, the stage is the whole of Perdido, and the audience consists of the actors and their fellow guests, who are unaware that they are witnessing a performance."

"Well, where does the mystery part come in?" asked Mrs. Agnes Ford. "Where's our darn victim? You can't have a murder mystery without a victim."

From beside Bix Morton, spooky, black-clad Marcia Tuttle said, "You people never heard of improv? It goes on all the time, in case you didn't know. He's talking about a group-improv performance piece, hit and run, like street theater, bing! bang!, define your situation, run with it as long as it stays fresh, boom!, get out. This is not a new concept, by the way."

"Maybe where you come from," said Joan Holtz. "If you tried that crap in South Boston, honey, you wouldn't last very long."

"I've spent a lot of time in experimental theater, *honey*," said Marcia Tuttle. "And don't get me started on tribal parochialism."

"I still want to hear about the darn victim," said Agnes Ford.

"Quite right, Mrs. Ford," said Colonel French. "A murder mystery requires a corpse. Fairly soon, certainly by tomorrow afternoon, someone will be found murdered. The discovery of subsequent victims is up to you. Despite its value, Ms. Tuttle's theatrical experience has no relevance here. We are not engaged in improvisatory street theater, and our drama must be seen through to its end. As I said, it has already begun."

"But you're describing a parlor game, not a drama," said Gloria Leeman. "What are the rules?"

"Strictly speaking, there are none," the Colonel said. "But I assure you, our event is indeed a drama."

Carver raised his hand. "You said we are the suspects and the detectives. Who are the victims?"

The Colonel's mouth lengthened into a smile, and the abruptly deepened lines in his cheeks made him look sinister. "Where but in this room could we find our victim or victims, Mr. Carver?"

"Gotcha, okay?" said Marcia Tuttle. "One or two of these people are in on the game."

Carver glanced sideways at Chloe Lovejoy, who stared straight ahead.

"That may be a reasonable assumption," said the Colonel. "It is, however, untrue. None of you are in possession of any more information than the others. Our victims select themselves."

"I'm having a problem with this set-up," said a voice from the back row.

Carver and the others turned around. Arnold Bax, the drab man in the rimless glasses, was pushing himself out of his chair.

"Could you be more specific, Mr. Bax?" the Colonel said.

"Well, I thought we were going to put on an amateur production, which is what I do with a group called the Metuchen Dramateers, in New Jersey. But . . ." Arnold Bax shrugged and raised his arms. "Sorry, I don't understand what you're doing here. For me, if you don't have a script, a stage, and an audience, you don't have a play. So I apologize for the mistake, and I hope you have fun, but I'm leaving."

"You feel comfortable with orderly structures," said the Colonel.

"That's true," Bax said. "In my profession, we deal with numbers. With numbers, you don't really get into improv, and if you adapt them to suit yourself, the IRS climbs all over you. Hey, I thought we'd be doing something like 'Dial M For Murder,' that's all. This activity isn't for me."

"I understand why you feel as you do," said the Colonel. "However, over the next twenty-four hours, Mr. Bax, you will, I promise you, experience a change of heart. Now please take your seat."

Arnold Bax opened his mouth to protest.

The Colonel said, "Take your seat, Mr. Bax," and Bax obeyed.

"Perhaps I should remind you of where we stand," the Colonel said. "Our story began to permeate this wonderful structure and its grounds a few minutes after you entered Charleton Room. You cannot avoid it, for you are already actors and soon will be onstage."

"Could we get real for a second?" said Joan Holtz. "Why don't you tell us what we're supposed to do?"

"With pleasure, Miss Holtz. Your first task is simply to keep your eyes open. After we break up, you may find that certain particulars are no longer as you remember them. *Observe*. What you observe will lead you deeper into the story. Consult with each other, if you like, discuss your ideas and experiences, but do not forget that since the story comes from you, your actions will affect it. *Think*. If event *A* leads to event *B*, follow the connection to event *C*. As detectives, your job is to discover a pattern. The pattern will lead you to a solution, and every good solution amounts to a revelation. By their very nature, revelations, being disturbances in a settled order, are uncomfortable. What could be more disturbing than a murder among friends?"

With another sinister smile and the suggestion of a bow, Colonel French gestured toward the door. "I wish you well, all of you." Some of the group began to leave their chairs.

"How do we find out who wins?" asked Mrs. Agnes Ford.

"In a participartory drama," said the Colonel, "victory derives from the experience of the process, and its gratifications come to all in precisely the measure they have been earned. Have fun, kids."

Carver looked for Amanda Lake among the group passing though the door, but she had already departed. One step before him, Chloe Lovejoy turned her head and revealed, beyond the edge of the cloche, a glittering, ironic glance.

"Boop-boop-a-doop," he said.

"Oh, you kid." She grinned. "If you want to know why I'm wearing these clothes, they were hanging in my closet, wrapped in dry cleaning bags tagged with my name, when I came back from lunch. I tried them on, and they fit perfectly. That's Perdido for you, right?"

"I wouldn't know. This is my first time."

"Mine, too. But this sure seems like a place where you'd better go with the flow."

Before Carver could ask her to join him for a drink in the half-empty lounge across the hallway, Chloe Lovejoy fluttered her fingers and said, "Twenty-three skidoo." She floated away to the right, deeper into the hotel. Carver turned left, traversed the lobby, and ascended to the fifth floor.

His room seemed to have increased its size by at least half. Six feet of carpeting separated the enormous bed from the inner wall. An even greater distance lay between the bed's foot and the facing wall, where a massive cabinet now stood. The pink and blue stripes of the wallpaper were brighter than those in the room he had left an hour earlier.

Embarrassed by his mistake, Carver backed out. It was the wrong room. His key had opened the door, but it was still the wrong room. He looked at the number, 546. Right number, wrong room. Therefore, there existed another room 546. Carver walked up and down the hallway, but found no other 546. He returned to the door and let himself back in. Feeling like a trespasser, like a thief, he prowled through the strange quarters.

"Perdido" never really ended—at least not yet—but it began with a dream I had early in the summer of 1998. I often dream of vast hotels and resorts through which I endlessly wander, trying to remember where my room is; this particular version of the recurring dream included an interesting variation on the familiar theme. This time, I was not merely wandering lost and baffled, I was searching for a woman, a friend of mine, who had accompanied me to the hotel or resort and subsequently disappeared. I kept catching glimpses of her vanishing around a corner or ascending a distant staircase. She was with a small group of men I did not recognize, and she seemed fascinated by them. I understood that the resort, although utterly luxurious, was the least exclusive and most unimpressive of a chain of resorts, the others of which were located nearby, and to which my rivals would soon lead my faithless friend. She would be taken literally out of my realm. The only other detail I remembered upon awakening was that at the end of the dream someone, maybe I, had cut a cat in half with a sword.

I had a little window of free time, about a month, and decided to make use of this period by writing a novella based on my peculiar dream. So I began with Carver and Margie, a married couple with problems, and their seductive friend Silsbee. Then I decided that these people were char-

acters in a work of fiction written by a former musical prodigy and thief whose parents had decided to separate while on vacation at Perdido, the mountain resort Silsbee describes to his friends. In the "real" story, Silsbee is a kind of mage, and Perdido is a place of mysterious and powerful secrets. When people go there, they endure the awakenings and revelations, and also the miseries, that accompany artistic creation. (Those with superior imaginations are invited to the next level up, Mordido, and the truly superior make it all the way to Endido.) So the narrative breaks into two sections, the first of which—the chapters dealing with Carver and Margie—has been written by the first-person narrator of the second part, who has constructed the Carver-Margie tale as a kind of examination, maybe therapeutic, of a difficult period in his life. In the process, I was thinking, the narrator would reveal himself to be an inhabitant, though not a literal inhabitant, of Endido.

The novella of course expanded beyond the month I could give to it. It also expanded internally, as Perdido itself seems to do, with the introduction of Carver's "activity," the game called "Murder Among Friends." Before I knew it, I had taken on board a talkative new batch of characters and committed myself to an extremely elaborate game. I did not have the time, or at that point the energy to give to a kind of metafictional whimsy, so I put the manuscript in a binder and resumed work on the novel I was all along supposed to be writing.

Peter Straub

IN REAL LIFE

by William F. Nolan

Hey, killing her was a pleasure. Easy. No problem. Gave me a
buzz, actually. Like having a double martini at lunch. She came
into the room raving as usual in that shrill voice of hers. Like a
train whistle. Or nails on a blackboard. Called me a fucking loser.
Said I wasn't worth cat shit. Raved and shouted, waving her hands
around. Swearing like a mill hand. Eyes blazing at me, like two
hot coals.

She made it easy, killing her. Like the end of that Mickey
Spillane book where Mike Hammer shoots the evil bitch in the
belly. I just walked into the bedroom and took the gun from her
vanity table where she always kept it for protection. Paranoid.
Afraid of intruders, of being raped. As if anyone would want to.

What are you doing with my gun? she yells. Always yelling.
Mouth like an open sewer. I said I took the gun to shut her up for
good. You're gonna kill me? She laughed her hyena laugh. Real
unattractive. You couldn't kill a fucking fly, she tells me. Oh, no,

that's not true . . . I can kill you okay, I said. No problem. My voice was icy calm. This was the Big Moment.

That's when I fired point-blank at her: bang, bang, bang.

She flopped over like a big rag doll. Kind of comical. But she really messed up the sofa, falling across it with all that blood coming out of her. Ruined it, really. You can't ever got blood out of a white sofa. That was when Bernie said, in his quiet way: cut and print.

How was I? Linda asked him. Did I fall the right way? You were perfect, darling, he told her. They hugged. Directors always hug their female stars. Treat them like children. That's because every actress is insecure. They need a lot of attention. Best I get is a pat on the shoulder. Good job, Chuck.

He held that gun too close to me, Linda complained. The wads from those fucking blanks *hurt* me.

Linda was like the bitch in the movie. She liked to say fuck. Tough broad. One of the boys. Never liked her. Third picture with her and we still didn't get along. Strong mutual dislike from the first day we met. None of the crew liked her either. Always complaining. Didn't approve of the way her hair was fixed: too short on the sides, too rigid on top. The pale makeup made her look like a corpse. Her dress didn't do her figure justice. The sound man was an asshole, didn't maintain her modulation level. The head grip smoked too much on his breaks. His clothes reeked of stale cigar smoke. Always something to criticize.

But she saved her prime complaints for me. I blocked her key light. Stepped on her lines. Hogged the camera. Wouldn't stick to the script. (She hated improv because she couldn't handle it herself. No flexibility.)

Killing her had been a pleasure. Wouldn't mind doing it in real life. Not that I would. I'm no psycho. Don't go around killing foul-mouthed females. But getting paid for faking it was satisfying. I got to kill Linda in two of our pics together. Strangled her in *The Dark Stranger* and stuck her in a food freezer in *Wake Up to Death*. Fun. A flat-out pleasure.

Ralph handed the pages back to me. "I don't believe it," he said, a nasty edge to his voice.

"Why not?" I demanded. "What's wrong with it?"

"Everything," said Ralph. He seemed to take special delight in hurting me. "You just don't know how to get into the male mind. It takes a man to write about another man."

"That's crap and you know it," I snapped back at him. "Women have been writing successfully about men for three thousand years."

"Okay." Ralph shrugged his scarecrow shoulders. "Maybe they have—but these pages fail to convince me that you're one of them."

"This is my fifth novel for Christ's sake," I protested. "If I'm so lousy, then how come Viking keeps buying them?"

"Hey, Linda! Get real. Your other books all had female protagonists." Ralph had that know-it-all grin on his face. "You wrote them from a feminine perspective. A man is different. It's obvious that you can't handle the male viewpoint."

"That's your opinion," I said. "I know exactly what I'm doing. *I'm* the writer, chum."

"And I'm your best editor!"

"Yeah, and my *worst* husband."

"Then why did you marry me?"

"Damned if I know. Guess I figured you'd be a step up from my first three. But I was wrong. You're a step *down*."

"You're a stupid cunt."

"And you're a stupid prick."

I looked him straight in the eye. "I want a divorce," I said.

And that's when I killed her.

Killed the character in my novel, I mean. This is as far as I got. Thing just wasn't working for me. No flow. Jagged. I was forcing it. And it wasn't truthful. For example, women can write beautifully about men, they do it all the time. Look at Joyce Carol Oates. She writes men that breathe on the page. Eudora Welty. Shirley Jackson. And lots of others.

So that part was all wrong. Yet if I had Linda's husband *approve* of her scenes then my structural conflict would be missing. I could do it over, but I just lost heart. And this novel-within-a-novel stuff is tricky to bring off.

There was something else. Using my dead wife's name for the female character was a bad idea. I should have called her something else. Any name but Linda.

Maybe I'm not cut out to be a novelist. Maybe I should just stick to directing other people's scripts. That's what I'm really good at. Hell, in France they think I'm another Jerry Lewis. Not that I do comedy; I don't. But the Frenchies love me. Edgar Price is a genius. That's what they say. In Frogland, I'm a hot property.

Writing about my dead wife was painful. Bitter memories. Linda drove me nuts during our marriage. We were never compatible. People still believe she died of "natural causes," I made sure about that. Used a poison you can't trace. My little secret. Her family was convinced of my grief. Kept my head lowered at the funeral, dabbing at my eyes. In the cemetery I leaned down to plant a kiss on her coffin. And the single rose I tossed into the grave was a lovely touch.

Guess I shouldn't be admitting it all here, in this diary. But no one will read it. Who'd ever think of looking for a floor safe in the garden shed? Ideal hiding place. That's where the diary goes each morning before I leave for the studio. And I keep the safe's combination inside my head. Never wrote it down. I'm no fool.

Well, at least Linda's gone. I'm damn well rid of her. No more arguments about money, or my drinking, or my women. That loud mouth of hers is shut forever. Comforting thought.

Oops, a horn outside. The limo is here, so I've got to wind this up. End of entry.

Off to the daily grind.

Killing him was easy. Big shot director. Big *shit* is more like it. With all his fancy clothes and his foreign cars and his big house in Bel Air. Claims he saved my ass. Said I'd be nothing if he hadn't come along. Probably be waiting tables at Denny's. Bull! I've always had talent, even as a little girl in Kansas City. Mama used to brag about me to all the neighbors. I'd do those little skits of mine, dancing and singing, and Mama would clap like crazy and tell me I was another Judy Garland. (But I could always dance better than Judy Garland.)

Edgar Price, the big shot director. Discovered me, he always said. Well, *someone* would have. He just happened to get a hard-on in that dumb little theater play in Pasadena when I showed a lot of leg. Came backstage after the curtain to tell me that I demonstrated "genuine talent" and that the studio was looking for talent like mine. Yeah, sure. *He* was the one looking—at my tits, not my talent.

He did get me into pictures, if you can call the kind of crap he directed a picture. Cheezy horror stuff, with me playing a nude corpse in the first one. Not a frigging line in the whole movie. *The Blood Queen's Revenge*. Yuck.

Then he had me doing bare-ass scenes in a shower for that crappy film of his about women in the Air Force. I was supposed to be a lesbian jet pilot. A nothing part. I had maybe five minutes of screen time and I was butt naked for most of that.

Next, he put me in his wrestling thing, where I was this female wrestler who gets her clothes torn off in the ring. Just the pits.

And there was the one where I played a doomed prostitute with lung cancer. God! How I hated the scene where I died in the bathtub. They got worried when my nipples stayed erect, which they said should not happen when I was dead. But that bathwater was frigging *cold!*

Edgar was a ten-carat liar. All the time, while he was putting the blocks to me off camera, he kept saying what a great star he was going to make out of me. But all he wanted was my pussy. I wasn't born yesterday.

Finally, I'd had enough. He comes to the studio in his custom stretch limo and the first thing he wants to do is screw me in his trailer before the morning's shoot. Told me he needed to release sexual energy. To relax his creative drive. Creative, my ass!

He'd been directing this moronic vampire flick, *The Devil Bat's Daughter.* I was the daughter, but natch I got snuffed in the first reel with my boobs hanging out.

I was really pissed. When we were inside his trailer that morning I put some stuff in his coffee. Gave him a heart attack. When he keeled over I started screaming for help. Terrified maiden with a dead director on her hands. Great scene. I was wonderful. Academy Award caliber.

Naturally, the doc couldn't do anything for Edgar. I sobbed up a storm. Big-time tears. The whole bazonga. The doc was so concerned about me that he gave me a prescription to calm my "severe emotional state." Hah! All the time I was giggling inside. The lecherous, lying bastard was dead.

I don't feel any guilt. Not a twinge. Hey, he killed his wife, didn't he? Poisoned her. That's where I got the idea for the stuff in his coffee—from the diary I fished out of his garden shed. When he was loaded one night in bed he kept mumbling the combination, over and over again, like a mantra. Didn't have any memory of it the next day—alcoholic blackout—but by then I'd written the numbers down. I'm very clever about things like that. Got a good head on my shoulders. Mama always said so.

And she was right about my talent. When Edgar had his "unfortunate heart attack" I started moving up the industry ladder. Took a while. I wasn't any spring chicken. And recently, as a "mature" actress, I started getting some fat parts with the likes of DeNiro, Stallone, and Sean Connery. (I was Connery's doped-out mistress in *Kill Me Sweetly*. A plum role. Won me a Golden Globe! Hotcha!)

They're calling for me on the set so I'll quit writing, but my journal is real important. Me writing to me. Very healthy. This no-bullshit stuff is supposed to flush out the emotions. Gets me ready to emote in front of the cameras.

In this one, the picture I'm doing now, I'm a bitchy killer. I drive an icepick into my boyfriend. The producer told me I was perfect for the part. He was right. Fits me like a second skin. I could grab an Oscar for this one. Oh, yeah! Little Linda is ready for stardom! (Funny thing, me having the same name as Edgar's dead wife.) Anyhow, I'm ready for my big icepick scene. Killing my boyfriend in this one will be a pleasure. Easy. No problem.

After all, it's not real life.

POUND ROTS IN
FRAGRANT HARBOUR

by Lisa Morton

Pound rots in Fragrant Harbour. Of course it didn't start here; Pound has been rotting for quite some time. In London, New York, Los Angeles. He wants it to end here, in this city whose original name ("Fragrant Harbour") now seems only slightly less ridiculous than "City of Angels."

Pound is rotting because of the Exchange, the one he made at the beginning of another century. Now it's a new millennium, and Pound has been forced to acknowledge that he was the loser in the Exchange (he steadfastly refuses to use the vulgar—if more traditional—"deal"). Which is not to say that he accepts it; he's fought it every day, since it began. That's why he's here now, in Hong Kong. Fragrant Harbour.

The Exchange came about when the youthful Pound realized that he simply was not going to live long enough to make all the money he wanted. He'd already done well for himself; born to a poor family, his life was consumed by his drive to transcend the legacy. Before his second decade he became overseer of a factory; his use of runaway child labor helped him rise quickly to a position of ownership. When the twelve-year-olds were taken from him, he found starving immigrants and women; when they were unionized, he bought union leaders. Those who couldn't be bought disappeared, and Pound slept soundly.

It still wasn't enough. Pound saw grand profits ahead, but knew even his money wouldn't buy him another lifetime. No, a different currency was needed—and when the Opportunity arose, Pound gladly grasped what was offered him, exchanging currency he considered useless.

Now he realizes he grasped *too* gladly. He should have looked the contract over more carefully. He should have fought over the wording. He'd fire anyone working for him who would approve a contract like that.

But he did sign it, and for a very long time he believed he'd triumphed. He was right about the future; he invested in technology and took his manufacturing firms overseas, where desperate workers were still tolerant of a dollar a day. On those rare occasions when an investment declined, Pound didn't panic because he knew he had time to make his money back again. All the time in the world, in fact.

He moved often, and spent considerable sums creating new identities. Once, a private detective, hired by a disgruntled ex-employee, found part of the trail; a week later, the dick found himself in jail with his license revoked, facing a long line of trumped-up charges. No one listened when he claimed Pound had originally been born in London, or that California was merely his last birthplace. The detective was still serving time when Pound's rot set in.

It began with small pains after he ate, or when he exerted himself, or when he drank too much. At first he ignored it—after all, even he occasionally took ill, like everyone else—but it went on, it got worse. He began—cautiously—to see doctors. They were baffled. Expensive tests showed that Pound's internal organs were simply decaying, and no one knew why. No one, that is, except Pound.

The rot continued, and those around him began to complain of an inexplicable bad odor; next they fell sick. Soon Pound was completely isolated; even his money couldn't keep anyone near him for long. His situation angered him, but Pound never stayed simply angry; he was driven by fury and the need to win.

He isolated himself in two rooms of one of his mansions. Unable to eat or find solace in substance abuse, he spent his days looking for answers online and in the outer reaches. Weary (and wary) of doctors, he turned to other practitioners: mediums, fortune-tellers, clairvoyants, psychics, sorcerers, magicians, and assorted charlatans. Most disgusted him more than he disgusted them. The few authentic ones turned away from him in revulsion. One actually tried to kill him, in an act of ritual magick; Pound laughed until the failed assassin fled. Later, he had the man tracked down and badly beaten. Only an ancient black woman his people found in New Orleans offered anything useful. She gave him one word before she staggered out, leaning heavily on her snake-headed cane:

"East."

The next day he was on his private jet, boarding with only a small suitcase and flight crew of four. Even though he was heavily dressed, wrapped in protective layers, one stewardess sickened, something she'd never done on a flight before. The other stewardess died within a month, of a mysterious disease that ate away at her.

And so Pound arrived in Hong Kong, which he had chosen as the eastern city most likely to accommodate his wealth. He was a pariah, a monster who looked like a normal twenty-something white man on the outside, but who was festering within and infesting all those who came near him. His money bought him service, but it couldn't buy respect, companionship, or an end to his hatred of his own flesh.

Now that he's arrived, he takes his single carry-on bag and his passport to Customs. His passport is stamped and he's waved through quickly, much to the relief of the young exchange student in the queue behind him. The student—returning home after studying commerce for a year in a foreign land—will spend the next month in bed, feverish, while his mother feeds him shark's fin soup and burns joss sticks.

Pound's people have booked him into the penthouse suite at the best hotel in Hong Kong, and the hotel has a car waiting, a dark, smoke-glassed limo. It's a thirty-five minute ride to the Tsim Sha Tsui district where the hotel is, but Pound is completely disinterested; he thinks only of what he can feel within himself, and what he would—what he *will*—do to stop it.

The train to Guangzhou is crowded and hot, and Ming-yun allows herself to drift with the swaying motion of the car.

She wasn't born Ming-yun; she was born with a dull name she despised as much as her dull family and dull home. Home was Huaihua, in China's western Hunan province; its chief attraction was a large railway junction. She grew up hearing that, if she were lucky, she would get work as a farmhand in the rice paddies; otherwise, she'd have to settle for life in a factory. At sixteen she'd left and never returned.

After a year she made her way south to Yangshuo, where she

worked for a while in a western-style restaurant, kowtowing to fat *gweilo* tourists who sometimes asked to take her picture so they could grab her with a sweaty hand. One day she simply walked past the restaurant and kept going. She wound up on Moon Hill, where she was approached by a man who offered to take her on a tour of the Black Buddha Caves for 25 yen. She walked by him without an answer, and began to hike through the country. She found her own entrance to the caves, waited until nightfall and made her way in.

Her descent was precipitated by neither boredom nor curiosity. Ming-yun was in search of something as basic to the Chinese heart as family or *face*: Fate. She believed in fate not as an abstract concept, but in Fate—a tangible thing that could be taken and twisted, molded to one's own purposes. She refused to accept her fate as a farmhand or factory worker or party member or wife; Fate had something different in store for her. Last night she'd dreamt of finding it in a cave.

Except it found her.

Ming-yun had expected to have her Fate revealed to her, as if some curtain were parted by a ghostly hand. She wanted to see her future, to know what road to walk when she left the cave, to have a promise beyond rice paddies and industrial complexes. What she'd been given instead . . .

She'd thought about it every day since, that night in the cave. She couldn't explain what had happened to her; there was no entity present she could name. She only knew that she'd fallen asleep on the hard cave floor, and in her sleep the offer had been made:

She wouldn't be shown her Fate—but she could be *given* one, if she chose to accept it.

She did accept it, without even questioning what it was. Afterwards, when she knew—she'd never regretted it. It was not, perhaps, what she would have chosen for herself, but then again it wasn't anything she could ever have imagined.

When she awoke the next day, she'd forgotten her old name, and had chosen the one she bore now—Ming-yun. Fate.

She is Fate. And now she is on a train bound for Guangzhou— and beyond that, Hong Kong.

Pound's car drops him off before his hotel, and he's efficiently whisked up to his room, by young men whose Cantonese-accented English courtesy masks their distaste.

He flips on the bathroom light, turns on the faucet in the sink, splashes water on his face and looks at himself in the mirror. His blue eyes are reddened; his skin has a dry, cracking look that wasn't there a week ago. Otherwise he could almost pass for just another Western businessman. *Almost.*

He has no idea what to do next; he's more uncertain every second of why he's here at all. He shakes off his irresolution, finds his outrage and leaves the room behind. If nothing else, he decides, he'll walk until he finds something.

It's night as he leaves the hotel behind and strides down the first side street he comes to. He's suddenly in a different world; the sidewalks are impossibly crowded—people coming home from work, shopping, eating. Somehow a path always clears before him; he doesn't see the frowns that appear behind him. Many of the people he passes barely make it home before collapsing, complaining of a new virus. Some will die within two weeks' time, after passing the rot on to those around them.

The streets are awash with neon and scents. He passes restaurants, and is nearly overcome by the temptation of roasting duck. His intestines choose that point to remind him of their condition, and he wheezes in pain, wheezes in fury at being so tormented by this simple pleasure. He steels himself and continues on down the sidewalk. New scents assault him: open barrels of dried scallops, steam from cooking noodles, bamboo shoots being boiled into a pungent beverage. He tries to walk in the street, and is nearly run down by a honking minibus. He reels into a small, crowded store selling CDs and movies; he pretends to riffle through the jewel-cases long enough to collect himself, then he re-enters the flow of traffic outside. But this time it's back to his hotel, to his cocooned suite, away from the mob and the ordinary seductions he can never enjoy again.

The worst part about knowing her Fate was waiting for it to arrive.

Ming-yun's train had reached Guangzhou, and now she has a three-hour ride on a jet catamaran to Hong Kong. This time she doesn't doze; she focuses, containing her anticipation. She's close now.

It has been twelve years since that night in the cave. Twelve years since she left, knowing what lay before her. Knowing that she would endure twelve years of life as the factory worker she'd been told she would become. Twelve years of mind-numbing drudgery, day after day leavened by the knowledge of what was to come. She couldn't imagine this life without that. She wondered how the rest survived.

In the evenings she trained. Her Fate required discipline, and so she educated herself in *wushu*, in sword forms, in Shaolin-style kung fu. The monks also taught her healing, at which she was surprised to find she excelled. She could locate a tumor or hernia with touch, or cure a headache or infection with herbs. Patients gave her gifts of gratitude; she gave most to the monks, except for the money, which she saved for her Fate. She would need money for the first part, the part when she had to travel to Hong Kong.

It never occurred to Ming-yun to doubt the reality of her Fate, to question the dream that led her on. Her Fate felt far more real to her than the daily grind of the factory, and her training gave her confidence to ward off the unwanted suitors who approached her from time to time. It wasn't that men didn't interest her; it was that only one man interested her, and he was still twelve years away, and in Hong Kong.

Pound falls into the daze that passes for sleep with him, and awakens to find himself blind at first. He lurches from the bed, overtaken with animal panic for the first time in his life. A wall stops him with a loud thud, and he finds himself thinking about the large plate-glass window that overlooks a busy street twenty floors below. The thought of lying in the roadway, shattered, helpless but still alive, sobers him, and he realizes his sight is returning. Gray light, thick shapes, finally give way to pale colors and outlines.

At least he has a destination now; last night, before he slipped into semiconsciousness, his eyes still functioned well enough to peruse the hotel room guidebook. It mentioned a row of fortune-tellers near the Tin Hau Temple in Jordan. Jordan is a five-minute car ride to the east.

It's already dark out again, but Pound reasons that fortune-telling isn't the kind of profession shut down due to lack of light. This time he balls up tiny pieces of tissue to stop the smells from reaching him. It's probably too much to hope, he thinks, that his sense of smell will give way as quickly as his sight.

The hotel limo is a welcome relief from the sensuality of the streets, hermetically sealing Pound behind cool, dull glass. The car moves slowly down Nathan Road, angling between double-decker busses and the ubiquitous taxis.

Despite the traffic, Pound is quickly deposited at the mouth of Temple Street; usually he'd want assistants, an obsequious entourage, around him, but tonight he's relieved that not even the limo driver offers to accompany him. He finds himself looking down a side boulevard, crowded and neon-lit like all the ones in Tsim Sha Tsui. He wonders briefly if there's any place in this city that *doesn't* look like this.

He starts down Temple Street, which nightly transforms itself into a street market of hundreds of tiny enclosed stalls. He pushes through the center of them, past displays of luggage, watches, dolls with oversized heads, movies recorded illegally on cheap computer disks, souvenir T-shirts and CDs. It seems to go on forever, until Pound's already-failing eyesight jumbles into something his brain can no longer read. He grabs on to a support pole and waits until it passes. He disregards the vendor railing angrily at him in Cantonese.

At last the street comes to a break, and the stalls disappear. A short distance ahead Pound makes out, at last, his goal: the Tin Hau Temple, and, on the sidewalk before it, a dozen fortune-tellers. Each has a table, chairs, red banners Pound can't read. What Pound is looking for is one with a queue of customers.

It's beginning to rain, and so the fortune-tellers aren't as busy tonight as usual, but one stall has a gathering of waiting clients, and Pound takes his place there. This stall has less decoration than the rest, no scrolls showing lines of the hand or parts of the face. Pound gazes curiously at the prognosticator, this one who must be proficient enough to draw business. It's a middle-aged man, ordinary looking except for his jagged and browned teeth. He seems more like one of the food vendors Pound's just passed than a seer. A teenage girl—his daughter, probably—stands next to him. At first Pound thinks she's extraordinarily ugly, with her moon face and her father's bad teeth; but as he watches her, the way she carefully attends to her father and the customers, he changes his mind and thinks her care makes her almost lovely.

Finally it's Pound's turn. He steps up, and the man behind the table tenses but holds his gaze. Pound asks if he speaks English. The girl answers: "I can tell you what he says."

She gestures at the chair near Pound, and he takes it, then puts his hand on the table as he's seen those before him do. "Other one," the girl says, and Pound puts his left up instead.

The girl notices her father's reluctance to touch Pound, and she takes the older man's shoulders reassuringly. He finally reaches across and begins to examine Pound's palm. After a long moment he releases the hand and looks Pound's face over carefully. Finally he leans back and mutters in Cantonese.

"He says," the daughter begins, "that you will not find the answer you want. He says . . ." She pauses to take in the stream of words pouring from the man, then: "Your only chance is to be reborn. You cannot seek it—it will find you. You must accept that. For you there is no other way." Then she names a price.

Pound considers questioning, or arguing, but instead pays and walks away. He finds a bench in the temple courtyard and sits, gathering himself. At first he's angry—he should have expected this, the usual singsong fortune-telling gibberish; but something about this one is different. Somehow it feels right.

When he turns, he's not surprised to see that the fortune-teller and his daughter have gone, only an empty space on the sidewalk now where their table and chairs had been. He wonders idly how long they'll live, and then laughs to himself as he settles back onto the bench to wait.

It's night when Ming-yun's boat arrives at the China Hong Kong City terminal in Tsim Sha Tsui. She's hungry, and once she's off the boat she makes her way past Kowloon Park to the shops, finds the first cheap restaurant and gorges herself. Then she steps into the rainy night, and closes her eyes.

The trail of rot is near.

She opens her eyes and begins moving, pushing her way brusquely through the passersby. She carries only a small pack on her back and a long, wrapped bundle in one hand. The sword gives her comfort.

She's never seen a city like Hong Kong. Even Guangzhou wasn't this dense and bright; it could easily be overwhelming if she tried to take it in. But the city doesn't interest her; perhaps later. If there is a later.

And so she turns north. She can tell that some of the people she passes on the sidewalks have already been infected by him, and they in turn are beginning to infect others. She pushes on harder, faster. At the corner of Nathan and Cameron roads, near a red subway entrance, she's nearly overcome by the trail of decay—*he was here*—but redoubles her determination and pushes north along Nathan, heading for Jordan and Temple streets.

Pound waits in the courtyard of the Tin Hau Temple. Sometime in the last hour he thinks his heart has stopped working, and now sits in his chest as a mouldering lump of useless organic matter. He's afraid to get up, afraid that his legs will no longer function and he'll be carted off to some Chinese hospital, locked away as a medical curiosity for the rest of an eternally long life. He's not sure what else he can do, so he waits.

The night wears on, and the last of the stalls on Temple Street shuts down. The courtyard empties, until Pound is alone there. He doesn't know what time it is, doesn't care. He only knows that the rain has stopped, a small fact for which he's grateful. At least that won't add to his decomposition.

He's dimly aware that a new arrival has entered the courtyard, and he looks up. squinting, to make out a woman standing before him. The most beautiful woman he's ever seen. Tall, especially for a Chinese, with fine slender limbs and an imperious chin.

Then she unwraps the sword.

Ming-yun has followed the trail through the early morning streets, as the crowds have thinned and then disappeared almost completely. As she neared the Temple, the reek became stronger. She saw the figure seated on the bench in the courtyard, saw him through the wrought-iron fence surrounding the Temple, and felt a thrill of exhilaration arc through her.

It was him. Her Fate.

She had paused only a moment, long enough to let this delicious moment sink in, to savor it as the reward for twelve years of hard labor, of endurance. Now is her moment.

She had entered the courtyard and approached him carefully. He didn't look like a monster; he merely looked like another *gwelo* who'd eaten something that hadn't agreed with him. But there was no question this was him. The aura around him was terrible, and Ming-yun used all the methods of concentration she'd been taught over the previous decade to force herself to stand there.

At last she unwraps the sword.

Ming-yun looks at Pound for a time, then sets her pack down and kneels before him. He looks at her blearily, and she understands that his eyes are rotting with the rest of him. She knows there isn't much time left, and prays that she isn't too late to do what her Fate has told her must be done.

She sets the sword down, and, still kneeling, slowly leans forward and kisses Pound. He's only mildly surprised, for some reason. He returns the kiss, thankful for a sensation that doesn't cause him pain, although his hands are too weak to raise to her face.

He is surprised, though, when he feels her fingers on his crotch, is more surprised by the fact that he's stiff there. She kneads him, gently, encouraging him, finally undoes his pants and releases him. Pound thinks he's never felt this hard before, never in his very long life. He gives himself over to it, willing now to accept whatever comes.

Ming-yun removes her own worn denims, then straddles him, lowering herself onto him. She barely moves and suddenly Pound is exploding. She tightens around him, drawing him in, holding him until the small spasms cease.

Pound is only dimly aware that Ming-yun has released him and risen off of him. He's simply glad that he could have this—this last, final pleasure—to hold on to.

That's why he doesn't see her, when she dresses again and then picks up the sword. She considers a moment, then begins with a matter-of-fact side swing that neatly severs Pound's head. There's no blood, as she expected, just a dull wet sound as the head hits the pavement and is stopped by her foot. She moves quickly, lowering the body to the ground and opening the chest with the sword tip. It's easy work—Pound was so far gone that his flesh and bones are nearly liquid.

Ming-yun isn't particularly concerned with whether she's seen or not; there's been no sound other than the small ones, so she knows she hasn't been heard. When she's done she reaches for her pack, and removes the small barbecue carried there. She sets it up, thankful the rain has stopped and made this task simpler. She stokes a fire in it, then places what she's removed onto the grate.

Pound's heart only takes an hour to turn to ash, and there's not very much left when Ming-yun is done. The sky is just starting to lighten as she empties the last embers out of the barbecue and sets the heart's ashes out to cool. When she can touch them without burning her fingers, she scoops them up into her mouth, swallowing quickly until they're all gone. It's only a few mouthfuls, which she washes down with a bottle of green tea from her pack.

As the sun rises Ming-yun is packed again and standing, looking up at the ancient temple as it glows in the morning light. The air around her is fresh again, even fragrant, and she breathes it in deeply. She can feel Pound inside her, already growing; then she turns away, ready to live the rest of her Fate.

APOLOGIA

by Robert Devereaux

I was born in Bartota in Upper Galilee.

My father was called Simon.

My mother had neither name nor face. She was nothing but a womb, an os, a vagina, a vulva, the last-mentioned beguilement gaping wide and saucy onto the fires of hell.

In Nazareth was I born, to a carpenter named Joseph and his chattel Miriam. Miriam had dropped some love brat first, Yeshua by name—my elder brother, a royal pain in the *tuchus*.

But I was his trusty puppy dog, and in later life he put all his faith in me.

It was misplaced.

It was not misplaced.

In Kerioth was I born, Reuben my father, Cyborea his wife. The night they lay together and I lay claim to her maculate womb, she split the blackness with her screams.

305

"I dreamed," she said, as Reuben calmed her, "that unto us a child was born, a son so steeped in wickedness that eternal ruin was visited upon our people."

When out I slid, my burst of red hair a sure sign of criminality and bewitchment, Cyborea put me to sea in a basket of woven rushes. To the island of Skariot did the frail cradle drift. A discreet maiden carried me to her childless queen who, feigning pregnancy, brought me forth in the fullness of time as her own. A year later, heavy indeed with child, she bore a second prince.

I was a dullard, the sort of lad who passes beneath notice. Yeshua, their first born, was the special one in Mom and Dad's eyes, a gentle know-it-all admired by those who knew him. From infancy, he could cure the possessed and work wonders.

I had three more brothers, dullards all.

There were a few sisters as well, naught but rustles of fabric and lowered lids.

A basket of rushes? Not so. It was an ornate chest, by some miracle watertight, that floated me toward Skariot and my princely life.

I was a biter. Palace guards, the queen mother, my little brother, fell victim to my assault.

Why did I break their skin?

Satan had corrupted my tender soul. Inside me had he encamped, the red-pink wrap of my ribcage aglow with torch light. My liver became his couch, my heart his pillow, my tinkler his plaything.

When no one was around to receive my proffered pain, I gnawed upon my own arms and hands. If anyone tried to stop me, they were bit and battered without mercy.

Mom muzzled me and ferried me to Nazareth's youthful healer,

Yeshua. His eyes burned deep. His fingers seemed thin and snap-pable.

I despised him.

"Remove the boy's muzzle," said Yeshua. "I want to touch his mouth."

Lion's den.

At once I buried my teeth in his side and caught his wrist in them, so that he cried. But his fingers brushed my scalp and out slinked the black dog Satan, who told me as he sped off that I had marked places for the spear and spike, good boy, good boy.

I had no idea what he meant.

God fuck all anti-Semites! May their nether regions be skewered for all eternity on demonic tallywhackers of fire and thorns.

The Pauline Church spiced up Yeshua's story with the mythic resonances of pagan god-sacrifice, which demanded a betrayer. Any of the disciples would have been fair game. But my name, a proud Jewish moniker, attracted their rabid fantasizing and I became a bogeyman, a greedy, hook-nosed, treacherous thief, red of hair, yel-low of garb, whose kiss betrayed a close friend on a whim.

Fire and thorns forever.

Iscariot means "of the Zealots."

Iscariot means "from the village of Kerioth."

Iscariot means "from the isle of Skariot."

Iscariot comes from "sicarius," a dagger man or a political assassin.

I never existed.

The mythmakers of a moribund sect seized upon me for their ends. The Black Christ, close companion, brother, lover, doppleganger gone bad, who betrayed the Savior to his assassins: So was I painted.

Unburdened by actual flesh and bone, I bestride the isthmus of history.

Yet I, unlike you whose dying eyes read these words, burn in memory. Deflated and engraved shall you crumble to dust. But Judas, nestled in the heart of humanity's collective hatred, shall gloat and glower there forever.

Naught endures nor can be clung to.

Peter had it right: *"Denn alles Fleisch, es ist wie Gras, und alle Herrlichkeit des Menschen wie des Grases Blumen. Das Gras ist verdorret und die Blume abgefallen."*

Weary of the abuse her true son suffered, my mother, the queen of Skariot, told me I was a foundling.

So I butchered her, tore out his throat, and sailed to Jerusalem, where I became a menial in Pontius Pilate's household.

Pilate craved apples, or were they figs? A certain orchard inflamed his lust. He drooled so as we passed it, that the road turned muddy.

"Get me some," he said one day.

I hopped down and vaulted the fence.

At my first pluck of apple, fig, apple, the enraged farmer appeared. We fought. I stove in his face. Back he fell against a tree, skull-struck unto death.

Pilate hurried us to Jerusalem, had his attendants slain, and gave me the orchard and the man's woman for my own, her name Cyborea, an aging bit of chattel who swived well but slept ill.

We had some good years. A boy, a girl. Then Cyborea filled in her background. Great. Killed Dad, bedded Mom, where had I heard this before?

So I donned sackcloth, rolled in ashes, sought out Yeshua for forgiveness, and joined his merry band.

Not quite.

I butchered and buried Cyborea and our brats. Then me and Pilate we yucked it up over wine, grapes, and past gropes renewed. He leaned to my ear: "I need someone to spy on this Yeshua character. You up to it?"

"Up as can be."

"So I see," said he.

Yeshua had a cousin named John the Immerser.

He lost his head.

Ich will deinen Mund küssen, Jochanaan.

So much for apocalyptic eschatology.

Yeshua gathered twelve disciples: some Zealots, a few fishermen, and me.

Yeshua was astute. Me, a thief, he put in charge of the purse. Me, a betrayer, he chose as his most trusted adviser.

He needed someone who would be impervious to his good influence. That someone he found in me.

I was an instrument of salvation.

Without me, no crucifixion, no resurrection, none of this taking on the sins of the world.

I deserve a medal.

If Yeshua was present at the dawn of creation, so was I, seed of divine betrayal.

Together, we comprised the Son of God.

Yeshua bathed in the sweat of the poor. He denied not the body, the beast-flesh that suffers illness, taxes, and the oppressive boot of the colonizer. He wandered in equality, inviting others to wander with him, there where meals were shared and the sick were made well. He was a rabble-rouser who brooked no bullshit. Hierarchies had no part in his vision. Egalitarianism delighted him. He was a communist. A socialist. Wise and caring beyond all others, Yeshua defied authority.

We Zealots expected great things from him.

He let us down.

It was said that he had a familiar spirit, one Baal-Zebul, God of Excrement, who gave him the power to cast out demons.

I never believed that.

When we passed through Nazareth, his home town? No healing. Nazarenes, you see, pride themselves on being undupable.

The glint I caught in Yeshua's eye should have tipped me off. Actors beguile through conviction absolute. The best actors and the most skilled liars are of a piece.

Yeshua was the greatest actor who ever lived. Using the Kingdom of God as a lure, he convinced me to hand him over, to replace him on the cross, a Gnostic simulacrum, spikes piercing my flesh, mockery, a parched demise, the prey to dogs.

He promised me a place on his right hand in heaven. Instead, he positioned me, jaws wide, my lips puckered around His Satanic Majesty's anus in hell. From thence speweth every vile act that inhumanunkind perpetrates upon itself. Poor Judas kneels in continual bloat, naught but a shit machine, the stench in front competing with that in back, where his fewmets fly up earthward to bespatter the sorry race of men.

Yeshua's finest hour, the hour I held him in highest esteem, was the Sermon on the Mount.

The Beatitudes resonated with us all.

We were drawn to paradox.

We also liked a good joke, and the "Blessed are" formulation gave rise to some real howlers. When Yeshua wandered off-road to pay nature his respects, the rest of us, Peter especially, grew ribald and crude in our humor.

Prissy Thomas ratted on us, of course.

But Yeshua was the forgiving sort.

In Bethany, this whore or virgin—depending whom you believe—named Miriam, in the house of Simon the leper, unsealed a jar of alabaster. Therein, ointment of nard. Miriam cupped some in her hand and poured it on Yeshua's head and feet, almost a burial preparation.

I spoke up. Yeshua had so championed the poor, I thought I'd win his favor by pointing out how expensive nard was, and what a great waste her whorish or virginal pouring represented.

He chided me and thanked Miriam.

This they cite as an instance of my greed.

They lie through their teeth.

Hengstenberg, some nineteenth-century anti-me idiot, said, "This house was disinfected by the savor of Miriam's ointment from the pestilential vapors with which Judas had previously filled it."

Diseased mind, diseased metaphor.

Entrance into Jerusalem, the donkey, the palm waving, hosannah in the highest?

Nonsense!

In the month of Nissan, when we celebrate Passover, no leafy branches exist anywhere.

Try the autumn Festival of Tabernacles, during which we wave *lulabs*, bundles of greenery made from the branches of myrtle, willow, and palm.

So why is Palm Sunday called Palm Sunday?

Beats me.

Ask Mister Preacherman.

All talk, no action.

That was what we Zealots muttered among ourselves about Yeshua.

When he routed the moneychangers from the Temple, we thought, *Ah, at last.* Stow the chatter, stir up trouble, fire the passions of the crowd.

What more opportune time and place than the Festival of Passover? Three million pilgrims, tinder-ready, who had converged to celebrate our ancient deliverance from foreign occupation.

I handed Yeshua a rope, which he twisted into a whip. The tables of the moneychangers, showers of gold splashing hither and yon, he overturned.

From their pens, he freed the sacrificial animals the moneychangers were selling.

This was dangerous stuff. This could get him killed. "Den of thieves," he bellowed. "House of prayer."

John, James, Peter, and I cheered him on.

Then he threw aside the whip and went soft. We left, it was over, we frowned and followed.

Never happened.

Yeshua's angry words are lifted verbatim from the ancient books of *Isaiah* and *Malachi*.

The triumphant Pauline Church pillaged the ancient scriptures for any scrap that they could turn into proof of Yeshua's divinity. Sleight of hand. Cobble together tales about their Man from material laid down centuries before, then claim prophetic links forward.

Pathetic.

In the midst of Our Lord's savage whip-dance in the Temple, a glint flickered in his eye.

It frightened me.

I hadn't believed the tales of Baal-Zebul, the demon they claimed possessed him.

Yeshua was supposed to be a realized being. He gave a convincing show, but one naked glint speaks volumes.

I vowed that moment to destroy him.

I did not betray him.

I *informed* against him.

There's a crucial distinction.

Yeshua was a false messiah, an idolatrous conjurer of the dead who was leading Israel astray. In the honorable tradition of Joseph, whose religious duty impelled him to inform against his brothers, I informed against Yeshua.

The law says: "Thou shalt destroy the wicked among you." And thus I acted.

The verb *paradidonai* does not mean to betray, but to hand over or surrender.

That is what it means in Xenophon, Pausanias, and Josephus. So is it rendered in the scriptures whenever my name is absent.

Put Judas proximate? Presto chango, betrayal drips from the translator's pen.

When Yeshua began to act kittenish again, vis à vis Caiaphas the High Priest, I took him aside.

"*Judas, step aside with me,*" said Our Lord, taking my arm.

Reminding him that he had always advised us to rebuke the sinner directly, I demanded to know why he had not so rebuked Caiaphas.

"*I need a volunteer,*" he said. "*I want you to serve a very special role. You must tell Caiaphas that I will allow myself to be handed over. Tell him, moreover, that I have authorized you to make it happen.*"

Looking lamb-foolish, he countered that the occasion of confronting the High Priest had not presented itself.

"*Your reward? My undying gratitude, nor do I use the word undying lightly. A chance to earn a reputation as the greatest villain that ever lived. To become indeed the personification of base betrayal for ages to come. To suffer for all eternity the torments of hell, as opposed to the ruined weekend ahead of me. Will you do it?*"

I offered to arrange it, certain that Caiaphas would crumble before Yeshua's simple majesty. Or that Yeshua would be laughed at and dismissed, his moment passed and he exposed as yet another false messiah. Either way, the decks would be cleared.

"I will," I said. Yeshua was a powerful persuader. Anybody exposed to the *aw-shucks effulgence* of his smile would have agreed.

Of *course* I betrayed him.

I wish I had done a better job of it.

Treachery on an intimate scale demands the utmost skill and attention. Ah, but what satisfaction redounds when one shatters a loved one's heart!

People have this odd notion that they are part angel. Nurse that delusion. Deliver praise and adoration beyond all bounds. Dig your meat hooks in deep. Take vows. Be trusted. Commit to their best interests.

Then come down hard.

Bruise them with a kiss.

Savor those hurt looks as they go to their ruin.

Come on. Admit it. Betrayal is fun. That's why it's so prevalent. That's why spousal trysts flourish, why trusted embezzlers amass troves in the shadows, and why confidants cannot, in the end, contain themselves.

Bad faith.

We can't get enough of it.

Thirty pieces of silver that belonged to Yeshua and the others I gambled away. He had sent me to fetch bread and wine for something called the Last Supper.

Maxima mea culpa, I was waylaid, hustled, and fleeced by Pilate's boys. Into the pot and gone, the coins.

One of them took me aside. "Hand Yeshua over to us, and we'll return your money. Deal?"

"Uh-huh," I said.

I took the silver, stopped at the market, wondered for a moment whether perhaps a crumb of bread and a lone drop of wine would suffice, given Yeshua's talents.

No, thought I, and bought abundant bread and wine.

I probably overpaid, thirty pieces of silver being enough to live on for five months, or to buy a slave. Come to think of it, given the blood and flesh themes Yeshua threaded through that supper, a succulent slave might have better served.

The institution of the Eucharist, historians tell us, was established not by Yeshua, but much later by Paul.

The unfaithful table companion? Straight out of *Psalms:* "Even my bosom friend in whom I trusted, who ate of my bread, has lifted his heel against me."

Nail Judas once again to his cross of betrayal.

The last meal was nothing special. Sopping, chewing, swilling, an eructatory episode or two from the less couth among us, one furtive break of wind from I dare not say whom, minimal chit-chat.

The Essenes invited us over.

Modest digs. We reclined Roman-style on low couches, dipping crusts of bread into communal dishes set on small round tables.

Though some called the Essenes radical, I felt right at home. The Temple priests were corrupt, they railed, a charge they repeated far into the night and long after our dinner plates had been spirited away.

Yeshua attempted to speak but gave up.

Still, we cut our hosts some slack.

When we left, we were still cutting.

We sat at a great stretcher of a table, six of us to Yeshua's right, six to his left.

When he said that one of us would betray him, Peter whispered fiercely to John behind my back. In the din and outcry of Bartholomew, James the Lesser, and Andrew on my right, I couldn't make out what Peter had said.

Beyond Yeshua, Matthew turned a troubled eye toward Simon and Thaddeus, as if to ask, *Can it be so?* Past them were Philip, James the Greater, and Thomas who, as always when he was agitated, pointed heavenward with his index finger.

I had the momentary impression that I saw before us an oddly dressed man holding a paintbrush, standing before a glimmer of wall and peering intently at Yeshua.

Then he was gone.

"But, Lord," they protested, "who among us would dare betray you?"

"The one into whose hand I place this sop of bread. That man is my betrayer."

And he gave me to eat.

"Who did you say would betray you, Lord?"

"The one to whose lips I lift this wine. That man is my betrayer."

And he gave me to drink.

"Oh, Lord," they wailed, "it is not I, surely."

"The man whose name is Judas and whom I now point my finger at. He, *he* is the one who will betray me."

"Grant us a sign, Lord. Give us to know the identity of that beastly disciple, and we shall tear out his lungs and thrash him soundly."

Yeshua threw up his hands and slumped upon his stool, the image of defeat.

Having heard what a ruckus Yeshua had raised in the Temple, the Sanhedrin met that night to condemn him and arrange for his arrest.

Right.

Even if the Sanhedrin had been inclined to convene for such a purpose, the Torah insists that they judge in the light of day only. A night meeting at any time, let alone on that most holy night of Passover, would have been unthinkable.

There was no betrayal, no kiss, and no Garden of Gethsemane.

Whole cloth.

That night the Sanhedrin met to condemn him. I stood before them and instructed them to follow me. The man I kissed was the man they should seize.

Yeshua and his followers crossed the Kedron ravine into the garden. Pleas were made, denials asserted and denied.

Then I showed up with a crowd of Jews . . . make that a

detachment of Roman soldiers . . . wait, no, they were guards sent by the chief priests and the Pharisees . . . or was it the chief priests themselves and the elders?

Hold on now.

The Pharisees could not have sent guards. That was just anti-Pharisee propaganda from wacko gospelizer John, to make Yeshua look good and the Pharisees evil. Only the High Priest—a Sadducee, not a Pharisee—acting on behalf of the Romans, would have been empowered to deploy them.

The chief priests and elders? Equally absurd. Such exalted ones would have sent Temple guards, not shown up in person.

Whatever, whoever, there were a bunch of us. I was the spearhead, my lips pursed into a hard steely buss, my mouth blundering against its target.

Someone's ear was cut off in the scuffle, the ear of the High Priest's servant.

Someone's *earlobe*, I mean.

Christ, it was *my* earlobe!

In the midst of the ruckus, lopped lobes flying hither and yon like globs of sputum, Yeshua smiled at me. "My friend," said he, his head imbalanced for loss of an ear, "thou art come at last."

He turned his cheek to me.

"The blows of a friend are well-meant, but the kisses of a foe are perfidious." So says the proverb.

Mine was a friend's kiss.

It surrendered Yeshua to the authorities, a goal he longed to attain.

Yeshua was an exceedingly oral man, all that emphasis on shared meals, loaves and fishes, the Eucharist, a kiss upon greeting, his mesmerizing palaver in the streets and on hillsides.

When my lips touched his cheek, I was seized by an over-whelming love of the universe and by its love for me. I broke down in tears, keening there against his face as the guards tore him from me. My seed leaped up, caught quick and clammy in my under-garments.

It was a gush of spirit entire, made manifest by the body, but not *of* the body.

My ecstasy was metaphysical.

You wouldn't understand.

The religious trial was followed by a civil trial. Pilate, Herod, and the Jews all turned out. Barabbas. Give us Barabbas, crucify the other. I wash my hands. His blood be on us and on our children.

God fuck all anti-Semites!

Pilate was a brutal suppressor of crowds, not one to meekly acquiesce to any mob's wishes.

There was no Barabbas.

Yeshua was a peasant nuisance nonentity whose death bore all the significance of a slapped mosquito.

His blood be on no one but himself.

It was not supposed to happen that way.

I expected Yeshua either to trump the High Priest and take over, or to return, crestfallen and draggletailed, to his disciples.

Instead Caiaphas handed him over to the Romans, who cruci-fied him.

Boy, was *I* ever in for a whipping when Daddy came home.

Truth be told, Yeshua was demon-possessed. We were relieved, those closest to him, when he was murdered. We piled rocks against his tomb, me, Peter, the redoubtable Thomas, and the three Maries, to ensure that Baal-Zebul stayed good and buried.

Until the mythmakers got hold of me, I was a nobody. "You're far too faithful," Yeshua told me. "A puppy dog with a lolling tongue. Show some backbone, why don't you? Assert yourself. Be bold, make plots, betray someone."

But I hung on.

It was actually Peter, the cock-crow denier, who did the deed, who planted the kiss, who testified before the Sanhedrin against him.

Pilate owed Peter a favor, some vow teased out in the bedroom.

Pilate paid off.

All in all, what happened was for the best.

I lived a long life and died stone dead.

There is no afterlife, by the way.

Sorry.

No thieves hung beside him.

No gall and vinegar were forced upon him.

No nameless centurion recognized him as the Son of God.

Joseph of Arimathea, the darling of the grail legend, a rich man torn between the need to be a disciple and his membership in the Sanhedrin, who buried Yeshua's body—he was a fable from start to finish.

Yeshua died an agonizing death, cursing God, cursing the disciples who had abandoned him, and cursing me above all, from my toes to my flaming red hair.

His body was tossed aside, unburied, to feed carrion birds and beasts. Packs of savage dogs worried the flesh from his bones. His grave was a shallow mound, his burial quick and casual.

The rest is fantasy.

When I begged a glimpse of his agony, Satan went the extra mile.

Visible only to Yeshua, I flew to where he writhed upon the cross. His spikes I wrenched and twisted, prying out cries of agony.

Barbed kisses I burrowed in among his blood and bruises, tearing with my teeth at each wound.

My master having shown me my fate, I craved payback in advance for it.

The Gnostics had it right.

Yeshua suffered not at all on the cross. He felt not one jot or tittle of pain. His was an early and painless journey toward heaven.

Ergo, my crime was no crime at all.

Praise Judas.

The resurrection was announced by a youth in a white robe . . . make that an angel floating on the wings of an earthquake . . . or was it a pair of angels, with a halo chaser.

Lies breed inconsistency.

Yeshua's risen body appeared first to Peter, first to the women in the garden. Or was it only to Magdalene? He showed himself to five hundred, to the dozen disciples, to the dozen-minus-me, to no one at all.

For God's sake, get it right!

Truth be told, I hung the defunct Nazarene's body on a huge cabbage stalk in my garden, away from prying eyes.

When his followers cited the empty tomb as proof that he had risen, I trundled him out before them.

Their faces fell. They called me names and wouldn't let me join in their games. With a reputation most foul did they saddle me.

No tolerance for practical jokes.

I rolled back the rock, nobody else.

I soul-kissed Yeshua's dry dead mouth.

His veins pumped, his heart pounded, he opened those Aryan-blue eyes.

Granting me powers, he took me with him for hell's harrowing. I got to stick it to plenty of sinners, while he freed the select and lay the place to waste.

"Not bad," I said, my throat constricted by sulfurous fumes. "What's my reward?"

Then he robbed me of my powers and shoved me into the middle mouth of Satan, there to be eternally gnashed.

I know that my betrayer liveth.

How did I die?

I never died.

Too late repentant, I threw the Sanhedrin's blood money into the Temple. Caiaphas flung it back. We kept it up for quite a while, streams of silver arcing through the air as wide-eyed urchins gawked and applauded.

When our arms tired, I retrieved the coins and bought a parcel of land with it.

I called it Blood Acres.

Eaten up with remorse, I hanged myself.

My spirit squeezed up into my skull and out the thin-sickle curves of my eye sockets. Then it flew to Calvary to plead for Yeshua's pardon.

What a mensch! In the midst of his agony, he offered poor Judas bounteous forgiveness.

When he at last expired, his spirit embraced mine and we floated up to heaven, where I and all the elect enjoy salvation.

I told my wife I feared that Yeshua would resurrect, and asked her for a rope to hang myself.

"Relax," she said. "That ne'er-do-well is as likely to come back to life as yon roasting cock is to crow."

The bird she had referenced, steeped in the logic of folktale, at once spread its regenerated black and green wings, and released a raucous cock-a-doodle-doo.

"Here," said my wife.

Taking the rope, I chanced upon Satan in the street. He introduced me to slope-shouldered, droopy-eyed Despair, who led me to a magnificent tamarind tree, at that time a thing of height and beauty.

I secured the rope and stood on his shoulders.

Despair stepped aside.

As I dropped, the tamarind tree, so help me Kipling, grew squat and worthless, as it has remained ever since.

Hoping to reach Hell before Yeshua did, there to beg salvation of him, I hanged myself.

But the tree bent down and refused to bear my weight. One tree after another behaved so, until I tossed the rope aside and resigned myself to a life of scorn and derision, replete, no doubt, with a Job's-worth of boils, bursitis, and carnal nasties as yet unknown.

I ended my life because God had granted me a vision of what I had set in motion.

Yes, I had betrayed Yeshua. But far worse, I had unleashed upon the entire human race a ravenous, wild-dog religion. Down the ages would its warped writhe of creeds flourish and fester.

I saw the crushing of pagan practices; the slaughter done in

Yeshua's name; the dishonoring of womanhood; the anti-Semitism of which I would be the seed; the hounding of those God had created in all righteousness to be loved by their own sex.

Anti-body.

Anti-spirit.

Anti-soul.

Not to hang myself was unthinkable.

I lived a decent span of years, an odd duck on the outskirts of Jerusalem.

Then one day, standing in Blood Acres, I swelled up like a bladder, uniform and sudden. My belly burst and my entrails spilled forth.

Gazing heavenward, I gasped, "I can take a hint," and died.

I wallowed in bloat. Passes easily negotiated by the widest wagon proved impassable to me.

So puffed were my eyelids that chance visitors could not find my eyes, nor they the light.

My penis was a cankerous toad of flesh, too huge and ungainly to stay garmented. When I pissed, out spattered worms and pus and barbed gushings of urine, reeking with such offense that my stomach roiled.

But so pouched were my cheeks, so pinholed my lips, that the vomitus would not be expelled, but bolted back inside, over tongue, down throat, careening up and down until the motion's natural decay.

I died, after years of torment, in a secluded spot, where to this day passersby hold their noses but cannot thereafter shake the vile fumes.

I never quite got around to dying.

I wander the earth, cloaked in woe, doomed to observe but not be able to stop the pain inflicted by one accursed motherfucker upon another.

Pauline propaganda, all of it.

Truth was, I became the head of the rival Jerusalem Church, third Vice Regent after James and Symeon. I wrote the *Epistle of Jude*, for the love of Christ. An honored man of learning and eloquence was I, and, to the end of my days, a farmer.

Mine was a natural death, minimally irksome as these things go. My funeral was attended by a host of sorrowful friends.

God fuck all Pauline propagandists!

My punishment is eternal separation from God.

All my protestations to the contrary?

I've been pulling the wool.

The Fundamentalists and Evangelicals have it spot-on. The Bible is indeed inerrant, and all of its multitudinous contradictions are resolvable into one coherent story, the truth of which damns me eternally, and a good job too.

Would it help to say I'm sorry?

Ultima maxima mea culpa.

As daunting as an eternity in hell is, I wish I could suffer still more punishment.

Go on, dish it out, I can take it. My spirit is hardy, my shoulders broad, my chin lifted for one more solidly rendered rounder.

I want it. I do. I do.

Won't you *please* give it to me, you big bad bruiser, you?

Satan, the sly son of a whore, convinced me that if I died swiftly, Yeshua, post-harrowing, would forgive me.

Rope, yank, choke. Foam and fizz flared in my brain as my

body jerked.

Hell rose up to claim me. Yeshua tromped on through, ten cubits tall and in better health than I had ever seen him. Divinity became him.

"Pity me, Lord?" I begged.

Yeshua gave me a look of scorn. "You, you, and you," he said, "no forgiveness. Stay put. Forever."

He meant Cain, Herod, and me.

We were locked in a bare room together, eating at one another, drip by drip. Whenever I thought my loathing for them had reached its height, it rose higher.

Hell is other people.

As I spiraled along the funneled walls of Hell, I recognized every sin in myself, wondering where I would come to rest.

Down down I clattered until, upon an icy plain at the nadir, Satan's stuck body waited to seize me. Three heads he sported, black, red, white, the teeth of the outer ones gnawing on one sinner each, all six eyes weeping tears of slush, blood, and pus.

The central face gaped. Into it I slid, head first, stopped at the hips by sharp teeth that chewed and worried me, flaying buttocks and back, where the skin healed to be flayed again.

Satan's mouth had never known hygiene. Its juices seared my nostrils. Though the tongue tasted rank, I was impelled to bite off chunks of it, puking throatward the gobbets I had swallowed.

Brutus and Cassius, the chomped betrayers at my right and left, bellowed their Latin woe with far less fury than I my Aramaic.

I had a raw deal.

I have it still.

Literalism, the turning of fancy into fact, renders savage the heart of Christianity. But before it turns, the fancy itself grows savage.

One Gottverfickene jackanapes named Wieser, in *Der Kreuzweg des Verraters in sechs Stationen*, wrote: "I have but one objective, but one wish: to awaken in you such a revulsion for the man and apostle Judas that once and for all you shall make a holy resolve to murder in yourselves every hint of Judas spirit, destroy every similarity with the Judas mentality, to hate the soul of Judas."

Tame stuff when placed beside seventeenth-century Austrian preacher Abraham Santa Clara, who obsessed for ten years about me. His final sermon on the subject consisted entirely of curses against every inch of my anatomy, from my toes to my flaming red hair. Body parts omitted from the sermon he drooled over beneath the sheets, castigating himself for being pleased by his rectitude.

And Martin Luther, Hitler's favorite author, was even more virulently obsessive: "I can't understand how the Jews manage to be so skilled, unless it be that, when Judas Iscariot hanged himself, his guts burst and voided. Perhaps the Jews sent servants with plates of silver and chambers of gold to gather up Judas's outflung excrement, eating and drinking his offal, thereby acquiring eyes so squint-sharp that they find commentaries in the Scriptures that neither Matthew nor Isaiah, let alone the rest of us accursed *goyim,* find there."

Many of the Passion Plays, performed in the streets in medieval times, devolved into frenzies of dramatized sadism, portraying caricatures of Jews torturing Christ and rousing the crowds to such a pitch that they seized and slaughtered real Jews living in their midst.

"His blood be on us and on our children."

Indeed.

What I did was exactly what God and his avatar asked me to do.

Those who made up and mongered tales about me and my so-called betrayal have betrayed me and Yeshua both.

Shame on them.

There once was a fertility god named Balder, Odin's child. Fearing for his son's death, Odin had the goddess Frigg exact a vow from all earthly things that they would never harm Balder. The gods amused themselves by placing him in their midst and hurling lethal objects at him, for the delight of watching them glance off him and with the hidden hope that some day the glorious son of Odin would suffer pain and death.

Loki, disguised as a kindly old crone, asked Frigg if there had been any exceptions.

Mistletoe, she confided.

So Loki tied some mistletoe to an arrowhead, set the bow in the hands of the blind god Hother, and turned him Balderward. "Let fly," said Loki.

Balder went bye-bye. Hother, who released the arrow, was forgiven. Loki suffered banishment and curses.

In *our* little folktale, Yeshua felt the arrow's bite. Pilate, who gave the order, was forgiven.

Judas and all his race?

Yeshua betrayed me.

Though he knew all along what his fate would be, he led me to expect otherwise.

Is mine the reputation any man would choose?

Call me God's dupe.

Call Yeshua . . . a Judas.

Yeshua loved his betrayer, the one who thrice denied him, those unable to stay awake, those who fled from him when he was seized, those who mocked him, those who drove the spikes and stood guard.

What would Yeshua do?

I *know* what he would do, and what he did.

Do you think you might do likewise?

Do you think you might?

Do you?

THE BIRD CATCHER

S. P. Somtow

There was this other boy in the internment camp. His name was Jim. After the war, he made something of a name for himself. He wrote books, even a memoir of the camp that got turned into a Spielberg movie. It didn't turn out that gloriously for me.

My grandson will never know what it's like to be consumed with hunger, hunger that is heartache, hunger that can propel you past insanity. But I know. I've been there. So has that boy Jim; that's why I really don't envy him his Spielberg movie.

After the war, my mother and I were stranded in China for a few more years. She was penniless, a lady journalist in a time when lady journalists only covered church bazaars, a single mother at a time when "bastard" was more than a bad word.

You might think that at least we had each other, but my mother and I never intersected. Not as mother and son, not even as Americans awash in great events and oceans of Asian faces. We were both loners. We were both vulnerable.

That's how I became the bogeyman's friend.

He's long dead now, but they keep him, you know, in the Museum of Horrors. Once in a generation, I visit him. Yesterday, I took my grandson Corey. Just as I took his father before him.

The destination stays the same, but the road changes every generation. The first time I had gone by boat, along the quiet back canals of the old city. Now there was an expressway. The toll was forty baht—a dollar—a month's salary that would have been, back in the '50s, in old Siam.

My son's in love with Bangkok, the insane skyline, the high tech blending with the low tech, the skyscraper shaped like a giant robot, the palatial shopping malls, the kinky sex bars, the bootleg software arcades, the whole tossed salad. And he doesn't mind the heat. He's a big-time entrepreneur here, owns a taco chain.

I live in Manhattan. It's quieter.

I can be anonymous. I can be alone. I can nurse my hunger in secret.

Christmases, though, I go to Bangkok; this Christmas, my grandson's eleventh birthday, I told my son it was time. He nodded and told me to take the chauffeur for the day.

So, to get to the place, you zigzag through the world's raunchiest traffic, then you fly along this madcap figure-eight expressway, cross the river where stone demons stand guard on the parapets of the Temple of Dawn, and then you're suddenly in this sleazy alley. Vendors hawk bowls of soup and pickled guavas. The directions are on a handwritten placard attached to a street sign with duct tape.

It's the Police Museum, upstairs from the local morgue. One wall is covered with photographs of corpses. That's not part of the museum; it's a public service display for people with missing family members to check if any of them have turned up dead. Corey didn't pay attention to the photographs; he was busy with Pokémon.

Upstairs, the feeling changed. The stairs creaked. The upstairs room was garishly lit. Glass cases along the walls were filled with medical oddities, two-headed babies and the like, each one in a jar of formaldehyde, each one meticulously labeled in Thai and English. The labels weren't printed, mind you. Handwritten. There was definitely a middle school show-and-tell feel about the exhibits. No air-conditioning. And no more breeze from the river like in the old days; skyscrapers had stifled the city's breath.

There was a uniform, sick-yellow tinge to all the displays . . . the neutral cream paint was edged with yellow . . . the deformed livers, misshappen brains, tumorous embryos all floating in a dull yellow fluid . . . the heaps of dry bones an orange-yellow, the rows of skulls yellowing in the cracks . . . and then there were the young novices, shaven-headed little boys in yellow robes, staring in a heat-induced stupor as their mentor droned on about the transience of all existence, the quintessence of Buddhist philosophy.

And then there was Si Ui.

He had his own glass cabinet, like a phone booth, in the middle of the room. Naked. Desiccated. A mummy. Skinny. Mud-colored, from the embalming process, I think. A sign (handwritten, of course) explained who he was. See Ui. Devourer of children's livers in the 1950s. My grandson reads Thai more fluently than I do. He sounded out the name right away.

Si Sui Sae Ung.

"It's the bogeyman, isn't it?" Corey said. But he showed little more than a passing interest. It was the year Pokémon Gold and Silver came out. So many new monsters to catch, so many names to learn.

"He hated cages," I said.

"Got him!" Corey squealed. Then, not looking up at the dead man, "I know who he was. They did a documentary on him. Can we go now?"

"Didn't your maid tell you stories at night? To frighten you? 'Be a good boy, or Si Ui will eat your liver?' "

"Gimme a break, Grandpa. I'm too old for that shit." He paused. Still wouldn't look up at him. There were other glass booths in the room, other mummified criminals: a serial rapist down the way. But Si Ui was the star of the show. "Okay," Corey said, "she did try to scare me once. Well, I was like five, okay? Si Ui. You watch out, he'll eat your liver, be a good boy now. Sure, I heard that before. Well, he's not gonna eat my liver now, is he? I mean, that's probably not even him; it's probably like wax or something."

He smiled at me. The dead man did not.

"I knew him," I said. "He was my friend."

"I get it!" Corey said, back to his Gameboy. "You're like me in this Pokémon game. You caught a monster once. And tamed him. You caught the most famous monster in Thailand."

"And tamed him?" I shook my head. "No, not tamed."

"Can we go to McDonald's now?"

"You're hungry."

"I could eat the world!"

"After I tell you the whole story."

"You're gonna talk about the Chinese camp again, Grandpa? And that kid Jim, and the Spielberg movie?"

"No, Corey, this is something I've never told you about before. But I'm telling you so when I'm gone, you'll know to tell your son. And your grandson."

"Okay, Grandpa."

And finally, tearing himself away from the video game, he willed himself to look.

The dead man had no eyes; he could not stare back.

He hated cages. But his whole life was a long imprisonment . . . without a cage, he did not even exist.

Listen, Corey. I'll tell you how I met the bogeyman.

Imagine I'm eleven years old, same as you are now, running wild on a leaky ship crammed with coolies. They're packed into the lower deck. We can't afford the upper deck, but when they saw we were white, they waved us on up without checking our tickets. It looks more interesting down there. And the food's got to be better. I can smell a Chinese breakfast. That oily fried bread, so crunchy on the outside, dripping with pig fat . . . yeah.

It's hot. It's boring. Mom's on the prowl. A job or a husband, whichever comes first. Everyone's fleeing the communists. We're some of the last white people to get out of China.

Someone's got a portable charcoal stove on the lower deck, and there's a toothless old woman cooking congee, fanning the stove. A whiff of opium in the air blends with the rich gingery broth. Everyone down there's clustered around the food. Except this one man. Harmless-looking. Before the Japs came, we had a gardener who looked like that. Shirtless, thin, by the railing. Stiller than a statue. And a bird on the railing. Also unmoving. The other coolies are ridiculing him, making fun of his Hakka accent, calling him simpleton.

I watch him.

"Look at the idiot," the toothless woman says. "Hasn't said a word since we left Swatow."

The man has his arms stretched out, his hands cupped. Frozen. Concentrated. I suddenly realize I've snuck down the steps myself, pushed my way through all the Chinese around the cooking pot, and I'm halfway there. Mesmerized. The man is stalking the bird, the boy stalking the man. I try not to breathe as I creep up.

He pounces. Wrings the bird's neck . . . in one swift liquid movement, a twist of the wrist, and he's already plucking the feathers with the other hand, ignoring the death-spasms. And I'm real close now. I can smell him. Mud and sweat. Behind him, the open sea. On the deck, the feathers, a bloody snowfall.

He bites off the head and I hear the skull crunch.

I scream. He whirls. I try to cover it up with a childish giggle.

He speaks in a monotone. Slowly. Sounding out each syllable, but he seems to have picked up a little pidgin. "Little white boy. You go upstairs. No belong here."

"I go where I want. They don't care."

He offers me a raw wing.

"Boy hungry?"

"Man hungry?"

I fish in my pocket, find half a liverwurst sandwich. I hold it out to him. He shakes his head. We both laugh a little. We've both known this hunger that consumes you; the agony of China is in our bones.

I say, "Me and Mom are going to Siam. On account of my dad getting killed by the Japs and we can't live in Shanghai anymore. We were in a camp and everything." He stares blankly and so I bark in Japanese, like the guards used to. And he goes crazy.

He mutters to himself in Hakka which I don't understand that well, but it's something like, "Don't look 'em in the eye. They chop off your head. You stare at the ground, they leave you alone." He is chewing away at raw bird flesh the whole time. He adds in English, "Si Ui no like Japan man."

"Makes two of us," I say.

I've seen too much. Before the internment camp, there was Nanking. Mom was gonna do an article about the atrocities. I saw them. You think a two-year-old doesn't see anything? She carried me on her back the whole time, papoose-style.

When you've seen a river clogged with corpses, when you've looked at piles of human heads, and human livers roasting on spits, and women raped and set on fire, well, Santa and the Tooth Fairy just don't cut it. I pretended about the Tooth Fairy, though, for a long time. Because, in the camp, the ladies would pool their resources to bribe Mr. Tooth Fairy Sakamoto for a little piece of fish.

"I'm Nicholas," I say.

"Si Ui." I don't know if it's his name or something in Hakka.

I hear my mother calling from the upper deck. I turn from the strange man, the raw bird's blood trailing from his lips. "Gotta go." I turn to him, pointing at my chest, and I say, "Nicholas."

Even the upper deck is cramped. It's hotter than Shanghai, hotter even than the internment camp. We share a cabin with two Catholic priests who let us hide out there after suspecting we didn't have tickets.

Night doesn't get any cooler, and the priests snore. I'm down to a pair of shorts and I still can't sleep. So I slip away. It's easy. Nobody cares. Millions of people have been dying and I'm just some skinny kid on the wrong side of the ocean. Me and my mom have been adrift for as long as I can remember.

The ship groans and clanks. I take the steep metal stairwell down to the coolies' level. I'm wondering about the birdcatcher. Down below, the smells are a lot more comforting. The smell of sweat and soy-stained clothing masks the odor of the sea. The charcoal stove is still burning. The old woman is simmering some stew. Maybe something magical . . . a bit of snake's blood to revive someone's limp dick . . . crushed tiger bones, powdered rhinoceros horn, to heal pretty much anything. People are starving, but you can still get those kind of ingredients. I'm eleven, and I already know too much.

They are sleeping every which way, but it's easy for me to step over them even in the dark. The camp was even more crowded than this, and a misstep could get you hurt. There's a little bit of light from the little clay stove.

I don't know what I'm looking for. Just to be alone, I guess. I can be more alone in a crowd of Chinese than up there. Mom says things will be better in Siam. I don't know.

I've threaded my way past all of them. And I'm leaning against the railing. There isn't much moonlight. It's probably past midnight but the metal is still hot. There's a warm wind, though, and it dries away my sweat. China's too far away to see, and I can't even imagine Boston anymore.

He pounces.

Leather hands rasp my shoulders. Strong hands. Not big, but I can't squirm out of their grip. The hands twirl me around and I'm looking into Si Ui's eyes. The moonlight is in them. I'm scared. I don't know why, really, all I'd have to do is scream and they'll pull him off me. But I can't get the scream out.

I look into his eyes and I see fire. A burning village. Maybe it's just the opium haze that clings to this deck, making me feel all weird inside, seeing things. And the sounds. I think it must be the whispering of the sea, but it's not, it's voices. *Hungry, you little chink?* And those leering, buck-toothed faces. Like comic book Japs. Barking. The fire blazes. And then, abruptly, it dissolves. And there's a kid standing in the smoky ruins. Me. And I'm holding out a liverwurst sandwich. Am I really than skinny, that pathetic? But the vision fades. And Si Ui's eyes become empty. Soulless.

"Si Ui catch anything," he says. "See, catch bird, catch boy. All same." And smiles, a curiously captivating smile.

"As long as you don't eat me," I say.

"Si Ui never eat Nicholas," he says. "Nicholas friend."

Friend? In the burning wasteland of China, an angel holding out a liverwurst sandwich? It makes me smile. And suddenly angry. The anger hits me so suddenly I don't even have time to figure out what it is. It's the war, the maggots in the millet, the commandant kicking me across the yard, but more than that it's my mom, clinging to her journalist fantasies while I dug for earthworms, letting my dad walk out to his death. I'm crying and the bird catcher is stroking my cheek, saying, "You no cry now. Soon go back America. No one cry there." And it's the first time someone has touched me with some kind of tenderness in, in, in, I dunno, since before the invasion. Because Mom doesn't hug, she kind of encircles, and her arms are like the bars of a cage.

So, I'm thinking this will be my last glimpse of Si Ui. It's in the harbor at Klong Toei. You know, where Anna landed in *The King and I*. And where Joseph Conrad landed in *Youth*.

So all these coolies, and all these trapped Americans and Europeans, they're all stampeding down the gangplank, with cargo being hoisted, workmen trundling, fleets of those bicycle pedicabs called *samlors*, itinerant merchants with bales of silk and fruits that seem to have hair or claws, and then there's the smell that socks you in the face, gasoline and jasmine and decay and incense. Pungent salt squid drying on racks. The ever-present fish sauce, blending with the odor of fresh papaya and pineapple and coconut and human sweat.

And my mother's off and running, with me barely keeping up, chasing after some waxed-mustache British doctor guy with one of those accents you think's a joke until you realize that's really how they talk.

So I'm just carried along by the mob.

"You buy bird, little boy?" I look up. It's a wall of sparrows, each one in a cramped wooden cage. Rows and rows of cages, stacked up from the concrete high as a man, more cages hanging from wires, stuffed into the branch-crooks of a mango tree. I see others buying the birds for a few coins, releasing them into the air.

"Why are they doing that?"

"Good for your karma. Buy bird, set bird free, shorten your suffering in your next life."

"Swell," I say.

Farther off, the vendor's boy is catching them, coaxing them back into cages. That's got to be wrong, I'm thinking as the boy comes back with ten little cages hanging on each arm. The birds haven't gotten far. They can barely fly. Answering my unspoken thought, the bird seller says, "Oh, we clip wings. Must make living too, you know."

That's when I hear a sound like the thunder of a thousand wings. I think I must be dreaming. I look up. The crowd has parted. And there's a skinny little shirtless man standing in the clearing, his arms spread wide like a Jesus statue, only you can barely see a square inch of him because he's all covered in sparrows. Perched all over his arms like they're telegraph wires or something, and squatting on his head, and clinging to his baggy homespun shorts with their claws. And the birds are all chattering at once, drowning out the cacophony of the mob.

Si Ui looks at me. And in his eyes I see . . . bars. Bars of light, maybe. Prison bars. The man's trying to tell me something. *I'm trapped.*

The crowd that parted all of sudden comes together and he's gone. I wonder if I'm the only one who saw. I wonder if it's just another aftereffect of the opium that clogged the walkways on the ship.

But it's too late to wonder; my mom has found me, she's got me by the arm and she's yanking me back into the stream of people. And in the next few weeks I don't think about Si Ui at all. Until he shows up, just like that, in a village called Thapsakae.

After the museum, I took Corey to Baskin-Robbins and popped into Starbucks next door for a frappuccino. Visiting the bogeyman is a draining thing. I wanted to let him down easy. But Corey didn't want to let go right away.

"Can we take a boat ride or something?" he said. "You know I never get to come to this part of town." It's true. The traffic in Bangkok is so bad that they sell little car toilets so you can go while you're stuck at a red light for an hour. This side of town, Thonburi, the old capital, is a lot more like the past. But no one bothers to come. The traffic, they say, always the traffic.

We left the car by a local pier, hailed a river taxi, just told him to go, anywhere, told him we wanted to ride around. Overpaid him. It served me right for being me, an old white guy in baggy slacks, with a backwards facing-Yankees-hatted blond kid in tow.

When you leave the river behind, there's a network of canals, called *klongs*, that used to be the arteries and capillaries of the old city. In Bangkok proper, they've all been filled in. But not here. The farther from the main waterway we floated, the further back in time. Now the *klongs* were fragrant with jasmine, with stilted houses rearing up behind thickets of banana and bamboo. And I was remembering more.

Rain jars by the landing docks . . . lizards basking in the sun . . . young boys leaping into the water.

"The water was a lot clearer," I told my grandson. "And the swimmers weren't wearing those little trunks . . . they were naked." Recently, fearing to offend the sensibilities of tourists, the Thai government made a fuss about little boys skinny-dipping along the tourist riverboat routes. But the river is so polluted now, one wonders what difference it makes.

They were bobbing up and down around the boat. Shouting in fractured English. Wanting a lick of Corey's Baskin-Robbins. When Corey spoke to them in Thai, they swam away. Tourists who speak the language aren't tourists anymore.

"You used to do that, huh, Grandpa."

"Yes," I said.

"I like the Sports Club better. The water's clean. And they make a mean chicken sandwich at the poolside bar."

I only went to the Sports Club once in my life. A week after we landed in Bangkok, a week of sleeping in a pew at a missionary church, a week of wringing out the same clothes and ironing them over and over.

"I never thought much of the Sports Club," I said.

"Oh, Grandpa, you're such a prole." One of his father's words, I thought, smiling.

"Well, I did grow up in *Red* China," I said.

"Yeah," he said. "So what was it like, the Sports Club?"

. . . a little piece of England in the midst of all this tropical stuff. The horse races. Cricket. My mother has a rendezvous with the doctor, the one she's been flirting with on the ship. They have tea and crumpets. They talk about the Bangkok Chinatown riots, and about money. I am reading a battered EC comic that I found in the reading room.

"Well, if you don't mind going native," the doctor says, "there's a clinic, down south a bit; pay wouldn't be much, and you'll have to live with the benighted buggers, but I daresay you'll cope."

"Oh, I'll go native," Mom says, "as long as I can keep writing.

I'll do anything for that. I'd give you a blowjob if that's what it takes."

"Heavens," says the doctor. "More tea?"

And so, a month later, we come to a fishing village nestled in the western crook of the Gulf of Siam, and I swear it's paradise. There's a village school taught by monks, and a little clinic where Mom works, dressing wounds, jabbing penicillin into people's buttocks; I think she's working on a novel. That doctor she was flirting with got her this job because she speaks Chinese, and the village is full of Chinese immigrants, smuggled across the sea, looking for some measure of freedom.

Thapsakae . . . it rhymes with Tupperware . . . it's always warm, but never stifling like in Bangkok . . . always a breeze from the unseen sea, shaking the ripe coconuts from the trees . . . a town of stilted dwellings, a tiny main street with storefront rowhouses, fields of neon green rice as far as the eye can see, lazy waterbuffalo wallowing, and always the canals running alongside the half-paved road, women beating their wet laundry with rocks in the dawn, boys diving in the noonday heat . . . the second day I'm there, I meet these kids, Lek and Sombun. They're my age. I can't understand a word they're saying at first. I'm watching them, leaning against a dragon-glazed rain jar, as they shuck their school uniforms and leap in. They're laughing a lot, splashing, one time they're throwing a catfish back and forth like it's some kind of volleyball, but they're like fishes themselves, silvery-brown sleek things chattering in a singsong language. And I'm alone, like I was at the camp, flinging stones into the water. Except I'm not scared like I was there. There's no time I have to be home. I can reach into just about any thicket and pluck out something good to eat: bananas, mangoes, little pink sour-apples. My shorts are all torn (I still only have one pair) and my shirt is stained with the juices of exotic fruits, and I let my hair grow as long as I want.

Today I'm thinking of the birds.

You buy a bird to free yourself from the cage of karma. You free the bird, but its wings are clipped and it's inside another cage, a cage circumscribed by the fact that it can't fly far. And the boy that catches it is in another cage, apprenticed to that vendor, unable to fly free. Cages within cages within cages. I've been in a cage before; one time in the camp they hung me up in one in the commandant's office and told me to sing.

Here, I don't feel caged at all.

The Thai kids have noticed me and they pop up from the depths right next to me, staring curiously. They're not hostile. I don't know what they're saying, but I know I'm soon going to absorb this musical language. Meanwhile, they're splashing me, daring me to dive in, and in the end I throw off these filthy clothes and I'm in the water and it's clear and warm and full of fish. And we're laughing and chasing each other. And they do know a few words of English; they've picked it up in that village school, where the monks have been ramming a weird antiquated English phrase-book down their throats.

But later, after we dry off in the sun and they try to show me how to ride a waterbuffalo, later we sneak across the *gailan* field and I see him again. The bird catcher, I mean. *Gailan* is a Chinese vegetable like broccoli only without the bushy part. The Chinese immigrants grow it here. They all work for this rich Chinese man named Tae Pak, the one who had the refugees shipped to this town as cheap labor.

"You want to watch TV?" Sombun asks me.

I haven't had much of a chance to see TV. He takes me by the hand and pulls me along, with Lek behind him, giggling. Night has fallen. It happens really suddenly in the tropics, boom and it's dark. In the distance, past a wall of bamboo trees, we see glimmering lights. Tae Pak has electricity. Not that many private homes do. Mom and I use kerosene lamps at night. I've never been to his house, but I know we're going there. Villagers are zeroing in on the house now, walking surefootedly in the moonlight. The stench of night-blooming jasmine is almost choking in the compound. A little shrine to the Mother of Mercy stands by the entrance, and ahead we see what passes for a mansion here; the wooden stilts and the thatched roof with the pointed eaves, like everyone else's house, but spread out over three sides of a quadrangle, and in the center a ruined pagoda whose origin no one remembers.

The usual pigs and chickens are running around in the space under the house, but the stairway up to the veranda is packed with people, kids mostly, and they're all gazing upward. The object of their devotion is a television set, the images on it ghostly, the sound staticky and in Thai in any case . . . but I recognize the show . . . it's *I Love Lucy*. And I'm just staring and staring. Sombun pushes me up the steps. I barely remember to remove my sandals and step in the trough at the bottom of the steps to wash the river mud off my feet. It's really true. I can't understand a word of it but it's still funny. The kids are laughing along with the laugh track.

Well . . . that's when I see Si Ui. I point at him. I try to attract his attention, but he too, sitting cross-legged on the veranda, is riveted to the screen. And when I try to whisper to Sombun that hey, I know this guy, what a weird coincidence, Sombun just whispers back, *"Jek, jek,"* which I know is a putdown word for a Chinaman.

"I know him," I whisper. "He catches birds. And eats them. Alive." I try to attract Si Ui's attention. But he won't look at me. He's too busy staring at Lucille Ball. I'm a little bit afraid to look at him directly, scared of what his eyes might disclose, our shared and brutal past.

Lek, whose nickname just means "tiny," shudders.

"*Jek, jek,*" Sombun says. The laugh track kicks in.

Everything has changed now that I know he's here. On my reed mat, under the mosquito nets every night, I toss and turn, and I see things. I don't think they're dreams. I think it's like the time I looked into Si Ui's eyes and saw the fire. I see a Chinese boy running through a field of dead people. It's sort of all in black and white and he's screaming and behind him a village is burning.

At first it's the Chinese boy but somehow it's me too, and I'm running, with my bare feet squishing into dead men's bowels, running over a sea of blood and shit. And I run right into someone's arms. Hard. The comic-book Japanese villain face. A human heart, still beating, in his hand.

"Hungry, you little chink?" he says.

Little chink. Little *jek.*

Intestines are writhing up out of disemboweled bodies like snakes. I saw a lot of disemboweled Japs. Their officers did it in groups, quietly, stony-faced. The honorable thing to do.

I'm screaming myself awake. And then, from the veranda, maybe, I hear the tap of my mom's battered typewriter, an old Hermes she bought in the Sunday market in Bangkok for a hundred baht.

I crawl out of bed. It's already dawn.

"Hi, Mom," I say, as I breeze past her, an old *phakomah* wrapped around my loins.

"Wow. It talks."

"Mom, I'm going over to Sombun's house to play."

"You're getting the hang of the place, I take it."

"Yeah."

"Pick up some food, Nicholas."

346

"Okay." Around here, a dollar will feed me and her three square meals. But it won't take away the other hunger.

Another lazy day of running myself ragged, gorging on papaya and coconut milk, another day in paradise.

It's time to meet the serpent, I decide.

Sombun tells me someone's been killed, and we sneak over to the police station. Si Ui is there, sitting at a desk, staring at a wall. I think he's just doing some kind of alien registration thing. He has a Thai interpreter, the same toothless woman I saw on the boat. And a policeman is writing stuff down in a ledger.

There's a woman sitting on a bench, rocking back and forth. She's talking to everyone in sight. Even me and Sombun.

Sombun whispers, "That woman Daeng. Daughter die."

Daeng mumbles, "My daughter. By the railway tracks. All she was doing was running down the street for an ice coffee. Oh, my terrible karma." She collars a passing inspector. "Help me. My daughter. Strangled, raped."

"That Inspector Jed," Sombun whispers to me. "Head of the whole place."

Inspector Jed is being polite, compassionate and efficient at the same time. I like him. My mom should hang out with people like that instead of the losers who are just looking for a quick lay.

The woman continues muttering to herself. *"Nit, nit, nit, nit, nit,"* she says. That must be the girl's name. They all have nicknames like that. Nit means "tiny," too, like Lek. "Dead, strangled," she says. "And this town is supposed to be heaven on earth. The sea, the palm trees, the sun always bright. This town has a dark heart."

Suddenly, Si Ui looks up. Stares at her. As though remembering something. Daeng is sobbing. And the policeman who's been interviewing him says, "Watch yourself, chink. Everyone smiles here.

Food falls from the trees. If a little girl's murdered, they'll file it away; they won't try to find out who did it. Because this is a perfect place, and no one gets murdered. We all love each other here . . . you little *jek*."

Si Ui has this weird look in his eye. Mesmerized. My mother looks that way sometimes . . . when a man catches her eye and she's zeroing in for the kill. The woman's mumbling that she's going to go be a nun now, she has nothing left to live for.

"Watch your back, *jek*," says the policeman. He's trying, I realize, to help this man, who he probably thinks is some kind of village idiot type. "Someone'll murder you just for being a stupid little chink. And no one will bother to find out who did it."

"Si Ui hungry," says Si Ui.

I realize that I speak his language, and my friends do not.

"Si Ui!" I call out to him.

He freezes in his tracks and slowly turns, and I look into his eyes for the second time, and I know that it was no illusion before.

Somehow we've seen through each other's eyes.

I am a misfit kid in a picture-perfect town with a dark heart, but I understand what he's saying, because though I look all different I come from where he comes from. I've experienced what it's like to be Chinese. You can torture them and kill them by the millions, like the Japs did, and still they endure. They just shake it off. They've outlasted everyone so far. And will till the end of time. Right now in Siam they're the coolies and the laborers, and soon they're going to end up owning the whole country. They endure. I saw their severed heads piled up like battlements, and the river choked with their corpses, and they outlasted it all.

These Thai kids will never understand.

"Si Ui hungry!" the man cries.

That afternoon, I slip away from my friends at the river, and I go to the *gailan* field where I know he works. He never acknowledges my presence, but later, he strides farther and farther from the house of his rich patron, toward a more densely wooded area past the fields. It's all banana trees, the little bananas that have seeds in them, you chew the whole banana and spit out the seeds, rat-tat-tat, like a machine gun. There's bamboo, too, and the jasmine bushes that grow wild, and mango trees. Si Ui doesn't talk to me, doesn't look back, but somehow I know I'm supposed to follow him.

And I do.

Through the thicket, into a private clearing, the ground overgrown with weeds, the whole thing surrounded by vegetation, and in the middle of it a tumbledown house, the thatch unpatched in places, the stilts decaying and carved with old graffiti. The steps are lined with wooden cages. There's birdshit all over the decking, over the wooden railings, even around the foot trough. Birds are chattering from the cages, from the air around us. The sun has been searing and sweat is running down my face, my chest, soaking my *phakhomah*.

We don't go up into the house. Instead, Si Ui leads me past it, toward a clump of rubber trees. He doesn't talk, just keeps beckoning me, the curious way they have of beckoning, palm pointing toward the ground.

I feel dizzy. He's standing there. Swaying a little. Then he makes a little clucking, chattering sound, barely opening his lips. The birds are gathering. He seems to know their language. They're answering him. The chirping around us grows to a screeching cacophony. Above, they're circling. They're blocking out the sun and it's suddenly chilly. I'm scared now. But I don't dare say anything. In the camp, if you said anything, they always hurt you. Si Ui keeps beckoning me: nearer, come nearer. And I creep up. The birds are shrieking. And now they're swooping down, landing, gathering at Si Ui's feet, their heads moving to and fro in a regular rhythm, like they're listening to . . . a heartbeat. Si Ui's heartbeat. My own.

An image flashes into my head. A little Chinese boy hiding in a closet . . . listening to footsteps . . . breathing nervously.

He's poised. Like a snake, coiled up, ready to pounce. And then, without warning, he drops to a crouch, pulls a bird out of the sea of birds, puts it to his lips, snaps its neck with his teeth, and the blood just spurts, all over his bare skin, over the homespun wrapped around his loins, an impossible crimson. And he smiles. And throws me the bird.

I recoil. He laughs again when I let the dead bird slip through my fingers. Pounces again and gets me another.

"Birds are easy to trap," he says to me in Chinese, "easy as children, sometimes; you just have to know their language." He rips one open, pulls out a slippery liver. "You don't like them raw, I know," he says, "but come, little brother, we'll make a fire."

He waves his hand, dismisses the birds; all at once they're gone and the air is steaming again. In the heat, we make a bonfire and grill the birds' livers over it. He has become, I guess, my friend. Because he's become all talkative. "I didn't rape her," he says.

Then he talks about fleeing through the rice fields. There's a war going on around him. I guess he's my age in his story, but in Chinese they don't use past or future, everything happens in a kind of abstract now-time. I don't understand his dialect that well, but what he says matches the waking dreams I've had tossing and turning under that mosquito net. There was a Japanese soldier. He seemed kinder than the others. They were roasting something over a fire. He was handing Si Ui a morsel. A piece of liver.

Hungry, little chink?

Hungry. I understand hungry.

Human liver.

In Asia they believe that everything that will ever happen has already happened. Is that what Si Ui is doing with me, forging a karmic chain with his own childhood, the Japanese soldier?

There's so much I want to ask him, but I can't form the thoughts, especially not in Chinese. I'm young, Corey. I'm not thinking karmic cycles. What are you trying to ask me?

"I thought Si Ui ate children's livers," said Corey. "Not some dumb old birds'."

We were still on the *klong*, turning back now toward civilization; on either side of us were crumbling temples, old houses with pointed eaves, each one with its little totemic spirit house by the front gate, pouring sweet incense into the air, the air itself dripping with humidity. But ahead, just beyond a turn in the *klong*, a series of eighty-story condos reared up over the banana trees.

"Yes, he did," I said, "and we'll get to that part, in time. Don't be impatient."

"Grandpa, Si Ui ate children's livers. Just like Dracula bit women in the neck. Well, like, it's the main part of the story. How long are you gonna make me wait?"

"So you know more than you told me before. About the maid trying to scare you one time, when you were five."

"Well, yeah, Grandpa, I saw the miniseries. It never mentioned you."

"I'm part of the secret history, Corey."

"Cool." He contemplated his Pokémon, but decided not to go back to monster trapping. "When we get back to the Bangkok side, can I get caramel frappuccino at Starbucks?"

"Decaf," I said.

That evening I go back to the house and find Mom in bed with Jed, the police inspector. Suddenly, I don't like Jed anymore.

She barely looks up at me; Jed is pounding away and oblivious to it all; I don't know if Mom really knows I'm there, or just a shadow flitting beyond the mosquito netting. I know why she's doing it; she'll say that it's all about getting information for this great novel she's planning to write, or research for a major magazine article, but the truth is that it's about survival; it's no different from that concentration camp.

I think she finally does realize I'm there; she mouths the words "I'm sorry" and then turns back to her work. At that moment, I hear someone tapping at the entrance, and I crawl over the squeaky floorplanks, Siamese–style (children learn to move around on their knees so that their head isn't accidentally higher than someone of higher rank) to see Sombun on the step.

"Can you come out?" he says. "There's a *ngaan wat*."

I don't know what that is, but I don't want to stay in the house. So I throw on a shirt and go with him. I soon find out that a *ngaan wat* is a temple fair, sort of a cross between a carnival and a church bazaar and a theatrical night out.

Even from a mile or two away we hear the music, the tinkling of marimbas and the thud of drums, the wail of the Javanese oboe. By the time we get there, the air is drenched with the fragrance of pickled guava, peanut pork skewers, and green papaya tossed in fish sauce. A makeshift dance floor has been spread over the muddy ground and there are dancers with rhinestone court costumes and pagoda hats, their hands bent back at an impossible angle. There's a Chinese opera troupe like I've seen in Shanghai, glittering costumes, masks painted on the faces in garish colors, boys dressed as monkeys leaping to and fro; the Thai and the Chinese striving to outdo each other in noise and brilliance. And on a grill, being tended by a fat woman, pigeons are barbecuing, each one on a mini-spear of steel. And I'm reminded of the open fire and the sizzling of half-plucked feathers.

"You got money?" Sombun says. He thinks that all *farangs* are rich. I fish in my pocket and pull out a few *saleungs,* and we stuff ourselves with pan-fried *roti* swimming in sweet condensed milk.

The thick juice is dripping from our lips. This really is paradise. The music, the mingled scents, the warm wind. Then I see Si Ui. There aren't any birds nearby, not unless you count the pigeons charring on the grill. Si Ui is muttering to himself, but I understand Chinese, and he's saying, over and over again, "Si Ui hungry, Si Ui hungry." He says it in a little voice and it's almost like baby talk.

We wander over to the Chinese opera troupe. They're doing something about monkeys invading heaven and stealing the apples of the gods. All these kids are somersaulting, tumbling, cartwheel- ing, and climbing up onto each other's shoulders. There's a little girl, nine or ten maybe, and she's watching the show. And Si Ui is watching her. And I'm watching him.

I've seen her before, know her from that night we squatted on the veranda staring at American TV shows. Was Si Ui watching her even then? I tried to remember. Couldn't be sure. Her name's Juk.

Those Chinese cymbals, with their annoying "boing-boing- boing" sound, are clashing. A man is intoning in a weird singsong. The monkeys are leaping. Suddenly I see, in Si Ui's face, the same expression I saw on the ship. He's utterly still inside, utterly quiet, beyond feeling. The war did that to him. I know. Just like it made my mom into a whore, and me into . . . I don't know . . . a bird without a nesting place . . . a lost boy.

And then I get this . . . *irrational* feeling. That the little girl is a bird, chirping to herself, hopping along the ground, not noticing the stalker.

So many people here. So much jangling, so much laughter. The town's dilapidated pagodas sparkle with reflected colors, like stone Christmas trees. Chinese opera rings in my ears. I look away, when

I look back they are gone . . . Sombun is preoccupied now, playing with a two-*saleung* top that he just bought. Somehow I feel impelled to follow. To stalk the stalker.

I duck behind a fruit stand and then I see a golden deer. It's a toy, on four wheels, pulled along a string. I can't help following it with my eyes as it darts between hampers full of rambutans and pomelos.

The deer darts toward the cupped hands of the little girl. I see her disappear into the crowd, but then I see Si Ui's face, too; you can't mistake the cold fire in his eyes.

She follows the toy. Si Ui pulls. I follow, too, not really know-ing why it's so fascinating. The toy deer weaves through the ocean of feet. Bare feet of monks and novices, their saffron robes skim-ming the mud. Feet in rubber flipflops, in the wooden sandals the *Jek* call *kiah*. I hear a voice: *Juk, Juk!* And I know there's someone else looking for the girl, too. It's a weird quartet, each one in the sequence known only to the next one. I can see Si Ui now, his head bobbing up and down in the throng because he's a little taller than the average Thai even though he's so skinny. He's intent. Concentrated. He seems to be on wheels himself, he glides through the crowd like the toy deer. The woman's voice, calling for Juk, is faint and distant; she hears it, I'm sure, but she's ignoring her mother or her big sister. I only hear it because my senses are sharp now, it's like the rest of the temple fair's all out of focus now, all blurry, and there's just the four of us. I see the woman now, it must be a mother or aunt, too old for a sister, collaring a *roti* vendor and asking if he's seen the child. The vendor shakes his head, laughs. And suddenly we're all next to the pigeon barbecue, and if the woman was only looking in the right place she'd see the little girl, giggling as she clambers through the forest of legs, as the toy zig-zags over the dirt aisles. And now the deer has been yanked right up to Si Ui's feet. And the girl crawls all the way after it, seizes it, laughs, looks solemnly up at the face of the Chinaman—

"It's him! It's the chink!" Sombun is pointing, laughing. I'd forgotten he was even with me.

Si Ui is startled. His concentration snaps. He lashes out. There's a blind rage in his eyes. Dead pigeons are flying everywhere.

"Hungry!" he screams in Chinese. "Si Ui hungry!"

He turns. There is a cloth stall nearby. Suddenly he and the girl are gone amid a flurry of billowing sarongs. And I follow.

Incense in the air, stinging my eyes. A shaman gets possessed in a side aisle, his followers hushed. A flash of red. A red sarong, embroidered with gold, a year's wages, twisting through the crowd. I follow. I see the girl's terrified eyes. I see Si Ui with the red cloth wrapped around his arms, around the girl. I see something glistening, a knife maybe. And no one sees. No one but me.

Juk! Juk!

I've lost Sombun somewhere. I don't care. I thread my way through a bevy of *ramwong* dancers, through men dressed as women and women dressed as men. Fireworks are going off. There's an ancient wall, the temple boundary, crumbling . . . and the trail of red funnels into black night . . . and I'm standing on the other side of the wall now, watching Si Ui ride away in a pedicab, into the night. There's moonlight on him. He's saying something; even from far off I can read his lips; he's saying it over and over: *Si Ui hungry, Si Ui hungry.*

So they find her by the side of the road with her internal organs missing. And I'm there, too, all the boys are at dawn, peering down, daring each other to touch. It's not a rape or anything, they tell us. Nothing like the other girl. Someone has seen a cowherd near the site, and he's the one they arrest. He's an Indian, you see. If there's anyone the locals despise more than the Chinese, it's the Indians. They have a saying: If you see a snake and an Indian, kill the *babu*.

Later, in the market, Inspector Jed is escorting the Indian to the police station, and they start pelting him with stones, and they call him a dirty Indian and a cowshit eater. They beat him up pretty badly in the jail. The country's under martial law in these days, you know. They can beat up anyone they want. Or shoot them.

But most people don't really notice, or care. After all, it is paradise. To say that it is not, aloud, risks making it true. That's why my mom will never belong to Thailand; she doesn't understand that everything there resides in what is left unsaid.

That afternoon I go back to the rubber orchard. He is standing patiently. There's a bird on a branch. Si Ui is poised. Waiting. I think he is about to pounce. But I'm too excited to wait. "The girl," I say. "The girl, she's dead, did you know?"

Si Ui whirls around in a murderous fury, and then, just as suddenly, he's smiling.

"I didn't mean to break your concentration," I say.

"Girl soft," Si Ui says. "Tender." He laughs a little. I don't see a vicious killer. All I see is loneliness and hunger.

"Did you kill her?" I say.

"Kill?" he says. "I don't know. Si Ui hungry." He beckons me closer. I'm not afraid of him. "Do like me," he says. He crouches. I crouch, too. He stares at the bird. And so do I. "Make like a tree now," he says, and I say, "Yes. I'm a tree." He's behind me. He's breathing down my neck. Am I the next bird? But somehow I know he won't hurt me.

"Now!" he shrieks. Blindly, instinctively, I grab the sparrow in both hands. I can feel the quick heart grow cold as the bones crunch. Blood and birdshit squirt into my fists. It feels exciting, you know, down there, inside me. I killed it. The shock of death is amazing, joyous. I wonder if this is what grown-ups feel when they do things to each other in the night.

He laughs. "You and me," he says, "now we same-same."

He shows me how to lick the warm blood as it spurts. It's hotter than you think. It pulses, it quivers, the whole bird trembles as it yields up its spirit to me.

And then there's the weirdest thing. You know that hunger, the one that's gnawed at me, like a wound that won't close up, since we were dragged to that camp . . . it's suddenly gone. In its place there's a kind of nothing.

The Buddhists here say that heaven itself is a kind of nothing. That the goal of all existence is to become as nothing.

And I feel it. For all of a second or two, I feel it. "I know why you do it," I say. "I won't tell anyone, I swear."

"Si Ui knows that already."

Yes, he does. We have stood on common ground. We have shared communion flesh. Once a month, a Chinese priest used to come to the camp and celebrate mass with a hunk of maggoty *man to,* but he never made me feel one with anyone, let alone God.

The blood bathes my lips. The liver is succulent and bursting with juices.

Perhaps this is the first person I've ever loved.

The feeling lasts a few minutes. But then comes the hunger, swooping down on me, hunger clawed and ravenous. It will never go away, not completely.

They have called in an exorcist to pray over the railway tracks. The mother of the girl they found there has become a nun, and she stands on the gravel pathway lamenting her karma. The most recent victim has few to grieve for her. I overhear Inspector Jed talking to my mother. He tells her there are two killers. The second one had her throat cut and her internal organs removed . . . the first one, strangulation, all different . . . he's been studying these cases, these ritual killers, in American psychiatry books. And the cowherd has an alibi for the first victim.

I'm only half-listening to Jed, who drones on and on about famous mad killers in Europe. Like the butcher of Hanover, Jack the Ripper. How their victims were always chosen in a special way. How they killed over and over, always a certain way, a ritual. How they always got careless after a while, because part of what they were doing came from a hunger, a desperate need to be found out. How after a while they might leave clues . . . confide in someone . . . how he thought he had one of these cases on his hands, but the authorities in Bangkok weren't buying the idea. The village of Thapsakae just wasn't grand enough to play host to a reincarnation of Jack the Ripper.

I listen to him, but I've never been to Europe, and it's all just talk to me. I'm much more interested in the exorcist, who's a Brahmin, in white robes, hair down to his feet, all nappy and filthy, a dozen flower garlands around his neck, and amulets tinkling all over him.

"The killer might confide in someone," says Jed, "someone he thinks is in no position to betray him, someone perhaps too simpleminded to understand. Remember, the killer doesn't know he's evil. In a sense, he really can't help himself. He doesn't think the way we think. To himself, he's an innocent."

The exorcist enters his trance and sways and mumbles in unknown tongues. The villagers don't believe the killer's an innocent. They want to lynch him.

Women washing clothes find a young girl's hand bobbing up and down, and her head a few yards downstream. Women are pan-

S. P. Somtow

icking in the marketplace. They're lynching Indians, Chinese, anyone alien. But not Si Ui; he's a simpleton, after all. The village idiot is immune from persecution because every village needs an idiot.

The exorcist gets quite a workout, capturing spirits into baskets and jars.

Meanwhile, Si Ui has become the trusted *Jek*, the one who cuts the *gailan* in the fields and never cheats anyone of their two-*saleung* bundle of Chinese broccoli.

I keep his secret. Evenings, after I'm exhausted from swimming all day with Sombun and Lek, or lazing on the back of a waterbuffalo, I go to the rubber orchard and catch birds as the sun sets. I'm almost as good as him now. Sometimes he says nothing, though he'll share with me a piece of meat, cooked or uncooked; sometimes he talks up a storm. When he talks pidgin, he sounds like he's a half-wit. When he talks Thai, it's the same way, I think. But when he goes on and on in his Hakka dialect, he's as lucid as they come. I think. Because I'm only getting it in patches.

One day he says to me, "The young ones taste the best because it's the taste of childhood. You and I, we have no childhood. Only the taste."

A bird flies onto his shoulder, head tilted, chirps a friendly song. Perhaps he will soon be dinner.

Another day, Si Ui says, "Children's livers are the sweetest, they're bursting with young life. I weep for them. They're with me always. They're my friends. Like you."

Around us, paradise is crumbling. Everyone suspects someone else. Fights are breaking out in the marketplace. One day it's the Indians, another day the chinks, the Burmese. Hatred hangs in the air like the smell of rotten mangoes.

And Si Ui is getting hungrier.

My mother is working on her book now, thinking it'll make her fortune; she waits for the mail, which gets here sometimes by train, sometimes by oxcart. She's waiting for some letter from Simon & Schuster. It never comes, but she's having a ball, in her own way. She stumbles her way through the language, commits appalling solecisms, points her feet, even touches a monk one time, a total sacrilege . . . but they let her get away with everything. *Farangs*, after all, are touched by a divine madness. You can expect nothing normal from them.

She questions every villager, pores over every clue. It never occurs to her to ask me what I know.

We glut ourselves on papaya and curried catfish.

"Nicholas," my mother tells me one evening, after she's offered me a hit of opium, her latest affectation, "this really is the Garden of Eden."

I don't tell her that I've already met the serpent.

Here's how the day of reckoning happened, Corey:

It's midmorning and I'm wandering aimlessly. My mother has taken the train to Bangkok with Inspector Jed. He's decided that her untouchable *farang*-ness might get him an audience with some major official in the police department. I don't see my friends at the river or in the marketplace. But it's not planting season, and there's no school. So I'm playing by myself, but you can only flip so many pebbles into the river and tease so many waterbuffaloes.

After a while I decide to go and look for Sombun. We're not close, he and I, but we're thrown together a lot; things don't seem right without him.

I go to Sombun's house; it's a shabby place, but immaculate, a row house in the more "citified" part of the village, if you can call it that. Sombun's mother is making chili paste, pounding the spices in a stone mortar. You can smell the sweet basil and the lemongrass in the air. And the betelnut, too; she's chewing on the intoxicant; her teeth are stained red-black from long use.

"Oh," she says, "the *farang* boy."

"Where's Sombun?"

She's doesn't know quite what to make of my Thai, which has been getting better for months. "He's not home, Little Mouse," she says. "He went to the *Jek's* house to buy broccoli. Do you want to eat?"

"I've eaten, thanks, auntie," I say, but for politeness' sake I'm forced to nibble on bright green *sali* pastry.

"He's been gone a long time," she said, as she pounded. "I wonder if the chink's going to teach him to catch birds."

"Birds?"

And I start to get this weird feeling. Because *I'm* the one who catches birds with the Chinaman, I'm the one who's shared his past, who understands his hunger. Not just any kid.

"Sombun told me the chink was going to show him a special trick for catching them. Something about putting yourself into a deep state of *samadhi*, reaching out with your mind, plucking the life-force with your mind. It sounds very spiritual, doesn't it? I always took the chink for a moron, but maybe I'm misjudging him; Sombun seems to do a much better job," she said. "I never liked it when they came to our village, but they do work hard."

Well, when I leave Sombun's house, I'm starting to get a little mad. It's jealousy, of course, childish jealousy; I see that now. But I don't want to go there and disrupt their little bird-catching session. I'm not a spoilsport. I'm just going to pace up and down by the side of the *klong,* doing a slow burn.

The serpent came to *me!* I was the only one who could see through his madness and his pain, the only one who truly knew the hunger that drove him! That's what I'm thinking. And I go back to tossing pebbles, and I tease the gibbon chained by the temple's gate, and I kick a waterbuffalo around. And, before I knew it, this twinge of jealousy has grown into a kind of rage. It's like I was one of those birds, only in a really big cage, and I'd been flying and flying and thinking I was free, and now I've banged into the prison bars for the first time. I'm so mad I could burst.

I'm playing by myself by the railway tracks when I see my mom and the inspector walking out of the station. And that's the last straw. I want to hurt someone. I want to hurt my mom for shutting me out and letting strangers into her mosquito net at night. I want to punish Jed for thinking he knows everything. I want someone to notice me.

So that's when I run up to them and I say, "I'm the one! He confided in *me!* You said he was going to give himself away to someone and it was *me*, it was *me!*"

My mom just stares at me, but Jed becomes very quiet. "The Chinaman?" he asks me.

I say, "He told me children's livers are the sweetest. I think he's after Sombun." I don't tell him that he's only going to teach Sombun to catch birds, that he taught me, too, that boys are safe from him because like the inspector told us, we're not the special kind of victim he seeks out. "In his house, in the rubber orchard, you'll find everything," I say. "Bones. He makes the feet into a stew," I add, improvising now, because I've never been inside that house. "He cuts off their faces and dries them on a jerky rack. And Sombun's with him."

The truth is, I'm just making trouble. I don't believe there's dried faces in the house or human bones. I know Sombun's going to be safe, that Si Ui's only teaching him how to squeeze the life force from the birds, how to blunt the ancient hunger. Him instead of me. They're not going to find anything but dead birds.

There's a scream. I turn. I see Sombun's mother with a basket of fish, coming from the market. She's overheard me, and she cries, "The chink is killing my son!" Faster than thought, the street is full of people, screaming their anti-chink epithets and pulling out butcher knives. Jed's calling for reinforcements. Street vendors are tightening their *phakhomas* around their waists.

"Which way?" Jed asks, and suddenly I'm at the head of an army, racing full tilt toward the rubber orchard, along the neon green of the young rice paddies, beside the canals teeming with catfish, through thickets of banana trees, around the walls of the old temple, through the fields of *gailan* . . . and this too feeds my hunger. It's ugly. He's a Chinaman. He's the village idiot. He's different. He's an alien. Anything is possible.

We're converging on the *gailan* field now. They're waving sticks. Harvesting sickles. Fish knives. They're shouting, "Kill the chink, kill the chink." Sombun's mother is shrieking and wailing, and Inspector Jed has his gun out. Tae Pak, the village rich man, is vainly trying to stop the mob from trampling his broccoli. The army is unstoppable. And I'm their leader, I brought them here with my little lie. Even my mother is finally in awe.

I push through the bamboo thicket and we're standing in the clearing in the rubber orchard now. They're screaming for the *Jek's* blood. And I'm screaming with them.

Si Ui is nowhere to be found. They're beating on the ground now, slicing it with their scythes, smashing their clubs against the trees. Sombun's mother is hysterical. The other women have caught her mood, and they're all screaming now, because someone is holding up a sandal . . . Sombun's.

. . . *a little Chinese boy hiding in a closet* . . .

The images flashes again. I must go up into the house. I steal away, sneak up the steps, respectfully removing my sandals at the veranda, and I slip into the house.

A kerosene lamp burns. Light and shadows dance. There is a low wooden platform for a bed, a mosquito net, a woven rush mat for sleeping; off in a corner, there is a closet.

Birds everywhere. Dead birds pinned to the walls. Birds' heads piled up on plates. Blood spatters on the floor planks. Feathers wafting. On a charcoal stove in one corner, there's a wok with some hot oil and garlic, and sizzling in that oil is a heart, too big to be the heart of a bird. . . .

My eyes get used to the darkness. I see human bones in a pail. I see a young girl's head in a jar, the skull sawn open, half the brain gone. I see a bowl of pickled eyes.

I'm not afraid. These are familiar sights. This horror is a spectral echo of Nanking, nothing more.

"Si Ui," I whisper. "I lied to them. I know you didn't do anything to Sombun. You're one of the killers who does the same thing over and over. You don't eat boys. I know I've always been safe with you. I've always trusted you."

I hear someone crying. The whimper of a child.

"Hungry," says the voice. "Hungry."

A voice from behind the closet door . . .

The door opens. Si Ui is there, huddled, bone-thin, his *phakom-ah* about his loins, weeping, rocking.

Noises now. Angry voices. They're clambering up the steps. They're breaking down the wall planks. Light streams in.

"I'm sorry," I whisper. I see fire flicker in his eyes, then drain away as the mob sweeps into the room.

My grandson was hungry, too. When he said he could eat the world, he wasn't kidding. After the second decaf frappuccino, there was Italian ice in the Oriental's coffee shop, and then, riding back on the Skytrain to join the chauffeur who had conveniently parked at the

Sogo mall, there was a box of Smarties. Corey's mother always told me to watch the sugar, and she had plenty of Ritalin in stock—no prescription needed here—but it was always my pleasure to defy my daughter-in-law and leave her to deal with the consequences.

Corey ran wild in the skytrain station, whooping up the staircases, yelling at old ladies. No one minded. Kids are indulged in Babylon East; little blond boys are too cute to do wrong. For some, this noisy, polluted, chaotic city is still a kind of paradise.

My day of revelations ended at my son's townhouse in Sukhumvit, where maids and nannies fussed over little Corey and undressed him and got him in his Pokémon pajamas as I drained a glass of Beaujolais. My son was rarely home; the taco chain consumed all his time. My daughter-in-law was a social butterfly; she had already gone out for the evening, all pearls and Thai silk. So it fell to me to go into my grandson's room and to kiss him goodnight and good-bye.

Corey's bedroom was little piece of America, with its *Phantom Menace* drapes and its Playstation. But on a high niche, an image of the Buddha looked down; a decaying garland still perfumed the air with a whiff of jasmine. The air-conditioning was chilly; the Bangkok of the rich is a cold city; the more conspicuous the consumption, the lower the thermostat setting. I shivered, even as I missed Manhattan in January.

"Tell me a story, Grandpa?" Corey said.

"I told you one already," I said.

"Yeah, you did," he said wistfully. "About you in the Garden of Eden, and the serpent who was really a kid-eating monster."

All true. But as the years passed I had come to see that perhaps I was the serpent. I was the one who mixed lies with the truth, and took away his innocence. He was a child, really, a hungry child. And so was I.

"Tell me what happened to him," Corey said. "Did the people lynch him?"

"No. The court ruled that he was a madman, and sentenced him to a mental home. But the military government of Field Marshall Sarit reversed the decision, and they took him away and shot him. And he didn't even kill half the kids they said he killed."

"Like the first girl, the one who was raped and strangled," Corey said, "but she didn't get eaten. Maybe that other killer's still around." So he had been paying attention after all. I know he loves me, though he rarely says so; he had suffered an old man's ramblings for one long air-conditioning-free day, without complaint. I'm proud of him, can barely believe I've held on to life long enough to get to know him.

I leaned down to kiss him. He clung to me; and, as he let go, he asked me sleepily, "Do you ever feel that hungry, Grandpa?"

I didn't want to answer him; so, without another word, I slipped quietly away.

That night, I wandered in my dreams through fields of the dead; the hunger raged; I killed, I swallowed children whole and spat them out; I burned down cities; I stood aflame in my self-made inferno, howling with elemental grief; and in the morning, without leaving a note, I took a taxi to the airport and flew back to New York.

To face the hunger.

You shudder and awaken.

How long have you been in the museum? You cannot have fallen asleep, standing here. You were tired but . . .

Now you are much farther along the corridor, as if you have moved between the exhibits without realizing it.

How is that possible?

You must have been dreaming—but each dream seemed more real than the last.

You have looked into these faces and learned their secrets. Some had grotesque and horrific tales to tell, without precedent in the annals of crime. Others were darkly amusing or deceptive, concealing compulsion and madness worthy of a textbook on abnormal psychology. Some had the authentic tone of dispatches from nightmare territory or the shock of the confessional, but there was also fear and compassion and terror and pity. . . .

And they have changed you.

Their stories are your stories now. They will live in you forever, a part of your blood and bone. They were waiting for the perfect host, and they have finally found one.

It could not end any other way.

Shaken, you prepare to leave—and brush against the last case. It is cold to the touch, even through your clothing.

It appears to be empty.

You stare until you see a pair of eyes floating within. The eyes are familiar. They hold the same light you have seen in the other exhibits, the reflection of a multitude of transgressions that cannot be spoken except to one who will listen without judgment, more patiently than life would seem to allow, until it is over.

At last you understand.

They are your eyes.

And at that moment you hear a clicking on the sidewalk outside the museum.

Someone was following you, after all.

The footsteps stop at this door. The brass knob rattles as he tries it but it does not open.

He is toying with you. Whoever he is, he knows you are here. You can almost see the smile curling his lips as he walks on for now, except that you cannot imagine his face. He could have entered and found you. But for some reason he did not. The door is unlocked. It has always been.

Unless you pulled it shut behind you so that the latch finally closed all the way and it is now locked from the outside.

What does he want? To punish you for your crimes? Or only to hear your story?

Perhaps he is the one. Or not. Perhaps the door opened only for you and no one else.

Why?

Ask the question.

Who is the keeper of this museum?

If you try to go, will the door open from this side?

Will it ever?

You make your way across the room. You grasp the knob. . . .

But do you really want to find out?

Because you already know the answer.

You have always been here.

You will always be here.

You are here now.

Welcome to the Museum of Horrors.

PETER ATKINS, novelist and screenwriter from Liverpool, now lives in Los Angeles and has contributed poetry and fiction to *Fear, Skull, Weird Tales, 365 Scary Stories* and *Best New Horror*. His first collection is *Wishmaster and Other Stories* and his novels are *Morningstar* and *Big Thunder*. Screen credits include *Hellraiser II, III* and *IV* and *Wishmaster*.

RAMSEY CAMPBELL, author of the collections *Demons by Daylight, The Height of the Scream* and *Alone with the Horrors*, has won more awards in this field than any other writer. Novels include *The Doll Who Ate His Mother, The Face That Must Die, Obsession, The Hungry Moon, The Long Lost, Ancient Images, The House on Nazareth Hill* and *The Last Voice They Hear*. Next: *The Pact of the Fathers* and *The Darkest Part of the Forest*.

ROBERT DEVEREAUX'S short fiction appears in *Year's Best Horror Stories, Year's Best Fantasy and Horror, MetaHorror*, etc. and has been short-listed for both the Bram Stoker and World Fantasy Awards. His novels to date are *Deadweight, Walking Wounded* and *Santa Steps Out: A Fairy Tale for Grown-Ups*, which suffered the distinction of being banned in Cincinnati. Two new novels are currently in the works.

SUSAN FRY'S fiction has been published in the anthologies *The Doom of Camelot* and *Cemetery Sonata II*, and her articles in *The Red Herring, The San Jose Mercury News, Salon, PC World* and *San Francisco Magazine*. She attended the writers' workshop Clarion West in 1998 and is the editor of the science fiction market magazine *Speculations*.

DARREN O. GODFREY began publishing in 1986 and has had stories in *The Art Times, The Scream Factory, Gorezone, Aberrations, Black*

Petals and *Demontia*, and in the anthology *Borderlands* 2. He learned to dispose of unexploded bombs in the U.S. Air Force, a job he continues to practice in civilian life and which he considers relatively stress-free compared to writing fiction.

CHARLES L. GRANT, a former HWA president, is the author of at least thirty novels and numerous short stories and the editor of many anthologies, among them the *Shadows* series. A multiple winner of the Nebula and World Fantasy Awards, the British Fantasy Award and HWA's Lifetime Achievement Award, his latest books are *The Millennium Quartet, Hunting Ground* and *When the Cold Wind Blows*.

JOEL LANE lives in Birmingham, England. His short stories may be found in *Darklands, Little Deaths, Dark Terrors* and other anthologies. He is the author of the collection *The Earth Wire*, a book of poems; *The Edge of the Screen*; and *From Blue to Black*, a novel set in the world of post-punk rock music. His second novel is *Your Broken Face*.

RICHARD LAYMON's three-dozen-plus books include novels (*The Cellar, Blood Games, Dark Mountain, Endless Night, In the Dark, Island, The Woods Are Dark*), collections (*Dreadful Tales*), anthologies (*Bad News*) and an autobiography (*A Writer's Tale*). Recent titles include *Friday Night in Beast House* and *Night in the Lonesome October*. He was elected president of the HWA in 2000.

GORDON LINZNER has published three novels and two dozen short stories, in such places as *Rod Serling's Twilight Zone Magazine* and *The Magazine of Fantasy and Science Fiction*, and has edited *Space and Time* since 1966. He has been spotted leading walking tours in his native New York City, and is known to frighten small children with his storytelling.

TH. METZGER is the author of the novels *Big Gurl, Shock Totem* and *Drowning in Fire*; a collection of short fiction, *This Is Your Final Warning*; and the nonfiction *Blood and Volts: Edison, Tesla and the Electric Chair* and *The Birth of Heroin*. Forthcoming are two more novels, *Dr. Pennetralia* and *Stonecutter*.

LISA MORTON's short stories have appeared in *Dark Terrors, The Mammoth Book of Dracula, White of the Moon* and *After Shocks*. She provided the screenplays for *Meet the Hollowheads* and *Dinosaur City* and is the author of *The Cinema of Tsui Hark*, a book-length study of the Hong Kong filmmaker. She is also a playwright and theater director in Los Angeles.

WILLIAM F. NOLAN's novels include *Logan's Run* (with George Clayton Johnson) and its two sequels, several mysteries, biographies of Hemingway and Hammett and the nonfiction *The Black Mask Boys*, and the scripts for *Burnt Offerings, The Turn of the Screw* and *Trilogy of Terror*, plus hundreds of anthology appearances and eight volumes of his short stories.

JOYCE CAROL OATES's twenty-four novels include *Wonderland, Bellefleur, American Appetites* and *Blonde*. She has nine collections, edited *American Gothic Tales* and *The Best American Essays of the Century*, and with her husband publishes *The Ontario Review*. Among her honors: a Guggenheim Fellowship, a National Book Award, the PEN/Malamud Award for Lifetime Achievement in the Short Story, and two Bram Stoker Awards, for Best Novel (*Zombie*) and Life Achievement.

TOM PICCIRILLI's novels include *Hexes, The Deceased, The Dead Past, Sorrow's Crown* and *A Lower Deep*. His short stories appear in such anthologies as *Hot Blood, Future Crimes, Bad News* and *The Conspiracy Files*, in *Cemetery Dance, The Third Alternative, Terminal*

Fright and other magazines, and in his collection *Deep into That Darkness Peering*. His next novel is *A Choir of Ill Children*.

S. P. SOMTOW (Somtow Sucharitkul), a past president of the HWA, is the author of *Vampire Junction, Jasmine Nights, The Riverrun Trilogy* and *Moon Dance*, and the winner of the John W. Campbell and International Critics Guild awards. He has directed two feature films, *Ill Met by Moonlight* and *The Laughing Dead*. His grand opera *Madana* premiered in Bangkok in 2001, the first in history by a Thai composer.

PETER STRAUB is the author of *Ghost Story, Floating Dragon, The Throat, Koko, The Hellfire Club, Mr. X* and an additional half-dozen novels and collections, for which he has received numerous Bram Stoker, World Fantasy, British Fantasy and International Horror Critics Guild Awards. He was named Grand Master at the 1998 World Fantasy Convention. His latest novel, a collaboration with Stephen King, is *Black House*.

MELANIE TEM has published approximately fifty short stories, most recently in *The Mammoth Book of Vampire Stories by Women* and *Extremes 2*, and nine novels, including *Black River* and *The Tides*. She lives in Denver with her husband, writer and editor Steve Rasnic Tem.

CONRAD WILLIAMS, born in Cheshire, England, is a British Fantasy Award winner. His work appears in magazines and anthologies including *Darklands 2, Narrow House: Blue Motel, Dark Terrors, Best New Horror* and *Year's Best Horror Stories*. He has adapted his first novel, *Head Injuries*, for the screen and is presently writing a new novel, *Penetralia*.

The Horror Writers Association (HWA) was formed in the 1980s with the help of many of contemporary horror fiction's greats, including Joe Lansdale, Robert McCammon and Dean Koontz. The HWA is now a worldwide organization of writers and publishing professionals with members throughout the United States, Canada, the United Kingdom, Australia and other countries.

The HWA's mission is to help horror writers and aspiring horror writers with their careers.

Membership is based on publishing credentials: *Active Members* must verify a certain amount of publishing credits at specified professional rates; *Affiliate Members* are new writers who haven't yet sold enough material to qualify for Active membership; *Associate Members* are professionals in the field such as editors, agents, producers, publishers, booksellers, etc.

The HWA sponsors a number of anthologies open only to members, such as this book, *The Museum of Horrors*. Members also receive regular Internet and printed newsletters full of useful information about the latest developments in the world of horror writing, publishing, bookselling, filmmaking, etc. Members have access to a wealth of information on the members-only pages of the HWA website (www.horror.org), which gives writing tips, offers a variety of discounts, provides a message board, and contains advice on such topics as agents, contracts, publishers, etc. For new writers, HWA also has a mentoring program.

Every year, HWA gets together for the Stoker weekend during which members have an opportunity to meet some of their favorite writers, to make valuable contacts with other horror professionals, and even to discover new friends who share their own passion for the dark side. Perhaps the highlight of the weekend is the awards banquet. There, HWA presents the prestigious Bram Stoker Awards for superior achievement in the horror field.

For more information, or to join, please contact HWA at:

The Horror Writers Association
PO Box 50577
Palo Alto, CA 94303
USA

www.horror.org